Dickens | Oliver Twist

Fremdsprachentexte | Englisch

Charles Dickens

Oliver Twist; or, The Parish Boy's Progress

Abridged Edition

Herausgegeben von Axel Monte

Reclam

RECLAMS UNIVERSAL-BIBLIOTHEK Nr. 19841

Umschlagabbildung: Barney Clark als Oliver in der Verfilmung des Romans von Roman Polanski (2005)
Gestaltung: Cornelia Feyll, Friedrich Forssman
Gesamtherstellung: Reclam, Ditzingen. Printed in Germany 2012

ISBN 978-3-15-019841-4
www.reclam.de

Chapter I

Treats of the Place where Oliver Twist was Born; and of the Circumstances Attending his Birth

Among other public buildings in a certain town, which for many reasons it will be prudent to refrain from mentioning, and to which I will assign no fictitious name, there is one anciently common to most towns, great or small: to wit, a workhouse; and in this workhouse was born: on a day and date which I need not trouble myself to repeat, inasmuch as it can be of no possible consequence to the reader, in this stage of the business at all events: the item of mortality whose name is prefixed to the head of this chapter.

For a long time after it was ushered into this world of sorrow and trouble, by the parish surgeon, it remained a matter of considerable doubt whether the child could survive to bear any name at all; in which case it is somewhat more than probable that these memoirs would never have appeared; or, if they had, that being comprised within a couple of pages, they would have possessed the inestimable merit of being the most

[Titel] **parish:** Kirchspiel, (politische) Gemeinde, Verwaltungsbezirk. | 3 **to attend:** begleiten. | 5 **prudent:** klug, vernünftig, besonnen. | **to refrain from doing s.th.:** Abstand davon nehmen, davon absehen, etwas zu tun. | 6 **to assign:** zuteilen, zuschreiben, zuordnen. | **fictitious:** Phantasie…, erfunden. | 6 f. **anciently:** alt, aus alter Zeit. | 7 **to wit:** das heißt, nämlich. | 7 f. **workhouse:** Armenhaus. | 9 **inasmuch as:** insofern als. | 10 **in this stage:** zu diesem Zeitpunkt. | 11 **at all events** (pl.): jedenfalls. | **mortality:** Sterblichkeit. | 11 f. **to prefix s.th.:** etwas voranstellen. | 13 **to usher s.o. into s.th.:** jdn. in etwas hineinführen, hineingeleiten. | 13 f. **sorrow:** Kummer, Leid. | 14 **surgeon:** Wundarzt. | 17 **memoirs:** Lebenserinnerungen, Bericht. | 18 **to comprise:** umfassen, enthalten. | 19 **inestimable:** unschätzbar. | **merit:** Verdienst, Vorzug.

concise and faithful specimen of biography, extant in the literature of any age or country.

Although I am not disposed to maintain that the being born in a workhouse, is in itself the most fortunate and enviable circumstance that can possibly befall a human being, I do mean to say that in this particular instance, it was the best thing for Oliver Twist that could by possibility have occurred. The fact is, that there was considerable difficulty in inducing Oliver to take upon himself the office of respiration, – a troublesome practice, but one which custom has rendered necessary to our easy existence; and for some time he lay gasping on a little flock mattress, rather unequally poised between this world and the next: the balance being decidedly in favour of the latter. Now, if, during this brief period, Oliver had been surrounded by careful grandmothers, anxious aunts, experienced nurses, and doctors of profound wisdom, he would most inevitably and indubitably have been killed in no time. There being nobody by, however, but a pauper old woman, who was rendered rather misty by an unwonted allowance of beer; and a parish surgeon

1 **concise:** knapp, bündig. | **faithful:** getreu, gewissenhaft. | **specimen:** Exemplar. | **(to be) extant:** vorhanden sein. | 3 **to be disposed to do s.th.:** geneigt sein, etwas zu tun. | 4 **enviable:** beneidenswert. | 5 **to befall s.o.:** jdm. widerfahren. | 6 **instance:** Fall, Gelegenheit, Beispiel. | 7 **to occur:** geschehen. | 8 **to induce s.o. to do s.th.:** jdn. dazu veranlassen, bewegen, etwas zu tun. | 9 **office:** Aufgabe. | **respiration:** Atmung. | **troublesome:** mühsam, beschwerlich. | 10 **custom:** Gewohnheit, Brauch, Sitte. | **to render:** machen, werden lassen. | 11 **to gasp:** keuchen, nach Luft ringen. | **flock:** Wollflocken. | 12 **to poise:** balancieren, schweben. | 13 **decidedly:** entschieden. | 14 **brief:** kurz. | 15 **nurse:** Kinderfrau, Pflegerin. | 16 **profound:** tief. | **wisdom:** Weisheit. | **inevitably:** unausweichlich, unabwendbar. | 16 f. **indubitably:** zweifellos. | 18 **pauper:** arm. | 19 **misty:** benebelt. | **unwonted:** ungewohnt. | **allowance:** Ration, Quantum.

who did such matters by contract; Oliver and Nature fought out the point between them. The result was, that, after a few struggles, Oliver breathed, sneezed, and proceeded to advertise to the inmates of the workhouse the fact of a new burden having been imposed upon the parish, by setting up as loud a cry as could reasonably have been expected from a male infant who had not been possessed of that very useful appendage, a voice, for a much longer space of time than three minutes and a quarter.

As Oliver gave this first proof of the free and proper action of his lungs, the patchwork coverlet which was carelessly flung over the iron bedstead, rustled; the pale face of a young woman was raised feebly from the pillow; and a faint voice imperfectly articulated the words, "Let me see the child, and die."

The surgeon had been sitting with his face turned towards the fire: giving the palms of his hands, a warm and a rub alternately. As the young woman spoke, he rose, and advancing to the bed's head, said, with more kindness than might have been expected of him:

"Oh, you must not talk about dying yet."

"Lor bless her dear heart, no!" interposed the nurse, hastily depositing in her pocket a green glass bottle, the contents of which she had been tasting in a corner with evident satisfaction. "Lor bless her dear heart, when she has lived as long as

1 **contract:** Vertrag, Verpflichtung. | 3 **to proceed to do s.th.:** damit fortfahren, weitermachen, etwas zu tun; damit beginnen, etwas zu tun. | 3 f. **to advertise:** ankündigen, verkünden. | 4 **inmates:** Insassen, Bewohner. | **burden:** Last, Kosten, Bürde. | 5 **to impose:** auferlegen, aufbürden. | 6 **infant:** Säugling. | 7 **appendage:** Anhängsel, Beigabe. | 11 **coverlet:** Bettdecke. | **to fling:** werfen. | 12 **bedstead:** Bettgestell. | **to rustle:** rascheln. | **pale:** bleich, blass. | 13 **feebly:** schwach, kraftlos. | **faint:** matt, schwach. | 16 f. **alternately:** abwechselnd. | 21 **Lor:** *Lord:* Herr, Gott. | **to interpose:** (Bemerkung, Frage) einwerfen.

I have, sir, and had thirteen children of her own, and all on 'em dead except two, and them in the wurkus with me, she'll know better than to take on in that way, bless her dear heart! Think what it is to be a mother, there's a dear young lamb, do."

Apparently this consolatory perspective of a mother's prospects failed in producing its due effect. The patient shook her head, and stretched out her hand towards the child.

The surgeon deposited it in her arms. She imprinted her cold white lips passionately on its forehead; passed her hands over her face; gazed wildly round; shuddered; fell back – and died. They chafed her breast, hands, and temples; but the blood had stopped for ever. They talked of hope and comfort. They had been strangers too long.

"It's all over, Mrs. Thingummy!" said the surgeon at last.

"Ah, poor dear, so it is!" said the nurse, picking up the cork of the green bottle, which had fallen out on the pillow, as she stooped to take up the child. "Poor dear!"

"You needn't mind sending up to me, if the child cries, nurse," said the surgeon, putting on his gloves with great deliberation. "It's very likely it *will* be troublesome. Give it a little gruel if it is." He put on his hat, and, pausing by the bedside on his way to the door, added "She was a good-looking girl, too; where did she come from?"

"She was brought here last night," replied the old woman, "by the overseer's order. She was found lying in the street. She had walked some distance, for her shoes were worn to pieces;

2 **wurkus:** *workhouse.* | 6 **consolatory:** tröstlich. | 6 f. **prospect:** Aussicht. | 7 **due:** gebührend, erwartet, angemessen. | 9 **to imprint:** aufdrücken. | 11 **to gaze:** starr blicken. | **to shudder:** erschaudern, beben. | 12 **to chafe:** reiben. | **temple:** Schläfe. | 18 **to stoop:** sich bücken. | 20 f. **deliberation:** Bedächtigkeit. | 22 **gruel:** Haferschleim. | 26 **overseer:** Aufseher(in) (*overseer of the poor:* Armenpfleger[in]).

but where she came from, or where she was going to, nobody knows."

The surgeon leaned over the body, and raised the left hand. "The old story," he said, shaking his head: "no wedding-ring, I see. Ah! Good night!"

The medical gentleman walked away to dinner; and the nurse, having once more applied herself to the green bottle, sat down on a low chair before the fire, and proceeded to dress the infant.

What an excellent example of the power of dress, young Oliver Twist was! Wrapped in the blanket which had hitherto formed his only covering, he might have been the child of a nobleman or a beggar; it would have been hard for the haughtiest stranger to have assigned him his proper station in society. But now that he was enveloped in the old calico robes which had grown yellow in the same service, he was badged and ticketed, and fell into his place at once – a parish child – the orphan of a workhouse – the humble half-starved drudge – to be cuffed and buffeted through the world – despised by all, and pitied by none.

Oliver cried lustily. If he could have known that he was an orphan, left to the tender mercies of churchwardens and overseers, perhaps he would have cried the louder.

7 **to apply o.s. to s.th.:** sich einer Sache widmen. | 11 **hitherto:** bisher, bis dato. | 12 f. **nobleman:** Edelmann, Adliger. | 13 **haughty:** hochmütig, überheblich. | 14 **station:** Rang, Stellung. | 15 **to envelop:** einhüllen, einwickeln. | **calico:** Kattun (Baumwollstoff). | **robe:** hier: Tragkleidchen für Säuglinge. | 16 **to badge:** kennzeichnen. | **to ticket:** etikettieren. | 17 **orphan:** Waisenkind. | 18 **humble:** niedrig, demütig. | **half-starved:** halb verhungert (*to starve s.o.:* jdn. verhungern lassen). | **drudge:** Arbeitstier. | **to cuff:** knuffen, ohrfeigen. | 19 **to buffet:** herumstoßen. | **to despise:** verachten. | 21 **lustily:** kräftig, herzhaft. | 22 **tender:** zärtlich, liebevoll. | **mercy:** Gnade. | **churchwarden:** Kirchenvorsteher.

Chapter II

Treats of Oliver Twist's Growth, Education, and Board

For the next eight or ten months, Oliver was the victim of a systematic course of treachery and deception. He was brought up by hand. The hungry and destitute situation of the infant orphan was duly reported by the workhouse authorities to the parish authorities. The parish authorities inquired with dignity of the workhouse authorities, whether there was no female then domiciled in "the house" who was in a situation to impart to Oliver Twist, the consolation and nourishment of which he stood in need. The workhouse authorities replied with humility, that there was not. Upon this, the parish authorities magnanimously and humanely resolved, that Oliver should be "farmed," or, in other words, that he should be despatched to a branch-workhouse some three miles off, where twenty or thirty other juvenile offenders against the poor-laws, rolled about the floor all day, without the inconvenience of too much food or too much clothing, under the parental superintendence of an elderly female, who received the

2 **board:** Verpflegung. | 4 **course:** Ablauf, Verlauf, Abfolge. | **treachery:** Verrat. | **deception:** Betrug, Täuschung. | 4 f. **to bring s.o. up by hand:** jdn. ohne Muttermilch aufziehen. | 5 **destitute:** trostlos. | 6 **duly:** pflichtgemäß. | 9 **domiciled:** wohnhaft. | 10 **to impart:** gewähren. | **consolation:** Trost. | **nourishment:** Nahrung. | 12 **humility:** Demut, Ergebenheit. | 13 **magnanimously:** großmütig. | **humanely:** menschlich. | **to resolve:** beschließen. | 14 **to farm:** in Pflege geben. | 15 **to despatch s.o. to s.th.:** jdn. in, zu etwas schicken, befördern. | **branch-workhouse:** Zweigstelle des Armenhauses. | 16 **juvenile:** jugendlich, kindlich. | **offender:** Rechtsbrecher, Straftäter. | 17 **poor-laws:** Armengesetze. | 17 f. **inconvenience:** Belästigung, Unannehmlichkeit. | 18 f. **parental:** elterlich. | 19 **superintendence:** Aufsicht.

culprits at and for the consideration of sevenpence-halfpenny per small head per week. Sevenpence-halfpenny's worth per week is a good round diet for a child; a great deal may be got for sevenpence-halfpenny: quite enough to overload its stomach, and make it uncomfortable. The elderly female was a woman of wisdom and experience; she knew what was good for children; and she had a very accurate perception of what was good for herself. So, she appropriated the greater part of the weekly stipend to her own use, and consigned the rising parochial generation to even a shorter allowance than was originally provided for them. [...]

It cannot be expected that this system of farming would produce any very extraordinary or luxuriant crop. Oliver Twist's ninth birth-day found him a pale thin child, somewhat diminutive in stature, and decidedly small in circumference. But nature or inheritance had implanted a good sturdy spirit in Oliver's breast. It had had plenty of room to expand, thanks to the spare diet of the establishment; and perhaps to this circumstance may be attributed his having any ninth birth-day at all. Be this as it may, however, it *was* his ninth birth-day; and he

1 **culprit:** Übeltäter, Schuldiger. | **consideration:** hier: Gegenleistung. | **sevenpence-halfpenny:** In der alten britischen Währung entsprach 1 Pfund = 20 Shilling = 240 Pence. | 3 **round:** beachtlich. | **diet:** Kost, Speiseration. | 4 **to overload:** überlasten. | 5 **uncomfortable:** unbehaglich, unwohl. | 7 **perception:** Vorstellung, Wahrnehmung. | 8 **to appropriate:** bestimmen, verwenden. | 8 f. **stipend:** Bezüge, Kostgeld. | 9 **to consign:** bestimmen, übergeben, anvertrauen. | **parochial:** Gemeinde…, die Gemeinde betreffend. | 10 **allowance:** Ration, Zuteilung. | 13 **luxuriant:** üppig, prächtig. | **crop:** Ernte. | 14 f. **diminutive:** klein. | 15 **circumference:** Umfang. | 16 **inheritance:** Vererbung. | **to implant:** einpflanzen. | **sturdy:** unbeugsam, kräftig. | 17 **to expand:** (sich) ausdehnen, ausweiten. | 18 **spare:** spärlich. | **establishment:** Anstalt. | 19 **to attribute:** zuschreiben.

was keeping it in the coal-cellar with a select party of two other young gentlemen, who, after participating with him in a sound threshing, had been locked up therein for atrociously presuming to be hungry, when Mrs. Mann, the good lady of the house, was unexpectedly startled by the apparition of Mr. Bumble, the beadle, striving to undo the wicket of the garden-gate.

"Goodness gracious! is that you, Mr. Bumble, sir?" said Mrs. Mann, thrusting her head out of the window in well-affected ecstasies of joy. "(Susan, take Oliver and them two brats up stairs, and wash 'em directly.) – My heart alive! Mr. Bumble, how glad I am to see you, sure-ly!"

Now, Mr. Bumble was a fat man, and a choleric; so, instead of responding to this open-hearted salutation in a kindred spirit, he gave the little wicket a tremendous shake, and then bestowed upon it a kick which could have emanated from no leg but a beadle's.

"Lor, only think," said Mrs. Mann, running out, – for the three boys had been removed by this time, – "only think of that! That I should have forgotten that the gate was bolted on

1 **select:** ausgewählt. | **party:** Gesellschaft. | 2 **sound:** gehörig, kräftig. | 3 **threshing:** Dresche, Tracht Prügel. | **to lock s.o. up:** jdn. einsperren. | **atrociously:** ungeheuerlich. | 3f. **to presume:** sich erdreisten, sich erlauben. | 5 **to startle:** aufschrecken. | **apparition:** Erscheinung. | 6 **beadle:** Büttel, Gemeindediener, der auch Aufgaben als »Hilfspolizist« übernahm. | **to strive to do s.th.:** sich ab-, bemühen, etwas zu tun. | **wicket:** Pförtchen. | 7 **goodness gracious!:** ach du lieber Himmel! | 8 **to thrust:** stecken, schieben. | **well-affected:** vorgespielt, vorgetäuscht (*to affect:* vortäuschen). | 9 **ecstasy:** Verzückung. | **them:** *those.* | **brat:** Balg, Göre. | 10 **'em:** *them.* | 12 **choleric:** reizbar, aufbrausend. | 13 **to respond to s.th.:** etwas erwidern. | **salutation:** Begrüßung. | **kindred:** verwandt, gleichartig. | 14 **tremendous:** furchtbar, ungeheuer. | 15 **to bestow:** gewähren, verleihen. | **to emanate:** herrühren, entspringen. | 18 **to remove:** entfernen. | 19 **to bolt:** verriegeln.

the inside, on account of them dear children! Walk in sir; walk in, pray, Mr. Bumble, do sir."

[…]

"Do you think this respectful or proper conduct, Mrs. Mann," inquired Mr. Bumble, grasping his cane, "to keep the parish officers a-waiting at your garden-gate, when they come here upon porochial business connected with the porochial orphans? Are you aweer, Mrs. Mann, that you are, as I may say, a porochial delegate, and a stipendiary?"

"I'm sure, Mr. Bumble, that I was only a-telling one or two of the dear children as is so fond of you, that it was you a-coming," replied Mrs. Mann with great humility.

Mr. Bumble had a great idea of his oratorical powers and his importance. He had displayed the one, and vindicated the other. He relaxed.

"Well, well, Mrs. Mann," he replied in a calmer tone; "it may be as you say; it may be. Lead the way in, Mrs. Mann, for I come on business, and have something to say."

Mrs. Mann ushered the beadle into a small parlour with a brick floor; placed a seat for him; and officiously deposited his cocked hat and cane on the table before him. Mr. Bumble wiped from his forehead the perspiration which his walk had engen-

1 **on account of:** wegen. | 2 **pray:** bitte. | 4 **proper conduct:** angemessenes Benehmen. | 5 **to grasp:** (an)packen, (er)greifen. | **cane:** Stock. | 7 **porochial:** *parochial.* | **business:** Angelegenheit. | 8 **aweer:** *aware.* | 9 **delegate:** Beauftragte(r). | **stipendiary:** Gehaltsempfänger(in). | 11 **to be fond of s.o.:** jdn. mögen. | 12 **humility:** Bescheidenheit, Demut. | 13 **oratorical:** rednerisch. | 14 **to display:** zeigen, offenbaren. | **to vindicate:** verteidigen. | 19 **parlour:** Stube, Wohnzimmer. | 20 **to place s.th.:** etwas hinstellen. | **officiously:** dienstbeflissen. | **to deposit:** deponieren. | 21 **cocked hat:** Dreispitz. | **to wipe:** (ab)wischen. | 22 **perspiration:** Schweiß. | 22 f. **to engender:** erzeugen.

dered; glanced complacently at the cocked hat, and smiled. Yes, he smiled. Beadles are but men; and Mr. Bumble smiled.

"Now don't you be offended at what I'm a-going to say," observed Mrs. Mann, with captivating sweetness. "You've had a long walk, you know, or I wouldn't mention it. Now, will you take a little drop of somethink, Mr. Bumble?"

"Not a drop. Not a drop," said Mr. Bumble, waving his right hand in a dignified, but placid manner.

"I think you will," said Mrs. Mann, who had noticed the tone of the refusal, and the gesture that had accompanied it. "Just a leetle drop, with a little cold water, and a lump of sugar."

Mr. Bumble coughed.

"Now, just a leetle drop," said Mrs. Mann persuasively.

"What is it?" inquired the beadle.

"Why, it's what I'm obliged to keep a little of in the house to put into the blessed infants' Daffy, when they ain't well, Mr. Bumble," replied Mrs. Mann as she opened a corner cupboard, and took down a bottle and glass. "It's gin. I'll not deceive you, Mr. B. It's gin."

"Do you give the children Daffy, Mrs. Mann?" inquired Bumble, following with his eyes the interesting process of mixing.

1 **to glance:** blicken. | **complacently:** selbstgefällig. | 3 **to be offended at s.th.:** über etwas aufgebracht sein, etwas als Ärgernis empfinden. | 3 f. **to observe:** bemerken. | 4 **to captivate s.o.:** jdn. berücken, bezaubern. | 7 **to wave s.th.:** mit etwas wedeln. | 8 **dignified:** würdevoll. | **placid:** milde, gelassen. | 10 **gesture:** Geste, Handbewegung. | **to accompany s.th.:** mit etwas einhergehen. | 11 **leetle:** *little.* | **lump:** Klümpchen. | 13 **persuasively:** überzeugend. | 15 **why:** nun. | **to be obliged to do s.th.:** gehalten sein, etwas zu tun. | 16 **blessed:** gesegnet. | **Daffy:** *Daffy's elixir* war ursprünglich eine Medizin, die u. a. auch Gin enthielt; später wurde *daffy* oft gleichbedeutend mit »Gin« verwendet. | 18 **to deceive:** täuschen.

"Ah, bless 'em, that I do, dear as it is," replied the nurse. "I couldn't see 'em suffer before my very eyes, you know, sir."

"No," said Mr. Bumble approvingly; "no, you could not. You are a humane woman, Mrs. Mann." (Here she set down the glass.) "I shall take a early opportunity of mentioning it to the board, Mrs. Mann." (He drew it towards him.) "You feel as a mother, Mrs. Mann." (He stirred the gin-and-water.) "I – I drink your health with cheerfulness, Mrs. Mann;" and he swallowed half of it.

"And now about business," said the beadle, taking out a leathern pocket-book. "The child that was half-baptized Oliver Twist, is nine year old to-day."

"Bless him!" interposed Mrs. Mann, inflaming her left eye with the corner of her apron.

"And notwithstanding a offered reward of ten pound, which was afterwards increased to twenty pound. Notwithstanding the most superlative, and, I may say, supernat'ral exertions on the part of this parish," said Bumble, "we have never been able to discover who is his father, or what was his mother's settlement, name, or con – dition."

Mrs. Mann raised her hands in astonishment; but added, after a moment's reflection, "How comes he to have any name at all, then?"

The beadle drew himself up with great pride, and said, "I inwented it."

3 **approvingly:** zustimmend. | 6 **board:** Vorstand, Direktorium. | 7 **to stir:** umrühren. | 8 **cheerfulness:** Fröhlichkeit. | 11 **to half-baptize s.o.:** jdn. nottaufen. | 13 **to inflame:** entzünden, wund reiben. | 14 **apron:** Schürze. | 15 **notwithstanding:** ungeachtet. | 17 **superlative:** äußerste(r, s). | **supernat'ral:** übermenschlich. | **exertion:** Anstrengung. | 19 f. **settlement:** Wohnort. | 20 **condition:** Stellung, Verhältnisse. | 22 **reflection:** Besinnung, Nachdenken. | 24 **to draw o.s. up with pride:** sich voller Stolz aufrichten. | 24 f. **to inwent:** *invent.*

"You, Mr. Bumble!"

"I, Mrs. Mann. We name our fondlins in alphabetical order. The last was a S, – Swubble, I named him. This was a T, – Twist, I named *him*. The next one as comes will be Unwin, and the next Vilkins. I have got names ready made to the end of the alphabet, and all the way through it again, when we come to Z."

"Why, you're quite a literary character, sir!" said Mrs. Mann.

"Well, well," said the beadle, evidently gratified with the compliment; "perhaps I may be. Perhaps I may be, Mrs. Mann." He finished the gin-and-water, and added, "Oliver being now too old to remain here, the board have determined to have him back into the house. I have come out myself to take him there. So let me see him at once."

"I'll fetch him directly," said Mrs. Mann, leaving the room for that purpose. Oliver, having had by this time as much of the outer coat of dirt, which encrusted his face and hands, removed, as could be scrubbed off in one washing, was led into the room by his benevolent protectress.

"Make a bow to the gentleman, Oliver," said Mrs. Mann.

Oliver made a bow, which was divided between the beadle on the chair, and the cocked hat on the table.

"Will you go along with me, Oliver?" said Mr. Bumble in a majestic voice.

Oliver was about to say that he would go along with anybody with great readiness, when, glancing upward, he caught sight of Mrs. Mann, who had got behind the beadle's chair, and

2 **fondlin:** *foundling:* Findelkind. | 7 **literary:** dichterisch. | **character:** Person, Persönlichkeit. | 8 **evidently:** offenkundig. | **to gratify s.o.:** jdn. erfreuen, befriedigen. | 11 **to determine:** bestimmen, beschließen. | 16 **to encrust:** verkrusten. | 16 f. **to remove:** ablösen, beseitigen. | 17 **to scrub s.th. off:** etwas abschrubben. | 18 **benevolent:** wohlwollend, gütig. | **protectress:** Beschützerin. | 19 **bow:** Verbeugung. | 23 **majestic:** hoheitsvoll, majestätisch. | 25 **readiness:** Bereitwilligkeit.

was shaking her fist at him with a furious countenance. He took the hint at once, for the fist had been too often impressed upon his body not to be deeply impressed upon his recollection.

"Will *she* go with me?" inquired poor Oliver.

"No, she can't," replied Mr. Bumble. "But she'll come and see you sometimes."

This was no very great consolation to the child. Young as he was, however, he had sense enough to make a feint of feeling great regret at going away. [...]

Mr. Bumble walked on with long strides; little Oliver, firmly grasping his gold-laced cuff, trotted beside him, inquiring at the end of every quarter of a mile whether they were "nearly there." To these interrogations Mr. Bumble returned very brief and snappish replies; for the temporary blandness which gin-and-water awakens in some bosoms had by this time evaporated: and he was once again a beadle.

Oliver had not been within the walls of the workhouse a quarter of an hour [...] when Mr. Bumble, who had handed him over to the care of an old woman, returned; and, telling him it was a board night, informed him that the board had said he was to appear before it forthwith.

1 **furious:** wütend, zornig. | **countenance:** Miene, Angesicht. | 2 f. **to impress: 1.** eindrücken; **2.** Eindruck machen. | 3 f. **recollection:** Erinnerung. | 9 **to have sense enough to do s.th.:** genug Verstand haben, etwas zu tun. | **feint:** Vortäuschung, Verstellung. | 11 **stride:** Schritt. | **firmly:** fest. | 12 **gold-laced:** goldbetresst (*lace:* Tresse). | **cuff:** Ärmelaufschlag. | **to trot:** traben. | 14 **interrogation:** Frage. | 14 f. **to return a reply:** eine Antwort geben. | 15 **snappish:** bissig. | **temporary:** zeitweilig. | **blandness:** Milde. | 16 **to awaken:** erwecken, entfachen. | **bosom:** Busen, Brust, Herz. | 16 f. **to evaporate:** verdunsten, sich verflüchtigen. | 21 **board night:** abendliche Vorstandssitzung. | 22 **forthwith:** umgehend, unverzüglich.

Not having a very clearly defined notion of what a live board was, Oliver was rather astounded by this intelligence, and was not quite certain whether he ought to laugh or cry. He had no time to think about the matter, however; for Mr. Bumble gave him a tap on the head, with his cane, to wake him up: and another on the back to make him lively: and bidding him follow, conducted him into a large whitewashed room, where eight or ten fat gentlemen were sitting round a table. At the top of the table, seated in an arm-chair rather higher than the rest, was a particularly fat gentleman with a very round, red face.

"Bow to the board," said Bumble. Oliver brushed away two or three tears that were lingering in his eyes; and seeing no board but the table, fortunately bowed to that.

"What's your name, boy?" said the gentleman in the high chair.

Oliver was frightened at the sight of so many gentlemen, which made him tremble; and the beadle gave him another tap behind, which made him cry; and these two causes made him answer in a very low and hesitating voice; whereupon a gentleman in a white waistcoat said he was a fool. Which was a capital way of raising his spirits, and putting him quite at his ease.

"Boy," said the gentleman in the high chair, "listen to me. You know you're an orphan, I suppose?"

"What's that, sir?" inquired poor Oliver.

1 **defined:** bestimmt, klar. | **notion:** Vorstellung, Begriff. | **live board:** Oliver kennt *board* nur in der Bedeutung »Brett«. | 2 **to be astounded by s.th.:** über etwas höchst erstaunt sein. | **intelligence:** Nachricht. | 5 **tap:** leichter Schlag, Klopfen. | 6 **lively:** lebhaft, lebendig. | **to bid s.o. do s.th.:** jdn. heißen, etwas zu tun. | 7 **to conduct:** führen, leiten. | **whitewashed:** getüncht, gekalkt. | 12 **to linger:** bleiben, verweilen. | 19 **hesitating:** zögerlich. | 20 **waistcoat:** Weste. | 20 f. **capital:** großartig. | 21 **to raise s.o.'s spirits:** jdn. aufheitern. | **to put s.o. at his, her ease:** jdn. beruhigen.

"The boy *is* a fool – I thought he was," said the gentleman in the white waistcoat.

"Hush!" said the gentleman who had spoken first. "You know you've got no father or mother, and that you were brought up by the parish, don't you?"

"Yes, sir," replied Oliver, weeping bitterly.

"What are you crying for?" inquired the gentleman in the white waistcoat. And to be sure it was very extraordinary. What *could* the boy be crying for?

[…]

"Well! You have come here to be educated, and taught a useful trade," said the red-faced gentleman in the high chair.

"So you'll begin to pick oakum to-morrow morning at six o'clock," added the surly one in the white waistcoat.

For the combination of both these blessings in the one simple process of picking oakum, Oliver bowed low by the direction of the beadle, and was then hurried away to a large ward: where, on a rough hard bed, he sobbed himself to sleep. […]

For the first six months after Oliver Twist was removed, the system was in full operation. It was rather expensive at first, in consequence of the increase in the undertaker's bill, and the necessity of taking in the clothes of all the paupers, which fluttered loosely on their wasted, shrunken forms, after a week or two's gruel. But the number of workhouse inmates got thin as well as the paupers; and the board were in ecstasies.

The room in which the boys were fed, was a large stone hall, with a copper at one end: out of which the master, dressed in

3 **hush!:** Ruhe!, pst! | 12 **trade:** Handwerk, Gewerbe. | 13 **to pick oakum:** Werg zupfen. | 14 **surly:** bärbeißig. | 15 **blessing:** Segen. | 17 **ward:** Saal. | 18 **to sob:** schluchzen. | 21 **undertaker:** Leichenbestatter. | 22 **pauper:** Arme(r), Bedürftige(r). | 23 **shrunken:** verhutzelt, ausgemergelt. | **form:** Gestalt. | 27 **copper:** Kupferkessel. | **master:** Hausherr, Vorsteher.

an apron for the purpose, and assisted by one or two women, ladled the gruel at meal-times. Of this festive composition each boy had one porringer, and no more – except on occasions of great public rejoicing, when he had two ounces and a quarter of bread besides. The bowls never wanted washing. The boys polished them with their spoons till they shone again; and when they had performed this operation (which never took very long, the spoons being nearly as large as the bowls,) they would sit staring at the copper, with such eager eyes, as if they could have devoured the very bricks of which it was composed; employing themselves, meanwhile, in sucking their fingers most assiduously, with the view of catching up any stray splashes of gruel that might have been cast thereon. Boys have generally excellent appetites. Oliver Twist and his companions suffered the tortures of slow starvation for three months; at last they got so voracious and wild with hunger, that one boy: who was tall for his age, and hadn't been used to that sort of thing, (for his father had kept a small cook's shop): hinted darkly to his companions, that unless he had another basin of gruel *per diem*, he was afraid he might some night happen to eat the boy who slept next him, who happened to be a weakly youth of

2 **to ladle:** schöpfen. | **festive:** feierlich, festlich. | **composition:** Zubereitung. | 3 **porringer:** Napf. | 4 **rejoicing:** Freude, Jubel. | **ounce:** Unze (etwa 30 g). | 5 **to want s.th.:** etwas benötigen. | 6 **to shine:** glänzen. | 7 **to perform:** verrichten. | **operation:** Tätigkeit, Handlung. | 9 **eager:** begierig. | 10 **to devour:** verschlingen. | **to be composed of s.th.:** aus etwas zusammengesetzt sein. | 10 f. **to employ o.s.:** sich beschäftigen. | 12 **assiduously:** eifrig. | **stray:** verirrt, vereinzelt. | **splash:** Spritzer. | 14 **companion:** Gefährte, Kamerad. | 15 **torture:** Folter, Qual. | **starvation:** Verhungern. | 16 **voracious:** gierig. | 18 **cook's shop:** Garküche. | **to hint:** andeuten. | 19 **basin:** Schale. | 19 f. **per diem** (Lat.): pro Tag. | 20 **to happen to do s.th.:** zufällig etwas tun.

tender age. He had a wild, hungry, eye; and they implicitly believed him. A council was held; lots were cast who should walk up to the master after supper that evening, and ask for more; and it fell to Oliver Twist.

The evening arrived; the boys took their places. The master, in his cook's uniform, stationed himself at the copper; his pauper assistants ranged themselves behind him; the gruel was served out; and a long grace was said over the short commons. The gruel disappeared; the boys whispered each other, and winked at Oliver; while his next neighbours nudged him. Child as he was, he was desperate with hunger, and reckless with misery. He rose from the table; and advancing to the master, basin and spoon in hand, said: somewhat alarmed at his own temerity:

"Please, sir, I want some more."

The master was a fat, healthy man; but he turned very pale. He gazed in stupefied astonishment on the small rebel for some seconds; and then clung for support to the copper. The assistants were paralysed with wonder; the boys with fear.

"What!" said the master at length, in a faint voice.

"Please, sir," replied Oliver, "I want some more."

The master aimed a blow at Oliver's head with the ladle; pinioned him in his arms; and shrieked aloud for the beadle.

1 **tender:** zart. | **implicitly:** unbedingt. | 2 **to cast a lot:** (aus)losen (*lot:* Los). | 6 **to station o.s.:** sich aufstellen, postieren. | 7 **to range o.s.:** sich einordnen. | 8 **grace:** Tischgebet. | **short commons** (pl.): schmale Kost. | 10 **to wink at s.o.:** jdm. zublinzeln. | **to nudge s.o.:** jdn. anstoßen. | 11 **desperate:** verzweifelt. | **reckless:** verwegen. | 12 **misery:** Elend. | 13 **(to be) alarmed at s.th.:** über etwas erschrocken sein. | 14 **temerity:** Kühnheit. | 17 **stupefied:** verblüfft, betäubt. | **rebel:** Aufrührer, Rebell. | 18 **to cling for s.th.:** sich an etwas festhalten. | 19 **to be paralysed with s.th.:** vor etwas gelähmt sein. | 20 **at length:** schließlich. | 22 **ladle:** Schöpfkelle. | 23 **to pinion:** fesseln. | **to shriek:** schreien.

The board were sitting in solemn conclave, when Mr. Bumble rushed into the room in great excitement, and addressing the gentleman in the high chair, said,

"Mr. Limbkins, I beg your pardon, sir! Oliver Twist has asked for more!"

There was a general start. Horror was depicted on every countenance.

"For *more*!" said Mr. Limbkins. "Compose yourself, Bumble, and answer me distinctly. Do I understand that he asked for more, after he had eaten the supper allotted by the dietary?"

"He did, sir," replied Bumble.

"That boy will be hung," said the gentleman in the white waistcoat. "I know that boy will be hung."

Nobody controverted the prophetic gentleman's opinion. An animated discussion took place. Oliver was ordered into instant confinement; and a bill was next morning pasted on the outside of the gate, offering a reward of five pounds to anybody who would take Oliver Twist off the hands of the parish. In other words, five pounds and Oliver Twist were offered to any man or woman who wanted an apprentice to any trade, business, or calling.

"I never was more convinced of anything in my life," said the gentleman in the white waistcoat, as he knocked at the gate

1 **solemn:** feierlich. | **conclave:** vertrauliche Beratung. |
2 **excitement:** Aufregung. | **to address s.o.:** jdn. ansprechen. |
6 **start:** Zusammenschrecken. | **to depict:** (sich) abzeichnen. | 8 **to compose o.s.:** sich beruhigen. | 9 **distinctly:** klar, deutlich. |
10 **to allot:** zuteilen, bewilligen. | 10 f. **dietary:** Speiseration. |
15 **to controvert:** widersprechen. | 16 **animated:** lebhaft. |
17 **instant:** augenblicklich. | **confinement:** Arrest. | **bill:** Plakat, Anschlag. | **to paste:** kleben. | 21 **apprentice:** Lehrling, Lehrbursche, Gehilfe. | 22 **calling:** Beruf.

and read the bill next morning: "I never was more convinced of anything in my life, than I am, that that boy will come to be hung."

[…]

Chapter III

Relates how Oliver Twist was very near getting a Place, which would not have been a Sinecure

For a week after the commission of the impious and profane offence of asking for more, Oliver remained a close prisoner in the dark and solitary room to which he had been consigned by the wisdom and mercy of the board. […]

It chanced one morning, while Oliver's affairs were in this auspicious and comfortable state, that Mr. Gamfield, chimney-sweeper, was wending his way adown the High Street, deeply cogitating in his mind, his ways and means of paying certain arrears of rent, for which his landlord had become rather pressing. Mr. Gamfield's most sanguine estimate of his finances could not raise them within full five pounds of the desired amount; and, in a species of arithmetical desperation, he was

6 **to relate:** berichten. | 7 **sinecure:** Pfründe, Ruheposten. | 8 **commission:** Verübung. | **impious:** gottlos. | **profane:** frevelhaft. | 9 **offence:** Vergehen. | 10 **solitary:** einsam. | 12 **it chanced:** es traf sich. | 13 **auspicious:** vielversprechend. | **comfortable:** angenehm, tröstlich. | **state:** Zustand. | 13 f. **chimney-sweeper:** Schornsteinfeger. | 14 **to wend one's way:** sich auf den Weg machen. | 15 **to cogitate:** nachdenken. | 16 **arrear:** Rückstand. | **landlord:** Wirt, Vermieter. | 16 f. **pressing:** bedrängend. | 17 **sanguine:** zuversichtlich, optimistisch. | **estimate:** Schätzung. | 18 **to desire:** wünschen, verlangen. | 19 **species:** Art. | **arithmetical:** rechnerisch. | **desperation:** Verzweiflung.

alternately cudgelling his brains and his donkey, when, passing the workhouse, his eyes encountered the bill on the gate.

"Wo – o!" said Mr. Gamfield to the donkey.

The donkey was in a state of profound abstraction: wondering, probably, whether he was destined to be regaled with a cabbage-stalk or two, when he had disposed of the two sacks of soot with which the little cart was laden; so, without noticing the word of command, he jogged onward.

Mr. Gamfield growled a fierce imprecation on the donkey generally, but more particularly on his eyes; and, running after him, bestowed a blow on his head, which would inevitably have beaten in any skull but a donkey's. Then, catching hold of the bridle, he gave his jaw a sharp wrench, by way of gentle reminder that he was not his own master; and by these means turned him round. He then gave him another blow on the head, just to stun him till he came back again. Having completed these arrangements, he walked up to the gate, to read the bill.

The gentleman with the white waistcoat, was standing at the gate with his hands behind him, after having delivered himself of some profound sentiments in the board-room. Hav-

1 **to cudgel:** prügeln. | **brains** (pl.): Verstand, Grips. | 2 **to encounter s.th.:** auf etwas stoßen. | 4 **abstraction:** Geistesabwesenheit. | 5 **probably:** wahrscheinlich. | **to be destined:** ausersehen sein. | **to regale s.o.:** jdn. verwöhnen, fürstlich bewirten. | 6 **cabbage-stalk:** Kohlstrunk. | **to dispose of s.th.:** etwas loswerden. | 7 **soot:** Ruß. | **cart:** Karre. | **laden:** beladen. | 8 **to jog:** trotten. | 9 **to growl:** knurren. | **fierce:** wild, grimmig. | **imprecation:** Fluch, Verwünschung. | 11 **inevitably:** unweigerlich. | 12 **skull:** Schädel. | 13 **bridle:** Zaumzeug. | **jaw:** Kiefer. | **wrench:** drehender Ruck. | 13 f. **reminder:** Mahnung, Gedächtnisstütze. | 14 **master:** Herr, Meister. | 16 **to stun:** betäuben. | 20 f. **to deliver o.s. of s.th.:** etwas zum besten geben. | 21 **sentiment:** Gedanke, Meinung.

ing witnessed the little dispute between Mr. Gamfield and the donkey, he smiled joyously when that person came up to read the bill, for he saw at once that Mr. Gamfield was exactly the sort of master Oliver Twist wanted. Mr. Gamfield smiled, too, as he perused the document, for five pounds was just the sum he had been wishing for; and, as to the boy with which it was encumbered, Mr. Gamfield, knowing what the dietary of the workhouse was, well knew he would be a nice small pattern: just the very thing for register stoves. So, he spelt the bill through again, from beginning to end; and then, touching his fur cap in token of humility, accosted the gentleman in the white waistcoat.

"This here boy, sir, wot the parish wants to 'prentice," said Mr. Gamfield.

"Aye my man," said the gentleman in the white waistcoat, with a condescending smile. "What of him?"

"If the parish vould like him to learn a light pleasant trade, in a good 'spectable chimbley-sweepin' bisness," said Mr. Gamfield, "I wants a 'prentice, and I'm ready to take him."

"Walk in," said the gentleman in the white waistcoat. [...]

The bargain was made. Mr. Bumble was at once instructed that Oliver Twist and his indentures were to be conveyed be-

1 **to witness s.th:** Zeuge, Zeugin von etwas sein. | **dispute:** Streit, Auseinandersetzung. | 5 **to peruse:** durchlesen, studieren. | 7 **to encumber:** belasten, beschweren. | 9 **register stove:** Ofen mit Ventilklappen zur Regulierung der Temperatur. | 11 **fur cap:** Pelzmütze. | **in token of:** als Zeichen von. | **to accost s.o.:** jdn. ansprechen. | 13 **wot:** *what.* | **to 'prentice:** *to apprentice s.o.:* jdn. in die Lehre geben. | 15 **aye:** ja. | 16 **condescending:** herablassend. | 18 **'spectable:** *respectable:* ehrbar. | **chimbley-sweepin' bisness:** *chimney-sweeping business.* | 21 **to make** (auch: *to strike*) **a bargain:** einen Handel abschließen. | 21 **to instruct s.o.:** jdn. anweisen, belehren. | 22 **indenture:** Lehrvertrag. | **to convey s.o.:** jdn. bringen, führen.

fore the magistrate, for signature and approval, that very afternoon.

[…]

On their way to the magistrate, Mr. Bumble instructed Oliver that all he would have to do, would be to look very happy, and say, when the gentleman asked him if he wanted to be apprenticed, that he should like it very much indeed; both of which injunctions Oliver promised to obey: the rather as Mr. Bumble threw in a gentle hint, that if he failed in either particular, there was no telling what would be done to him. […]

Behind a desk, sat two old gentlemen with powdered heads: one of whom was reading the newspaper: while the other was perusing, with the aid of a pair of tortoise-shell spectacles, a small piece of parchment which lay before him. Mr. Limbkins was standing in front of the desk on one side; and Mr. Gamfield, with a partially washed face, on the other; while two or three bluff-looking men, in top-boots, were lounging about.

The old gentleman with the spectacles, gradually dozed off, over the little bit of parchment; and there was a short pause, after Oliver had been stationed by Mr. Bumble in front of the desk.

"This is the boy, your worship," said Mr. Bumble.

The old gentleman who was reading the newspaper, raised his head for a moment, and pulled the other old gentleman

1 **magistrate:** Richter, richterlicher Beamter. | **approval:** Genehmigung. | 8 **injunction:** Anweisung, Befehl. | 9 **to fail:** fehl gehen, säumig sein. | 9 f. **particular:** Einzelheit. | 10 **there was no telling:** es ließ sich nicht absehen. | 11 **to powder:** (be)pudern. | 13 **tortoise-shell:** Schildpatt. | 14 **parchment:** Pergament. | 16 **partially:** teilweise. | 17 **bluff-looking:** derb aussehend. | **top-boots** (pl.): Stulpenstiefel. | 17 f. **to lounge about:** umherlungern. | 19 **gradually:** allmählich. | **to doze off:** einnicken. | 23 **your worship:** Euer Gnaden.

by the sleeve; whereupon, the last-mentioned old gentleman woke up.

"Oh, is this the boy?" said the old gentleman.

"This is him, sir," replied Mr. Bumble. "Bow to the magistrate, my dear."

[…]

"And this man that's to be his master – you, sir – you'll treat him well, and feed him, and do all that sort of thing, – will you?" said the old gentleman.

"When I says I will, I means I will," replied Mr. Gamfield doggedly.

"You're a rough speaker, my friend, but you look an honest, open-hearted man," said the old gentleman: turning his spectacles in the direction of the candidate for Oliver's premium, whose villanous countenance was a regular stamped receipt for cruelty. But, the magistrate was half blind and half childish, so he couldn't reasonably be expected to discern what other people did.

"I hope I am, sir," said Mr. Gamfield, with an ugly leer.

"I have no doubt you are, my friend," replied the old gentleman […].

The old gentleman stopped, laid down his pen, and looked from Oliver to Mr. Limbkins: who attempted to take snuff with a cheerful and unconcerned aspect.

"My boy!" said the old gentleman, leaning over the desk.

1 **sleeve:** Ärmel. | **whereupon:** woraufhin. | 8 **to feed s.o.:** jdn. ernähren. | 11 **doggedly:** verbissen. | 13 **open-hearted:** aufrichtig. | 14 **premium:** Lehrgeld, das der Lehrherr erhält. | 15 **villanous:** *villainous:* schurkisch. | **regular:** ordnungsgemäß. | **to stamp:** (ab)stempeln. | **receipt:** Beleg, Quittung. | 16 **cruelty:** Grausamkeit. | 17 **to discern:** erkennen. | 19 **leer:** gehässiger Seitenblick. | 23 **to take snuff:** eine Prise Schnupftabak nehmen. | 24 **cheerful:** fröhlich, freundlich. | **unconcerned:** unbekümmert. | **aspect:** Miene.

Oliver started at the sound. He might be excused for doing so; for the words were kindly said; and strange sounds frighten one. He trembled violently, and burst into tears.

"My boy!" said the old gentleman, "you look pale and alarmed. What is the matter?"

"Stand a little away from him, Beadle," said the other magistrate: laying aside the paper, and leaning forward with an expression of interest. "Now, boy, tell us what's the matter: don't be afraid."

Oliver fell on his knees, and clasping his hands together, prayed that they would order him back to the dark room – that they would starve him – beat him – kill him if they pleased – rather than send him away with that dreadful man.

"Well!" said Mr. Bumble, raising his hands and eyes with most impressive solemnity, "Well! of all the artful and designing orphans that ever I see, Oliver, you are one of the most bare-facedest."

"Hold your tongue, Beadle," said the second old gentleman, when Mr. Bumble had given vent to this compound adjective.

[…]

The old gentleman in the tortoise-shell spectacles, looked at his companion; he nodded significantly.

[…]

"Take the boy back to the workhouse, and treat him kindly. He seems to want it."

[…]

10 **to clasp one's hands:** die Hände falten. | 11 **to pray:** flehen. | 13 **dreadful:** schrecklich. | 15 **impressive:** beeindruckend. | **solemnity:** Feierlichkeit. | **artful:** gerissen, gewievt. | 15 f. **designing:** hinterhältig. | 17 **bare-faced:** schamlos. | 18 **to hold one's tongue:** den Mund halten, schweigen. | 19 **to give vent to s.th.:** etwas äußern, einer Sache Luft machen. | **compound adjective:** zusammengesetztes Eigenschaftswort. | 22 **to nod:** nicken. | **significantly:** bedeutsam.

The next morning, the public were once more informed that Oliver Twist was again To Let; and that five pounds would be paid to anybody who would take possession of him.

Chapter IV

Oliver, being offered another Place, makes his first entry into Public Life

[…] The more the case presented itself to the board, […] they came to the conclusion, that the only way of providing for Oliver effectually, was to send him to sea without delay.

Mr. Bumble had been despatched to make various preliminary inquiries, with the view of finding out some captain or other who wanted a cabin-boy without any friends; and was returning to the workhouse to communicate the result of his mission; when he encountered, just at the gate, no less a person than Mr. Sowerberry, the parochial undertaker.

[…]

"By the bye," said Mr. Bumble, "you don't know anybody who wants a boy, do you? A porochial 'prentice, who is at present a deadweight; a millstone, as I may say; round the porochi-

1 **the public:** die Öffentlichkeit. | 2 **to let:** zu vergeben. | 3 **to take possession of s.o.:** von jdm. Besitz nehmen. | 5 **place:** Anstellung, (Arbeits-)Stelle. | **entry:** Eintritt. | 8 **conclusion:** Ergebnis, Schlussfolgerung. | 9 **effectually:** erfolgreich, wirksam. | **to send s.o. to sea:** jdn. zur See(fahrt) schicken, jdm. eine Heuer auf einem Schiff verschaffen. | 10 **to despatch s.o.:** jdn. entsenden. | 10 f. **preliminary:** vorausgehend, vorbereitend, einleitend. | 11 **view:** Absicht. | 12 **cabin-boy:** Schiffsjunge. | 13 **to communicate:** mitteilen, kundtun. | 14 **mission:** Auftrag. | **to encounter s.o.:** jdm. begegnen. | 14 f. **no less a person:** kein(e) Geringere(r). | 17 **by the bye:** übrigens. | 19 **deadweight:** Ballast.

al throat? Liberal terms, Mr. Sowerberry, liberal terms!" As Mr. Bumble spoke, he raised his cane to the bill above him, and gave three distinct raps upon the words "five pounds:" which were printed thereon in Roman capitals of gigantic size.

"Gadso!" said the undertaker: taking Mr. Bumble by the gilt-edged lappel of his official coat; "that's just the very thing I wanted to speak to you about. [...]"

"[...] you know, Mr. Bumble, I pay a good deal towards the poor's rates."

"Hem!" said Mr. Bumble. "Well?"

"Well," replied the undertaker, "I was thinking that if I pay so much towards 'em, I've a right to get as much out of 'em as I can, Mr. Bumble; and so – and so – I think I'll take the boy myself."

Mr. Bumble grasped the undertaker by arm, and led him into the building. Mr. Sowerberry was closeted with the board for five minutes; and it was arranged that Oliver should go to him that evening "upon liking" – a phrase which means, in the case of a parish apprentice, that if the master find, upon a short trial, that he can get enough work out of a boy without putting too much food into him, he shall have him for a term of years, to do what he likes with.

When little Oliver was taken before "the gentlemen" that evening; and informed that he was to go, that night, as general house-lad to a coffin-maker's; and that if he complained of his

1 **liberal terms:** günstige Bedingungen. | 3 **distinct:** deutlich, vernehmlich. | **rap:** Schlag, Klopfen. | 4 **Roman:** Antiqua (Schrifttyp). | **capitals:** Großbuchstaben. | **gigantic:** riesenhaft. | 5 **Gadso!:** Alle Wetter! | 5 f. **gilt-edged:** goldgerändert. | 6 **lappel:** Rockaufschlag. | 9 **poor's rates** (pl.): Armensteuer. | 16 **to be closeted with s.o.:** eine vertrauliche Unterredung mit jdm. haben. | 18 **upon liking:** auf Probe. | **phrase:** Ausdruck, Wendung. | 19 **master:** Lehrherr. | **trial:** Probezeit. | 21 **term:** Dauer, Zeitspanne. | 25 **coffin-maker:** Sargmacher.

situation, or ever came back to the parish again, he would be sent to sea: there to be drowned, or knocked on the head, as the case might be; he evinced so little emotion, that they, by common consent, pronounced him a hardened young rascal, and ordered Mr. Bumble to remove him forthwith.

[...]

The undertaker, who had just put up the shutters of his shop, was making some entries in his day-book by the light of a most appropriately dismal candle, when Mr. Bumble entered.

"Aha!" said the undertaker: looking up from the book, and pausing in the middle of a word; "is that you, Bumble?"

"No one else, Mr. Sowerberry," replied the beadle. "Here! I've brought the boy." Oliver made a bow.

"Oh! that's the boy, is it?" said the undertaker: raising the candle above his head, to get a better view of Oliver. "Mrs. Sowerberry, will you have the goodness to come here a moment, my dear?"

Mrs. Sowerberry emerged from a little room behind the shop, and presented the form of a short, thin, squeezed-up woman, with a vixenish countenance.

"My dear," said Mr. Sowerberry, deferentially, "this is the boy from the workhouse that I told you of." Oliver bowed again.

"Dear me!" said the undertaker's wife, "he's very small."

2 **to be drowned:** ertränkt werden. | 3 **to evince:** zeigen, bekunden. | 4 **consent:** Übereinstimmung, Einverständnis. | **to pronounce s.o. s.th.:** jdn. für etwas erklären. | **hardened:** verhärtet, abgebrüht. | **rascal:** Schurke, Halunke. | 7 **shutter:** Fensterladen. | 8 **entry:** Eintrag. | **day-book:** Kassenbuch. | 9 **appropriately:** angemessen, passend. | **dismal:** trostlos, trübe. | 16 **goodness:** Güte, Freundlichkeit. | 18 **to emerge from s.th.:** aus etwas auftauchen, hervortreten, herauskommen. | 19 **squeezed-up:** verkniffen. | 20 **vixenish:** zänkisch. | 21 **deferentially:** ehrerbietig. | 24 **Dear me!:** Ach du meine Güte!

"Why, he *is* rather small," replied Mr. Bumble: looking at Oliver as if it were his fault that he was no bigger; "he *is* small. There's no denying it. But he'll grow, Mrs. Sowerberry – he'll grow."

"Ah! I dare say he will," replied the lady pettishly, "on our victuals and our drink. I see no saving in parish children, not I; for they always cost more to keep, than they're worth. However, men always think they know best. [...]"

[...]

"Then come with me," said Mrs. Sowerberry: taking up a dim and dirty lamp [...]; "your bed's under the counter. You don't mind sleeping among the coffins, I suppose? But it doesn't much matter whether you do or don't, for you can't sleep anywhere else. Come; don't keep me here all night!"

Oliver lingered no longer, but meekly followed his new mistress.

3 **to deny:** leugnen, abstreiten. | 5 **pettishly:** launisch, reizbar. | 6 **victuals** (pl.): Lebensmittel, Verpflegung. | **saving:** Ersparnis. | 11 **dim:** trübe, matt. | **counter:** Ladentheke. | 15 **meekly:** demütig, widerspruchslos. | 15 f. **mistress:** Herrin.

Chapter V

Oliver mingles with new Associates. Going to a Funeral for the first time, he forms an unfavourable Notion of his Master's Business

Oliver, being left to himself in the undertaker's shop, set the lamp down on a workman's bench, and gazed timidly about him with a feeling of awe and dread, which many people a good deal older than he will be at no loss to understand. An unfinished coffin on black tressels, which stood in the middle of the shop, looked so gloomy and deathlike that a cold tremble came over him, every time his eyes wandered in the direction of the dismal object: from which he almost expected to see some frightful form slowly rear its head, to drive him mad with terror. [...]

Oliver was awakened in the morning, by a loud kicking at the outside of the shop-door: which, before he could huddle on his clothes, was repeated, in an angry and impetuous manner, about twenty-five times. When he began to undo the chain, the legs desisted, and a voice began.

"Open the door, will yer?" cried the voice which belonged to the legs which had kicked at the door.

2 **to mingle with s.o.:** mit jdm. Umgang haben. | **associate:** Kollege, Mitarbeiter. | **funeral:** Beerdigung. | 3 **unfavourable:** ungünstig. | 6 **workman's bench:** Werkbank. | **timidly:** ängstlich, scheu. | 7 **awe:** Schauer, Furcht. | **dread:** Grauen, Schrecken. | 8 **to be at no loss to do s.th.:** keine Schwierigkeiten haben, etwas zu tun. | 9 **tressel:** Gestell, Bock. | 10 **gloomy:** düster. | **tremble:** Zittern. | 12 **dismal:** trostlos, bedrückend. | 13 **frightful:** schrecklich, grässlich. | **to rear one's head:** den Kopf heben. | 16 f. **to huddle s.th. on:** etwas flüchtig überstreifen. | 17 **impetuous:** ungestüm. | 18 **to undo:** aufmachen, öffnen. | 19 **to desist:** einhalten, innehalten. | 20 **yer:** *you.*

"I will, directly, sir," replied Oliver: undoing the chain, and turning the key.

"I suppose yer the new boy, a'n't yer?" said the voice, through the keyhole.

"Yes, sir," replied Oliver.

"How old are yer?" inquired the voice.

"Ten, sir," replied Oliver.

"Then I'll whop yer when I get in," said the voice; "you just see if I don't, that's all, my work'us brat!" and having made this obliging promise, the voice began to whistle.

Oliver had been too often subjected to the process to which the very expressive monosyllable just recorded bears reference, to entertain the smallest doubt that the owner of the voice, whoever he might be, would redeem his pledge, most honourably. He drew back the bolts with a trembling hand, and opened the door.

For a second or two, Oliver glanced up the street, and down the street, and over the way: impressed with the belief that the unknown, who had addressed him through the keyhole, had walked a few paces off, to warm himself; for nobody did he see but a big charity-boy, sitting on a post in front of the house,

1 **directly:** sofort. | 3 **yer:** *you are.* | 8 **to whop s.o.:** jdn. verdreschen. | 9 **work'us:** *workhouse.* | 10 **obliging:** verbindlich. | 11 **to subject s.o. to s.th.:** jdn. einer Sache aussetzen. | 12 **expressive:** ausdrucksstark. | **monosyllable:** einsilbiges Wort. | **to record:** verzeichnen. | **to bear reference to s.th.:** Bezug haben zu etwas. | 13 **to entertain doubt:** Zweifel hegen. | 14 **to redeem:** einlösen. | **pledge:** Versprechen, Zusage. | 14 f. **honourably:** ehrenhaft. | 15 **bolt:** Riegel. | 20 **pace:** Schritt. | 21 **charity-boy:** Armenschüler. Armenschulen (*charity schools*) waren Einrichtungen, in denen die ärmsten Kinder vor und nach ihrer täglichen Arbeit neben Unterricht auch Essen, Kleidung und Unterkunft erhielten. Oliver erkennt den Jungen an seiner Kleidung als Armenschüler (*charity:* Almosen; Barmherzigkeit). | **post:** Pfosten.

eating a slice of bread and butter: which he cut into wedges, the size of his mouth, with a clasp-knife, and then consumed with great dexterity.

"I beg your pardon, sir," said Oliver, at length: seeing that no other visitor made his appearance; "did you knock?"

"I kicked," replied the charity-boy.

"Did you want a coffin, sir?" inquired Oliver, innocently.

At this, the charity-boy looked monstrous fierce; and said that Oliver would want one before long, if he cut jokes with his superiors in that way.

"Yer don't know who I am, I suppose, Work'us?" said the charity-boy, in continuation: descending from the top of the post, meanwhile, with edifying gravity.

"No, sir," rejoined Oliver.

"I'm Mister Noah Claypole," said the charity-boy, "and you're under me. Take down the shutters, yer idle young ruffian!" [...]

Noah was a charity-boy, but not a workhouse orphan. No chance-child was he, for he could trace his genealogy all the way back to his parents, who lived hard by; his mother being a washerwoman, and his father a drunken soldier: discharged with a wooden leg, and a diurnal pension of twopence-half-

1 **wedge:** (keilförmiges) Stück. | 2 **clasp-knife:** Klappmesser. | 3 **dexterity:** Geschicklichkeit. | 4 **I beg your pardon:** Ich bitte um Verzeihung. | 5 **to make one's appearance:** erscheinen, auftauchen. | 8 **monstrous:** ungeheuer. | 9 **to cut jokes:** Witze reißen. | 10 **superior:** Vorgesetzter. | 12 **continuation:** Fortführung. | **to descend:** herabsteigen. | 13 **edifying:** erbaulich. | **gravity:** Ernsthaftigkeit, Feierlichkeit. | 14 **to rejoin:** erwidern. | 16 **idle:** faul. | 16 f. **ruffian:** Halunke. | 19 **chance-child:** uneheliches Kind. | **to trace s.th. back:** etwas zurückverfolgen. | **genealogy:** Abstammung. | 20 **hard by:** ganz nahe. | 21 **to discharge s.o.:** jdn. entlassen. | 22 **diurnal:** täglich.

penny and an unstateable fraction. The shop-boys in the neighbourhood had long been in the habit of branding Noah, in the public streets, with the ignominious epithets of "leathers," "charity," and the like; and Noah had borne them without reply. But, now that fortune had cast in his way a nameless orphan, at whom even the meanest could point the finger of scorn, he retorted on him with interest. This affords charming food for contemplation. It shows us what a beautiful thing human nature sometimes is; and how impartially the same amiable qualities are developed in the finest lord and the dirtiest charity-boy.

Oliver had been sojourning at the undertaker's some three weeks or a month. Mr. and Mrs. Sowerberry: the shop being shut up: were taking their supper in the little back-parlour, when Mr. Sowerberry, after several deferential glances at his wife, said,

"My dear –" He was going to say more; but, Mrs. Sowerberry looking up, with a peculiarly unpropitious aspect, he stopped short.

"Well," said Mrs. Sowerberry, sharply.

"Nothing, my dear, nothing," said Mr. Sowerberry.

1 **unstateable:** nicht nennbar. | **fraction:** Bruchzahl. | 2 **to be in the habit of doing s.th.:** die Angewohnheit haben, etwas zu tun. | **to brand s.o.:** jdn. brandmarken. | 3 **ignominious:** schimpflich, schmählich. | **epithet:** Beiname. | 3 f. **leathers** (pl.): Lederhose (bezieht sich auf die Kleidung der Armenschüler). | 5 **fortune:** Schicksal. | 6 **mean:** gering, niedrig. | 7 **scorn:** Verachtung. | **to retort on s.o.:** jdm. (etwas) zurückgeben, heimzahlen. | **interest:** Zins(en). | **to afford s.th.:** etwas bieten. | 8 **contemplation:** Betrachtung, Nachdenken. | 9 **impartially:** unabhängig. | 9 f. **amiable:** liebenswert. | 12 **to sojourn:** verweilen. | 14 **back-parlour:** Hinterstübchen. | 15 **glance:** Blick. | 18 **peculiarly:** besonders. | **unpropitious:** ungünstig. | 18 f. **to stop short:** plötzlich innehalten.

[…]

"It's only about young Twist, my dear," said Mr. Sowerberry. "A very good-looking boy, that, my dear."

"He need be, for he eats enough," observed the lady.

"There's an expression of melancholy in his face, my dear," resumed Mr. Sowerberry, "which is very interesting. He would make a delightful mute, my love."

[…]

"I don't mean a regular mute to attend grown-up people, my dear, but only for children's practice. It would be very new to have a mute in proportion, my dear. You may depend upon it, it would have a superb effect."

Mrs. Sowerberry, who had a good deal of taste in the undertaking way, was much struck by the novelty of this idea; […] it was speedily determined, therefore, that Oliver should be at once initiated into the mysteries of the trade; and, with this view, that he should accompany his master on the very next occasion of his services being required.

The occasion was not long in coming. Half an hour after breakfast next morning, Mr. Bumble entered the shop; and supporting his cane against the counter, drew forth his large leathern pocket-book: from which he selected a small scrap of paper, which he handed over to Sowerberry.

"Aha!" said the undertaker, glancing over it with a lively

6 **to resume:** fortfahren, weiterreden. | 7 **delightful:** entzückend, wunderbar. | **mute:** Begleiter bei Leichenzügen. | 9 **to attend s.o.:** jdm. beiwohnen, beistehen; jdn. begleiten. | 11 **in proportion:** in passender Größe. | **to depend upon s.th.:** sich auf etwas verlassen. | 12 **superb:** hervorragend. | 14 **to strike s.o.:** jdn. beeindrucken. | **novelty:** Neuartigkeit, Neuheit. | 15 **speedily:** schnell, rasch. | 16 **to initiate s.o. into s.th.:** jdn. in etwas einweihen. | 21 **to support:** (an)lehnen. | **forth:** heraus, hervor. | 22 f. **scrap of paper:** Papierfetzen, Stückchen Papier.

countenance; "an order for a coffin, eh?" "For a coffin first, and a porochial funeral afterwards," replied Mr. Bumble, fastening the strap of the leathern pocket-book: which, like himself, was very corpulent.

[…]

"Well," said Mr. Sowerberry, taking up his hat, "the sooner this job is done, the better. Noah, look after the shop. Oliver, put on your cap, and come with me." Oliver obeyed, and followed his master on his professional mission.

They walked on, for some time, through the most crowded and densely inhabited part of the town; and then, striking down a narrow street more dirty and miserable than any they had yet passed through, paused to look for the house which was the object of their search. […]

There was neither knocker nor bell-handle at the open door where Oliver and his master stopped; so, groping his way cautiously through the dark passage, and bidding Oliver keep close to him and not be afraid, the undertaker mounted to the top of the first flight of stairs; and stumbling against a door on the landing, rapped at it with his knuckles.

It was opened by a young girl of thirteen or fourteen. The undertaker at once saw enough of what the room contained, to know it was the apartment to which he had been directed. He stepped in; and Oliver followed him.

There was no fire in the room; but a man was crouching,

3 **strap:** Riemen. | 4 **corpulent:** füllig, beleibt. | 7 **to look after s.th.:** auf etwas aufpassen. | 11 **densely inhabited:** dicht besiedelt. | 11 f. **to strike down s.th.:** etwas hinabgehen. | 12 **miserable:** elend, armselig. | 15 **knocker:** Klopfer. | **bell-handle:** Klingelzug. | 16 **to grope:** ertasten. | 16 f. **cautiously:** vorsichtig. | 17 **passage:** Korridor, Flur. | 18 **to mount s.th.:** etwas hinaufsteigen. | 19 **flight of stairs:** Treppenflucht. | **to stumble:** stolpern. | 20 **landing:** Treppenabsatz. | **to rap at s.th.:** an etwas klopfen. | **knuckle:** (Finger-)Knöchel. | 25 **to crouch:** kauern.

mechanically, over the empty stove. An old woman, too, had drawn a low stool to the cold hearth: and was sitting beside him. There were some ragged children in another corner; and in a small recess, opposite the door, there lay upon the ground, something covered with an old blanket. Oliver shuddered as he cast his eyes towards the place: and crept involuntarily closer to his master; for though it was covered up, the boy felt that it was a corpse.

[...]

"Nobody shall go near her," said the man, starting fiercely up, as the undertaker approached the recess. "Keep back! d–n you, keep back, if you've a life to lose!"

"Nonsense, my good man," said the undertaker, who was pretty well used to misery in all its shapes. "Nonsense!"

"I tell you," said the man: clenching his hands, and stamping furiously on the floor, – "I tell you I won't have her put into the ground. She couldn't rest there. The worms would worry her: not eat her: she is so worn away."

The undertaker offered no reply to this raving; but, producing a tape from his pocket, knelt down for a moment by the side of the body.

"Ah!" said the man: bursting into tears, and sinking on his knees at the feet of the dead woman; "kneel down, kneel down – kneel round her, every one of you, and mark my words! I say

1 **mechanically:** mechanisch. | **stove:** Küchenherd, Ofen. | 2 **stool:** Hocker, Schemel. | **hearth:** Feuerstelle. | 3 **ragged:** zerlumpt. | 4 **recess:** Nische. | 6 **to creep:** kriechen. | **involuntarily:** unfreiwillig. | 8 **corpse:** Leichnam. | 10 f. **to start up:** aufspringen, hochfahren. | 11 **to approach s.th.:** an etwas herangehen. | **keep back!:** weg da! | 11 f. **d–n you:** *damn you:* scher dich zum Teufel! | 15 **to clench one's hands:** die Fäuste ballen. | **to stamp:** stampfen, trampeln. | 18 **worn away:** ausgemergelt. | 19 **raving:** Raserei. | 19 f. **to produce:** hervorziehen, -holen. | 23 **to kneel down:** niederknien. | 24 **mark my words!:** hört, was ich sage!

she was starved to death. I never knew how bad she was, till the fever came upon her; and then her bones were starting through the skin. There was neither fire nor candle; she died in the dark – in the dark. She couldn't even see her children's faces, though we heard her gasping out their names. I begged for her in the streets: and they sent me to prison. When I came back, she was dying; and all the blood in my heart has dried up, for they starved her to death. I swear it before the God that saw it! They starved her!" He twined his hands in his hair; and, with a loud scream, rolled grovelling upon the floor: his eyes fixed: and the foam gushing from his lips.

[…]

The next day, (the family having been meanwhile relieved with a half-quartern loaf and a piece of cheese: left with them by Mr. Bumble himself,) Oliver and his master returned to the miserable abode; where Mr. Bumble had already arrived, accompanied by four men from the workhouse: who were to act as bearers. An old black cloak had been thrown over the rags of the old woman and the man; and the bare coffin having been screwed down, was hoisted on the shoulders of the bearers, and carried into the street.

"Now, you must put your best leg foremost, old lady!" whispered Sowerberry in the old woman's ear; "we are rather late; and it won't do, to keep the clergyman waiting. Move on, my men, – as quick as you like!"

2 **to start:** hervortreten. | 7 **to dry up:** austrocknen, versiegen. | 9 **to twine one's hands:** die Hände ringen. | 10 **to grovel:** kriechen. | 11 **fixed:** starr. | **foam:** Schaum. | **to gush:** strömen, schießen. | 13 **to relieve s.o.:** jdn. unterstützen. | 14 **half-quartern loaf:** halbes Viertelpfundbrot. | 16 **abode:** Behausung, Wohnstätte. | 18 **cloak:** Mantel, Umhang. | **rags** (pl.): Lumpen. | 20 **to screw s.th. down:** etwas zuschrauben. | **to hoist:** hieven. | 22 **to put one's best leg foremost:** sein Bestes geben, einen Schritt zulegen. | 24 **clergyman:** Geistlicher.

Thus directed, the bearers trotted on under their light burden; and the two mourners kept as near them, as they could. Mr. Bumble and Sowerberry walked at a good smart pace in front; and Oliver, whose legs were not so long as his master's, ran by the side.

There was not so great a necessity for hurrying as Mr. Sowerberry had anticipated, however; for when they reached the obscure corner of the churchyard in which the nettles grew, and where the parish graves were made, the clergyman had not arrived; and the clerk, who was sitting by the vestry-room fire, seemed to think it by no means improbable that it might be an hour or so, before he came. So, they put the bier on the brink of the grave; and the two mourners waited patiently in the damp clay, with a cold rain drizzling down: while the ragged boys, whom the spectacle had attracted into the churchyard, played a noisy game at hide-and-seek among the tombstones: or varied their amusements by jumping backwards and forwards over the coffin. Mr. Sowerberry and Bumble, being personal friends of the clerk, sat by the fire with him, and read the paper.

At length, after a lapse of something more than an hour, Mr. Bumble, and Sowerberry, and the clerk, were seen running towards the grave. Immediately afterwards, the clergyman appeared: putting on his surplice as he came along. Mr. Bumble

2 **mourner:** Trauernde(r), Trauergast. | 3 **smart:** zügig. | **pace:** Tempo. | 6 **necessity:** Notwendigkeit. | 7 **to anticipate:** erwarten, annehmen. | 8 **obscure:** dunkel, düster. | **churchyard:** Friedhof. | **nettles:** Nesseln. | 10 **clerk:** hier: Küster. | **vestry-room:** Sakristei. | 11 **improbable:** unwahrscheinlich. | 12 **bier:** (Toten-)Bahre. | 13 **brink:** Rand, Kante. | 14 **damp:** feucht, klamm. | **clay:** Lehm. | **to drizzle:** nieseln. | 15 **spectacle:** Schauspiel. | 16 f. **tombstone:** Grabstein. | 17 **to vary:** abwandeln, wechseln. | 21 **lapse:** Zeitspanne, Ablauf. | 24 **surplice:** Chorhemd.

then threshed a boy or two, to keep up appearances; and the reverend gentleman, having read as much of the burial service as could be compressed into four minutes, gave his surplice to the clerk, and walked away again.

"Now, Bill!" said Sowerberry to the grave-digger, "fill up!"

It was no very difficult task; for the grave was so full, that the uppermost coffin was within a few feet of the surface. The grave-digger shovelled in the earth; stamped it loosely down with his feet; shouldered his spade; and walked off [...].

"Well, Oliver," said Sowerberry, as they walked home, "how do you like it?"

"Pretty well, thank you, sir," replied Oliver, with considerable hesitation. "Not very much, sir."

"Ah, you'll get used to it in time, Oliver," said Sowerberry. "Nothing when you *are* used to it, my boy."

Oliver wondered, in his own mind, whether it had taken a very long time to get Mr. Sowerberry used to it. But he thought it better not to ask the question; and walked back to the shop: thinking over all he had seen and heard.

1 **to thresh s.o.:** jdn. verdreschen. | **appearance:** Anschein, äußerer Schein. | 2 **reverend:** ehrwürdig. | **burial service:** Begräbnisgottesdienst. | 3 **to compress:** pressen. | 8 **grave-digger:** Totengräber. | **to shovel:** schaufeln. | 9 **spade:** Spaten. | 13 **hesitation:** Zögern. | 14 **to get used to s.th.:** sich an etwas gewöhnen.

Chapter VI

Oliver, being goaded by the Taunts of Noah, rouses into Action, and rather astonishes him

The month's trial over, Oliver was formally apprenticed. It was a nice sickly season just at this time. In commercial phrase, coffins were looking up; and, in the course of a few weeks, Oliver had acquired a great deal of experience. [...]

[...] for many months he continued meekly to submit to the domination and ill-treatment of Noah Claypole: who used him far worse than before, now that his jealousy was roused by seeing the new boy promoted to the black stick and hat-band, while he, the old one, remained stationary in the muffin-cap and leathers. Charlotte treated him badly, because Noah did; and Mrs. Sowerberry was his decided enemy, because Mr. Sowerberry was disposed to be his friend [...].

One day, Oliver and Noah had descended into the kitchen at the usual dinner-hour, to banquet upon a small joint of mutton – a pound and a half of the worst end of the neck – when, Charlotte being called out of the way, there ensued a brief interval of time, which Noah Claypole, being hungry and vicious, consid-

2 **to goad s.o.:** jdn. reizen, anstacheln. | **taunt:** Hohn Spott, Stichelei. | 3 **to rouse into action:** wach werden, zur Tat schreiten. | 4 **formally:** offiziell, in aller Form. | 5 **sickly:** ungesund. | **commercial:** geschäftlich, kaufmännisch. | 6 **to be looking up:** sich im Aufwärtstrend befinden. | 7 **to acquire:** erwerben. | 8 **to submit to s.th.:** etwas über sich ergehen lassen. | 9 **domination:** Herrschaft. | **ill-treatment:** Misshandlung. | 10 **to rouse s.th.:** etwas wecken. | 11 **to promote s.o.:** jdn. befördern. | **hat-band** (auch: *hatband*): Hutband. | 12 **to remain stationary:** unverändert bleiben. | **muffin-cap:** flache, runde Mütze. | 17 **to banquet:** schmausen, tafeln. | **joint:** Braten. | **mutton:** Hammel. | 19 **to ensue:** folgen. | 19 f. **interval of time:** Zeitspanne, Pause. | 20 **vicious:** bösartig.

ered he could not possibly devote to a worthier purpose than aggravating and tantalising young Oliver Twist.

[…]

"Work'us," said Noah, "how's your mother?"

"She's dead," replied Oliver; "don't you say anything about her to me!"

Oliver's colour rose as he said this; he breathed quickly; and there was a curious working of the mouth and nostrils, which Mr. Claypole thought must be the immediate precursor of a violent fit of crying. Under this impression he returned to the charge.

[…]

"Yer know, Work'us," continued Noah, emboldened by Oliver's silence; and speaking in a jeering tone of affected pity: of all tones the most annoying: "Yer know, Work'us, it carn't be helped now; and of course yer couldn't help it then; and I'm very sorry for it; and I'm sure we all are: and pity yer very much. But yer must know, Work'us, yer mother was a regular right-down bad 'un."

"What did you say?" inquired Oliver, looking up very quickly.

"A regular right-down bad 'un, Work'us," replied Noah, coolly. […]

Crimson with fury, Oliver started up; overthrew the chair

1 **to devote:** (sich) widmen. | **purpose:** Zweck. | 2 **to aggravate:** ärgern. | **to tantalise:** peinigen. | 8 **nostrils:** Nasenlöcher. | 9 **precursor:** Vorläufer, Vorbote. | 10 **fit of crying:** Weinkrampf. | 10 f. **to return to the charge:** zur Sache zurückkommen. | 13 **emboldened:** ermutigt. | 14 **jeering:** höhnisch, spöttisch. | 15 f. **it carn't be helped:** es lässt sich nicht ändern. | 16 f. **to be sorry for s.th.:** etwas bedauern. | 18 **regular:** regelrecht, ausgesprochen. | 19 **right-down:** regelrecht, ausgesprochen. | **bad 'un:** *bad one:* Taugenichts. | 23 **coolly:** unverfroren. | 24 **crimson:** hochrot. | **fury:** große Wut. | **to overthrow:** umwerfen, -stoßen.

and table; seized Noah by the throat; shook him, in the violence of his rage, till his teeth chattered in his head; and, collecting his whole force into one heavy blow, felled him to the ground.

[…]

"He'll murder me!" blubbered Noah. "Charlotte! missis! Here's the new boy a-murdering of me! Help! help! Oliver's gone mad! Char – lotte!"

Noah's shouts were responded to, by a loud scream from Charlotte, and a louder from Mrs. Sowerberry; the former of whom rushed into the kitchen by a side-door: while the latter paused on the staircase till she was quite certain that it was consistent with the preservation of human life, to come further down.

"Oh, you little wretch!" screamed Charlotte; seizing Oliver with her utmost force, which was about equal to that of a moderately strong man in particularly good training, "Oh, you little un-grate-ful, mur-de-rous, hor-rid vil-lain!" And between every syllable, Charlotte gave Oliver a blow with all her might: accompanying it with a scream, for the benefit of society.

Charlotte's fist was by no means a light one; but, lest it should not be effectual in calming Oliver's wrath, Mrs. Sower-

1 **to seize:** anpacken, greifen. | 2 **rage:** Wut, Rasen, Toben. | **to chatter:** klappern (Zähne). | 3 **to fell s.o.:** jdn. niederstrecken. | 6 **to blubber:** plärren, flennen. | **missis:** gnädige Frau, Frau des Hauses. | 13 **consistent:** vereinbar, übereinstimmend. | **preservation:** Erhaltung, Bewahrung. | 15 **wretch:** Halunke, Bösewicht. | 16 **utmost:** äußerste(r, s), allergrößte(r, s). | 17 **moderately:** mäßig. | 18 **ungrateful:** undankbar. | **horrid:** abscheulich, fürchterlich. | **villain:** Schurke. | 20 **might:** Macht. | **benefit:** Nutzen, Gefallen. | 22 **by no means:** keineswegs, keinesfalls. | **lest:** aus Furcht, dass; für den Fall, dass. | 23 **to calm:** beruhigen, besänftigen. | **wrath:** Zorn, Wut.

berry plunged into the kitchen, and assisted to hold him with one hand, while she scratched his face with the other. In this favourable position of affairs, Noah rose from the ground: and pommelled him behind.

This was rather too violent exercise to last long. When they were all three wearied out, and could tear and beat no longer, they dragged Oliver, struggling and shouting, but nothing daunted, into the dust-cellar, and there locked him up […].

"What's to be done!" exclaimed Mrs. Sowerberry. "Your master's not at home: there's not a man in the house; and he'll kick that door down, in ten minutes." Oliver's vigorous plunges against the bit of timber in question, rendered this occurrence highly probable.

[…] "Run to Mr. Bumble, Noah, and tell him to come here directly, and not to lose a minute; never mind your cap! Make haste! […]"

[…]

1 **to plunge:** stürzen. | 2 **to scratch:** zerkratzen. | 3 **favourable:** günstig. | **position of affairs:** Lage der Dinge. | 4 **to pommel:** schlagen, prügeln. | 6 **to be wearied out:** erschöpft sein. | 7 **to drag:** schleifen, zerren. | 8 **daunted:** eingeschüchtert. | **dust-cellar:** Rumpelkammer. | 11 **vigorous:** kräftig. | 11 f. **plunge:** Ausschlagen (eines Pferdes), Tritt. | 12 **bit of timber:** Stückchen Holz. | **in question:** fraglich, betreffend. | 12 f. **occurrence:** Ereignis. | 15 f. **make haste!:** Beeilung!

Chapter VII

Oliver continues refractory

Noah Claypole ran along the streets at his swiftest pace; and paused not once for breath, until he reached the workhouse-gate. [...]

"Oh, Mr. Bumble, sir!" said Noah: "Oliver, sir, – Oliver has –"

"What? What?" interposed Mr. Bumble: with a gleam of pleasure in his metallic eyes. "Not run away; he hasn't run away, has he, Noah?"

"No, sir, no. Not run away, sir, but he's turned wicious," replied Noah. "He tried to murder me, sir; and then he tried to murder Charlotte; and then missis. [...]"

"By Jove!" exclaimed the gentleman in the white waistcoat, [...]. "I knew it! I felt a strange presentiment from the very first, that that audacious young savage would come to be hung!"

[...]

"Yes, sir," replied Noah. "And please, sir, missis wants to know whether Mr. Bumble can spare time to step up there, directly, and flog him: 'cause master's out."

"Certainly, my boy; certainly," said the gentleman in the white waistcoat: smiling benignly: and patting Noah's head, which was about three inches higher than his own. "You're a good boy – a very good boy. Here's a penny for you. Bumble,

2 **refractory:** widerspenstig. | 3 **swift:** flink, geschwind. | 8 **gleam:** Leuchten, Glanz. | 11 **wicious:** *vicious*. | 14 **By Jove!:** Um Himmels willen! (*Jove:* Jupiter). | 15 **presentiment:** Vorahnung. | 16 **audacious:** dreist, frech. | **savage:** Wilder, Barbar. | 19 **to be able to spare time:** Zeit erübrigen können. | **to step up:** hingehen. | 20 **to flog s.o.:** jdn. auspeitschen. | 22 **benignly:** wohlwollend, gütig. | **to pat s.th.:** etwas tätscheln. | 23 **inch:** Längenmaß; entspricht 2,54 cm.

just step up to Sowerberry's with your cane, and see what's best to be done. Don't spare him, Bumble."

"No, I will not, sir," replied the beadle: adjusting the wax-end which was twisted round the bottom of his cane, for purposes of parochial flagellation.

"Tell Sowerberry not to spare him either. They'll never do anything with him, without stripes and bruises," said the gentleman in the white waistcoat.

"I'll take care, sir," replied the beadle. And the cocked hat and cane having been, by this time, adjusted to their owner's satisfaction: Mr. Bumble and Noah Claypole betook themselves with all speed to the undertaker's shop.

Here the position of affairs had not at all improved. Sowerberry had not yet returned: and Oliver continued to kick, with undiminished vigour, at the cellar-door. The accounts of his ferocity, as related by Mrs. Sowerberry and Charlotte, were of so startling a nature, that Mr. Bumble judged it prudent to parley, before opening the door. With this view, he gave a kick at the outside, by way of prelude; and, then, applying his mouth to the keyhole, said, in a deep and impressive tone:

"Oliver!"

"Come; you let me out!" replied Oliver, from the inside.

"Do you know this here voice, Oliver?" said Mr. Bumble.

"Yes," replied Oliver.

"Ain't you afraid of it, sir? Ain't you a-trembling while I speak, sir?" said Mr. Bumble.

5 **flagellation:** Auspeitschen, Züchtigung. | 6 **to spare s.o.:** jdn. verschonen. | 7 **bruise:** blauer Fleck, Bluterguss. | 10 **to adjust:** ordnen, arrangieren. | 11 f. **to betake o.s. to s.th:** sich auf den Weg zu etwas machen, sich zu etwas begeben. | 15 **undiminished:** unvermindert. | **vigour:** Kraft. | **account:** Bericht. | 15 f. **ferocity:** Wildheit. | 16 **as related:** wie berichtet. | 17 **startling:** erschreckend. | **to parley:** verhandeln. | 19 **prelude:** Vorspiel, Auftakt. | **to apply:** (an)legen.

“No!” replied Oliver, boldly.

An answer so different from the one he had expected to elicit, and was in the habit of receiving, staggered Mr. Bumble not a little. He stepped back from the keyhole; drew himself up to his full height; and looked from one to another of the three bystanders, in mute astonishment.

“Oh, you know, Mr. Bumble, he must be mad,” said Mrs. Sowerberry. “No boy in half his senses could venture to speak so to you.”

[...]

“Ah!” said Mr. Bumble, when the lady brought her eyes down to earth again; “the only thing that can be done now, that I know of, is to leave him in the cellar for a day or so, till he's a little starved down; and then to take him out, and keep him on gruel all through his apprenticeship. He comes of a bad family. Excitable natures, Mrs. Sowerberry! Both the nurse and doctor said, that that mother of his made her way here, against difficulties and pain that would have killed any well-disposed woman weeks before.”

At this point of Mr. Bumble's discourse, Oliver, just hearing enough to know that some further allusion was being made to his mother, recommenced kicking, with a violence that rendered every other sound inaudible. Sowerberry returned at this juncture; and Oliver's offence having been explained to him, with such exaggerations as the ladies thought best calcu-

1 **boldly:** mutig, kühn, verwegen. | 2 f. **to elicit:** entlocken, hervorrufen. | 3 **to stagger s.o.:** jdn. überraschen. | 5 f. **bystander:** Zuschauer. | 6 **mute:** stumm, sprachlos. | 8 **in half one's senses:** halb bei Sinnen. | **to venture:** wagen. | 16 **excitable:** erregbar, reizbar. | 18 **well-disposed:** gutgesinnt. | 20 **discourse:** Rede, Vortrag. | 21 **allusion:** Anspielung. | 22 **to recommence:** wieder beginnen. | 23 **inaudible:** unhörbar. | 23 f. **at this juncture:** in diesem Augenblick. | 25 **exaggeration:** Übertreibung. | 25 f. **calculated:** berechnet, geeignet.

lated to rouse his ire: he unlocked the cellar-door in a twinkling, and dragged his rebellious apprentice out, by the collar.

Oliver's clothes had been torn in the beating he had received; his face was bruised and scratched; and his hair scattered over his forehead. The angry flush had not disappeared, however; and when he was pulled out of his prison, he scowled boldly on Noah, and looked quite undismayed.

"Now, you are a nice young fellow, ain't you?" said Sowerberry: giving Oliver a shake, and a box on the ear.

"He called my mother names," replied Oliver.

"Well, and what if he did, you little ungrateful wretch?" said Mrs. Sowerberry. "She deserved what he said, and worse."

[…] For the rest of the day, he was shut up in the back kitchen, in company with a pump and a slice of bread; and, at night, Mrs. Sowerberry, after making various remarks outside the door, by no means complimentary to the memory of his mother, looked into the room: and, amidst the jeers and pointings of Noah and Charlotte, ordered him up stairs to his dismal bed.

[…]

With the first ray of light that struggled through the crevices in the shutters, Oliver rose, and again unbarred the door. One timid look around, – one moment's pause of hesitation, – he had closed it behind him, and was in the open street.

He looked to the right and to the left, uncertain whither to

1 **ire:** Zorn. | 1 f. **in a twinkling:** augenblicklich, im Handumdrehen, im Nu. | 2 **rebellious:** widerspenstig. | 4 **bruised:** zerschrammt. | 4 f. **to scatter:** hier: wirr hängen. | 5 **angry flush:** Zornesröte. | 6 **to scowl:** finster blicken. | 7 **undismayed:** unverzagt. | 9 **box:** Schlag mit der Hand. | 10 **to call s.o. names:** jdn. beschimpfen. | 14 **pump:** Pumpe. | 16 **complimentary:** schmeichelhaft. | **memory:** Angedenken. | 17 **amidst:** inmitten, mitten unter. | **jeer:** Spott. | 20 **ray of light:** Lichtstrahl. | **crevice:** Spalt. | 21 **to unbar:** entriegeln. | 24 **whither:** wohin.

fly. He remembered to have seen the waggons, as they went out, toiling up the hill. He took the same route; and arriving at a footpath across the fields: which he knew, after some distance, led out again into the road: struck into it, and walked quickly on.

[…]

Chapter VIII

Oliver walks to London. He encounters on the road, a strange sort of young Gentleman

Oliver reached the stile at which the by-path terminated; and once more gained the high-road. It was eight o'clock now. […]

The stone by which he was seated, bore, in large characters, an intimation that it was just seventy miles from that spot to London. The name awakened a new train of ideas in the boy's mind. London! – that great large place! – nobody – not even Mr. Bumble – could ever find him there! He had often heard the old men in the workhouse, too, say that no lad of spirit need want in London; and that there were ways of living in that vast city, which those who had been bred up in country parts had no idea of. It was the very place for a homeless boy, who must die in the streets, unless some one helped him. As these things

1 **to fly:** fliehen. | **waggon:** Fuhrwerk. | 2 **to toil:** sich quälen. | 4 **to strike into s.th.:** in etwas einbiegen. | 10 **stile:** Zaunübertritt. | **by-path:** Seitenweg. | **to terminate:** aufhören, enden. | 11 **to gain:** erreichen. | **high-road:** Landstraße. | 12 **characters:** Buchstaben. | 13 **intimation:** Hinweis. | 14 **train of ideas:** Gedankengang. | 17 **lad of spirit:** beherzter Bursche. | **to need want:** Mangel leiden, darben müssen. | 18 **vast:** riesig. | 19 **to breed s.o. up:** jdn. großziehen. | 20 **the very place:** genau der richtige Ort. | **homeless:** obdachlos.

passed through his thoughts, he jumped upon his feet, and again walked forward.

[...]

Early on the seventh morning after he had left his native place, Oliver limped slowly into the little town of Barnet. The window-shutters were closed; the street was empty; not a soul had awakened to the business of the day. The sun was rising in all its splendid beauty; but the light only served to shew the boy his own lonesomeness and desolation, as he sat, with bleeding feet and covered with dust, upon a cold door-step.

[...]

He had been crouching on the step for some time: [...] when he was roused by observing that a boy, who had passed him carelessly some minutes before, had returned, and was now surveying him most earnestly from the opposite side of the way. He took little heed of this at first; but the boy remained in the same attitude of close observation so long, that Oliver raised his head, and returned his steady look. Upon this, the boy crossed over; and, walking close up to Oliver, said,

"Hullo! my covey, what's the row?"

The boy who addressed this inquiry to the young wayfarer, was about his own age: but one of the queerest-looking boys that Oliver had ever seen. He was a snub-nosed, flat-browed,

4 f. **native place:** Heimatort. | 5 **to limp:** humpeln, hinken. | **Barnet:** heute innerhalb des Gebiets von Greater London befindlich. | 8 **splendid:** glänzend, prächtig. | **to shew:** *to show.* | 9 **lonesomeness:** Einsamkeit. | **desolation:** Trostlosigkeit. | 15 **to survey s.th.:** etwas genau betrachten. | 16 **to take heed of s.th.:** etwas beachten. | 17 **close observation:** genaues Beobachten. | 19 **to cross over:** die Straße überqueren. | 20 **covey:** Diminutiv von *cove:* Bursche, Kerl. | **what's the row?:** was ist denn los? | 21 **wayfarer:** Wanderer. | 22 **queer-looking:** seltsam, wunderlich aussehend. | 23 **snub-nosed:** stupsnasig. | **flat-browed:** mit flacher Stirn (*brow:* Stirn).

common-faced boy enough; and as dirty a juvenile as one would wish to see; but he had about him all the airs and manners of a man. He was short of his age: with rather bow-legs: and little, sharp, ugly eyes. His hat was stuck on the top of his head so lightly, that it threatened to fall off every moment; and would have done so, very often, if the wearer had not had a knack of every now and then giving his head a sudden twitch: which brought it back to its old place again. He wore a man's coat, which reached nearly to his heels. He had turned the cuffs back, halfway up his arm, to get his hands out of the sleeves: apparently with the ultimate view of thrusting them into the pockets of his corduroy trousers; for there he kept them. He was, altogether, as roystering and swaggering a young gentleman as ever stood four feet six, or something less, in his bluchers.

"Hullo, my covey, what's the row?" said this strange young gentleman to Oliver.

"I am very hungry and tired," replied Oliver: the tears standing in his eyes as he spoke. "I have walked a long way. I have been walking these seven days."

"Walking for sivin days!" said the young gentleman. "Oh, I see. Beak's order, eh? But," he added, noticing Oliver's look of surprise, "I suppose you don't know what a beak is, my flash com-pan-i-on."

Oliver mildly replied, that he had always heard a bird's mouth described by the term in question.

1 **juvenile:** Jugendlicher, Halbwüchsiger. 2 **airs** (pl.): Gebaren. | 2 f. **manners** (pl.): Benehmen. | 3 **bow-legs:** O-Beine, Säbelbeine. | 7 **knack:** Dreh, Kniff. | **twitch:** Ruck. | 11 **ultimate:** letztendlich. | 12 **corduroy trousers** (pl.): Kordhose. | 13 **to royster:** laut prahlen. | **to swagger:** großtun, angeben. | 15 **bluchers** (pl.): Schaftstiefel. | 21 **sivin:** *seven.* | 22 **beak:** Schnabel; hier: Kadi (Richter). | 23 **flash:** Gauner…; (hum.) schick. | 26 **term:** Begriff.

"My eyes, how green!" exclaimed the young gentleman. "Why, a beak's a madgst'rate; and when you walk by a beak's order, it's not straight forerd, but always a going up, and nivir a-coming down agin. Was you never on the mill?"

"What mill?" inquired Oliver.

"What mill! – why, *the* mill – the mill as takes up so little room that it'll work inside a Stone Jug; and always goes better when the wind's low with people, than when it's high: acos then they can't get workmen. But come," said the young gentleman; "you want grub, and you shall have it. I'm at low-water-mark myself – only one bob and a magpie; but, *as* far *as* it goes, I'll fork out and stump. Up with you on your pins. There! […]"

[…] the young gentleman turned into a small public-house: and led the way to a tap-room in the rear of the premises. Here, a pot of beer was brought in, by direction of the mysterious youth; and Oliver: falling to, at his new friend's bidding: made a long and hearty meal; during the progress of which, the strange boy eyed him from time to time with great attention.

"Going to London?" said the strange boy, when Oliver had at length concluded.

1 **green:** (fig.) grün, unbedarft. | 2 **madgst'rate:** *magistrate.* | 3 **forerd:** *forward.* | **nivir:** *never.* | 4 **mill:** Gemeint ist hier die Tretmühle, eine von Menschen betriebene mechanische Vorrichtung zur Erzeugung von Energie, in der die Häftlinge in Schichten antreten mussten. | 7 **stone jug:** wörtl.: Steinkrug; hier: Kerkerzelle. | 8 **when the wind's low/high:** wenn der Wind ungünstig/günstig steht. | **acos:** *because.* | 10 **grub:** Essen, Fressalien. | 10 f. **to be at low-water-mark** (fig.): pleite sein (*low-water-mark:* Niedrigwassermarke). | 11 **bob:** Shilling. | **magpie:** Halfpenny. | 12 **to fork out and stump:** die Zeche zahlen. | **pins:** Beine. | 13 **public-house:** Wirtshaus. | 14 **tap-room:** Schankstube. | **rear:** hinterer Teil. | **premises:** Räumlichkeit(en), Lokal. | 15 **direction:** Anweisung. | 16 **to fall to s.th.:** mit etwas beginnen. | **bidding:** Geheiß. | 18 **to eye s.o.:** jdn. beäugen. | 20 **to conclude:** zum Schluss kommen.

"Yes."

"Got any lodgings?"

"No."

"Money?"

"No."

The strange boy whistled; and put his arms into his pockets, as far as the big coat-sleeves would let them go.

"Do you live in London?" inquired Oliver.

"Yes. I do, when I'm at home," replied the boy. "I suppose you want some place to sleep in to-night, don't you?"

"I do, indeed," answered Oliver. "I have not slept under a roof since I left the country."

"Don't fret your eyelids on that score," said the young gentleman. "I've got to be in London to-night; and I know a 'spectable old genelman as lives there, wot'll give you lodgings for nothink, and never ask for the change; that is, if any genelman he knows interduces you. And don't he know me? Oh, no! Not in the least! By no means. Certainly not!"

The young gentleman smiled, as if to intimate that the latter fragments of discourse were playfully ironical; and finished the beer as he did so.

This unexpected offer of shelter, was too tempting to be resisted: especially as it was immediately followed up, by the assurance that the old gentleman already referred to, would doubtless provide Oliver with a comfortable place, without loss of time. This led to a more friendly and confidential dia-

2 **lodgings** (pl.): Unterkunft. | 13 **don't fret your eyelids on that score:** lass dir deshalb mal keine grauen Haare wachsen. | 17 **interduces:** *introduces.* | 19 **to intimate:** andeuten. | 20 **fragments of discourse:** Gesprächsfetzen, -brocken. | **playfully:** scherzhaft. | 22 **shelter:** Obdach, Schutz. | **tempting:** verlockend. | 22 f. **to resist:** widerstehen. | 23 f. **assurance:** Beteuerung, Versicherung. | 25 **doubtless:** zweifellos. | 26 **confidential:** vertraulich.

logue; from which Oliver discovered that his friend's name was Jack Dawkins: and that he was a peculiar pet and *protégé* of the elderly gentleman before mentioned.

Mr. Dawkins's appearance did not say a vast deal in favour of the comforts which his patron's interest obtained for those whom he took under his protection; but as he had a rather flighty and dissolute mode of conversing: and furthermore avowed that among his intimate friends he was better known by the *sobriquet* of "The Artful Dodger:" Oliver concluded that, being of a dissipated and careless turn, the moral precepts of his benefactor had hitherto been thrown away upon him. [...]

As John Dawkins objected to their entering London before nightfall, it was nearly eleven o'clock when they reached the turnpike at Islington. [...]

Although Oliver had enough to occupy his attention in keeping sight of his leader, he could not help bestowing a few hasty glances on either side of the way, as he passed along. A dirtier or more wretched place he had never seen. The street

2 **pet:** Liebling. | **protégé:** Schützling. | 4 **in favour of:** zugunsten von. | 5 **comforts:** Annehmlichkeiten. | **patron:** Gönner, Förderer. | **to obtain:** erhalten. | 6 **protection:** Schutz, Begünstigung. | 7 **flighty:** flatterhaft. | **dissolute:** liederlich. | **mode:** Art, Form. | **to converse:** sich unterhalten. | 8 **to avow:** bekennen, eingestehen. | **intimate:** innig, vertraut. | 9 **sobriquet:** Spitzname. | **dodger:** Schwindler. | 10 **dissipated:** zügellos, ausschweifend. | **turn:** Einstellung, Lebenswandel. | **precept:** Regel, Gebot. | 11 **benefactor:** Wohltäter. | **to throw s.th. away upon s.o.:** etwas an jdm. verschwenden. | 13 **to object to s.th.:** etwas ablehnen. | 14 **nightfall:** Einbruch der Dunkelheit. | 15 **turnpike:** Schlagbaum, Zollschranke (in Islington befand sich damals ein Zolltor nach London). | 17 **to keep sight of s.o.:** jdn. nicht aus den Augen verlieren. | 18 **hasty:** flüchtig, hastig. | 19 **wretched:** elend, erbärmlich.

was very narrow and muddy; and the air was impregnated with filthy odours. [...]

Oliver was just considering whether he hadn't better run away, when they reached the bottom of the hill. His conductor, catching him by the arm, pushed open the door of a house near Field-Lane; and, drawing him into the passage, closed it behind them.

[...]

Oliver, groping his way with one hand; and having the other firmly grasped by his companion; ascended with much difficulty the dark and broken stairs: which his conductor mounted with an ease and expedition that shewed he was well acquainted with them. He threw open the door of a back-room, and drew Oliver in after him.

The walls and ceiling of the room were perfectly black, with age and dirt. There was a deal table before the fire: upon which were a candle, stuck in a ginger-beer bottle: two or three pewter pots: a loaf and butter: and a plate. In a frying-pan, which was on the fire, and which was secured to the mantelshelf by a string, some sausages were cooking; and standing over them, with a toasting-fork in his hand, was a very old shrivelled Jew, whose villanous-looking and repulsive face was obscured by a quantity of matted red hair. He was dressed in a greasy flannel

1 **muddy:** schlammig, schmutzig. | **impregnated:** geschwängert. | 2 **filthy:** ekelhaft. | **odour:** Geruch. | 4 **conductor:** Führer. | 10 **to ascend s.th.:** etwas hinaufsteigen. | 12 **with ease:** mit Leichtigkeit. | **expedition:** Schnelligkeit. | 12 f. **to be acquainted with s.th.:** mit etwas vertraut sein. | 16 **deal:** Fichten-, Kiefernholz. | 17 **ginger-beer:** Ingwer-Bier. | 17 f. **pewter pot:** Zinngefäß. | 19 **to secure:** befestigen. | **mantelshelf:** Kaminsims. | 21 **toasting-fork:** Röstgabel. | **shrivelled:** runzelig, verschrumpelt. | 22 **repulsive:** abstoßend. | **to obscure s.th.:** etwas verdecken. | 23 **matted:** verfilzt. | **greasy:** fettig, schmierig. | 23 f. **flannel gown:** Flanellkittel, -umhang.

gown, with his throat bare; and seemed to be dividing his attention between the frying-pan and a clothes-horse, over which a great number of silk handkerchiefs were hanging. Several rough beds made of old sacks, were huddled side by side on the floor; and seated round the table were four or five boys: none older than the Dodger: smoking long clay pipes, and drinking spirits, with the air of middle-aged men. These all crowded about their associate as he whispered a few words to the Jew; and then turned round and grinned at Oliver; as did the Jew himself, toasting-fork in hand.

"This is him, Fagin," said Jack Dawkins; "my friend Oliver Twist."

[...]

"We are very glad to see you, Oliver – very," said the Jew. "Dodger, take off the sausages; and draw a tub near the fire for Oliver. Ah, you're a-staring at the pocket-handkerchiefs! eh, my dear! There are a good many of 'em, ain't there? We've just looked 'em out, ready for the wash; that's all, Oliver; that's all. Ha! ha! ha!"

The latter part of this speech was hailed by a boisterous shout from all the hopeful pupils of the merry old gentleman. In the midst of which, they went to supper.

Oliver ate his share, and the Jew then mixed him a glass of hot gin-and-water: telling him he must drink it off directly, because another gentleman wanted the tumbler. Oliver did

1 **bare:** bloß, nackt. | 2 **clothes-horse:** Wäscheständer. | 3 **silk handkerchiefs:** seidene Schnupftücher. | 4 **to huddle:** sich zusammendrängen. | 6 **clay pipe:** Tonpfeife. | 7 **spirits:** alkoholische Getränke, Spirituosen. | **air:** Miene, Betragen. | 8 **to crowd about s.o.:** sich um jdn. drängen. | 15 **tub:** Fass, Tonne. | 18 **to look out s.th.:** etwas heraussuchen, aussortieren. | 20 **to hail s.th.:** etwas begrüßen, bejubeln. | **boisterous:** wild, ungestüm. | 21 **merry:** fröhlich. | 25 **tumbler:** Becher, Trinkglas.

as he was desired. Immediately afterwards, he felt himself gently lifted on to one of the sacks; and then he sunk into a deep sleep.

Chapter IX

Containing further Particulars concerning the pleasant old Gentleman, and his hopeful Pupils

It was late next morning when Oliver awoke, from a sound, long sleep. There was no other person in the room but the old Jew; who was boiling some coffee in a saucepan for breakfast; and whistling softly to himself as he stirred it round and round, with an iron spoon. He would stop every now and then to listen when there was the least noise below; and, when he had satisfied himself, he would go on, whistling and stirring again, as before.

[...]

When the coffee was done, the Jew drew the saucepan to the hob; and, standing in an irresolute attitude for a few minutes, as if he did not well know how to employ himself; turned round and looked at Oliver, and called him by his name. He did not answer; and was to all appearance asleep.

After satisfying himself upon this head, the Jew stepped gently to the door: which he fastened. He then drew forth: as it seemed to Oliver, from some trap in the floor: a small box, which he placed carefully on the table. His eyes glistened as he

7 **sound:** tief (Schlaf). | 9 **saucepan:** Kochtopf, Stieltopf. | 17 **hob:** Ofen-, Kaminvorsprung zum Abstellen von Geschirr. | **irresolute:** unentschlossen. | 21 **upon this head:** in diesem Punkt, in dieser Sache. | 22 **to draw forth:** hervorholen. | 23 **trap:** Klappe. | 24 **to glisten:** funkeln, glitzern.

raised the lid, and looked in. Dragging an old chair to the table, he sat down; and took from it a magnificent gold watch, sparkling with jewels.

[…]

Oliver thought the old gentleman must be a decided miser to live in such a dirty place, with so many watches; but, thinking that perhaps his fondness for the Dodger and the other boys, cost him a good deal of money, he only cast a deferential look at the Jew, and asked if he might get up.

"Certainly, my dear – certainly," replied the old gentleman. […]

He had scarcely washed himself: and made everything tidy, by emptying the basin out of the window, agreeably to the Jew's directions; when the Dodger returned; accompanied by a very sprightly young friend, whom Oliver had seen smoking on the previous night; and who was now formally introduced to him as Charley Bates. The four sat down, to breakfast, on the coffee, and some hot rolls and ham, which the Dodger had brought home in the crown of his hat.

"Well," said the Jew, glancing slyly at Oliver, and addressing himself to the Dodger, "I hope you've been at work this morning, my dears?"

"Hard," replied the Dodger.

"As Nails," added Charley Bates.

"Good boys, good boys!" said the Jew. "What have *you* got, Dodger?"

"A couple of pocket-books," replied that young gentleman.

1 **lid:** Deckel. | 2 **magnificent:** prächtig, herrlich. | 2f. **to sparkle:** funkeln, glitzern. | 5 **miser:** Geizhals. | 7 **fondness:** Zuneigung. | 13 **basin:** Waschschüssel. | **agreeably to:** gemäß, in Übereinstimmung mit. | 15 **sprightly:** munter, lebhaft. | 18 **rolls** (pl.): Brötchen. | 19 **crown:** (Hut-)Wölbung, Kopfteil. | 20 **slyly:** schlau, verschlagen. | 27 **pocket-book:** Brieftasche.

"Lined?" inquired the Jew, with eagerness.

"Pretty well," replied the Dodger, producing two pocket-books: one green: and the other red.

"Not so heavy as they might be," said the Jew, after looking at the insides carefully; "but very neat and nicely made. Ingenious workman, ain't he, Oliver?"

"Very, indeed, sir," said Oliver. At which Mr. Charles Bates laughed uproariously; very much to the amazement of Oliver, who saw nothing to laugh at, in anything that had passed.

"And what have you got, my dear?" said Fagin to Charley Bates.

"Wipes," replied Master Bates; at the same time producing four pocket-handkerchiefs.

"Well," said the Jew, inspecting them closely; "they're very good ones – very. You haven't marked them well, though, Charley; so the marks shall be picked out with a needle, and we'll teach Oliver how to do it. Shall us, Oliver, eh? Ha! ha! ha!"

"If you please, sir," said Oliver.

"You'd like to be able to make pocket-handkerchiefs as easy as Charley Bates, wouldn't you, my dear?" said the Jew.

"Very much indeed, if you'll teach me, sir," replied Oliver.

Master Bates saw something so exquisitely ludicrous in this reply, that he burst into another laugh; which laugh, meeting the coffee he was drinking, and carrying it down some

1 **lined:** (mit Stoff) gefüttert. | **eagerness:** Eifer, Begierde. | 5 f. **ingenious:** geschickt. | 8 **uproariously:** brüllend. | **amazement:** Erstaunen, Verwunderung. | 13 **wipe:** Rotzfahne. | 15 **to inspect:** untersuchen. | 16 **to mark s.th.:** etwas kennzeichnen. | 17 **marks:** Kennzeichen (gemeint sind die eingestickten Monogramme). | **to pick out:** herauslösen. | 24 **exquisitely:** höchst, ungemein. | **ludicrous:** witzig, drollig.

wrong channel, very nearly terminated in his premature suffocation.

"He is so jolly green!" said Charley when he recovered: as an apology to the company for his unpolite behaviour.

[...]

When the breakfast was cleared away, the merry old gentleman and the two boys played at a very curious and uncommon game, which was performed in this way: The merry old gentleman: placing a snuff-box in one pocket of his trousers, a note-case in the other, and a watch in his waistcoat-pocket: with a guard-chain round his neck: and sticking a mock diamond pin in his shirt: buttoned his coat tight round him, and putting his spectacle-case and handkerchief in his pockets, trotted up and down the room with a stick, in imitation of the manner in which old gentlemen walk about the streets any hour in the day. Sometimes he stopped at the fire-place, and sometimes at the door; making belief that he was staring with all his might into shop-windows. At such times, he would look constantly round him, for fear of thieves; and would keep slapping all his pockets in turn, to see that he hadn't lost anything; in such a very funny and natural manner, that Oliver laughed till the tears ran down his face. All this time, the two boys followed him closely about: getting out of his sight, so nimbly,

1 **channel:** hier (hum.): (Speise-, Luft-)Röhre. | **premature:** vorzeitig. | 1 f. **suffocation:** Erstickungstod. | 3 **jolly:** herrlich. | **to recover:** sich erholen. | 4 **apology:** Entschuldigung. | 6 **to clear away s.th.:** etwas abräumen. | 7 **curious:** seltsam, sonderbar, wunderlich. | **uncommon:** ungewöhnlich. | 9 **snuff-box:** Schnupftabaksdose. | 10 **note-case:** Brieftasche. | 11 **guard-chain:** Sicherungskette (für die Uhr). | 11 f. **mock diamond pin:** unechte Diamantennadel. | 13 **spectacle-case:** Brillenetui. | 19 **constantly:** ständig, andauernd. | 19 f. **to slap s.th.:** etwas beklopfen, auf etwas klopfen, schlagen. | 20 **in turn:** der Reihe nach. | 23 **nimbly:** flink, behende.

every time he turned round, that it was impossible to follow their motions. At last, the Dodger trod upon his toes, or ran upon his boot accidentally, while Charley Bates stumbled up against him behind; and in that one moment they took from him, with the most extraordinary rapidity, snuff-box, note-case, watch, guard-chain, shirt-pin, pocket-handkerchief; even the spectacle-case. If the old gentleman felt a hand in any one of his pockets, he cried out where it was; and then the game began all over again.

When this game had been played a great many times, a couple of young ladies called to see the young gentlemen; one of whom was named Bet, and the other Nancy. They wore a good deal of hair: not very neatly turned up behind; and were rather untidy about the shoes and stockings. They were not exactly pretty, perhaps; but they had a great deal of colour in their faces; and looked quite stout and hearty. Being remarkably free and agreeable in their manners, Oliver thought them very nice girls indeed. As there is no doubt they were.

[...]

2 **motion:** Bewegung. | **to tread:** treten. | 3 **accidentally:** zufällig, aus Versehen. | 5 **rapidity:** Schnelligkeit. | 11 **to call:** vorbeischauen, einen kurzen Besuch machen. | 13 **neatly:** ordentlich. | 16 **stout:** kräftig, drall. | **hearty:** herzlich. | **remarkably:** bemerkenswert. | 17 **agreeable:** angenehm, liebenswürdig.

Chapter X

Oliver becomes better acquainted with the Characters of his new Associates; and purchases experience at a high price. Being a short, but very important Chapter, in this History

For many days, Oliver remained in the Jew's room, picking the marks out of the pocket-handkerchiefs, (of which a great number were brought home,) and sometimes taking part in the game already described: which the two boys and the Jew played, regularly, every morning. At length, he began to languish for fresh air; and took many occasions of earnestly entreating the old gentleman to allow him to go out to work, with his two companions.

[…]

At length, one morning, Oliver obtained the permission he had so eagerly sought. There had been no handkerchiefs to work upon, for two or three days; and the dinners had been rather meagre. Perhaps these were reasons for the old gentleman's giving his assent; but, whether they were or no, he told Oliver he might go; and placed him under the joint guardianship of Charley Bates, and his friend the Dodger.

[…]

They were just emerging from a narrow court not far from the open square in Clerkenwell, […] when the Dodger made a sudden stop; and, laying his finger on his lip, drew his com-

2 **to become acquainted with s.o.:** mit jdm. bekanntwerden. | 3 **to purchase:** erwerben. | 10 f. **to languish for s.th.:** sich nach etwas sehnen. | 11 f. **to entreat:** ersuchen. | 16 **to seek s.th.:** etwas begehren. | 18 **meagre:** kärglich, dürftig. | 19 **assent:** Zustimmung, Genehmigung. | 20 **joint:** gemeinsam. | 20 f. **guardianship:** Aufsicht, Obhut. | 23 **court:** hier: Hintergässchen.

panions back again, with the greatest caution and circumspection.

"What's the matter?" demanded Oliver.

"Hush!" replied the Dodger. "Do you see that old cove at the book-stall?"

"The old gentleman over the way?" said Oliver. "Yes, I see him."

[...]

What was Oliver's horror and alarm as he stood a few paces off, looking on with his eyelids as wide open as they would possibly go, to see the Dodger plunge his hand into the old gentleman's pocket; and draw from thence a handkerchief! To see him hand the same to Charley Bates; and finally to behold them, both, running away round the corner at full speed!

In an instant the whole mystery of the handkerchiefs, and the watches, and the jewels, and the Jew, rushed upon the boy's mind. He stood, for a moment, with the blood so tingling through all his veins from terror, that he felt as if he were in a burning fire; then, confused and frightened, he took to his heels; and, not knowing what he did, made off as fast as he could lay his feet to the ground.

This was all done in a minute's space. In the very instant when Oliver began to run; the old gentleman, putting his hand to his pocket, and missing his handkerchief, turned sharp round. Seeing the boy scudding away at such a rapid pace, he very naturally concluded him to be the depredator; and, shout-

1 **caution:** Vorsicht. | 1 f. **circumspection:** Umsicht, Behutsamkeit. | 5 **book-stall:** Bücherverkaufsstand, Bücherbude. | 9 **alarm:** Schrecken. | 9 f. **to stand off:** Abstand halten. | 10 **eyelids:** Augenlider. | 11 **to plunge:** stecken. | 12 **from thence:** von dort. | 13 **to behold:** sehen. | 15 **instant:** Augenblick. | 16 **to rush:** anstürmen. | 17 **to tingle:** kribbeln. | 25 **to scud away:** davoneilen. | **rapid:** rasch, schnell. | 26 **depredator:** Plünderer.

ing "Stop thief!" with all his might, made off after him, book in hand.

But the old gentleman was not the only person who raised the hue-and-cry. The Dodger and Master Bates, unwilling to attract public attention by running down the open street, had merely retired into the very first doorway round the corner. They no sooner heard the cry, and saw Oliver running, than, guessing exactly how the matter stood, they issued forth with great promptitude; and, shouting "Stop thief!" too, joined in the pursuit like good citizens.

[...]

"Stop thief! Stop thief!" There is a passion *for hunting something* deeply implanted in the human breast. One wretched breathless child, panting with exhaustion; terror in his looks; agony in his eye; large drops of perspiration streaming down his face; strains every nerve to make head upon his pursuers; and as they follow on his track, and gain upon him every instant, they hail his decreasing strength with still louder shouts: and whoop and scream with joy. "Stop thief!" Aye, stop him for God's sake, were it only in mercy!

Stopped at last! A clever blow. He is down upon the pavement; and the crowd eagerly gather round him: each newcomer, jostling and struggling with the others to catch a glimpse. "Stand aside!" "Give him a little air!" "Nonsense! he

1 **to make off:** davonlaufen. | 3f. **to raise a hue-and-cry:** Zeter und Mordio schreien. | 6 **to retire:** sich zurückziehen. | **doorway:** Eingang. | 8 **to issue forth:** hervorkommen. | 9 **promptitude:** Schnelligkeit, Bereitwilligkeit. | 10 **pursuit:** Verfolgungsjagd. | 14 **to pant:** keuchen. | **exhaustion:** Erschöpfung. | 15 **agony:** großer Schmerz, Pein, Qual. | **to stream:** fließen, strömen. | 16 **to strain:** anspannen. | **to make head:** Vorsprung gewinnen. | **pursuer:** Verfolger. | 17 **track:** Spur, Fährte. | **to gain upon s.o.:** jdn. einholen, jdm. näher kommen. | 20 **for God's sake:** um Gottes willen. | 23 **to jostle:** drängeln. | 24 **glimpse:** flüchtiger Blick.

don't deserve it." "Where's the gentleman?" "Here he is, c ing down the street." "Make room there for the gentlema..!" "Is this the boy, sir?" "Yes."

Oliver lay, covered with mud and dust: and bleeding from the mouth, looking wildly round upon the heap of faces that surrounded him: when the old gentleman was officiously dragged and pushed into the circle by the foremost of the pursuers.

[…]

Oliver, who could hardly stand, made a shift to raise himself on his feet; and was at once lugged along the streets by the jacket-collar, at a rapid pace. […]

Chapter XI

Treats of Mr. Fang the Police Magistrate; and furnishes a slight specimen of his mode of administering Justice

The offence had been committed within the district, and indeed in the immediate neighbourhood of, a very notorious metropolitan police-office. The crowd had only the satisfaction of accompanying Oliver through two or three streets, and down a place called Mutton-hill, when he was led beneath a low archway, and up a dirty court, into this dispensary of

4 **mud:** Dreck, Matsch. | 5 **heap:** Menge. | 7 **foremost:** vorderste(r, s), führend. | 10 **shift:** Verlagerung, Bewegung. | 11 **to lug:** schleppen, zerren. | 14 **to furnish:** geben, liefern, bereitstellen. | 15 **slight specimen:** kleine Kostprobe. | **to administer justice:** Gerechtigkeit üben, walten lassen. | 16 **to commit s.th.:** etwas verüben. | 17 **notorious:** berüchtigt. | 18 **metropolitan:** hauptstädtisch (*the Metropolis* ist eine Bezeichnung für London, vgl. die Überschrift zu Kap. 42, S. 233). | 21 **archway:** Torbogen. | **dispensary:** Ambulanz, (Armen-)Apotheke.

summary justice, by the back way. It was a small paved yard into which they turned; and here, they encountered a stout man with a bunch of whiskers on his face, and a bunch of keys in his hand.

"What's the matter now?" said the man carelessly.

"A young fogle-hunter," replied the man who had Oliver in charge.

"Are you the party that's been robbed, sir?" inquired the man with the keys.

"Yes, I am," replied the old gentleman; "but I am not sure that this boy actually took the handkerchief. I – I would rather not press the case."

"Must go before the magistrate now, sir," replied the man. "His worship will be disengaged in half a minute. [...]"

[...]

The office was a front-parlour, with a panelled wall. Mr. Fang sat behind a bar at the upper end; and on one side the door was a sort of wooden pen in which poor little Oliver was already deposited: trembling very much at the awfulness of the scene.

Mr. Fang was a lean, long-backed, stiff-necked, middle-sized man, with no great quantity of hair: and what he had, growing on the back and sides of his head. His face was stern, and much flushed. If he were really not in the habit of drinking rather more than was exactly good for him, he might have brought an

1 **summary justice:** juristisches Schnellverfahren. | **paved:** gepflastert. | 2 **stout:** stämmig, beleibt. | 3 **whiskers:** Barthaare. | 6 **fogle-hunter:** Taschentuchjäger. | 6 f. **to have s.o. in charge:** jdn. in Obhut haben. | 12 **to press the case:** die Sache weiterverfolgen. | 14 **his worship:** Seiner Ehren. | **disengaged:** frei, unbeschäftigt. | 16 **panelled:** getäfelt. | 17 **bar:** Schranke. | 18 **pen:** Verschlag. | 21 **lean:** hager. | 23 **stern:** ernst, streng. | 24 **flushed:** gerötet. | 25 f. **to bring an action:** Klage erheben.

action against his countenance for libel, and have recovered heavy damages.

The old gentleman bowed respectfully; and, advancing to the magistrate's desk, said, suiting the action to the word, "That is my name and address, sir." He then withdrew a pace or two; and, with another polite and gentlemanly inclination of the head, waited to be questioned.

[…]

"Officer!" said Mr. Fang, throwing the paper on one side, "what's this fellow charged with?"

"He's not charged at all, your worship," replied the officer. "He appears against the boy, your worship."

[…]

"Now," said Fang, "what's the charge against this boy? What have you got to say, sir?"

"I was standing at a book-stall –" Mr. Brownlow began.

[…]

With many interruptions, and repeated insults, Mr. Brownlow contrived to state his case; observing that, in the surprise of the moment, he had run after the boy because he saw him running away; and expressing his hope that, if the magistrate should believe him, although not actually the thief, to be connected with thieves; he would deal as leniently with him as justice would allow.

"He has been hurt already," said the old gentleman in con-

1 **libel:** Verleumdung. | 1 f. **to recover damages:** Schadensersatz erhalten. | 4 **to suit the action to the word:** das Wort in die Tat umsetzen (d. h., der alte Herr überreicht dem Polizeirichter seine Visitenkarte). | 5 **to withdraw:** sich zurückziehen. | 10 **to charge s.o. with s.th.:** jdm. etwas zur Last legen. | 12 **to appear against s.o.:** als Kläger gegen jdn. auftreten. | 18 **insult:** Beleidigung. | 19 **to contrive to do s.th.:** es fertigbringen, etwas zu tun. | 23 **leniently:** milde, nachsichtig.

clusion. "And I fear," he added, with great energy, looking towards the bar, "I really fear that he is very ill."

"Oh! yes; I dare say!" said Mr. Fang, with a sneer. "Come; none of your tricks here, you young vagabond; they won't do. What's your name?"

Oliver tried to reply, but his tongue failed him. He was deadly pale; and the whole place seemed turning round and round.

"What's your name, you hardened scoundrel?" demanded Mr. Fang. "Officer, what's his name?"

This was addressed to a bluff old fellow, in a striped waistcoat: who was standing by the bar. He bent over Oliver, and repeated the inquiry; but finding him really incapable of understanding the question; and knowing that his not replying would only infuriate the magistrate the more, and add to the severity of his sentence; he hazarded a guess.

"He says his name's Tom White, your worship," said this kind-hearted thief-taker.

[...]

"How do you propose to deal with the case, sir?" inquired the clerk in a low voice.

"Summarily," replied Mr. Fang. "He stands committed for three months, – hard labour of course. Clear the office."

The door was opened for this purpose; and a couple of men were preparing to carry the insensible boy to his cell; when an

3 **I dare say!:** Das glaube ich gern! | **sneer:** spöttisches Lächeln. | 9 **hardened scoundrel:** abgebrühter Schurke. | 11 **bluff:** gutmütig-derb. | 13 **incapable:** außerstande, unfähig. | 15 **to infuriate s.o.:** jdn. aufbringen, wütend machen. | 16 **severity:** Härte, Schwere. | **to hazard s.th.:** etwas wagen. | 18 **thief-taker:** Diebesfänger. | 20 **to propose:** beabsichtigen. | 21 **clerk:** Gerichtsschreiber. | 22 **summarily:** im Schnellverfahren. | **to stand committed for s.th.:** zu etwas verurteilt werden. | 23 **to clear:** räumen. | 25 **insensible:** bewusstlos.

elderly man of decent but poor appearance, clad in an old suit of black, rushed hastily into the office: and advanced towards the bench.

"Stop, stop! Don't take him away! For Heaven's sake stop a moment!" cried the new-comer: breathless with haste.

[…]

"What is this? Who is this? Turn this man out. Clear the office!" cried Mr. Fang.

"I will speak," cried the man; "I will not be turned out. I saw it all. I keep the book-stall. I demand to be sworn. I will not be put down. Mr. Fang, you must hear me. You must not refuse, sir."

The man was right. His manner was bold and determined; and the matter was growing rather too serious to be hushed up.

"Swear the fellow," growled Mr. Fang, with a very ill grace. "Now, man, what have you got to say?"

"This," said the man: "I saw three boys: two others and the prisoner here: loitering on the opposite side of the way, when this gentleman was reading. The robbery was committed by another boy. I saw it done; and I saw that this boy was perfectly amazed and stupefied by it." Having by this time recovered a little breath, the worthy book-stall keeper proceeded to relate, in a more coherent manner, the exact circumstances of the robbery.

"Why didn't you come here before?" said Fang, after a pause.

[…]

1 **decent:** anständig, ehrbar. | **clad:** gekleidet. | 3 **bench:** Richterbank. | 7 **to turn s.o. out:** jdn. hinauswerfen. | 10 **to swear s.o.:** jdn. vereidigen. | 11 **to put s.o. down:** jdn. abweisen. | 13 **determined:** bestimmt, entschlossen. | 14 **to hush s.th. up:** etwas vertuschen. | 15 **with ill grace:** ungnädig, missmutig. | 18 **to loiter:** trödeln, lungern. | 19 **robbery:** Raub(überfall). | 23 **coherent:** zusammenhängend, verständlich.

"[…] The boy is discharged. Clear the office."

[…]

The mandate was obeyed; and the indignant Mr. Brownlow was conveyed out […]. He reached the yard; and it vanished in a moment. Little Oliver Twist lay on his back on the pavement, with his shirt unbuttoned, and his temples bathed with water; his face a deadly white; and a cold tremble convulsing his whole frame.

"Poor boy, poor boy!" said Mr. Brownlow, bending over him. "Call a coach, somebody, pray. Directly!"

A coach was obtained, and Oliver, having been carefully laid on one seat, the old gentleman got in and sat himself on the other.

[…]

Chapter XII

In which Oliver is taken better care of, than he ever was before. And in which the Narrative reverts to the merry old Gentleman and his youthful Friends

The coach rattled away, down Mount Pleasant and up Exmouth-street: over nearly the same ground as that which Oliver had traversed when he first entered London in company with the Dodger; and, turning a different way when it reached the Angel at Islington, stopped at length before a neat house, in

1 **to discharge s.o.:** jdn. entlasten, freilassen. | 3 **mandate:** Befehl. | **indignant:** empört. | 4 **to vanish:** verschwinden. | 7 **to convulse:** krampfhaft zusammenziehen, erschüttern. | 8 **frame:** Gestalt, Körper. | 17 **narrative:** Erzählung. | **to revert to s.o.:** zu jdm. zurückkehren. | 19 **to rattle:** klappern, rasseln. | 21 **to traverse:** überqueren. | 23 **Angel:** Name eines Gasthofes.

a quiet shady street near Pentonville. Here, a bed was prepared, without loss of time, in which Mr. Brownlow saw his young charge carefully and comfortably deposited; and here, he was tended with a kindness and solicitude that knew no bounds.

[…]

Weak, and thin, and pallid, he awoke at last from what seemed to have been a long and troubled dream. Feebly raising himself in the bed, with his head resting on his trembling arm, he looked anxiously round.

"What room is this? Where have I been brought to?" said Oliver. "This is not the place I went to sleep in."

He uttered these words in a feeble voice: being very faint and weak; but they were overheard at once; for the curtain at the bed's head was hastily drawn back: and a motherly old lady, very neatly and precisely dressed, rose as she undrew it, from an arm-chair close by, in which she had been sitting at needle-work.

"Hush, my dear," said the old lady softly. "You must be very quiet, or you will be ill again; and you have been very bad, – as bad as bad could be, pretty nigh. Lie down again; there's a dear!" With these words, the old lady very gently placed Oliver's head upon the pillow; […].

In three days' time, he was able to sit in an easy-chair, well propped up with pillows; and, as he was still too weak to walk, Mrs. Bedwin had him carried down stairs into the little housekeeper's room, which belonged to her […].

1 **shady:** schattig. | 3 **charge:** Schützling. | 4 **to tend s.o.:** jdn. pflegen. | **solicitude:** Fürsorglichkeit. | **bounds:** Grenzen. | 6 **pallid:** blass. | 12 **to utter:** aussprechen. | 13 **to overhear s.th.:** etwas vernehmen. | 15 **precisely:** akkurat. | **to undraw s.th.:** etwas aufmachen, öffnen. | 16 f. **needle-work:** Handarbeit. | 20 **nigh:** nahe (am Tod). | 20 f. **there's a dear!:** sei ein braves Kind! | 23 **easy-chair:** Polstersessel. | 24 **to prop up:** stützen. | 25 f. **housekeeper:** Haushälterin.

“You’re very, very kind to me, ma’am,” said Oliver.

“Well, never you mind that, my dear,” said the old lady; “that’s got nothing to do with your broth; and it’s full time you had it; for the doctor says Mr. Brownlow may come in to see you this morning: and we must get up our best looks, because the better we look, the more he’ll be pleased.” And with this, the old lady applied herself to warming up in a little saucepan, a basin full of broth: strong enough to furnish an ample dinner, when reduced to the regulation strength: for three hundred and fifty paupers, at the very lowest computation.

“Are you fond of pictures, dear?” inquired the old lady, seeing that Oliver had fixed his eyes, most intently, on a portrait which hung against the wall: just opposite his chair.

“I don’t quite know, ma’am,” said Oliver, without taking his eyes from the canvas; “I have seen so few that I hardly know. What a beautiful, mild face that lady’s is!”

[...] Mrs. Bedwin, satisfied that he felt more comfortable, salted and broke bits of toasted bread into the broth, with all the bustle befitting so solemn a preparation. Oliver got through it with extraordinary expedition: and had scarcely swallowed the last spoonful, when there came a soft tap at the door. “Come in,” said the old lady; and in walked Mr. Brownlow.

[...]

“Good boy,” said Mr. Brownlow, stoutly. “Have you given him any nourishment, Bedwin? Any slops, eh?”

1 **ma’am:** *madam:* gnädige Frau. | 3 **broth:** (Fleisch-)Brühe. | 8 **ample:** reichlich, üppig. | 9 **to reduce:** abschwächen, vermindern. | **regulation strength:** vorgeschriebene Stärke. | 10 **computation:** Schätzung, Berechnung. | 12 **to fix:** (Blick) richten, heften. | **intently:** aufmerksam. | 15 **canvas:** Leinwand; Gemälde. | 19 **bustle:** Betriebsamkeit. | **to befit s.th.:** einer Sache gebühren. | **preparation:** Zubereitung. | 24 **stoutly:** hier: tapfer. | 25 **slop:** Krankenspeise, -süppchen.

“He has just had a basin of beautiful strong broth, sir,” replied Mrs. Bedwin: drawing herself up slightly, and laying a strong emphasis on the last word: to intimate that between slops, and broth well compounded, there existed no affinity or connection whatsoever.

“Ugh!” said Mr. Brownlow, with a slight shudder; “a couple of glasses of port wine would have done him a great deal more good. Wouldn’t they, Tom White, eh?”

“My name is Oliver, sir,” replied the little invalid: with a look of great astonishment.

“Oliver,” said Mr. Brownlow; “Oliver what? Oliver White, eh?”

“No, sir, Twist, Oliver Twist.”

“Queer name!” said the old gentleman. “What made you tell the magistrate your name was White?”

“I never told him so, sir,” returned Oliver in amazement.

This sounded so like a falsehood, that the old gentleman looked somewhat sternly in Oliver’s face. It was impossible to doubt him; there was truth in every one of its thin and sharpened lineaments.

[…]

“I hope you are not angry with me, sir?” said Oliver, raising his eyes beseechingly.

“No, no,” replied the old gentleman. “Why! what’s this? Bedwin, look there!”

As he spoke, he pointed hastily to the picture above Oliver’s head; and then to the boy’s face. There was its living copy. The eyes, the head, the mouth; every feature was the same. The ex-

3 **emphasis:** Betonung, Nachdruck. | 4 **to compound:** anrühren, mischen. | **affinity:** Ähnlichkeit, Wesensverwandtschaft. | 6 **shudder:** Schaudern. | 9 **invalid:** Kranker, Patient. | 17 **falsehood:** Unwahrheit, Lüge. | 19 f. **sharpened:** spitz. | 20 **lineaments:** (Gesichts-)Züge. | 23 **beseechingly:** flehentlich. | 28 **feature:** Gesichtszug.

pression was, for the instant, so precisely alike, that the minutest line seemed copied with startling accuracy.

Oliver knew not the cause of this sudden exclamation; for, not being strong enough to bear the start it gave him, he fainted away. A weakness on his part, which affords the narrative an opportunity of relieving the reader from suspense, in behalf of the two young pupils of the Merry Old Gentleman; and of recording

That when the Dodger, and his accomplished friend Master Bates, joined in the hue-and-cry which was raised at Oliver's heels, in consequence of their executing an illegal conveyance of Mr. Brownlow's personal property, as has been already described, they were actuated by a very laudable and becoming regard for themselves […].

It was not until the two boys had scoured, with great rapidity, through a most intricate maze of narrow streets and courts, that they ventured to halt, by one consent, beneath a low and dark archway. Having remained silent here, just long enough to recover breath to speak, Master Bates uttered an exclamation of amusement and delight; and, bursting into an uncontrollable fit of laughter, flung himself upon a door-step, and rolled thereon in a transport of mirth.

"What's the matter?" inquired the Dodger.

1 f. **minutest:** kleinste(r, s). | 2 **accuracy:** Genauigkeit. | 4 f. **to faint away:** ohnmächtig werden. | 6 **to relieve s.o. from s.th.:** jdn. von etwas befreien, erlösen. | **suspense:** Spannung, Ungewissheit. | **in behalf of:** betreffs. | 9 **accomplished:** fein, vorzüglich. | 11 **to execute:** ausführen, vollziehen. | **conveyance:** Überführung. | 13 **to actuate s.o.:** jdn. antreiben. | **laudable:** lobenswert. | **becoming:** geziemend, passend. | 14 **regard:** Beachtung, Aufmerksamkeit. | 15 **to scour:** (umher)eilen, (umher)jagen. | 16 **intricate:** verschlungen. | **maze:** Labyrinth. | 20 **delight:** Freude, Vergnügen. | 21 **fit of laughter:** Lachanfall, Lachkrampf. | 22 **transport of mirth:** Ausbruch unbändiger Fröhlichkeit.

"Ha! ha! ha!" roared Charley Bates.

"Hold your noise," remonstrated the Dodger, looking cautiously round. "Do you want to be grabbed, stupid?"

"I can't help it," said Charley, "I can't help it! To see him a-splitting away at that pace; and cutting round the corners; and knocking up again the posts; and starting on again as if he was made of iron as well as them; and me with the wipe in my pocket, singing out arter him – oh, my eye!" The vivid imagination of Master Bates, presented the scene before him in too strong colours. As he arrived at this apostrophe, he again rolled upon the door-step, and laughed louder than before.

"What'll Fagin say?" inquired the Dodger; taking advantage of the next interval of breathlessness on the part of his friend to propound the question.

"What?" repeated Charley Bates.

"Ah, what?" said the Dodger.

"Why, what should he say?" inquired Charley: stopping rather suddenly in his merriment; for the Dodger's manner was impressive. "What should he say?"

[...]

The noise of footsteps on the creaking stairs, a few minutes after the occurrence of this conversation, roused the merry old gentleman as he sat over the fire with a saveloy and a small loaf in his left hand; a pocket-knife in his right; and a pewter pot on the trivet. There was a rascally smile on his white face as he

2 **hold your noise:** halt den Mund. | **to remonstrate:** protestieren. | 3 **to be grabbed:** gefasst, geschnappt werden. | 5 **to split away:** stiften gehen. | 8 **singing out arter him:** etwa: schreiend hinter ihm her. | **oh, my eye!:** ach herrje! | **vivid:** lebhaft. | 10 **at this apostrophe:** an dieser Stelle. | 12 **to take advantage of s.th.:** etwas ausnutzen. | 13 **on the part of:** seitens. | 14 **to propound s.th.:** etwas vorbringen. | 18 **merriment:** Fröhlichkeit. | 21 **to creak:** knarren. | 23 **saveloy:** Zervelatwurst. 25 **trivet:** Dreifuß. | **rascally:** schurkisch.

turned round; and, looking sharply out from under his thick red eyebrows, bent his ear towards the door, and listened intently.

"Why, how's this?" muttered the Jew: changing countenance, "only two of 'em? Where's the third? They can't have got into trouble. Hark!"

The footsteps approached nearer; they reached the landing. The door was slowly opened; and the Dodger and Charley Bates entered: closing it behind them.

Chapter XIII

Some new Acquaintances are introduced to the intelligent Reader; connected with whom, various pleasant Matters are related, appertaining to this History

"Where's Oliver?" said the Jew, rising with a menacing look. "Where's the boy?"

The young thieves eyed their preceptor as if they were alarmed at his violence; and looked uneasily at each other. But they made no reply.

"What's become of the boy?" said the Jew, seizing the Dodger tightly by the collar, and threatening him with horrid imprecations. "Speak out, or I'll throttle you!"

[...] thundered the Jew: shaking the Dodger so much that his keeping in the big coat at all, seemed perfectly miraculous.

4 **to mutter:** murmeln, brummen. | 6 **hark!:** horch! | 11 **acquaintance:** Bekanntschaft. | **intelligent:** verständig. | 13 **to appertain to s.th.:** zu etwas gehören. | 14 **menacing:** bedrohlich. | 16 **preceptor:** Lehrer. | 17 **uneasily:** unbehaglich, ängstlich. | 20 **to threat s.o.:** jdm. drohen. | 21 **to throttle:** erdrosseln. | 22 **to thunder:** donnern. | 23 **miraculous:** wunderbar, verwunderlich.

"Why, the traps have got him, and that's all about it," said the Dodger, sullenly. "Come, let go o' me, will you!" And, swinging himself, at one jerk, clean out of the big coat, which he left in the Jew's hands: the Dodger snatched up the toasting-fork, and made a pass at the merry old gentleman's waistcoat; which, if it had taken effect, would have let a little more merriment out, than could have been easily replaced in a month or two.

The Jew stepped back, in this emergency, with more agility than could have been anticipated in a man of his apparent decrepitude; and, seizing up the pot, prepared to hurl it at his assailant's head. But, Charley Bates, at this moment, calling his attention by a perfectly terrific howl, he suddenly altered its destination, and flung it full at that young gentleman.

"Why, what the blazes is in the wind now!" growled a deep voice. "Who pitched that 'ere at me? It's well it's the beer, and not the pot, as hit me, or I'd have settled somebody. […] Wot's it all about, Fagin? D–me, if my neckankercher an't lined with beer! Come in, you sneaking warmint; wot are you stopping outside for, as if you was ashamed of your master! Come in!"

1 **trap:** Greifer, Diebesfänger, Polizist. | 2 **sullenly:** mürrisch, missmutig. | 3 **to swing o.s.:** sich drehen. | **jerk:** Ruck. | 4 **to snatch up s.th.:** sich etwas schnappen. | 5 **pass:** Stoß, Ausfall. | 6 **to take effect:** Wirkung haben. | 7 **to replace s.th.:** etwas erneuern, ersetzen. | 9 **emergency:** Notlage, Gefahr. | **agility:** Wendigkeit. | 10 f. **decrepitude:** Hinfälligkeit, Altersschwäche. | 11 **to hurl:** werfen, schleudern. | 11 f. **assailant:** Angreifer. | 13 **terrific:** fürchterlich. | **howl:** Geheul. | **to alter:** (ab-, ver-) ändern. | 14 **destination:** Ziel. | 15 **What the blazes is in the wind?:** Was zum Teufel ist hier los? | 16 **to pitch:** werfen. | **'ere:** *here.* | 17 **as:** *that has.* | **to settle s.o.:** jdn. vertrimmen. | **wot's:** *what is.* | 18 **d–me:** *damme: damn me.* | **neckankercher:** *neck-handkerchief:* Halstuch. | **an't:** *ain't.* | **lined:** hier: getränkt, befleckt. | 19 **to sneak:** schleichen. | **warmint:** *varmint:* Schädling, Racker.

The man who growled out these words, was a stoutly-built fellow of about five-and-thirty, in a black velveteen coat, very soiled drab breeches, lace-up half boots, and grey cotton stockings, which inclosed a very bulky pair of legs, with large swelling calves; – the kind of legs, that in such costume, always look in an unfinished and incomplete state without a set of fetters to garnish them. [...]

"Come in, d'ye hear?" growled this engaging ruffian.

A white shaggy dog, with his face scratched and torn in twenty different places, skulked into the room.

"Why didn't you come in afore?" said the man. "You're getting too proud to own me afore company, are you? Lie down!"

This command was accompanied with a kick, which sent the animal to the other end of the room. He appeared well used to it, however; for he coiled himself up in a corner very quietly, without uttering a sound; and winking his very ill-looking eyes twenty times in a minute, appeared to occupy himself in taking a survey of the apartment.

"What are you up to? Ill-treating the boys, you covetous, avaricious, in-sa-ti-a-ble old fence?" said the man, seating himself deliberately. "I wonder they don't murder you; [...]."

2 **velveteen:** Baumwollsamt. | 3 **soiled:** schmutzig. | **drab:** graubraun. | **breeches** (pl.): Kniebundhose. | **lace-up half boots:** Schnürschuhe. | 4 **bulky:** dick. | 4 f. **swelling calves:** dicke Waden. | 5 **costume:** Kleidung. | 6 **incomplete:** unvollständig, mangelhaft. | **set of fetters:** Garnitur von Fußfesseln. | 7 **to garnish:** verzieren. | 8 **engaging:** reizend, bezaubernd. | 9 **shaggy:** struppig. | 10 **to skulk:** schleichen. | 11 **afore:** *before.* | 16 **to coil o.s. up:** sich zusammenrollen. | 17 f. **to wink one's eyes:** blinzeln. | 19 **survey:** Begutachtung, Erkundung. | 20 f. **covetous:** habgierig, lüstern. | 21 **avaricious:** geizig. | **insatiable:** unersättlich. | **fence:** Hehler. | 22 **deliberately:** bedächtig.

"Hush! hush! Mr. Sikes," said the Jew, trembling; "don't speak so loud."

[...]

After swallowing two or three glasses of spirits, Mr. Sikes condescended to take some notice of the young gentlemen; which gracious act led to a conversation, in which the cause and manner of Oliver's capture were circumstantially detailed; with such alterations and improvements on the truth, as to the Dodger appeared most advisable under the circumstances.

"I'm afraid," said the Jew, "that he may say something which will get us into trouble."

[...]

"Somebody must find out wot's been done at the office," said Mr. Sikes in a much lower tone than he had taken since he came in.

The Jew nodded assent.

[...]

The prudence of this line of action, indeed, was obvious; but unfortunately there was one very strong objection to its being adopted; and this was, that the Dodger, and Charley Bates, and Fagin, and Mr. William Sikes, happened, one and all, to entertain a most violent and deeply-rooted antipathy to going near a police-office, on any ground or pretext whatever.

How long they might have sat and looked at each other, in a state of uncertainty not the most pleasant of its kind, it is diffi-

5 **to condescend to do s.th.:** sich dazu herablassen, geruhen, etwas zu tun. | 6 **gracious:** gnädig. | 7 **capture:** Gefangennahme. | **circumstantially:** ausführlich. | **to detail s.th.:** etwas genau schildern. | 8 **alteration:** Abänderung. | **improvement:** Verbesserung, Beschönigung. | 9 **advisable:** ratsam. | 13 **office:** (Polizei-)Wache. | 18 **prudence:** Klugheit. | **line of action:** Vorgehensweise. | 19 **objection:** Einwand. | 20 **to adopt:** anwenden. | 21 f. **to entertain:** (Gefühl) hegen. | 23 **ground:** Veranlassung. | **pretext:** Vorwand. | 25 **uncertainty:** Ungewissheit.

cult to say. It is not necessary to make any guesses on the subject, however; for the sudden entrance of the two young ladies whom Oliver had seen on a former occasion, caused the conversation to flow afresh.

"The very thing!" said the Jew. "Bet will go; won't you, my dear?"

"Wheres?" inquired the young lady.

"Only just up to the office, my dear," said the Jew coaxingly.

It is due to the young lady to say that she did not positively affirm that she would not, but that she merely expressed an emphatic and earnest desire to be "blessed" if she would; [...].

The Jew's countenance fell; and he turned from this young lady: who was gaily, not to say gorgeously attired, in a red gown, green boots, and yellow curl-papers; to the other female.

"Nancy, my dear," said the Jew in a soothing manner, "what do *you* say?"

"That it won't do; so it's no use a-trying it on, Fagin," replied Nancy.

[...]

"She'll go, Fagin," said Sikes.

"No, she won't, Fagin," said Nancy.

"Yes she will, Fagin," said Sikes.

And Mr. Sikes was right. By dint of alternate threats, prom-

1 f. **subject:** Thema. | 3 **to cause:** veranlassen; bewirken. | 4 **afresh:** erneut. | 5 **The very thing!:** Das ist es! | 8 **coaxingly:** einschmeichelnd. | 9 **to be due to s.o.:** jdm. gebühren. | **positively:** bestimmt, eindeutig. | 10 **to affirm s.th.:** etwas beteuern, versichern. | 11 **emphatic:** nachdrücklich. | **to be "blessed":** verdammt sein. | 12 **the Jew's countenance fell:** der Jude machte ein langes Gesicht. | 13 **gaily:** fröhlich, bunt. | **gorgeously:** prächtig. | **attired:** gekleidet. | 14 **curl-paper:** Haarschleifchen. | 16 **soothing:** besänftigend. | 24 **by dint of:** durch, mit Hilfe von.

ises, and bribes, the lady in question was ultimately prevailed upon to undertake the commission. […]

[…] Nancy made straight up to the bluff officer in the striped waistcoat; and with the most piteous wailings and lamentations […] demanded her own dear brother.

"I haven't got him, my dear," said the old man.

"Where is he?" screamed Nancy, in a distracted manner.

"Why, the gentleman's got him," replied the officer.

"What gentleman? Oh, gracious heavins! what gentleman?" exclaimed Nancy.

In reply to this incoherent questioning, the old man informed the deeply affected sister that Oliver had been taken ill in the office, and discharged in consequence of a witness having proved the robbery to have been committed by another boy, not in custody; and that the prosecutor had carried him away, in an insensible condition, to his own residence: of and concerning which, all the informant knew was, that it was somewhere at Pentonville: he having heard that word mentioned in the directions to the coachman.

[…]

Mr. Bill Sikes no sooner heard the account of the expedition delivered, than he very hastily called up the white dog; and, putting on his hat, expeditiously departed: without devoting

1 **bribe:** Bestechung. | 1 f. **to prevail upon s.o. to do s.th.:** jdn. dazu bewegen, etwas zu tun. | 2 **to undertake:** durchführen. | **commission:** Auftrag. | 4 **piteous:** kläglich, erbärmlich. | **wailing:** Jammern. | 4 f. **lamentation:** Wehklagen. | 7 **distracted:** verwirrt, verstört. | 11 **incoherent:** zusammenhanglos. | 12 **affected:** betroffen. | 13 **witness:** Zeuge, Zeugin. | 14 **to prove:** bekunden. | 15 **in custody:** in Haft. | **prosecutor:** Kläger. | 16 **residence:** Wohnsitz. | 21 **expedition:** Erkundungsreise, Ausflug, Unternehmung. | 22 **to deliver s.th.:** etwas abliefern, abgeben. | 23 **expeditiously:** eilig.

any time to the formality of wishing the company good morning.

"We must know where he is, my dears; he must be found," said the Jew, greatly excited. "Charley, do nothing but skulk about, till you bring home some news of him! Nancy, my dear, I must have him found. I trust to you, my dear, – to you and the Artful for everything! Stay, stay," added the Jew, unlocking a drawer with a shaking hand; "there's money, my dears. I shall shut up this shop to-night. You'll know where to find me! Don't stop here a minute. Not an instant, my dears!"

[...]

Chapter XIV

Comprising further Particulars of Oliver's stay at Mr. Brownlow's. With the remarkable Prediction which one Mr. Grimwig uttered concerning him, when he went out on an Errand

Oliver soon recovered from the fainting fit into which Mr. Brownlow's abrupt exclamation had thrown him; and the subject of the picture was carefully avoided, both by the old gentleman and Mrs. Bedwin [...].

They were happy days, those of Oliver's recovery. Everything was so quiet, and neat, and orderly; everybody was kind and gentle; that after the noise and turbulence in the midst of which he had always lived, it seemed like Heaven itself. He was

1 **formality:** Förmlichkeit. | 6 **to trust to s.o.:** sich auf jdn. verlassen. | 13 **stay:** Aufenthalt. | 14 **prediction:** Vorhersage, Prophezeiung. | 16 **errand:** Botengang, Besorgung. | 17 **fainting fit:** Ohnmachtsanfall. | 18 **abrupt:** plötzlich. | 21 **recovery:** Erholung, Genesung. | 23 **turbulence:** Unruhe.

no sooner strong enough to put his clothes on, properly, than Mr. Brownlow caused a complete new suit, and a new cap, and a new pair of shoes, to be provided for him. As Oliver was told that he might do what he liked with the old clothes, he gave them to a servant who had been very kind to him: and asked her to sell them to a Jew: and keep the money for herself. This she very readily did; and, as Oliver looked out of the parlour-window, and saw the Jew roll them up in his bag and walk away, he felt quite delighted to think that they were safely gone, and that there was now no possible danger of his ever being able to wear them again. They were sad rags, to tell the truth; and Oliver had never had a new suit before.

One evening, about a week after the affair of the picture, as he was sitting talking to Mrs. Bedwin, there came a message down from Mr. Brownlow, that if Oliver Twist felt pretty well, he should like to see him in his study, and talk to him a little while.

[...] Oliver tapped at the study-door. On Mr. Brownlow calling to him to come in, he found himself in a little back room, quite full of books: with a window, looking into some pleasant little gardens. [...]

"Now," said Mr. Brownlow, speaking if possible in a kinder, but at the same time in a much more serious manner, than Oliver had ever known him assume yet, "I want you to pay great attention, my boy, to what I am going to say. I shall talk to you without any reserve; because I am sure you are as well able to understand me, as many older persons would be."

"Oh, don't tell me you are going to send me away, sir, pray!"

1 **properly:** ordentlich, richtig. | 3 **to provide s.th.:** etwas beschaffen, besorgen. | 6 **Jew:** Der Beruf des Kleidertrödlers wurde damals häufig von Juden ausgeübt. | 7 **readily:** bereitwillig. | 16 **study:** Arbeitszimmer. | 18 **to tap at s.th.:** an etwas klopfen. | 24 **to assume:** annehmen. | 26 **reserve:** Zurückhaltung.

exclaimed Oliver, alarmed at the serious tone of the old gentleman's commencement; "Don't turn me out of doors to wander in the streets again. Let me stay here, and be a servant. Don't send me back to the wretched place I came from. Have mercy upon a poor boy, sir!"

[...]

Oliver's sobs checked his utterance for some minutes; when he was on the point of beginning to relate how he had been brought up at the farm, and carried to the workhouse by Mr. Bumble, a peculiarly impatient little double-knock was heard at the street-door; and the servant, running up stairs, announced Mr. Grimwig.

"Is he coming up?" inquired Mr. Brownlow.

"Yes, sir," replied the servant. "He asked if there were any muffins in the house; and, when I told him yes, he said he had come to tea."

Mr. Brownlow smiled; and, turning to Oliver, said that Mr. Grimwig was an old friend of his, and he must not mind his being a little rough in his manners; for he was a worthy creature at bottom, as he had reason to know.

"Shall I go down stairs, sir?" inquired Oliver.

"No," replied Mr. Brownlow; "I would rather you remained here."

At this moment, there walked into the room: supporting himself by a thick stick: a stout old gentleman, rather lame in one leg, who was dressed in a blue coat, striped waistcoat, nankeen breeches and gaiters, and a broad-brimmed white hat,

2 **commencement:** Beginn, Anfang. | 7 **sob:** Schluchzer. | **utterance:** Äußerung. | 10 **impatient:** ungeduldig. | 15 **muffin:** Teekuchen. | 19 **worthy:** achtbar, trefflich. | 20 **at bottom:** im Grunde. | 25 **lame:** lahm. | 26 f. **nankeen breeches** (pl.): Nankinghose. | 27 **gaiters:** Gamaschen. | **broad-brimmed:** breitkrempig.

with the sides turned up with green. A very small-plaited shirt-frill, stuck out from his waistcoat; and a very long steel watch-chain, with nothing but a key at the end, dangled loosely below it. The ends of his white neckerchief were twisted into a ball about the size of an orange; the variety of shapes into which his countenance was twisted, defy description. He had a manner of screwing his head on one side when he spoke: and of looking out of the corners of his eyes at the same time: which irresistibly reminded the beholder of a parrot. […]

"That's the boy, is it?" said Mr. Grimwig, at length.

"That is the boy," replied Mr. Brownlow.

"How are you, boy?" said Mr. Grimwig.

"A great deal better, thank you, sir," replied Oliver.

Mr. Brownlow, seeming to apprehend that his singular friend was about to say something disagreeable, asked Oliver to step down stairs and tell Mrs. Bedwin they were ready fo tea; which, as he did not half like the visitor's manner, he was very happy to do.

[…]

"And when are you going to hear a full, true, and particular account of the life and adventures of Oliver Twist?" asked Grimwig of Mr. Brownlow, at the conclusion of the meal: looking sideways at Oliver, as he resumed the subject.

"To-morrow morning," replied Mr. Brownlow. "I would rather he was alone with me at the time. Come up to me tomorrow morning at ten o'clock, my dear."

1 **small-plaited:** mit kleinen Falten. | 2 **shirt-frill:** Hemdkrause. | 3 **to dangle:** baumeln. | 4 **neckerchief:** Halstuch. | 6 **to defy description:** jeder Beschreibung spotten. | 7 **to screw one's head:** den Kopf drehen. | 9 **irresistibly:** unwiderstehlich, unweigerlich. | **beholder:** Betrachter. | **parrot:** Papagei. | 14 **to apprehend:** befürchten. | **singular:** einzigartig, bemerkenswert. | 15 **disagreeable:** unangenehm. | 23 **sideways:** seitlich.

"Yes, sir," replied Oliver. He answered with some hesitation, because he was confused by Mr. Grimwig's looking so hard at him.

"I'll tell you what," whispered that gentleman to Mr. Brownlow; "he won't come up to you to-morrow morning. I saw him hesitate. He is deceiving you, my good friend."

"I'll swear he is not," replied Mr. Brownlow, warmly.

[…]

As fate would have it, Mrs. Bedwin chanced to bring in, at this moment, a small parcel of books: which Mr. Brownlow had that morning purchased of the identical book-stall keeper, who has already figured in this history; having laid them on the table, she prepared to leave the room.

"Stop the boy, Mrs. Bedwin!" said Mr. Brownlow; "there is something to go back."

"He has gone, sir," replied Mrs. Bedwin.

"Call after him," said Mr. Brownlow; "it's particular. He is a poor man, and they are not paid for. There are some books to be taken back, too."

The street-door was opened. Oliver ran one way; and the girl ran another; and Mrs. Bedwin stood on the step and screamed for the boy; but there was no boy in sight. Oliver and the girl returned, in a breathless state, to report that there were no tidings of him.

"Dear me, I am very sorry for that," exclaimed Mr. Brownlow; "I particularly wished those books to be returned to-night."

"Send Oliver with them," said Mr. Grimwig, with an ironical smile; "he will be sure to deliver them safely, you know."

3 **hard:** streng. | 9 **fate:** Schicksal. | 11 **identical:** gleich, nämlich. | 12 **to figure:** eine Rolle spielen. | 17 **particular:** wichtig. | 24 **tidings** (pl.): Kunde, Nachricht.

"Yes; do let me take them, if you please, sir," said Oliver. "I'll run all the way, sir."

The old gentleman was just going to say that Oliver should not go out on any account; when a most malicious cough from Mr. Grimwig determined him that he should; and that, by his prompt discharge of the commission, he should prove to him the injustice of his suspicions: on this head at least: at once.

"You *shall* go, my dear," said the old gentleman. "The books are on a chair by my table. Fetch them down."

Oliver, delighted to be of use, brought down the books under his arm in a great bustle; and waited, cap in hand, to hear what message he was to take.

"You are to say," said Mr. Brownlow, glancing steadily at Grimwig; "you are to say that you have brought those books back; and that you have come to pay the four pound ten I owe him. This is a five-pound note, so you will have to bring me back, ten shillings change."

"I won't be ten minutes, sir," replied Oliver, eagerly. Having buttoned up the bank-note in his jacket-pocket, and placed the books carefully under his arm, he made a respectful bow, and left the room. [...]

"Let me see; he'll be back in twenty minutes, at the longest," said Mr. Brownlow, pulling out his watch, and placing it on the table. "It will be dark by that time."

"Oh! you really expect him to come back, do you?" inquired Mr. Grimwig.

"Don't you?" asked Mr. Brownlow, smiling.

The spirit of contradiction was strong in Mr. Grimwig's

4 **not on any account:** auf keinen Fall. | **malicious:** boshaft. | 6 **prompt:** unverzüglich, sofortig. | **discharge:** Erfüllung, Ausführung. | 7 **head:** Thema. | 10 **to be of use:** nützlich, dienlich sein. | 28 **contradiction:** Widerspruch.

breast, at the moment; and it was rendered stronger by his friend's confident smile.

"No," he said, smiting the table with his fist, "I do not. The boy has a new suit of clothes on his back; a set of valuable books under his arm; and a five-pound note in his pocket. He'll join his old friends the thieves, and laugh at you. If ever that boy returns to this house, sir, I'll eat my head."

With these words, he drew his chair closer to the table; and there the two friends sat, in silent expectation, with the watch between them.

It is worthy of remark: as illustrating the importance we attach to our own judgments, and the pride with which we put forth our most rash and hasty conclusions: that, although Mr. Grimwig was not by any means a bad-hearted man; and though he would have been unfeignedly sorry to see his respected friend, duped and deceived; he really did, most earnestly and strongly hope, at that moment, that Oliver Twist might not come back.

It grew so dark, that the figures on the dial-plate were scarcely discernible; but there the two old gentlemen continued to sit, in silence: with the watch between them.

3 **to smite:** schlagen. | 4 **valuable:** wertvoll. | 15 **unfeignedly:** aufrichtig. | 16 **to dupe s.o.:** jdn. düpieren, übertölpeln. | 20 **discernible:** erkennbar, wahrnehmbar.

Chapter XV

Shewing how very fond of Oliver Twist, the merry old Jew and Miss Nancy were

[…]

Meanwhile, Oliver Twist, little dreaming that he was within so very short a distance of the merry old gentleman, was on his way to the book-stall. When he got into Clerkenwell, he accidentally turned down a by-street which was not exactly in his way; but not discovering his mistake until he had got half-way down it, and knowing it must lead in the right direction, he did not think it worth while to turn back; and so marched on, as quickly as he could, with the books under his arm.

He was walking along; thinking how happy and contented he ought to feel; and how much he would give for only one look at poor little Dick: who, starved and beaten, might be weeping bitterly at that very moment; when he was startled by a young woman screaming out very loud, "Oh, my dear brother!" And he had hardly looked up, to see what the matter was, when he was stopped by having a pair of arms thrown tight round his neck.

"Don't," cried Oliver, struggling. "Let go of me. Who is it? What are you stopping me for?"

The only reply to this, was a great number of loud lamentations from the young woman who had embraced him; and who had a little basket and a street-door key in her hand.

"Oh my gracious!" said the young woman, "I've found him! Oh! Oliver! Oliver! Oh you naughty boy, to make me suffer

8 **by-street:** Seiten-, Nebenstraße. | 11 **worth while:** lohnend, der Mühe wert. | 13 **contented:** zufrieden. | 24 **to embrace s.o.:** jdn. umarmen. | 27 **naughty:** böse, unartig.

sich distress on your account! Come home, dear, come. Oh, I've found him. Thank gracious goodness heavins, I've found him!" With these incoherent exclamations, the young woman burst into another fit of crying, and got so dreadfully hysterical, that a couple of women who came up at the moment asked a butcher's boy with a shiny head of hair anointed with suet, who was also looking on, whether he didn't think he had better run for the doctor. To which, the butcher's boy: who appeared of a lounging, not to say indolent disposition: replied, that he thought not.

"Oh, no, no, never mind," said the young woman, grasping Oliver's hand; "I'm better now. Come home directly, you cruel boy! Come!"

"What's the matter, ma'am?" inquired one of the women.

"Oh, ma'am," replied the young woman, "he ran away, near a month ago, from his parents, who are hard-working and respectable people; and went and joined a set of thieves and bad characters; and almost broke his mother's heart."

"Young wretch!" said one woman.

"Go home, do, you little brute," said the other.

"I'm not," replied Oliver, greatly alarmed. "I don't know her. I haven't any sister, or father and mother either. I'm an orphan; I live at Pentonville."

"Oh, only hear him, how he braves it out!" cried the young woman.

"Why, it's Nancy!" exclaimed Oliver; who now saw her face for the first time; and started back, in irrepressible astonishment.

1 **sich:** *such.* | **distress:** Kummer, Sorge. | 6 **shiny:** glänzend. | **to anoint:** einölen, einschmieren. | **suet:** Rindertalg. | 9 **lounging:** träge. | **indolent:** träge, faul. | **disposition:** Veranlagung, Naturell. | 17 **set:** Gruppe. | 20 **brute:** Rohling, Unmensch. | 24 **to brave it out:** sich trotzig benehmen, sich nicht einschüchtern lassen. | 27 **irrepressible:** unbezähmbar.

"You see he knows me!" cried Nancy, appealing to the bystanders. "He can't help himself. Make him come home, there's good people, or he'll kill his dear mother and father, and break my heart!"

"What the devil's this?" said a man, bursting out of a beer-shop, with a white dog at his heels; "young Oliver! Come home to your poor mother, you young dog! Come home directly."

"I don't belong to them. I don't know them. Help! help!" cried Oliver, struggling in the man's powerful grasp.

"Help!" repeated the man. "Yes; I'll help you, you young rascal! What books are these? You've been a-stealing 'em, have you? Give 'em here." With these words, the man tore the volumes from his grasp, and struck him on the head.

"That's right!" cried a looker-on, from a garret-window. "That's the only way of bringing him to his senses!"

"To be sure!" cried a sleepy-faced carpenter, casting an approving look at the garret-window.

"It'll do him good!" said the two women.

"And he shall have it, too!" rejoined the man, administering another blow, and seizing Oliver by the collar. "Come on, you young villain! Here, Bull's-eye, mind him, boy! Mind him!"

Weak with recent illness; stupefied by the blows and the suddenness of the attack; terrified by the fierce growling of the dog, and the brutality of the man; and overpowered by the

5 **to burst out of s.th.:** aus etwas herausstürmen. | 5f. **beer-shop:** Kneipe. | 14 **volume:** Buch, Band. | 15 **looker-on:** Zuschauer. | **garret-window:** Mansardenfenster. | 16 **to bring s.o. to his, her senses:** jdn. zur Vernunft bringen. | 20f. **to administer:** verabreichen, geben, austeilen. | 22 **Bull's-eye:** sprechender Name des Hundes; wörtl.: das Schwarze (einer Zielscheibe); Bullauge. | 24 **recent:** kürzlich. | 25 **terrified:** entsetzt, erschrocken. | 26 **overpowered:** überwältigt.

conviction of the bystanders that he really was the hardened little wretch he was described to be; what could one poor child do! Darkness had set in; it was a low neighbourhood; no help was near; resistance was useless. In another moment, he was dragged into a labyrinth of dark narrow courts: and forced along them, at a pace which rendered the few cries he dared to give utterance to, wholly unintelligible. It was of little moment, indeed, whether they were intelligible or no, for there was nobody to care for them, had they been ever so plain.

The gas-lamps were lighted; Mrs. Bedwin was waiting anxiously at the open door; the servant had run up the street twenty times to see if there were any traces of Oliver; and still the two old gentlemen sat, perseveringly, in the dark parlour: with the watch between them.

Chapter XVI

Relates what became of Oliver Twist, after he had been claimed by Nancy

The narrow streets and courts, at length, terminated in a large open space; scattered about which, were pens for beasts: and other indications of a cattle-market. Sikes slackened his pace when they reached this spot: the girl being quite unable to support, any longer, the rapid rate at which they had hitherto

1 **conviction:** Überzeugung. | 7 **unintelligible:** unverständlich. | 7 f. **moment:** Bedeutung, Belang. | 9 **plain:** deutlich. | 12 **trace:** Spur. | 13 **perseveringly:** ausdauernd, beharrlich. | 19 **to be scattered:** verstreut sein. | 20 **indication:** Hinweis, Zeichen. | **to slacken one's pace:** das Tempo, den Schritt verlangsamen. | 21 f. **to support:** aufrechterhalten.

walked. Turning to Oliver, he roughly commanded him to take hold of Nancy's hand.

[...]

They walked on, by little-frequented and dirty ways, for a full half-hour: meeting very few people: and those appearing from their looks to hold much the same position in society as Mr. Sikes himself. At length they turned into a very filthy narrow street, nearly full of old-clothes shops; the dog, running forward, as if conscious that there was now no further occasion for his keeping on guard, stopped before the door of a shop that was closed and apparently untenanted. The house was in a ruinous condition; and on the door was nailed a board, intimating that it was to let: which looked as if it had hung there, for many years.

"All right," said Sikes, glancing cautiously about.

Nancy stooped below the shutters; and Oliver heard the sound of a bell. They crossed to the opposite side of the street: and stood for a few moments under a lamp. A noise, as if a sash-window were gently raised, was heard; and soon afterwards the door softly opened. Mr. Sikes then seized the terrified boy by the collar with very little ceremony; and all three were quickly inside the house.

The passage was perfectly dark. They waited, while the person who had let them in, chained and barred the door.

"Anybody here?" inquired Sikes.

"No," replied a voice, which Oliver thought he had heard before.

4 **little-frequented:** wenig benutzt. | 7 **filthy:** dreckig, schmutzig. | 9 **(to be) conscious that ...:** wissen, dass ... | 10 **to keep on guard:** wachsam sein. | 11 **untenanted:** leerstehend, unverpachtet. | 12 **condition:** Zustand. | 13 **to let:** zu vermieten. | 19 **sash-window:** Schiebefenster. | 21 **ceremony:** Förmlichkeit, Umschweife. | 24 **to chain and bar a door:** eine Tür mit einer Kette sichern und verriegeln.

"Is the old 'un here?" asked the robber.

"Yes," replied the voice; "and precious down in the mouth he has been. Won't he be glad to see you? Oh, no!"

The style of this reply, as well as the voice which delivered it, seemed familiar to Oliver's ears; but it was impossible to distinguish even the form of the speaker in the darkness.

"Let's have a glim," said Sikes, "or we shall go breaking our necks, or treading on the dog. Look after your legs if you do! That's all."

"Stand still a moment, and I'll get you one," replied the voice. The receding footsteps of the speaker were heard; and, in another minute, the form of Mr. John Dawkins, otherwise the Artful Dodger, appeared. He bore in his right hand, a tallow candle stuck in the end of a cleft stick.

The young gentleman did not stop to bestow any other mark of recognition upon Oliver than a humorous grin; but, turning away, beckoned the visitors to follow him down a flight of stairs. They crossed an empty kitchen; and, opening the door of a low earthy-smelling room, which seemed to have been built in a small back-yard, were received with a shout of laughter.

"Oh, my wig, my wig!" cried Master Charles Bates, from whose lungs the laughter had proceeded; "here he is! oh, cry, here he is! Oh, Fagin, look at him; Fagin, do look at him! I can't bear it; it is such a jolly game, I can't bear it. Hold me, somebody, while I laugh it out."

With this irrepressible ebullition of mirth, Master Bates laid

2 **to be precious down in the mouth:** den Kopf ganz schön hängen lassen. | 4 **style:** Art und Weise. | 5 f. **to distinguish s.th.:** etwas klar erkennen. | 7 **glim:** Funzel. | 11 **to recede:** sich entfernen. | 13 f. **tallow candle:** Talgkerze. | 14 **cleft stick:** Gabelstock. | 17 **to beckon to s.o. to do s.th.:** jdm. ein Zeichen geben, etwas zu tun. | 21 **wig:** Perücke. | 22 **to proceed from s.th.:** von etwas ausgehen, herrühren. | 24 **game:** Ulk, Spaß. | 26 **ebullition:** Überschäumen, Aufwallen.

himself flat on the floor: and kicked convulsively, for five minutes, in an ecstasy of facetious joy. Then, jumping to his feet, he snatched the cleft stick from the Dodger: and, advancing to Oliver, viewed him round and round; while the Jew, taking off his nightcap, made a great number of low bows to the bewildered boy. The Artful meantime, who was of a rather saturnine disposition, and seldom gave way to merriment when it interfered with business, rifled Oliver's pockets with steady assiduity.

"Look at his togs, Fagin!" said Charley, putting the light so close to his new jacket as nearly to set him on fire. "Look at his togs! – superfine cloth, and the heavy-swell cut! Oh, my eye, what a game! And his books, too; nothing but a gentleman, Fagin!"

"Delighted to see you looking so well, my dear," said the Jew, bowing with mock humility. "The Artful shall give you another suit, my dear, for fear you should spoil that Sunday one. Why didn't you write, my dear, and say you were coming? We'd have got something warm for supper."

At this, Master Bates roared again; so loud, that Fagin himself relaxed: and even the Dodger smiled; but as the Artful drew forth the five-pound note at that instant, it is doubtful whether the sally or the discovery awakened his merriment.

[...]

"They belong to the old gentleman," said Oliver, wringing his hands; "to the good, kind, old gentleman who took me into

1 **convulsively:** krampfartig. | 2 **facetious:** drollig, witzig. | 5 **nightcap:** Nachtmütze. | 5f. **bewildered:** verwirrt. | 6 **saturnine:** mürrisch, finster. | 7 **to give way to s.th.:** einer Sache nachgeben. | 7f. **to interfere with s.th.:** etwas stören. | 8 **to rifle s.th.:** etwas durchwühlen. | 8f. **assiduity:** Eifer, Fleiß. | 10 **togs:** Klamotten. | 12 **heavy-swell:** todschick. | 16 **mock:** vorgetäuscht, gespielt, unecht. | 23 **sally:** Scherz. | 25f. **to wring one's hands:** die Hände ringen.

his house, and had me nursed, when I was near dying of the fever. Oh, pray send them back; send him back the books and money. Keep me here all my life long; but pray, pray send them back. He'll think I stole them; the old lady: all of them who were so kind to me: will think I stole them. Oh, do have mercy upon me, and send them back!"

With these words, which were uttered with all the energy of passionate grief, Oliver fell upon his knees at the Jew's feet; and beat his hands together, in perfect desperation.

"The boy's right," remarked Fagin, looking covertly round, and knitting his shaggy eyebrows into a hard knot. "You're right, Oliver, you're right; they *will* think you have stolen 'em. Ha! ha!" chuckled the Jew, rubbing his hands; "it couldn't have happened better, if we had chosen our time!"

[...]

"I suppose he'd better not wear his best clothes to-morrow, Fagin, had he?" inquired Charley Bates.

"Certainly not," replied the Jew, reciprocating the grin with which Charley put the question.

Master Bates, apparently much delighted with his commission, took the cleft stick: and led Oliver into an adjacent kitchen, where there were two or three of the beds on which he had slept before; and here, with many uncontrollable bursts of laughter, he produced the identical old suit of clothes which Oliver had so much congratulated himself upon leaving off at Mr. Brownlow's; and the accidental display of which, to Fagin, by the Jew who purchased them, had been the very first clue received, of his whereabout.

1 **to nurse:** pflegen. | 8 **grief:** Kummer. | 10 **covertly:** verstohlen, heimlich. | 11 **to knit one's eyebrows:** die Augenbrauen runzeln. | **knot:** Knoten. | 13 **to chuckle:** kichern. | 18 **to reciprocate:** erwidern. | 21 **adjacent:** angrenzend. | 26 **display:** Vorführung, Vorzeigen. | 27 **clue:** Hinweis, Anhaltspunkt. | 28 **whereabout:** Aufenthaltsort.

"Pull off the smart ones," said Charley, "and I'll give 'em to Fagin to take care of. What fun it is!"

Poor Oliver unwillingly complied. Master Bates rolling up the new clothes under his arm, departed from the room; leaving Oliver in the dark; and locking the door behind him.

[...]

Chapter XVII

Oliver's Destiny, continuing unpropitious,
brings a Great Man to London to injure his Reputation

[...]

Mr. Bumble emerged at early morning from the workhouse-gate; and walked, with portly carriage and commanding steps, up the High-street. He was in the full bloom and pride of beadlehood; his cocked hat and coat were dazzling in the morning sun; he clutched his cane with the vigorous tenacity of health and power. Mr. Bumble always carried his head high; but this morning it was higher than usual. There was an abstraction in his eye, an elevation in his air, which might have warned an observant stranger that thoughts were passing in the beadle's mind, too great for utterance.

Mr. Bumble stopped not to converse with the small shopkeepers and others who spoke to him, deferentially, as he

1 **smart:** schick. | 3 **to comply:** sich fügen. | 8 **destiny:** Schicksal. | **unpropitious:** ungünstig. | 9 **to injure:** verletzen, beschädigen. | **reputation:** (guter) Ruf. | 12 **portly:** würdevoll. | **carriage:** (Körper-)Haltung. | **commanding:** gebieterisch. | 13 **bloom:** Blüte. | **pride:** Stolz. | 14 **beadlehood:** Büttelamt. | **to dazzle:** funkeln. | 15 **to clutch:** fest anpacken, umklammern. | **tenacity:** Zähigkeit. | 17 f. **abstraction:** Entrücktheit. | 18 **elevation:** (fig.) Erhebung.

passed along. He merely returned their salutations with a wave of his hand; and relaxed not in his dignified pace, until he reached the farm where Mrs. Mann tended the infant paupers with parochial care.

"Drat that beadle!" said Mrs. Mann, hearing the well-known shaking at the garden-gate. "If it isn't him at this time in the morning! Lauk, Mr. Bumble, only think of its being you! Well, dear me, it *is* a pleasure, this is! Come into the parlour, sir, please."

The first sentence was addressed to Susan; and the exclamations of delight were uttered to Mr. Bumble: as the good lady unlocked the garden-gate: and shewed him, with great attention and respect, into the house.

[...]

"Mrs. Mann, I am a-going to London."

"Lauk, Mr. Bumble!" cried Mrs. Mann, starting back.

"To London, ma'am," resumed the inflexible beadle, "by coach. I and two paupers, Mrs. Mann! A legal action is a-coming on, about a settlement; and the board has appointed me – me, Mrs. Mann – to depose to the matter before the quarter-sessions at Clerkinwell. [...]

"You're going by coach, sir? I thought it was always usual to send them paupers in carts."

[...] "They are both in a very low state, and we find it would come two pound cheaper to move 'em than to bury 'em – that is, if we can throw 'em upon another parish, which I think we

5 **Drat that beadle!:** Dieser verflixte Büttel! | 7 **lauk!:** ach herrje! (Ausruf des Erstaunens). | 17 **inflexible:** unbeugsam. | 18 **legal action:** Gerichtsverfahren. | 19 **settlement:** Unterbringung (d. h., welcher Bezirk für den Unterhalt der Armen aufkommt). | **to appoint s.o.:** jdn. ernennen, bestimmen. | 20 **to depose:** unter Eid aussagen. | 20 f. **quarter-sessions:** vierteljährliche Gerichtssitzungen. | 26 **if we can throw 'em upon another parish:** ob wir sie einer anderen Gemeinde unterjubeln können.

shall be able to do, if they don't die upon the road to spite us. Ha! ha! ha!"

When Mr. Bumble had laughed a little while, his eyes again encountered the cocked hat; and he became grave.

"We are forgetting business, ma'am," said the beadle; "here is your porochial stipend for the month."

Mr. Bumble produced some silver money rolled up in paper, from his pocket-book; and requested a receipt: which Mrs. Mann wrote.

[...] Mr. Bumble shortly afterwards took himself off, to prepare for his journey.

At six o'clock next morning, Mr. Bumble: having exchanged his cocked hat for a round one, and encased his person in a blue great-coat with a cape to it: took his place on the outside of the coach, accompanied by the criminals whose settlement was disputed; with whom, in due course of time, he arrived in London. [...]

Having disposed of these evil-minded persons for the night, Mr. Bumble sat himself down in the house at which the coach stopped: and took a temperate dinner of steaks, oyster-sauce, and porter. Putting a glass of hot gin-and-water on the chimney-piece, he drew his chair to the fire; and, with sundry moral reflections on the too-prevalent sin of discontent and complaining, composed himself to read the paper.

1 **to spite s.o.:** jdn. ärgern. | 4 **grave:** ernst. | 8 **to request:** erbitten. | 13 **to encase:** einhüllen. | 14 **great-coat:** Überzieher. | **cape:** Pelerine, Schulterumhang. | 16 **disputed:** umstritten. | 18 **evil-minded:** übel gesinnt. | 20 **temperate:** maßvoll. | **oyster-sauce:** Austernsauce. | 21 **porter:** Porter (Biersorte). | 21 f. **chimney-piece:** Kaminsims. | 22 **sundry:** allerlei, verschiedene. | 23 **reflections:** Überlegungen. | **too-prevalent:** allzu verbreitet, vorherrschend. | **discontent:** Unzufriedenheit. | 24 **to compose o.s. to do s.th.:** sich anschicken, etwas zu tun.

The very first paragraph upon which Mr. Bumble's eye rested, was the following advertisement.

"Five Guineas Reward.

"Whereas a young boy, named Oliver Twist, absconded, or was enticed, on Thursday evening last, from his home, at Pentonville; and has not since been heard of. The above reward will be paid to any person who will give such information as will lead to the discovery of the said Oliver Twist, or tend to throw any light upon his previous history, in which the advertiser is, for many reasons, warmly interested."

And then followed a full description of Oliver's dress, person, appearance, and disappearance: with the name and address of Mr. Brownlow at full length.

Mr. Bumble opened his eyes; read the advertisement, slowly and carefully, three several times; and in something more than five minutes was on his way to Pentonville: having actually, in his excitement, left the glass of hot gin-and-water, untasted.

"Is Mr. Brownlow at home?" inquired Mr. Bumble of the girl who opened the door.

[…]

He was shown into the little back study, where sat Mr. Brownlow and his friend Mr. Grimwig, with decanters and glasses before them. […]

1 **paragraph:** (Text-)Abschnitt, Absatz. | 2 **advertisement:** Annonce, Inserat. | 3 **guinea:** Guinee (21 Shilling). | 4 **whereas:** in Sachen. | **to abscond:** fortlaufen, verschwinden. | 5 **to entice s.o.:** jdn. fortlocken. | 8 **to tend to do s.th.:** darauf abzielen, etwas zu tun. | 9 **previous history:** Vorgeschichte (*previous:* vorherig). | 9 f. **advertiser:** Inserent. | 16 f. **actually:** tatsächlich. | 17 f. **untasted:** hier: unberührt. | 23 **decanter:** Karaffe.

"Now, sir, you come in consequence of having seen the advertisement?"

"Yes, sir," said Mr. Bumble.

"And you *are* a beadle, are you not?" inquired Mr. Grimwig.

"I am a porochial beadle, gentlemen," rejoined Mr. Bumble, proudly.

"Of course," observed Mr. Grimwig aside to his friend, "I knew he was. A beadle all over!"

Mr. Brownlow gently shook his head to impose silence on his friend, and resumed:

"Do you know where this poor boy is now?"

"No more than nobody," replied Mr. Bumble.

"Well, what *do* you know of him?" inquired the old gentleman. "Speak out, my friend, if you have anything to say. What *do* you know of him?"

"You don't happen to know any good of him, do you?" said Mr. Grimwig, caustically; after an attentive perusal of Mr. Bumble's features.

Mr. Bumble, catching at the inquiry very quickly, shook his head with portentous solemnity.

"You see?" said Mr. Grimwig, looking triumphantly at Mr. Brownlow.

Mr. Brownlow looked apprehensively at Mr. Bumble's pursed-up countenance; and requested him to communicate what he knew regarding Oliver, in as few words as possible.

Mr. Bumble put down his hat; unbuttoned his coat; folded

17 **caustically:** in bissigem Ton. | **attentive:** aufmerksam. | **perusal:** Prüfung. | 19 **to catch at s.th.:** nach etwas greifen, etwas aufgreifen. | 20 **portentous:** unheilvoll. | 21 **triumphantly:** triumphierend. | 23 **apprehensively:** besorgt. | 24 **pursed-up:** gekräuselt, in Falten gelegt, verkniffen. | **to request:** bitten, ersuchen. | 25 **regarding:** bezüglich, hinsichtlich. | 26 f. **to fold one's arms:** die Arme verschränken.

his arms; inclined his head in a retrospective manner; and, after a few moments' reflection, commenced his story.

It would be tedious if given in the beadle's words: occupying, as it did, some twenty minutes in the telling; but the sum and substance of it was, That Oliver was a foundling, born of low and vicious parents. That he had, from his birth, displayed no better qualities than treachery, ingratitude, and malice. That he had terminated his brief career in the place of his birth, by making a sanguinary and cowardly attack on an unoffending lad; and running away in the night-time from his master's house. In proof of his really being the person he represented himself, Mr. Bumble laid upon the table the papers he had brought to town: and folding his arms again, awaited Mr. Brownlow's observations.

"I fear it is all too true," said the old gentleman sorrowfully, after looking over the papers. "This is not much for your intelligence; but I would gladly have given you treble the money, if it had been favourable to the boy."

It is not improbable that if Mr. Bumble had been possessed of this information at an earlier period of the interview, he might have imparted a very different colouring to his little history. It was too late to do it now, however; so he shook his head gravely: and, pocketing the five guineas, withdrew.

[...]

1 **to incline:** neigen. | **retrospective:** rückblickend. | 2 **to commence:** anfangen, beginnen. | 3 **tedious:** ermüdend. | 3 f. **to occupy s.th.:** etwas in Anspruch nehmen. | 4 f. **sum and substance:** das Wesentliche. | 7 **ingratitude:** Undankbarkeit. | **malice:** Bosheit, Bösartigkeit. | 8 **career:** Laufbahn. | 9 **sanguinary:** blutrünstig. | **cowardly:** feige. | **unoffending:** harmlos. | 11 **in proof of:** als Beweis für. | 11 f. **to represent o.s.:** sich darstellen. | 15 **sorrowfully:** betrübt, bekümmert. | 17 **treble:** dreifach. | 20 **period:** Zeitpunkt. | **interview:** Unterredung. | 21 **colouring:** (fig.) Anstrich. | 23 **to pocket:** einstecken.

There were sad hearts at Mr. Brownlow's that night.

Oliver's heart sank within him, when he thought of his good kind friends; it was well for him that he could not know what they had heard, or it might have broken outright.

Chapter XVIII

How Oliver passed his time, in the improving society of his reputable Friends

About noon next day, when the Dodger and Master Bates had gone out to pursue their customary avocations, Mr. Fagin took the opportunity of reading Oliver a long lecture on the crying sin of ingratitude: of which he clearly demonstrated he had been guilty, to no ordinary extent, in wilfully absenting himself from the society of his anxious friends; [...].

The Jew smiled hideously; patting Oliver on the head, said, that if he kept himself quiet, and applied himself to business, he saw they would be very good friends yet. Then, taking his hat; and covering himself with an old patched great-coat; he went out, and locked the room-door behind him.

And so Oliver remained all that day, and for the greater part of many subsequent days; seeing nobody, between early morning and midnight; and left, during the long hours, to commune

4 **outright:** ganz und gar. | 6 **to pass one's time:** die Zeit verbringen. | **improving:** förderlich. | 7 **reputable:** ehrenwert. | 9 **to pursue s.th.:** einer Sache nachgehen, etwas verfolgen. | **customary:** üblich, gewöhnlich. | **avocation:** Beschäftigung. | 11 **to demonstrate:** darlegen. | 12 **extent:** Ausmaß, Umfang. | **wilfully:** mutwillig, absichtlich. | 12 f. **to absent o.s.:** sich entfernen. | 14 **hideously:** abscheulich, grässlich, scheußlich. | 17 **patched:** geflickt. | 20 **subsequent:** folgend. | 21 f. **to commune with s.o.:** mit jdm. verkehren.

with his own thoughts: which, never failing to revert to his kind friends, and the opinion they must long ago have formed of him, were sad indeed.

[...]

One afternoon: the Dodger and Master Bates being engaged out that evening: the first-named young gentleman took it into his head to evince some anxiety regarding the decoration of his person (which, to do him justice, was by no means an habitual weakness with him;) and, with this end and aim, he condescendingly commanded Oliver to assist him in his toilet, straightway.

Oliver was but too glad to make himself useful; too happy to have some faces, however bad, to look upon; and too desirous to conciliate those about him when he could honestly do so; to throw any objection in the way of this proposal. So he at once expressed his readiness; and, kneeling on the floor, while the Dodger sat upon the table so that he could take his foot in his lap, he applied himself to a process which Mr. Dawkins designated as "japanning his trotter-cases." Which phrase, rendered into plain English, signifieth, cleaning his boots.

[...]

"You've been brought up bad," said the Dodger, surveying his boots with much satisfaction when Oliver had polished them. "Fagin will make something of you, though, or you'll be

5 **engaged:** beschäftigt. | 7 **anxiety:** Sorge. | **decoration:** Ausschmückung, Schmuck. | 8 **to do s.o. justice:** jdm. gerecht werden. | **habitual:** gewohnheitsmäßig. | 9 **end:** Ziel, Absicht. | 10 **to assist s.o. in s.th.:** jdm. bei etwas behilflich sein. | 11 **straightway:** auf der Stelle. | 13 **desirous:** begierig. | 14 **to conciliate s.o.:** jdn. versöhnlich stimmen. | 15 **proposal:** Vorschlag. | 18 **lap:** Schoß. | 18 f. **to designate:** bezeichnen. | 19 **japanning his trotter-cases:** etwa: das Wienern seiner Quadratlatschen. | **to render:** wiedergeben. | 20 **signifieth:** *signifies* (*to signify s.th.:* etwas bedeuten, besagen).

the first he ever had that turned out unprofitable. You'd better begin at once; for you'll come to the trade long before you think of it; and you're only losing time, Oliver."

Master Bates backed this advice with sundry moral admonitions of his own [...].

"And always put this in your pipe, Nolly," said the Dodger, as the Jew was heard unlocking the door above, "if you don't take fogles and tickers –"

"What's the good of talking in that way?" interposed Master Bates: "he don't know what you mean."

"If you don't take pocket hankechers and watches," said the Dodger, reducing his conversation to the level of Oliver's capacity, "some other cove will [...]."

"To be sure, to be sure!" said the Jew, who had entered, unseen by Oliver, "It all lies in a nutshell, my dear; in a nutshell, take the Dodger's word for it. Ha! ha! He understands the catechism of his trade."

The old man rubbed his hands gleefully together, as he corroborated the Dodger's reasoning in these terms; and chuckled with delight at his pupil's proficiency.

The conversation proceeded no farther at this time, for the Jew had returned home accompanied by Miss Betsy, and a gentleman whom Oliver had never seen before, but who was accosted by the Dodger as Tom Chitling [...].

From this day, Oliver was seldom left alone; but was placed

1 **to turn out s.th.:** sich als etwas erweisen. | **unprofitable:** unnütz, nicht gewinnbringend. | 4 f. **admonition:** Mahnung. | 6 **put this in your pipe!:** schreib dir das hinter die Ohren! | **Nolly:** Kurzform von *Oliver*. | 8 **ticker:** Uhr. | 12 **to reduce:** beschränken. | 12 f. **capacity:** Verständnis. | 14 **to be sure:** wohl wahr. | 15 **it all lies in a nutshell:** es ist auf den Punkt gebracht. | 16 f. **catechism:** Katechismus. | 18 **gleefully:** fröhlich, vergnügt. | 18 f. **to corroborate:** bekräftigen, untermauern. | 19 **reasoning:** Beweisführung. | 20 **proficiency:** Fertigkeit.

in almost constant communication with the two boys, who played the old game with the Jew every day: whether for their own improvement or Oliver's, Mr. Fagin best knew. At other times, the old man would tell them stories of robberies he had committed in his younger days: mixed up with so much that was droll and curious, that Oliver could not help laughing heartily, and showing that he was amused in spite of all his better feelings.

In short, the wily old Jew had the boy in his toils; and, having prepared his mind, by solitude and gloom, to prefer any society to the companionship of his own sad thoughts in such a dreary place, he was now slowly instilling into his soul the poison which he hoped would blacken it, and change its hue for ever.

Chapter XIX

In which a notable Plan is discussed and determined on

It was a chill, damp, windy night, when the Jew: buttoning his great-coat tight round his shrivelled body, and pulling the collar up over his ears so as completely to obscure the lower part of his face: emerged from his den. He paused on the step as the door was locked and chained behind him; and having listened while the boys made all secure, and until their retreating foot-

6 **droll:** drollig, lustig. | 7 **in spite of:** trotz, ungeachtet. | 9 **wily:** gerissen, verschlagen. | **to have s.o. in one's toils:** jdn. in der Mache haben. | 10 **solitude:** Einsamkeit. | **gloom:** Trübsinn. | 12 **dreary:** düster, trostlos. | **to instil:** einträufeln. | 13 **to blacken:** schwärzen. | **hue:** Farbe, Tönung. | 16 **notable:** bemerkenswert. | 17 **chill:** frostig, kalt. | 20 **den:** (Räuber-)Höhle, Schlupfwinkel. | 22 **to retreat:** sich zurückziehen, entfernen.

steps were no longer audible, slunk down the street as quickly as he could.

[…]

The Jew was evidently too familiar with the ground he traversed, however, to be at all bewildered, either by the darkness of the night, or the intricacies of the way. He hurried through several alleys and streets; and at length turned into one, lighted only by a single lamp at the farther end. At the door of a house in this street, he knocked; and having exchanged a few muttered words with the person who opened it, walked up stairs.

A dog growled as he touched the handle of a room-door; and a man's voice demanded who was there.

"Only me, Bill; only me, my dear," said the Jew, looking in.

"Bring in your body then," said Sikes. […]

"[…] Now, my dear, about that crib at Chertsey; when is it to be done, Bill, eh? When is it to be done? Such plate, my dears, such plate!" said the Jew: rubbing his hands, and elevating his eyebrows in a rapture of anticipation.

"Not at all," replied Sikes coldly.

"Not to be done at all!" echoed the Jew, leaning back in his chair.

"No, not at all," rejoined Sikes. "At least it can't be a put-up job, as we expected."

[…]

A long silence ensued; during which, the Jew was plunged in deep thought: with his face wrinkled into an expression of

1 **audible:** hörbar, vernehmlich. | **to slink:** schleichen. | 6 **intricacies** (pl.): Verschlungenheit. | 7 **alley:** Gasse. | 15 **crib:** Ding, Haus (Gaunersprache). | 17 **plate:** Beute (Gaunersprache). | **to elevate:** emporheben. | 18 **rapture:** Begeisterung, Verzückung. | **anticipation:** Erwartung, Vorfreude. | 22 f. **put-up job:** abgekartetes Spiel; Einbruch, an dem jemand vom Hauspersonal als Komplize beteiligt ist. | 25 **to be plunged:** (fig.) versunken sein. | 26 **to wrinkle:** sich in Falten legen, sich runzeln.

villany perfectly demoniacal. Sikes eyed him furtively from time to time; Nancy, apparently fearful of irritating the housebreaker, sat with her eyes fixed upon the fire, as if she had been deaf to all that passed.

"Fagin," said Sikes, abruptly breaking the stillness that prevailed, "is it worth fifty shiners extra, if it's safely done from the outside?"

"Yes," said the Jew, as suddenly rousing himself.

"Is it a bargain?" inquired Sikes.

"Yes, my dear, yes," rejoined the Jew; his eyes glistening, and every muscle in his face working, with the excitement that the inquiry had awakened.

"Then," said Sikes, thrusting aside the Jew's hand, with some disdain, "let it come off as soon as you like. Toby and me were over the garden-wall the night afore last, sounding the panels of the door and shutters. The crib's barred up at night like a jail; but there's one part we can crack, safe and softly."

[...]

"As you like my dear, as you like," replied the Jew. "Is there no help wanted, but yours and Toby's?"

"None," said Sikes. "'Cept a centre-bit and a boy. The first we've both got; the second you must find us."

[...]

"Now, Fagin," said Nancy with a laugh. "Tell Bill at once, about Oliver!"

1 **villany:** *villainy:* Schurkerei. | **demoniacal:** dämonisch. | **furtively:** heimlich, verstohlen. | 2 **to irritate:** reizen, erzürnen. | 2 f. **housebreaker:** Einbrecher. | 5 f. **to prevail:** vorherrschen. | 6 **shiner:** Goldmünze. | 9 **Is it a bargain?:** Abgemacht? | 14 **disdain:** Verachtung, Geringschätzung. | **to come off:** zustandekommen, stattfinden. | 15 **to sound:** überprüfen. | 16 **panel:** (Tür-)Füllung. | 17 **to crack:** aufknacken, aufbrechen. | 21 **'cept:** *except.* | **centre-bit:** Spezialbohrer.

"Ha! you're a clever one, my dear; the sharpest girl I ever saw!" said the Jew, patting her on the neck. "It *was* about Oliver I was going to speak, sure enough. Ha! ha! ha!"

"What about him?" demanded Sikes.

"He's the boy for you, my dear," replied the Jew in a hoarse whisper; laying his finger on the side of his nose; and grinning frightfully.

[...]

"Well, he is just the size I want," said Mr. Sikes, ruminating.

"And will do everything you want, Bill, my dear," interposed the Jew; "he can't help himself. That is, if you frighten him enough."

"Frighten him!" echoed Sikes. "It'll be no sham frightening, mind you. If there's anything queer about him when we once get into the work; in for a penny, in for a pound. You won't see him alive again, Fagin. Think of that, before you send him. Mark my words!" said the robber, poising a crowbar: which he had drawn from under the bedstead.

[...]

After some discussion, in which all three took an active part, it was decided that Nancy should repair to the Jew's next evening when the night had set in: and bring Oliver away with her [...].

1 **sharp:** scharfsinnig, gescheit. | 5 **hoarse:** heiser. | 9 **to ruminate:** sinnieren, grübeln. | 11 **to frighten s.o.:** jdm. Angst einjagen. | 13 **sham:** unecht, nur zum Schein. | 15 **in for a penny, in for a pound:** mitgefangen, mitgehangen. | 17 **crowbar:** Brechstange, Stemmeisen. | 21 **to repair to s.o.:** sich zu jdm. begeben.

Chapter XX

Wherein Oliver is delivered over to Mr. William Sikes

When Oliver awoke in the morning, he was a good deal surprised to find that a new pair of shoes, with strong thick soles, had been placed at his bedside; and that his old shoes had been removed. At first, he was pleased with the discovery: hoping that it might be the forerunner of his release; but such thoughts were quickly dispelled, on his sitting down to breakfast alone with the Jew, who told him, in a tone and manner which increased his alarm, that he was to be taken to the residence of Bill Sikes that night.

"To – to – stop there, sir?" asked Oliver, anxiously.

"No, no, my dear. Not to stop there," replied the Jew. "We shouldn't like to lose you. Don't be afraid, Oliver, you shall come back to us again. Ha! ha! ha! We won't be so cruel as to send you away, my dear. Oh no, no!"

The old man, who was stooping over the fire toasting a piece of bread, looked round as he bantered Oliver thus; and chuckled as if to shew that he knew he would still be very glad to get away if he could.

[...]

"You may burn a candle," said the Jew, putting one upon the table. "And here's a book for you to read, till they come to fetch you. Good night!"

"Good night!" replied Oliver, softly.

The Jew walked to the door: looking over his shoulder at the boy as he went. Suddenly stopping, he called him by his name.

7 **forerunner:** Vorbote. | **release:** Freilassung, Befreiung. |
8 **to dispel s.th.:** vertreiben, zerstreuen. | 18 **to banter:** necken, hänseln.

Oliver looked up; the Jew, pointing to the candle, motioned him to light it. He did so; and, as he placed the candlestick upon the table, saw that the Jew was gazing fixedly at him, with lowering and contracted brows, from the dark end of the room.

"Take heed, Oliver! take heed!" said the old man, shaking his right hand before him in a warning manner. "He's a rough man, and thinks nothing of blood when his own is up. Whatever falls out, say nothing; and do what he bids you. Mind!" Placing a strong emphasis on the last word, he suffered his features gradually to resolve themselves into a ghastly grin; and, nodding his head, left the room.

Oliver leaned his head upon his hand when the old man disappeared; and pondered, with a trembling heart, on the words he had just heard. [...]

He had concluded his prayer, but still remained with his head buried in his hands, when a rustling noise aroused him.

"What's that!" he cried, starting up, and catching sight of a figure standing by the door. "Who's there?"

"Me. Only me," replied a tremulous voice.

Oliver raised the candle above his head: and looked towards the door. It was Nancy.

"Put down the light," said the girl, turning away her head. "It hurts my eyes."

[...]

"Am I to go with you?" asked Oliver.

1 f. **to motion s.o. to do s.th.:** jdn. durch einen Wink auffordern, etwas zu tun. | 2 **candlestick:** Kerzenhalter. | 4 **lowering:** drohend. | **contracted:** zusammengezogen, gerunzelt (*to contract the brows:* die Augenbrauen runzeln). | 7 **to think nothing of s.th.:** etwas ganz normal finden. | **to be up:** in Wallung geraten. | 8 **to fall out:** sich ereignen. | 9 **to suffer:** zulassen. | 10 **to resolve o.s.:** sich auflösen. | **ghastly:** grausig. | 13 **to ponder on s.th.:** über etwas nachgrübeln. | 19 **tremulous:** bebend, zittrig.

"Yes; I have come from Bill," replied the girl. "You are to go with me."

[...]

She caught the hand which Oliver instinctively placed in hers; and, blowing out the light, drew him after her up the stairs. The door was opened, quickly, by some one shrouded in the darkness; and was as quickly closed, when they had passed out. A hackney-cabriolet was in waiting; [...].

[...] All was so quick and hurried, that he had scarcely time to recollect where he was, or how he came there, when the carriage stopped at the house to which the Jew's steps had been directed, on the previous evening.

[...]

"This way," said the girl, releasing her hold for the first time. "Bill!"

"Hallo!" replied Sikes: appearing at the head of the stairs, with a candle. "Oh! That's the time of day. Come on!"

This was a very strong expression of approbation: an uncommonly hearty welcome: from a person of Mr. Sikes's temperament. Nancy, appearing much gratified thereby, saluted him cordially.

"Bull's-eye's gone home with Tom," observed Sikes, as he lighted them up. "He'd have been in the way."

"That's right," rejoined Nancy.

"So you've got the kid," said Sikes, when they had all reached the room: closing the door as he spoke.

"Yes, here he is," replied Nancy.

4 **instinctively:** unwillkürlich. | 6 **to shroud s.o.:** jdn. verbergen. | 8 **hackney-cabriolet:** einspännige Mietdroschke. | 10 **to recollect:** sich besinnen. | 10 f. **carriage:** Kutsche. | 14 **to release:** lösen, lockern. | 17 **That's the time of day!:** etwa: Das ist aber schön! | 18 **approbation:** Billigung, Beifall. | 20 **to salute:** begrüßen. | 21 **cordially:** herzlich. | 23 **to light s.o.:** jdm. leuchten.

"Did he come quiet?" inquired Sikes.

"Like a lamb," rejoined Nancy.

"I'm glad to hear it," said Sikes, looking grimly at Oliver; "for the sake of his young carcase: as would otherwise have suffered for it. Come here, young un; and let me read you a lectur', which is as well got over at once."

Thus addressing his new pupil, Mr. Sikes pulled off Oliver's cap and threw it into a corner; and then, taking him by the shoulder, sat himself down by the table, and stood the boy in front of him.

"Now, first: do you know wot this is?" inquired Sikes, taking up a pocket-pistol which lay on the table.

Oliver replied in the affirmative.

"Well then, look here," continued Sikes. "This is powder; that 'ere's a bullet; and this is a little bit of a old hat for waddin'."

Oliver murmured his comprehension of the different bodies referred to; and Mr. Sikes proceeded to load the pistol, with great nicety and deliberation.

"Now it's loaded," said Mr. Sikes, when he had finished.

"Yes, I see it is, sir," replied Oliver.

"Well," said the robber, grasping Oliver's wrist tightly: and putting the barrel so close to his temple that they touched; at which moment the boy could not repress a start; "if you speak a word when you're out o' doors with me, except when I speak to you, that loading will be in your head without notice. So, if

3 **grimly:** grimmig. | 4 **carcase:** Gerippe, Leib. | 5 f. **to read s.o. a lecture:** jdm. eine Lektion erteilen. | 13 **in the affirmative:** bejahend. | 14 **powder:** *gunpowder:* Schießpulver. | 15 f. **waddin':** *wadding:* Ladepfropf. | 17 **to murmur:** murmeln. | **comprehension:** Verständnis, Begreifen. | **body:** Teil, Gegenstand. | 18 **to refer to s.th.:** etwas erwähnen. | 19 **nicety:** peinliche Genauigkeit. | 23 **barrel:** Lauf einer Waffe. | 26 **without notice:** ohne Ankündigung.

you *do* make up your mind to speak without leave; say your prayers first."

[…]

Supper being ended – it may be easily conceived that Oliver had no great appetite for it – Mr. Sikes disposed of a couple of glasses of spirits and water: and threw himself upon the bed; ordering Nancy, with many imprecations in case of failure, to call him at five precisely. Oliver stretched himself in his clothes, by command of the same authority, on a mattress upon the floor; […].

When he awoke, the table was covered with tea things; and Sikes was thrusting various articles into the pockets of his great-coat, which hung over the back of a chair: while Nancy was busily engaged in preparing breakfast. It was not yet daylight; for the candle was still burning; and it was quite dark outside. A sharp rain, too, was beating against the window-panes; and the sky looked black and cloudy.

[…]

1 **leave:** Erlaubnis. | 4 **to conceive:** sich (etwas) vorstellen. | 5 **to dispose of s.th.:** etwas beseitigen, entsorgen. | 11 **tea-things** (pl.): Teegeschirr. | 16 f. **window-pane:** Fensterscheibe.

Chapter XXI

The Expedition

It was a cheerless morning when they got into the street; blowing and raining hard; and the clouds looking dull and stormy. The night had been very wet: large pools of water had collected in the road: and the kennels were overflowing. […]

By the time they had turned into the Bethnal Green-road, the day had fairly begun to break. Many of the lamps were already extinguished; a few country waggons were slowly toiling on, towards London; and now and then, a stage-coach, covered with mud, rattled briskly by: […].

"Now, young un!" said Sikes, looking up at the clock of St. Andrew's Church, "hard upon seven! you must step out. Come, don't lag behind already, Lazy-legs!"

Mr. Sikes accompanied this speech with a jerk at his little companion's wrist; Oliver, quickening his pace into a kind of trot, between a fast walk and a run, kept up with the rapid strides of the housebreaker as well as he could.

They held their course at this rate, until they had passed Hyde Park corner, and were on their way to Kensington: when Sikes relaxed his pace, until an empty cart, which was at some little distance behind, came up. Seeing "Hounslow" written on it, he asked the driver with as much civility

2 **expedition:** Streifzug, Feldzug, Fußmarsch. | 3 **cheerless:** trübselig, freudlos. | 4 **dull:** düster. | 5 **pool:** Pfütze, Lache. | 6 **kennel:** Rinnstein, Gosse. | 9 **to extinguish:** löschen. | 10 **stage-coach:** Postkutsche. | 11 **briskly:** schnell. | 13 **hard upon seven:** kurz vor sieben (Uhr). | **to step out:** schnell gehen, ausschreiten. | 14 **to lag behind:** zurückbleiben. | **lazy-legs:** (hum.) lahme Ente, Schlafmütze. | 16 **to quicken:** beschleunigen. | 17 **trot:** Trab. | 19 **rate:** Geschwindigkeit. | 23 **civility:** Höflichkeit.

as he could assume, if he would give them a lift as far as Isleworth.

"Jump up," said the man. "Is that your boy?"

"Yes; he's my boy," replied Sikes, looking hard at Oliver, and putting his hand abstractedly into the pocket where the pistol was.

"Your father walks rather too quick for you, don't he, my man?" inquired the driver: seeing that Oliver was out of breath.

"Not a bit of it," replied Sikes, interposing. "He's used to it. Here, take hold of my hand, Ned. In with you!"

Thus addressing Oliver, he helped him into the cart; and the driver, pointing to a heap of sacks, told him to lie down there, and rest himself. As they passed the different mile-stones, Oliver wondered, more and more, where his companion meant to take him. Kensington, Hammersmith, Chiswick, Kew Bridge, Brentford, were all passed; and yet they went on as steadily as if they had only just begun their journey. […]

The night was very dark. A damp mist rose from the river, and the marshy ground about; and spread itself over the dreary fields. It was piercing cold, too; all was gloomy and black. Not a word was spoken; for the driver had grown sleepy; and Sikes was in no mood to lead him into conversation. Oliver sat huddled together, in a corner of the cart; bewildered with alarm and apprehension; and figuring strange objects in the gaunt trees, whose branches waved grimly to and fro, as if in some fantastic joy at the desolation of the scene.

[…]

1 **to assume:** vorgeben, heucheln. | **to give s.o. a lift:** jdn. mitnehmen, mitfahren lassen. | 5 **abstractedly:** beiläufig, zufällig. | 19 **mist:** Nebel, Dunst. | 20 **marshy:** sumpfig, morastig. | 21 **piercing:** schneidend. | 25 **apprehension:** Besorgnis, ängstliche Erwartung. | **to figure s.th.:** sich etwas vorstellen. | **gaunt:** dürr. | 26 **to and fro:** hin und her.

Sunbury was passed through; and they came again into the lonely road. Two or three miles more; and the cart stopped. Sikes alighted; and, taking Oliver by the hand, they once again walked on.

They turned into no house at Shepperton, as the weary boy had expected; but still kept walking on, in mud and darkness, through gloomy lanes and over cold open wastes, until they came within sight of the lights of a town at no great distance. On looking intently forward, Oliver saw that the water was just below them: and that they were coming to the foot of a bridge.

Sikes kept straight on, until they were close upon the bridge; and then turned suddenly down a bank upon the left.

"The water!" thought Oliver, turning sick with fear. "He has brought me to this lonely place to murder me!"

He was about to throw himself on the ground, and make one struggle for his young life, when he saw that they stood before a solitary house: all ruinous and decayed. There was a window on each side of the dilapidated entrance; and one story above; but no light was visible. It was dark, dismantled: and, to all appearance, uninhabited.

Sikes, with Oliver's hand still in his, softly approached the low porch, and raised the latch. The door yielded to the pressure; and they passed in, together.

3 **to alight:** absteigen. | 5 **weary:** erschöpft, müde. | 7 **lane:** Heckenweg, Feldweg. | **waste:** (Ein-)Öde, Brachland. | 13 **bank:** Ufer. |
18 **solitary:** einzeln. | **decayed:** verfallen. | 19 **dilapidated:** zerfallen. | **story:** Stockwerk. | 20 **dismantled:** ausgeräumt. | 21 **uninhabited:** unbewohnt. | 23 **porch:** Vordach. | **latch:** Riegel, Klinke. | **to yield to s.th.:** einer Sache nachgeben.

Chapter XXII

The Burglary

"Hallo!" cried a loud, hoarse voice, as soon as they had set foot in the passage.

"Don't make such a row," said Sykes, bolting the door. "Shew a glim, Toby."

"Aha! my pal!" cried the same voice; "a glim, Barney, a glim! Shew the gentleman in, Barney; and wake up first, if convenient."

[...]

A pair of slipshod feet shuffled, hastily, across the bare floor of the room, as this interrogatory was put; and there issued, from a door on the right hand: first, a feeble candle: and next, the form of the same individual who has been heretofore described as labouring under the infirmity of speaking through his nose, and officiating as waiter at the public-house on Saffron Hill.

"Bister Sikes!" exclaimed Barney, with real or counterfeit joy; "cub id, sir; cub id."

"Here! you get on first," said Sikes, putting Oliver in front of him. "Quicker! or I shall tread upon your heels."

Muttering a curse upon his tardiness, Sikes pushed Oliver before him; and they entered a low dark room with a smoky fire: two or three broken chairs, a table, and a very old couch:

2 **burglary:** Einbruch. | 5 **row:** Lärm, Krach. | **Sykes:** *Sikes.* | 7 **pal:** Kumpan. | 8 f. **if convenient:** wenn's recht ist. | 11 **slipshod:** schlampig, schludrig. | **to shuffle:** schlurfen. | 12 **interrogatory:** Frage. | 14 **heretofore:** vordem. | 15 **to labour under s.th.:** unter etwas leiden. | **infirmity:** Gebrechen, Schwäche. | 16 **to officiate as s.th.:** als etwas fungieren. | 18 **Bister:** *Mister.* | **counterfeit:** unecht, vorgetäuscht. | 19 **cub id:** *come in.* | 22 **tardiness:** Langsamkeit.

on which, with his legs much higher than his head, a man was reposing at full length, smoking a long clay pipe. He was dressed in a smartly-cut snuff-coloured coat, with large brass buttons; an orange neckerchief; a coarse, staring, shawl-pattern waistcoat; and drab breeches. Mr. Crackit (for he it was) had no very great quantity of hair, either upon his head or face; but what he had, was of a reddish dye, and tortured into long corkscrew curls, through which he occasionally thrust some very dirty fingers, ornamented with large common rings. […]

"Bill, my boy!" said this figure, turning his head towards the door, "I'm glad to see you. I was almost afraid you'd given it up: in which case I should have made a personal wentur. Hallo!"

Uttering this exclamation in a tone of great surprise, as his eye rested on Oliver, Mr. Toby Crackit brought himself into a sitting posture, and demanded who that was.

"The boy. Only the boy!" replied Sikes, drawing a chair towards the fire.

[…]

"Now," said Sikes, as he resumed his seat, "if you'll give us something to eat and drink while we're waiting, you'll put some heart in us; or in me, at all events. […]"

This done, and Sikes having satisfied his appetite (Oliver could eat nothing but a small crust of bread which they made him swallow), the two men laid themselves down on chairs for

2 **to repose:** ruhen. | 3 **snuff-coloured:** zimtfarben. | 3 f. **brass button:** Messingknopf. | 4 **coarse:** geschmacklos. | **staring:** grell, schreiend (Farbe). | 4 f. **shawl-pattern:** türkisches Muster (*shawl:* Umhängetuch). | 7 **reddish:** rötlich. | **dye:** Farbe. | **to torture:** quälen. | 8 **corkscrew curls:** Korkenzieherlocken. | 9 **ornamented:** geschmückt. | 13 **wentur:** *venture:* Wagnis, Unternehmen, Glück. | 17 **posture:** Haltung, Stellung. | 25 **crust of bread:** Stückchen hartes Brot.

a short nap. Oliver retained his stool by the fire; and Barney, wrapped in a blanket, stretched himself on the floor: close outside the fender.

They slept, or appeared to sleep, for some time; nobody stirring but Barney, who rose once or twice to throw coals upon the fire. Oliver fell into a heavy doze: imagining himself straying alone through the gloomy lanes, or wandering about the dark churchyard, or retracing some one or other of the scenes of the past day: when he was roused by Toby Crackit jumping up and declaring it was half-past one.

[...]

The two robbers issued forth with Oliver between them. [...]

Quickening their pace, they turned up a road upon the left hand. After walking about a quarter of a mile, they stopped before a detached house surrounded by a wall: to the top of which, Toby Crackit, scarcely pausing to take breath, climbed in a twinkling.

"The boy next," said Toby. "Hoist him up; I'll catch hold of him."

Before Oliver had time to look round, Sikes had caught him under the arms; and in three or four seconds he and Toby were lying on the grass on the other side. Sikes followed directly. And they stole cautiously towards the house.

And now, for the first time, Oliver, well nigh mad with grief and terror, saw that housebreaking and robbery, if not murder, were the objects of the expedition. He clasped his hands to-

1 **nap:** Schläfchen, Nickerchen. | **to retain:** beibehalten. | 3 **fender:** Kaminblech. | 4f. **to stir:** sich regen, sich rühren. | 6 **doze:** Schlummer. | 6f. **to stray:** irren, streifen. | 8 **to retrace:** nachvollziehen. | 16 **detached:** freistehend. | 24 **to steal towards s.th.:** sich an etwas heranschleichen. | 25 **well nigh:** nahezu. | 26 **housebreaking:** Einbruch. | 27 **object:** Ziel, Absicht.

gether, and involuntarily uttered a subdued exclamation of horror. A mist came before his eyes; the cold sweat stood upon his ashy face; his limbs failed him; and he sunk upon his knees.

"Get up!" murmured Sikes, trembling with rage, and drawing the pistol from his pocket; "get up, or I'll strew your brains upon the grass."

"Oh! for God's sake let me go!" cried Oliver; "let me run away and die in the fields. I will never come near London; never, never! Oh! pray have mercy on me, and do not make me steal. For the love of all the bright Angels that rest in Heaven, have mercy upon me!"

The man to whom this appeal was made, swore a dreadful oath, and had cocked the pistol, when Toby, striking it from his grasp, placed his hand upon the boy's mouth, and dragged him to the house.

[…]

Sikes, invoking terrific imprecations upon Fagin's head for sending Oliver on such an errand, plied the crowbar vigorously, but with little noise. After some delay, and some assistance from Toby, the shutter to which he had referred, swung open on its hinges.

It was a little lattice-window, about five feet and a half above the ground: at the back of the house: which belonged to a scullery, or small brewing-place, at the end of the passage. The aperture was so small, that the inmates had probably not thought it worth while to defend it more securely; but it was large

1 **subdued:** gedämpft, unterdrückt. | 3 **ashy:** aschfahl. | **limb:** Körperglied. | **to fail:** im Stich lassen. | 5 **to strew:** verstreuen. | 12 f. **to swear an oath:** einen Fluch ausstoßen. | 13 **to cock a pistol:** eine Pistole spannen. | **to strike:** schlagen. | 17 **to invoke s.th. upon s.o.:** etwas auf jdn. herabrufen. | 21 **hinge:** Angel, Scharnier. | 22 **lattice-window:** Gitterfenster. | 23 f. **scullery:** Spülküche. | 24 **brewing-place:** Braustube. | 24 f. **aperture:** Öffnung.

enough to admit a boy of Oliver's size, nevertheless. A very brief exercise of Mr. Sikes's art, sufficed to overcome the fastening of the lattice; and it soon stood wide open also.

"Now listen, you young limb," whispered Sikes, drawing a dark lantern from his pocket, and throwing the glare full on Oliver's face; "I'm a-going to put you through there. Take this light; go softly up the steps straight afore you; and along the little hall to the street-door; unfasten it, and let us in."

"There's a bolt at the top, you won't be able to reach," interposed Toby. "Stand upon one of the hall chairs. […]"

"Take this lantern," said Sikes, looking into the room. "You see the stairs afore you?"

Oliver, more dead than alive, gasped out, "Yes." Sikes, pointing to the street-door with the pistol-barrel, briefly advised him to take notice that he was within shot all the way; and that if he faltered, he would fall dead that instant.

"It's done in a minute," said Sikes, in the same low whisper. "Directly I leave go of you, do your work. Hark!"

"What's that?" whispered the other man.

They listened intently.

"Nothing," said Sikes, releasing his hold of Oliver. "Now!"

In the short time he had had to collect his senses, the boy had firmly resolved that, whether he died in the attempt or not, he would make one effort to dart up stairs from the hall, and alarm the family. Filled with this idea, he advanced at once, but stealthily.

"Come back!" suddenly cried Sikes aloud. "Back! back!"

4 **limb:** Racker. | 5 **dark lantern:** Blendlaterne. | **glare:** greller Lichtschein. | 8 **to unfasten:** öffnen, entriegeln. | 15 **within shot:** in Schussweite. | 16 **to falter:** wanken, zögern. | 18 **to leave go of s.o.:** jdn. loslassen. | 22 **to collect one's senses:** zur Besinnung kommen. | 24 **to dart:** losstürzen, flitzen. | 26 **stealthily:** verstohlen, heimlich.

Scared by the sudden breaking of the dead stillness of the place, and by a loud cry which followed it, Oliver let his lantern fall, and knew not whether to advance or fly.

The cry was repeated – a light appeared – a vision of two terrified half-dressed men at the top of the stairs swam before his eyes – a flash – a loud noise – a smoke – a crash somewhere, but where he knew not, – and he staggered back.

Sikes had disappeared for an instant; but he was up again, and had him by the collar before the smoke had cleared away. He fired his own pistol after the men, who were already retreating; and dragged the boy up.

"Clasp your arm tighter," said Sikes, as he drew him through the window. "Give me a shawl here. They've hit him. Quick! Damnation, how the boy bleeds!"

Then, came the loud ringing of a bell: mingled with the noise of fire-arms, and the shouts of men, and the sensation of being carried over uneven ground at a rapid pace. And then, the noises grew confused in the distance; and a cold deadly feeling crept over the boy's heart; and he saw or heard no more.

6 **crash:** Krach, Getöse. | 7 **to stagger:** schwanken, taumeln. | 9 **to clear away:** sich auflösen, sich verziehen. | 15 **to mingle with s.th.:** (sich) mit etwas (ver)mischen. | 16 **sensation:** Empfindung. | 17 **uneven:** uneben.

Chapter XXIII

Which contains the substance of a pleasant Conversation between Mr. Bumble and a Lady; and shews that even a Beadle may be susceptible on some points

The night was bitter cold. The snow lay on the ground, frozen into a hard thick crust; [...].

Such was the aspect of out-of-door affairs, when Mrs. Corney, the matron of the workhouse to which our readers have been already introduced as the birthplace of Oliver Twist, sat herself down before a cheerful fire in her own little room; and glanced, with no small degree of complacency, at a small round table: on which stood a tray of corresponding size, furnished with all necessary materials for the most grateful meal that matrons enjoy. In fact, Mrs. Corney was about to solace herself with a cup of tea. As she glanced from the table to the fire-place, where the smallest of all possible kettles was singing a small song in a small voice, her inward satisfaction evidently increased, – so much so, indeed, that Mrs. Corney smiled.

"Well!" said the matron, leaning her elbow on the table, and looking reflectively at the fire; "I'm sure we have all on us a great deal to be grateful for! A great deal, if we did but know it. Ah!"

2 **substance:** Inhalt, Wesentliches. | 4 **to be susceptible on s.th.:** für etwas empfänglich, anfällig sein. | 6 **crust:** (Eis-)Kruste. | 7 **aspect:** Anblick, Aussehen. | 8 **matron of the workhouse:** Vorsteherin des Armenhauses, Hausmutter. | 11 **complacency:** Wohlbehagen, Selbstzufriedenheit. | 12 **tray:** Tablett. | **corresponding:** entsprechend, passend. | 12 f. **to be furnished with s.th.:** mit etwas versehen sein. | 13 **grateful:** wohltuend. | 14 **matron:** würdige ältere Dame. | **to solace o.s.:** sich trösten. | 21 **reflectively:** nachdenklich.

Mrs. Corney shook her head mournfully, as if deploring the mental blindness of those paupers who did *not* know it; and thrusting a silver spoon (private property) into the inmost recesses of a two-ounce tin tea-caddy, proceeded to make the tea.

How slight a thing will disturb the equanimity of our frail minds! The black teapot, being very small and easily filled, ran over while Mrs. Corney was moralising; and the water slightly scalded Mrs. Corney's hand.

"Drat the pot!" said the worthy matron, setting it down very hastily on the hob; "a little stupid thing, that only holds a couple of cups! What use is it of, to anybody! Except," said Mrs. Corney, pausing, "except to a poor desolate creetur like me. Oh dear!"

With these words, the matron dropped into her chair; and, once more resting her elbow on the table, thought of her solitary fate. The small teapot, and the single cup, had awakened in her mind sad recollections of Mr. Corney (who had not been dead more than five-and-twenty years); and she was overpowered.

"I shall never get another!" said Mrs. Corney, pettishly; "I shall never get another – like him."

Whether this remark bore reference to the husband, or the teapot, is uncertain. It might have been the latter; for Mrs. Corney looked at it as she spoke: and took it up afterwards. She

1 **mournfully:** traurig. | **to deplore s.th.:** etwas bedauern, beklagen. | 2 **mental:** geistig, seelisch. | **blindness:** Blindheit, Verblendung. | 3 **inmost:** innerste(r, s), tiefste(r, s). | 4 **recesses:** Tiefen, Winkel. | **tea-caddy:** Teedose. | 6 **slight:** klein, gering(fügig), unerheblich, unbedeutend. | **equanimity:** Gleichmut, Fassung. | **frail:** empfindlich, zart, zerbrechlich. | 8 **to moralise:** moralisieren. | 9 **to scald:** verbrühen. | 13 **desolate:** einsam, unglücklich, trostlos. | **creetur:** *creature.*

had just tasted her first cup, when she was disturbed by a soft tap at the room-door.

"Oh, come in with you!" said Mrs. Corney, sharply. "Some of the old women dying, I suppose. They always die when I'm at meals. Don't stand there, letting the cold air in, don't. What's amiss now, eh?"

"Nothing, ma'am, nothing," replied a man's voice.

"Dear me!" exclaimed the matron, in a much sweeter tone, "is that Mr. Bumble?"

"At your service, ma'am," said Mr. Bumble, who had been stopping outside to rub his shoes clean, and to shake the snow off his coat; and who now made his appearance, bearing the cocked hat in one hand and a bundle in the other. "Shall I shut the door, ma'am?"

[…]

"Hard weather, Mr. Bumble," said the matron.

"Hard, indeed, ma'am," replied the beadle. […]

"[…] This is the port wine, ma'am, that the board ordered for the infirmary; real, fresh, genuine port wine; only out of the cask this forenoon; clear as a bell; and no sediment!"

[…]

The matron looked, from the little kettle, to the beadle, who was moving towards the door; and as the beadle coughed, preparatory to bidding her good night, bashfully inquired whether – whether he wouldn't take a cup of tea?

Mr. Bumble instantaneously turned back his collar again;

6 **What's amiss now?:** Was ist jetzt schon wieder los? | 10 **at your service:** zu Euren Diensten. | 19 **infirmary:** Krankenstube. | **genuine:** echt, unverfälscht. | 20 **cask:** Fass. | **forenoon:** Vormittag. | **sediment:** Bodensatz, Ablagerung, Ausfällung. | 23 f. **preparatory:** vorbereitend. | 24 **to bid s.o. good night:** jdm. gute Nacht wünschen. | **bashfully:** schüchtern, schamhaft, verlegen. | 26 **instantaneously:** unverzüglich, augenblicklich.

laid his hat and stick upon a chair; and drew another chair up to the table. As he slowly seated himself, he looked at the lady. She fixed her eyes upon the little teapot. Mr. Bumble coughed again, and slightly smiled.

Mrs. Corney rose to get another cup and saucer from the closet. As she sat down, her eyes once again encountered those of the gallant beadle; she coloured, and applied herself to the task of making his tea. Again Mr. Bumble coughed, – louder this time than he had coughed yet.

"Sweet? Mr. Bumble," inquired the matron, taking up the sugar-basin.

"Very sweet, indeed, ma'am," replied Mr. Bumble. He fixed his eyes on Mrs. Corney as he said this; and if ever a beadle looked tender, Mr. Bumble was that beadle at that moment.

[…]

The beadle drank his tea to the last drop; finished a piece of toast; whisked the crumbs off his knees; wiped his lips; and deliberately kissed the matron.

"Mr. Bumble!" cried that discreet lady in a whisper; for the fright was so great, that she had quite lost her voice, "Mr. Bumble, I shall scream!" Mr. Bumble made no reply; but, in a slow and dignified manner, put his arm round the matron's waist.

As the lady had stated her intention of screaming, of course she would have screamed at this additional boldness, but that the exertion was rendered unnecessary by a hasty knocking at the door: which was no sooner heard, than Mr. Bumble darted, with much agility, to the wine-bottles, and began dusting

5 **saucer:** Untertasse, Untersatz. | 6 **closet:** Schrank. | 7 **gallant:** stattlich. | **to colour:** erröten. | 11 **sugar-basin:** Zuckerdose. | 17 **to whisk off s.th.:** etwas wegwischen. | 19 **discreet:** besonnen. | 20 **fright:** Schreck. | 23 **to state s.th.:** etwas bekunden, etwas erklären. | 24 **additional:** zusätzlich. | **boldness:** Kühnheit. | 27 **to dust:** abstauben.

them with great violence: while the matron sharply demanded who was there. […]

“If you please, mistress,” said a withered old female pauper, hideously ugly: putting her head in at the door, “old Sally is a-going fast.”

“Well, what’s that to me?” angrily demanded the matron. “I can’t keep her alive, can I?”

“No, no, mistress,” replied the old woman, “nobody can; she’s far beyond the reach of help. I’ve seen a many people die; little babes and great strong men; and I know when death’s a-coming, well enough. But she’s troubled in her mind; and when the fits are not on her, – and that’s not often, for she is dying very hard, – she says she has got something to tell, which you must hear. She’ll never die quiet till you come, mistress.”

At this intelligence, the worthy Mrs. Corney muttered a variety of invectives against old women who couldn’t even die, without purposely annoying their betters; and, muffling herself in a thick shawl which she hastily caught up, briefly requested Mr. Bumble to stay till she came back, lest anything particular should occur; and, bidding the messenger walk fast, and not be all night hobbling up the stairs, followed her from the room with a very ill grace: scolding all the way.

Mr. Bumble’s conduct on being left to himself, was rather inexplicable. He opened the closet, counted the tea-spoons,

3 **withered:** verdorrt, hutzelig. | 4 f. **old Sally is a-going fast:** etwa: die alte Sally macht’s nicht mehr lang. | 12 **when the fits are not on her:** etwa: wenn sie bei klarem Verstand ist. | 16 f. **variety:** Vielzahl. | 17 **invective:** Schimpfwort, Schmähung. | 18 **purposely:** absichtlich, vorsätzlich. | **betters:** Vorgesetzte, Höhergestellte, Respektspersonen. | **to muffle o.s.:** sich einhüllen. | 21 **messenger:** Bote, Botin. | 22 **to hobble:** humpeln, hinken. | 23 **to scold:** schelten, schimpfen. | 24 **conduct:** Benehmen. | 24 f. **inexplicable:** unerklärlich.

farther end. There was another old woman watching by the bed; and the parish apothecary's apprentice was standing by the fire, making a toothpick out of a quill.

"Cold night, Mrs. Corney," said this young gentleman, as the matron entered.

"Very cold, indeed, sir," replied the mistress, in her most civil tones, and dropping a curtsey as she spoke.

[...]

The apothecary's apprentice, having completed the manufacture of the toothpick, planted himself in front of the fire and made good use of it for ten minutes or so: when, apparently growing rather dull, he wished Mrs. Corney joy of her job, and took himself off on tiptoe.

When they had sat in silence for some time, the two old women rose from the bed; and crouching over the fire, held out their withered hands to catch the heat. [...]

While they were thus employed, the matron, who had been impatiently watching until the dying woman should awaken from her stupor, joined them by the fire, and sharply asked how long she was to wait.

"Not long, mistress," replied the second woman, looking up into her face. "We have none of us long to wait for Death. Patience, patience! He'll be here soon enough for us all."

[...]

"Long or short," said the matron, snappishly, "she won't find me here when she does wake; and take care, both of you, how you worry me again for nothing. It's no part of my duty to see all the old women in the house die, and I won't – that's

2 **apothecary:** Apothekerdoktor. | 3 **toothpick:** Zahnstocher. | **quill:** Federkiel. | 7 **civil:** höflich. | **to drop a curtsey:** einen Knicks machen. | 9 f. **manufacture:** Herstellung, Fertigung. | 10 **to plant o.s. in front of s.th.:** sich vor etwas hinstellen. | 12 **dull:** langweilig, eintönig. | 13 **on tiptoe:** auf Zehenspitzen. | 19 **stupor:** Benommenheit.

weighed the sugar-tongs, closely inspected a silver milk-pot to ascertain that it was of the genuine metal; and, having satisfied his curiosity on these points, put on his cocked hat corner-wise, and danced with much gravity four distinct times round the table. Having gone through this very extraordinary performance, he took off the cocked hat again; and, spreading himself before the fire with his back towards it, seemed to be mentally engaged in taking an exact inventory of the furniture.

Chapter XXIV

Treats of a very poor Subject. But is a short one; and may be found of importance in this History

[…]

The old crone tottered along the passages, and up the stairs, muttering some indistinct answers to the chidings of her companion; and being at length compelled to pause for breath, gave the light into her hand, and remained behind to follow as she might: while the more nimble superior made her way to the room where the sick woman lay.

It was a bare garret-room, with a dim light burning at the

1 **to weigh s.th.:** etwas wiegen, prüfen. | **sugar-tongs** (pl.): Zuckerzange. | 2 **to ascertain:** sich vergewissern, herausfinden, feststellen. | 4 **corner-wise:** schräg, quer, diagonal. | **distinct:** verschieden. | 6 **performance:** Vorführung, Darbietung. | 6 f. **to spread o.s.:** sich ausbreiten. | 8 **inventory:** Bestandsaufnahme. | 11 **subject:** hier: (krankes) Geschöpf, Wesen. | 14 **crone:** altes Weib. | **to totter:** wacke torkeln. | 15 **indistinct:** undeutlich. | **chiding:** Schelte. | 16 **compelled:** gezwungen, genötigt. | 18 **nimble:** behend, flink. | 20 **garret-room:** Dachstube.

more. Mind that, you impudent old harridans. If you make a fool of me again, I'll soon cure you, I warrant you!"

She was bouncing away, when a cry from the two women, who had turned towards the bed, caused her to look round. The patient had raised herself upright, and was stretching her arms towards them.

"Who's that?" she cried, in a hollow voice.

"Hush, hush!" said one of the women, stooping over her. "Lie down, lie down!"

"I'll never lie down again alive!" said the woman, struggling. "I *will* tell her! Come here! Nearer! Let me whisper in your ear."

She clutched the matron by the arm; and forcing her into a chair by the bedside, was about to speak, when looking round, she caught sight of the two old women bending forward in the attitude of eager listeners.

"Turn them away," said the woman, drowsily; "make haste! Make haste!"

The two old crones, chiming in together, began pouring out many piteous lamentations that the poor dear was too far gone to know her best friends; and were uttering sundry protestations that they would never leave her, when the superior pushed them from the room, closed the door, and returned to the bedside. [...]

"Now listen to me," said the dying woman, aloud, as if making a great effort to revive one latent spark of energy. "In this

1 **impudent:** unverschämt, frech. | **harridan:** alter Drache, zänkisches Weib. | 2 **I'll soon cure you:** Das werde ich euch schon noch austreiben! | **to warrant:** zusichern, garantieren. | 3 **to bounce away:** davonstürmen. | 7 **hollow:** hohl, dumpf. | 16 **to turn away s.o.:** jdn. wegschicken. | **drowsily:** schläfrig. | 18 **to chime in:** (in einen Chor) einstimmen. | **to pour out:** ausschütten, hervorstoßen. | 20 f. **protestation:** Beteuerung. | 25 **to revive:** wiederbeleben, zum Leben erwecken. | **latent:** verborgen, ruhend. | **spark:** Funke.

very room – in this very bed – I once nursed a pretty young creetur, that was brought into the house with her feet cut and bruised with walking, and all soiled with dust and blood. She gave birth to a boy, and died. [...]

"I robbed her, so I did! She wasn't cold – I tell you she wasn't cold, when I stole it!"

"Stole what, for God's sake?" cried the matron, with a gesture as if she would call for help.

"*It*!" replied the woman, laying her hand over the other's mouth. "The only thing she had. She wanted clothes to keep her warm, and food to eat; but she had kept it safe, and had it in her bosom. It was gold, I tell you! Rich gold, that might have saved her life!"

"Gold!" echoed the matron, bending eagerly over the woman as she fell back. "Go on, go on – yes – what of it? Who was the mother? When was it?"

"She charged me to keep it safe," replied the woman, with a groan, "and trusted me as the only woman about her. I stole it in my heart when she first shewed it me hanging round her neck; and the child's death, perhaps, is on me besides! They would have treated him better, if they had known it all!"

"Known what?" asked the other. "Speak!"

"The boy grew so like his mother," said the woman, rambling on, and not heeding the question, "that I could never forget it when I saw his face. Poor girl! poor girl! She was so young, too! Such a gentle lamb! Wait; there's more to tell. I have not told you all, have I?"

"No, no," replied the matron, inclining her head to catch the

11 f. **had it in her bosom:** trug es an ihrem Busen. | 17 **to charge s.o. to do s.th.:** jdn. damit beauftragen, etwas zu tun. | 18 **groan:** Stöhnen, Ächzen. | 24 f. **to ramble:** faseln, schwafeln.

words, as they came more faintly from the dying woman. "Be quick, or it may be too late!"

"The mother," said the woman, making a more violent effort than before; "the mother, when the pains of death first came upon her, whispered in my ear that if her baby was born alive, and thrived, the day might come when it would not feel so much disgraced to hear its poor young mother named. "And oh, kind Heaven!" she said, folding her thin hands together, "whether it be boy or girl, raise up some friends for it in this troubled world; and take pity upon a lonely desolate child, abandoned to its mercy!""

"The boy's name?" demanded the matron.

"They *called* him Oliver," replied the woman, feebly. "The gold I stole was –"

"Yes, yes, – what?" cried the other.

She was bending eagerly over the woman to hear her reply; but drew back, instinctively, as she once again rose, slowly and stiffly, into a sitting posture; then, clutching the coverlet with both hands, muttered some indistinct sounds in her throat, and fell lifeless on the bed.

[...]

6 **to thrive:** gedeihen. | 7 **disgraced:** beschämt. | 9 **raise up some friends for it:** sende ihm ein paar Freunde. | 11 **(to be) abandoned to s.th.:** einer Sache preisgegeben sein. | 18 **stiffly:** steif, starr.

Chapter XXV

Wherein this History reverts to Mr. Fagin and Company

While these things were passing in the country workhouse, Mr. Fagin sat in the old den – the same from which Oliver had been removed by the girl – brooding over a dull, smoky fire. [...]

At a table behind him, sat the Artful Dodger, Master Charles Bates, and Mr. Chitling: all intent upon a game of whist; the Artful taking dummy against Master Bates and Mr. Chitling. [...]

"That's two doubles and the rub," said Mr. Chitling, with a very long face, as he drew half-a-crown from his waistcoat-pocket. "I never see such a feller as you, Jack; you win everything. Even when we've good cards, Charley and I can't make nothing of 'em."

Either the matter or the manner of this remark, which was made very ruefully, delighted Charley Bates so much, that his consequent shout of laughter roused the Jew from his reverie, and induced him to inquire what was the matter.

"Matter, Fagin!" cried Charley. "I wish you had watched the play. Tommy Chitling hasn't won a point; and I went partners with him against the Artful and dum."

"Aye, aye!" said the Jew, with a grin, which sufficiently demonstrated that he was at no loss to understand the reason. "Try 'em again, Tom; try 'em again."

5 **to brood:** brüten, grübeln, sinnieren. | 8 **whist:** Whist (Kartenspiel). | 8 f. **the Artful taking dummy:** d. h., der Dodger spielt mit einem Strohmann gegen die beiden anderen. | 11 **double:** doppelter Gewinn. | **rub:** *rubber:* Spielrunde im Whist. | 13 **feller:** *fellow.* | 17 **ruefully:** kläglich. | 18 **reverie:** Träumerei. | 22 **dum:** Strohmann. | 23 **sufficiently:** genügend, ausreichend. | 24 f. **to try s.o.:** jdn. herausfordern.

"No more of it for me, thankee, Fagin," replied Mr. Chitling; "I've had enough. That 'ere Dodger has such a run of luck that there's no standing again' him."

"Ha! ha! my dear," replied the Jew, "you must get up very early in the morning, to win against the Dodger."

[...]

"Hark!" cried the Dodger at this moment, "I heard the tinkler." Catching up the light, he crept softly up stairs.

The bell was rung again, with some impatience, while the party were in darkness. After a short pause, the Dodger reappeared; and whispered Fagin mysteriously.

"What!" cried the Jew, "alone?"

The Dodger nodded in the affirmative; and, shading the flame of the candle with his hand, gave Charley Bates a private intimation, in dumb show, that he had better not be funny just then. Having performed this friendly office, he fixed his eyes on the Jew's face, and awaited his directions.

The old man bit his yellow fingers, and meditated for some seconds; his face working with agitation, the while, as if he dreaded something, and feared to know the worst. At length he raised his head.

"Where is he?" he asked.

The Dodger pointed to the floor above; and made a gesture, as if to leave the room.

"Yes," said the Jew, answering the mute inquiry; "bring him down. [...]"

[...] the Dodger descended the stairs, bearing the light in his

1 **thankee:** *thank you.* | 3 **there's no standing again' him:** gegen den kommt man nicht an. | 7f. **tinkler:** Klingel. | 9 **impatience:** Ungeduld. | 11 **mysteriously:** geheimnisvoll. | 15 **dumb show:** Pantomime, Gebärdensprache, stumme Gesten. | 18 **to meditate:** nachdenken. | 19 **agitation:** Unruhe, Aufregung. | 20 **to dread s.th.:** sich vor etwas fürchten.

hand, and followed by a man in a coarse smock-frock; who, after casting a hurried glance round the room, pulled off a large wrapper which had concealed the lower portion of his face, and disclosed: all haggard, unwashed, and unshorn: the features of flash Toby Crackit.

[...]

"First and foremost, Fagey," said Toby.

"Yes, yes!" interposed the Jew, drawing up his chair.

Mr. Crackit stopped to take a draught of spirits and water, and to declare that the gin was excellent; and then, placing his feet against the low mantelpiece, so as to bring his boots to about the level of his eye, quietly resumed,

"First and foremost, Fagey," said the housebreaker, "how's Bill?"

"What!" screamed the Jew, starting from his seat.

"Why, you don't mean to say –" began Toby, turning pale.

"Mean!" cried the Jew, stamping furiously on the ground. "Where are they? Sikes and the boy! Where are they? Where have they been? Where are they hiding? Why have they not been here?"

"The crack failed," said Toby, faintly.

"I know it," replied the Jew, tearing a newspaper from his pocket, and pointing to it. "What more?"

"They fired and hit the boy. We cut over the fields at the back with him between us – straight as the crow flies – through hedge and ditch. They gave chase. D–me! the whole country was awake, and the dogs upon us."

1 **coarse:** grob. | **smock-frock:** Bauernkittel. | 3 **wrapper:** Tuch. | **to conceal:** verbergen. | **portion:** Teil. | 4 **to disclose:** preisgeben, enthüllen. | **haggard:** abgezehrt. | **unshorn:** unrasiert. | 7 **foremost:** zuallererst. | 25 **straight as the crow flies:** immer geradeaus. | 26 **hedge:** Hecke. | **ditch:** Graben. | **to give chase:** die Verfolgungsjagd aufnehmen.

"The boy!" gasped the Jew.

"Bill had him on his back, and scudded like the wind. We stopped to take him between us; his head hung down; and he was cold. They were close upon our heels; every man for himself, and each from the gallows! We parted company, and left the youngster lying in a ditch. Alive or dead, that's all I know about him."

The Jew stopped to hear no more; but uttering a loud yell, and twining his hands in his hair, rushed from the room, and from the house.

Chapter XXVI

In which, a mysterious Character appears upon the scene; and many things, inseparable from this History, are done and performed

The old man had gained the street corner, before he began to recover the effect of Toby Crackit's intelligence. [...]

After a brief reflection, he called a hack-cabriolet, and bade the man drive towards Bethnal Green. He dismissed him within some quarter of a mile of Mr. Sikes's residence; and performed the short remainder of the distance, on foot.

"Now," muttered the Jew, as he knocked at the door, "if there is any deep play here, I shall have it out of you, my girl, cunning as you are."

She was in her room, the woman said. Fagin crept softly up

5 **gallows** (pl.): Galgen. | **to part company:** sich trennen. | 8 **yell:** (Auf-) Schrei. | 13 **inseparable:** untrennbar. | 18 **to dismiss s.o.:** jdn. verabschieden. | 20 **remainder:** Rest. | 22 **deep play:** falsches Spiel. | 23 **cunning:** raffiniert, gerissen.

stairs, and entered it without any previous ceremony. The girl was alone; lying with her head upon the table, and her hair straggling over it.

"She has been drinking," thought the Jew, coolly, "or perhaps she is only miserable."

The old man turned to close the door, as he made this reflection; and the noise thus occasioned, roused the girl. She eyed his crafty face narrowly, as she inquired whether there was any news, and listened to his recital of Toby Crackit's story. When it was concluded, she sank into her former attitude, but spoke not a word. She pushed the candle impatiently away; and once or twice, as she feverishly changed her position, shuffled her feet upon the ground; but this was all.

During this silence, the Jew looked restlessly about the room, as if to assure himself that there were no appearances of Sikes having covertly returned. Apparently satisfied with his inspection, he coughed twice or thrice, and made as many efforts to open a conversation; but the girl heeded him no more than if he had been made of stone. At length he made another attempt; and, rubbing his hands together, said, in his most conciliatory tone,

"And where should you think Bill was now, my dear?"

The girl moaned out some half intelligible reply, that she could not tell; and seemed, from the smothered noise that escaped her, to be crying.

"And the boy, too," said the Jew, straining his eyes to catch a

3 **to straggle:** verstreut liegen. | 7 **to occasion:** hervorrufen, schaffen. | 8 **crafty:** schlau, gerissen. | 9 **recital:** Vortrag, Bericht, Schilderung. | 12 **feverishly:** wie im Fieber. | 12 f. **to shuffle one's feet:** mit den Füßen scharren. | 15 **to assure o.s. that …:** sich vergewissern, dass … | 16 **covertly:** heimlich. | 17 **inspection:** Prüfung. | **thrice:** dreimal. | 21 **conciliatory:** versöhnlich. | 23 **to moan:** stöhnen. | **intelligible:** verständlich. | 24 **smothered:** erstickt.

glimpse of her face. "Poor leetle child! Left in a ditch, Nance; only think!"

"The child," said the girl, suddenly looking up, "is better where he is, than among us; and if no harm comes to Bill from it, I hope he lies dead in the ditch, and that his young bones may rot there."

"What!" cried the Jew, in amazement.

"Aye, I do," returned the girl, meeting his gaze. "I shall be glad to have him away from my eyes, and to know that the worst is over. I can't bear to have him about me. The sight of him turns me against myself, and all of you."

"Pooh!" said the Jew, scornfully. "You're drunk."

"Am I?" cried the girl, bitterly. "It's no fault of yours, if I am not! you'd never have me anything else, if you had your will, except now; – the humour doesn't suit you, doesn't it?"

"No!" rejoined the Jew, furiously. "It does not."

"Change it, then!" responded the girl, with a laugh.

"Change it!" exclaimed the Jew, exasperated beyond all bounds by his companion's unexpected obstinacy, and the vexation of the night, "I will change it! Listen to me, you drab! Listen to me, who, with six words, can strangle Sikes as surely as if I had his bull's throat between my fingers now. If he comes back, and leaves that boy behind him, – if he gets off free; and, dead or alive, fails to restore him to me; murder him yourself if you would have him escape Jack Ketch: and do it the moment he sets foot in this room, or, mind me, it will be too late!"

6 **to rot:** verrotten, verfaulen. | 12 **scornfully:** verächtlich. | 15 **to suit s.o.:** jdm. passen, recht sein. | 18 **exasperated:** verärgert, gereizt, aufgebracht. | 18 f. **beyond all bounds:** grenzenlos, über alle Maßen. | 19 **obstinacy:** Sturheit, Eigensinn. | 20 **vexation:** Ärger, Verdruss. | **drab:** Schlampe, Hure. | 23 **to get off free:** ungeschoren davonkommen. | 24 **to restore s.o.:** jdn. zurückbringen. | 25 **Jack Ketch:** Henker (nach einem legendären Henker aus dem 17. Jh.).

"What is all this?" cried the girl, involuntarily.

"What is it?" pursued Fagin, mad with rage. "When the boy's worth hundreds of pounds to me, am I to lose what chance threw me in the way of getting safely, through the whims of a drunken gang that I could whistle away the lives of! And me bound, too, to a born devil that only wants the will, and has the power to, to –"

Panting for breath, the old man stammered for a word; and in that instant checked the torrent of his wrath, and changed his whole demeanour. A moment before, his clenched hands had grasped the air; his eyes had dilated; and his face grown livid with passion; but now, he shrunk into a chair, and, cowering together, trembled with the apprehension of having himself disclosed some hidden villany. After a short silence, he ventured to look round at his companion. He appeared somewhat reassured, on beholding her in the same listless attitude from which he had first roused her.

"Nancy, dear!" croaked the Jew, in his usual voice. "Did you mind me, dear?"

"Don't worry me now, Fagin!" replied the girl, raising her head languidly. "If Bill has not done it this time, he will another. He has done many a good job for you, and will do many more when he can; and when he can't, he won't, so no more about that."

2 **to pursue:** fortfahren, weitersprechen. | 4 **chance:** Zufall, Glück. | 5 **whims:** Launen, Narreteien. | **gang:** Bande. | **to whistle away:** verpfeifen, verraten. | 6 **bound:** gefesselt, verpflichtet. | **will:** Vermächtnis, Erbe, Testament. | 8 **to stammer:** stammeln, stottern. | 9 **to check s.th.:** etwas eindämmen, zügeln. | **torrent:** Sturzbach, reißender Strom. | 10 **demeanour:** Gebaren, Auftreten, Benehmen. | 11 **to dilate:** sich weiten. | 12 **livid:** aschfahl, bleich. | **to shrink:** zusammensinken. | 12 f. **to cower:** kauern. | 16 **reassured:** beruhigt, bestätigt. | **listless:** teilnahmslos, apathisch. | 18 **to croak:** krächzen. | 21 **languidly:** müde, träge.

"Regarding this boy, my dear?" said the Jew, rubbing the palms of his hands nervously together.

"The boy must take his chance with the rest," interrupted Nancy, hastily; "and I say again, I hope he is dead, and out of harm's way, and out of yours, – that is, if Bill comes to no harm. And if Toby got clear off, he's pretty sure to be safe; for he's worth two of him any time."

"And about what I was saying, my dear?" observed the Jew, keeping his glistening eye steadily upon her.

"You must say it all over again, if it's anything you want me to do," rejoined Nancy; "and if it is, you had better wait till to-morrow. You put me up for a minute; but now I'm stupid again."

Fagin put several other questions: all with the same drift of ascertaining whether the girl had profited by his unguarded hints; but she answered them so readily, and was withal so utterly unmoved by his searching looks, that his original impression of her being more than a trifle in liquor, was fully confirmed. [...]

Having eased his mind by this discovery; and having accomplished his twofold object of imparting to the girl what he had that night heard, and of ascertaining, with his own eyes, that Sikes had not returned; Mr. Fagin again turned his face homeward: leaving his young friend asleep, with her head upon the table.

[...]

6 **to get clear off:** verduften. | 12 **to put s.o. up:** jdn. aufrütteln. | 14 **drift:** Tendenz, Hintersinn. | 15 **unguarded:** unbedacht, unvorsichtig. | 16 **withal:** außerdem, obendrein. | 17 **unmoved:** ungerührt, gleichgültig. | 18 **a trifle:** ein wenig, etwas. | **to be in liquor:** angetrunken sein (*liquor:* Spirituosen, Alkohol). | 20 **to ease:** beruhigen. | 20 f. **to accomplish:** Erreichen, erfüllen. | 21 **twofold:** doppelt, zweifach. | **to impart:** mitteilen.

He had reached the corner of his own street, and was already fumbling in his pocket for the door-key, when a dark figure emerged from a projecting entrance which lay in deep shadow, and, crossing the road, glided up to him unperceived.

"Fagin!" whispered a voice close to his ear.

"Ah!" said the Jew, turning quickly round, "is that –"

"Yes!" interrupted the stranger, harshly. "I have been lingering here these two hours. Where the devil have you been?"

"On your business, my dear," replied the Jew, glancing uneasily at his companion, and slackening his pace as he spoke. "On your business all night."

"Oh, of course!" said the stranger, with a sneer. "Well; and what's come of it?"

"Nothing good," said the Jew.

"Nothing bad, I hope?" said the stranger, stopping short, and turning a startled look on his companion.

The Jew shook his head, and was about to reply, when the stranger, interrupting him, motioned to the house, before which they had by this time arrived: remarking, that he had better say what he had got to say, under cover: for his blood was chilled with standing about so long, and the wind blew through him.

Fagin looked as if he could have willingly excused himself from taking home a visitor at that unseasonable hour; and, indeed, muttered something about having no fire; but his companion repeating his request in a peremptory manner, he unlocked the door, and requested him to close it softly, while he got a light.

2 **to fumble:** fingern, herumtasten. | 3 **projecting:** vorspringend. | 4 **to glide:** gleiten. | **unperceived:** unbemerkt. | 18 **to motion to s.th.:** auf etwas deuten. | 21 **chilled:** kalt. | 23 **willingly:** bereitwillig, gerne. | 24 **unseasonable:** ungelegen, unzeitig. | 26 **peremptory:** gebieterisch, bestimmt.

"It's as dark as the grave," said the man, groping forward a few steps. "Make haste!"

"Shut the door," whispered Fagin from the end of the passage. As he spoke, it closed with a loud noise.

"That wasn't my doing," said the other man, feeling his way. "The wind blew it to, or it shut of its own accord; one or the other. Look sharp with the light, or I shall knock my brains out against something in this confounded hole."

Fagin stealthily descended the kitchen stairs. After a short absence, he returned with a lighted candle, and the intelligence that Toby Crackit was asleep in the back-room below, and the boys in the front one. Beckoning the other man to follow him, he led the way up stairs.

"We can say, the few words we've got to say in here, my dear," said the Jew, throwing open a door on the first floor; "and as there are holes in the shutters, and we never shew lights to our neighbours, we'll set the candle on the stairs. There!"

With these words, the Jew, stooping down, placed the candle on an upper flight of stairs, exactly opposite to the room-door. This done, he led the way into the apartment; which was destitute of all moveables save a broken arm-chair, and an old couch or sofa without covering, which stood behind the door. Upon this piece of furniture, the stranger flung himself with the air of a weary man; and, the Jew drawing up the arm-chair opposite, they sat face to face. It was not quite dark; for the door was partially open; and the candle outside, threw a feeble reflection on the opposite wall.

They conversed for some time in whispers. Though nothing

6 **of one's own accord:** von selbst. | 7 **look sharp:** mach schnell. | 8 **confounded:** verwünscht. | 22 **to be destitute of s.th.:** ohne etwas sein. | **movables** (pl.): Mobiliar. | **save:** außer, ausgenommen. | 23 **covering:** (Stoff-)Bezug.

of the conversation was distinguishable beyond a few disjointed words here and there, a listener might easily have perceived that Fagin appeared to be defending himself against some remarks of the stranger; and that the latter was in a state of considerable irritation. They might have been talking, thus, for a quarter of an hour or more, when Monks – by which name the Jew had designated the strange man several times in the course of their colloquy – said, raising his voice a little,

"I tell you again, it was badly planned. Why not have kept him here among the rest, and made a sneaking, snivelling pickpocket of him at once?"

[...]

"I saw it was not easy to train him to the business," replied the Jew; "he was not like other boys in the same circumstances."

"Curse him, no!" muttered the man, "or he would have been a thief, long ago."

"I had no hold upon him, to make him worse," pursued the Jew, anxiously watching the countenance of his companion. [...]

"[...] You want him made a thief. If he is alive, I can make him one from this time; and if – if –" said the Jew, drawing nearer to the other, – "it's not likely, mind, – but if the worst comes to the worst, and he is dead –"

"It's no fault of mine if he is!" interposed the other man, with a look of terror, and clasping the Jew's arm with trembling hands. "Mind that, Fagin! I had no hand in it. Anything but his death; I told you from the first. I won't shed blood; it's

1 **distinguishable:** hörbar, verständlich. | 1 f. **disjointed:** zusammenhanglos. | 2 **to perceive s.th.:** etwas wahrnehmen, erkennen, bemerken. | 5 **irritation:** Verärgerung. | 8 **colloquy:** Unterredung. | 10 **snivelling:** wehleidig. | 10 f. **pickpocket:** Taschendieb. | 13 **to train s.o. to s.th.:** jdn. in etwas ausbilden. | 18 **hold:** Einfluss. | 28 **to shed:** vergießen.

always found out, and haunts a man besides. If they shot him dead, I was not the cause; do you hear me? Fire this infernal den! What's that?"

"What!" cried the Jew, grasping the coward round the body, with both arms, as he sprung to his feet. "Where?"

"Yonder!" replied the man, glaring at the opposite wall. "The shadow! I saw the shadow of a woman, in a cloak and bonnet, pass along the wainscot like a breath!"

The Jew released his hold; and they rushed tumultuously from the room. The candle, wasted by the draught, was standing where it had been placed. It shewed them, only the empty staircase, and their own white faces. They listened intently; but a profound silence reigned throughout the house.

"It's your fancy," said the Jew, taking up the light, and turning to his companion.

"I'll swear I saw it!" replied Monks, trembling. "It was bending forward, when I saw it first; and when I spoke, it darted away."

The Jew glanced, contemptuously, at the pale face of his associate; and, telling him he could follow, if he pleased, ascended the stairs. They looked into all the rooms; they were cold, bare, and empty. They descended into the passage, and thence into the cellars below. The green damp hung upon the low walls; and the tracks of the snail and slug glistened in the light of the candle; but all was still as death.

[...]

1 **to haunt s.o.:** jdn. heimsuchen, verfolgen. | 2 f. **Fire this infernal den!:** Zum Teufel mit diesem Höllenloch! | 6 **yonder:** dort drüben. | **to glare at s.th.:** etwas anstarren. | 8 **bonnet:** Haube. | **wainscot:** Täfelung. | 9 **tumultuously:** Hals über Kopf. | 10 **wasted:** aufgezehrt. | **draught:** Zugluft. | 13 **to reign:** herrschen. | 14 **fancy:** Einbildung, Phantasie. | 19 **contemptuously:** verächtlich. | 23 **damp:** Feuchtigkeit. | 24 **snail:** Schnecke. | **slug:** Nacktschnecke.

Chapter XXVII

Atones for the unpoliteness of a former Chapter; which deserted a Lady, most unceremoniously

As it would be, by no means, seemly in a humble author to keep so mighty a personage as a beadle waiting, with his back to the fire, and the skirts of his coat gathered up under his arms, until such time as it might suit his pleasure to relieve him; and as it would still less become his station, or his gallantry, to involve in the same neglect a lady on whom that beadle had looked with an eye of tenderness and affection, and in whose ear he had whispered sweet words, which, coming from such a quarter, might well thrill the bosom of maid or matron of whatsoever degree; the historian whose pen traces these words [...] hastens to pay them that respect which their position demands, [...].

Mr. Bumble had re-counted the tea-spoons, re-weighed the sugar-tongs, made a closer inspection of the milk-pot, and ascertained to a nicety the exact condition of the furniture, down to the very horse-hair seats of the chairs; and had repeated each process full half a dozen times; before he began to think that it was time for Mrs. Corney to return. [...]

2 **to atone for s.th.:** für etwas Abbitte leisten. | 3 **to desert s.o.:** jdn. allein, im Stich lassen. | **unceremoniously:** rüde, unsanft. | 4 **seemly:** schicklich, geziemend. | 6 **skirts of his coat:** seine (Geh-) Rockschöße. | **to gather up s.th.:** etwas hochraffen. | 8 **to become s.th.:** einer Sache ziemen. | **gallantry:** Ritterlichkeit. | 8 f. **to involve s.o.:** jdn. einbeziehen. | 9 **neglect:** Nachlässigkeit, Versäumnis. | 10 **tenderness:** Zärtlichkeit. | **affection:** Zuneigung. | 12 **quarter:** Richtung; hier etwa: Sphäre. | **to thrill s.o.:** jdn. entzücken, erregen. | 13 **degree:** Rang, Stufe, Stand. | **to trace:** aufzeichnen. | 19 **horse-hair seats** (pl.): Rosshaarpolster.

He was still placidly engaged in this latter survey, when Mrs. Corney, hurrying into the room, threw herself, in a breathless state, on a chair by the fireside; and covering her eyes with one hand, placed the other over her heart, and gasped for breath.

"Mrs. Corney," said Mr. Bumble, stooping over the matron, "what is this, ma'am? has anything happened, ma'am? [...]"

"It's dreadful to think of!" said the lady, shuddering.

"Then *don't* think of it, ma'am," rejoined Mr. Bumble.

"I can't help it," whimpered the lady.

"Then take something, ma'am," said Mr. Bumble soothingly. "A little of the wine?"

"Not for the world!" replied Mrs. Corney. "I couldn't, – oh! The top shelf in the right-hand corner – oh!" Uttering these words, the good lady pointed, distractedly, to the cupboard; and underwent a convulsion from internal spasms. Mr. Bumble rushed to the closet; and, snatching a pint green-glass bottle from the shelf thus incoherently indicated, filled a tea-cup with its contents, and held it to the lady's lips.

"I'm better now," said Mrs. Corney, falling back, after drinking half of it.

[...]

"This is a very comfortable room, ma'am," said Mr. Bumble, looking round. "Another room and this, ma'am, would be a complete thing."

"It would be too much for one," murmured the lady.

"But not for two, ma'am," rejoined Mr. Bumble, in soft accents. "Eh, Mrs. Corney?"

9 **to whimper:** wimmern, winseln. | 15 **to undergo s.th.:** etwas erdulden, etwas erleben, etwas ertragen. | **convulsion:** Krampf, Zuckung. | **internal:** inwendig. | **spasm:** Krampf. | 16 **pint:** entspricht etwa einem halben Liter. | 17 **to indicate:** bezeichnen. | 22 **comfortable:** behaglich. | 26 f. **accent:** Ton.

Mrs. Corney drooped her head, when the beadle said this; the beadle drooped his, to get a view of Mrs. Corney's face. Mrs. Corney, with great propriety, turned her head away, and released her hand to get at her pocket-handkerchief; but insensibly replaced it in that of Mr. Bumble.

"The board allow you coals, don't they, Mrs. Corney?" inquired the beadle, affectionately pressing her hand.

"And candles," replied Mrs. Corney, slightly returning the pressure.

"Coals, candles, and house-rent free," said Mr. Bumble. "Oh, Mrs. Corney, what a Angel you are!"

The lady was not proof against this burst of feeling. She sunk into Mr. Bumble's arms; and that gentleman, in his agitation, imprinted a passionate kiss upon her chaste nose.

"Such porochial perfection!" exclaimed Mr. Bumble, rapturously. "You know that Mr. Slout is worse to-night, my fascinator?"

"Yes," replied Mrs. Corney, bashfully.

"He can't live a week, the doctor says," pursued Mr. Bumble. "He is the master of this establishment; his death will cause a wacancy; that wacancy must be filled up. Oh, Mrs. Corney, what a prospect this opens! What a opportunity for a jining of hearts and housekeepings!"

Mrs. Corney sobbed.

"The little word?" said Mr. Bumble, bending over the bashful beauty. "The one little, little, little word, my blessed Corney?"

1 **to droop one's head:** den Kopf hängen lassen. | 3 **propriety:** Schicklichkeit. | 4 f. **insensibly:** unmerklich. | 6 **to allow s.o. s.th.:** jdm. etwas bewilligen. | 9 **pressure:** Druck. | 12 **to be proof against s.th.:** gegen etwas gefeit sein. | **burst:** Ausbruch. | 14 **chaste:** keusch. | 15 f. **rapturously:** verzückt, hingerissen. | 16 f. **fascinator:** Betörende(r). | 21 **wacancy:** *vacancy:* freie Stelle. | 22 **jining:** *joining.*

"Ye–ye–yes!" sighed out the matron.

[...]

Matters being thus amicably and satisfactorily arranged, the contract was solemnly ratified in another tea-cupful of the peppermint mixture; which was rendered the more necessary, by the flutter and agitation of the lady's spirits. While it was being disposed of, she acquainted Mr. Bumble with the old woman's decease.

"Very good," said that gentleman, sipping his peppermint. "I'll call at Sowerberry's as I go home, and tell him to send to-morrow morning. Was it that as frightened you, love?"

"It wasn't anything particular, dear," said the lady, evasively.

"It must have been something, love," urged Mr. Bumble. "Won't you tell your own B.?"

"Not now," rejoined the lady; "one of these days. After we're married, dear."

"After we're married!" exclaimed Mr. Bumble. "It wasn't any impudence from any of them male paupers as –"

"No, no, love!" interposed the lady, hastily.

"If I thought it was," continued Mr. Bumble; "if I thought as any one of 'em had dared to lift his wulgar eyes to that lovely countenance –"

"They wouldn't have dared to do it, love," responded the lady.

"They had better not!" said Mr. Bumble, clenching his fist. "Let me see any man, porochial, or extra-porochial, as would

1 **to sigh out:** hauchen. | 3 **amicably:** einvernehmlich, gütlich. | 4 **to ratify:** besiegeln, bestätigen. | 6 **flutter:** Aufgeregtheit. | **spirits** (pl.): Gemütsverfassung. | 8 **decease:** Ableben. | 9 **to sip s.th.:** an etwas nippen. | 10 **to send:** vorbeikommen. | 12 **evasively:** ausweichend. | 15 **one of these days:** demnächst. | 18 **impudence:** Unverschämtheit, Frechheit. | 21 **to lift:** erheben. | **wulgar:** *vulgar:* gemein, ordinär.

presume to do it; and I can tell him that he wouldn't do it a second time!"

Unembellished by any violence of gesticulation, this might have seemed no very high compliment to the lady's charms; but, as Mr. Bumble accompanied the threat with many warlike gestures, she was much touched with this proof of his devotion; and protested, with great admiration, that he was indeed a dove.

The dove then turned up his coat-collar, and put on his cocked hat; and having exchanged a long and affectionate embrace with his future partner, once again braved the cold wind of the night, [...].

Chapter XXVIII

Looks after Oliver, and proceeds with his Adventures

"Wolves tear your throats!" muttered Sikes, grinding his teeth. "I wish I was among some of you; you'd howl the hoarser for it."

As Sikes growled forth this imprecation, with the most desperate ferocity that his desperate nature was capable of, he rested the body of the wounded boy across his bended knee; and turned his head, for an instant, to look back at his pursuers.

There was little to be made out, in the mist and darkness; but the loud shouting of men vibrated through the air; and the

3 **unembellished:** unverziert. | **gesticulation:** Gebärde. | 6 f. **devotion:** Hingabe, Ergebenheit. | 7 **admiration:** Bewunderung. | 8 **dove:** Taube, Täubchen, Herzchen. | 10 f. **embrace:** Umarmung. | 11 **to brave s.th.:** einer Sache trotzen. | 15 **to grind one's teeth:** mit den Zähnen knirschen. | 16 **to howl:** aufheulen, jaulen. | 20 **to rest:** legen. | **bended knee:** gebeugtes Knie. | 22 **to make out s.th.:** etwas erkennen.

barking of the neighbouring dogs, roused by the sound of the alarm-bell, resounded in every direction.

"Stop, you white-livered hound!" cried the robber, shouting after Toby Crackit, who, making the best use of his long legs, was already ahead. "Stop!"

The repetition of the word, brought Toby to a dead stand-still. For he was not quite satisfied that he was beyond the range of pistol-shot; and Sikes was in no mood to be played with.

"Bear a hand with the boy," roared Sikes, beckoning furiously to his confederate. "Come back!"

Toby made a show of returning; but ventured, in a low voice, broken for want of breath, to intimate considerable reluctance as he came slowly along.

"Quicker!" cried Sikes, laying the boy in a dry ditch at his feet, and drawing a pistol from his pocket. "Don't play booty with me."

At this moment the noise grew louder. Sikes, again looking round, could discern that the men who had given chase were already climbing the gate of the field in which he stood; and that a couple of dogs were some paces in advance of them.

"It's all up, Bill!" cried Toby; "drop the kid, and show 'em your heels." With this parting advice, Mr. Crackit: preferring the chance of being shot by his friend, to the certainty of being

2 **alarm bell:** Sturmglocke. | **to resound:** schallen, laut ertönen. | 3 **white-livered:** feige. | **hound:** Hund, Lump. | 6 f. **dead stand-still:** jähes Anhalten. | 8 **range:** Reichweite. | 10 **to bear a hand:** helfen. | 11 **confederate:** Komplize, Verbündeter. | 12 **to make a show of doing s.th.:** Anstalten machen, etwas zu tun. | 13 **reluctance:** Abneigung, Widerwille. | 16 **to play booty with s.o.:** mit jdm. falsches Spiel treiben. | 22 **it's all up:** es ist alles aus. | 22 f. **to show one's heels to s.o.:** Fersengeld geben. | 23 **parting advice:** Rat zum Abschied. | 24 **chance:** Möglichkeit. | **certainty:** Gewissheit.

taken by his enemies: fairly turned tail, and darted off at full speed. Sikes clenched his teeth; took one look round; threw over the prostrate form of Oliver, the cape in which he had been hurriedly muffled; ran along the front of the hedge, as if to distract the attention of those behind, from the spot where the boy lay; paused, for a second, before another hedge which met it at right angles; and whirling his pistol high into the air, cleared it at a bound, and was gone.

"Ho, ho, there!" cried a tremulous voice in the rear. "Pincher! Neptune! Come here, come here!"

The dogs, who, in common with their masters, seemed to have no particular relish for the sport in which they were engaged, readily answered to the command, and three men, who had by this time advanced some distance into the field, stopped to take counsel together.

"My advice, or, leastways, I should say, my *orders*, is," said the fattest man of the party, "that we 'mediately go home again."

"I am agreeable to anything which is agreeable to Mr. Giles," said a shorter man; who was by no means of a slim figure, and who was very pale in the face, and very polite: as frightened men frequently are.

[...]

"You are afraid, Brittles," said Mr. Giles.

"I a'n't," said Brittles.

1 **to turn tail:** die Flucht ergreifen. | 2 **to clench one's teeth:** die Zähne zusammenbeißen. | 3 **prostrate:** ausgestreckt daliegend. | 5 **to distract:** ablenken. | 7 **at right angles** (pl.): im rechten Winkel. | **to whirl:** wirbeln. | 8 **to clear s.th. at a bound:** etwas in, mit einem Satz überspringen. | 9 **in the rear:** hinten, im Hintergrund. | 12 **relish:** Geschmack, Genuss, Vorliebe. | **sport:** Zeitvertreib. | 15 **to take counsel:** zurate gehen. | 16 **leastways:** zumindest, wenigstens. | 17 **'mediately:** *immediately*.

"You are," said Giles.

"You're a falsehood, Mr. Giles," said Brittles.

"You're a lie, Brittles," said Mr. Giles.

Now, these four retorts arose from Mr. Giles's taunt; and Mr. Giles's taunt had arisen from his indignation at having the responsibility of going home again, imposed upon himself under cover of a compliment. The third man brought the dispute to a close, most philosophically.

"I'll tell you what it is, gentlemen," said he, "we're all afraid."

[...]

This dialogue was held between the two men who had surprised the burglars; and a travelling tinker, who had been sleeping in an outhouse: and who had been roused, together with his two mongrel curs, to join in the pursuit. Mr. Giles acted in the double capacity of butler and steward to the old lady of the mansion; and Brittles was a lad of all-work; who, having entered her service a mere child, was treated as a promising young boy still, though he was something past thirty.

Encouraging each other with such converse as this; but keeping very close together, notwithstanding; and looking apprehensively round, whenever a fresh gust rattled through the boughs; the three men hurried back to a tree, behind which

4 **retort:** (scharfe) Erwiderung. | **to arise from s.th.:** von etwas hervorgerufen werden. | **taunt:** Stichelei. | 5 **indignation:** Entrüstung, Empörung. | 7 f. **to bring s.th. to a close:** etwas zum Abschluss bringen. | 13 **travelling tinker:** wandernder Kesselflicker. | 14 **outhouse:** Nebengebäude. | 15 **mongrel cur:** Straßenköter, Promenadenmischung. | 16 **to act:** tätig sein. | **capacity:** Stellung, Amt. | **steward:** Hausverwalter. | 17 **mansion:** Herrenhaus, herrschaftlicher Wohnsitz. | **lad of all-work:** Faktotum, Mädchen für alles. | 18 **mere:** bloß. | 23 **gust:** Windstoß, Bö. | 24 **bough:** Zweig, Ast.

they had left their lantern, lest its light should inform the thieves in what direction to fire. Catching up the light, they made the best of their way home [...].

[...] Still Oliver lay motionless and insensible on the spot where Sikes had left him.

[...]

At length, a low cry of pain broke the stillness that prevailed; and uttering it, the boy awoke. His left arm, rudely bandaged in a shawl, hung heavy and useless at his side: and the bandage was saturated with blood. He was so weak, that he could scarcely raise himself into a sitting posture; when he had done so, he looked feebly round for help, and groaned with pain. Trembling in every joint, from cold and exhaustion, he made an effort to stand upright; but, shuddering from head to foot, fell prostrate on the ground.

After a short return of the stupor in which he had been so long plunged, Oliver: urged by a creeping sickness at his heart, which seemed to warn him that if he lay there, he must surely die: got upon his feet, and essayed to walk. His head was dizzy; and he staggered to and fro like a drunken man; but he kept up, nevertheless, and, with his head drooping languidly on his breast, went stumbling onward, he knew not whither.

[...]

He looked about; and saw that at no great distance there was a house, which perhaps he could reach. Pitying his condition, they might have compassion on him; and if they did not, it would be better, he thought, to die near human beings, than in

1 **lest:** damit nicht. | 3 **to make the best of one's way:** möglichst schnell gehen. | 8 **rudely:** grob, notdürftig. | **bandaged:** verbunden. | 9 **bandage:** Verband. | 10 **saturated:** durchtränkt, vollgesogen. | 12 **to groan:** stöhnen, ächzen. | 13 **joint:** Gelenk. | 19 **to essay:** versuchen. | **dizzy:** benommen, schwindlig. | 26 **compassion:** Mitleid, Erbarmen.

the lonely, open fields. He summoned up all his strength for one last trial; and bent his faltering steps towards it.

As he drew nearer to this house, a feeling came over him that he had seen it before. He remembered nothing of its details; but the shape and aspect of the building seemed familiar to him.

[…] He tottered across the lawn; climbed the steps; knocked faintly at the door; and his whole strength failing him, sunk down against one of the pillars of the little portico.

It happened that about this time, Mr. Giles, Brittles, and the tinker, were recruiting themselves, after the fatigues and terrors of the night, with tea and sundries, in the kitchen. […]

"It was about half-past two," said Mr. Giles, "or I wouldn't swear that it mightn't have been a little nearer three, when I woke up, and, turning round in my bed, as it might be so, (here Mr. Giles turned round in his chair, and pulled the corner of the table-cloth over him to imitate bed-clothes,) I fancied I heerd a noise."

At this point of the narrative the cook turned pale, and asked the housemaid to shut the door, who asked Brittles, who asked the tinker, who pretended not to hear.

[…]

"I heerd it now, quite apparent," resumed Mr. Giles. "'Somebody,' I says, 'is forcing of a door, or window; what's to be done? I'll call up that poor lad, Brittles, and save him from be-

1 **to summon up:** aufbieten, aufbringen. | 2 **trial:** Versuch. | **to bend one's steps towards s.th.:** seine Schritte in Richtung von etwas lenken. | 3 **to draw nearer to s.th.:** sich einer Sache nähern, näher an etwas herankommen. | 9 **portico:** Vorbau. | 11 **to recruit o.s.:** sich erholen. | **fatigue:** Müdigkeit, Erschöpfung. | 12 **sundries:** allerlei Häppchen. | 17 **to fancy:** sich einbilden. | 18 **heerd:** *heard.* | 20 **housemaid:** Hausmädchen. | 21 **to pretend:** vortäuschen, vorgeben. | 24 **to force:** aufbrechen.

ing murdered in his bed; or his throat,' I says, 'may be cut from his right ear to his left, without his ever knowing it.'"

Here, all eyes were turned upon Brittles, who fixed his upon the speaker, and stared at him, with his mouth wide open, and his face expressive of the most unmitigated horror.

[…]

"*Was* he frightened?" asked the cook.

"Not a bit of it," replied Mr. Giles. "He was as firm – ah! pretty near as firm as I was."

"I should have died at once, I'm sure, if it had been me," observed the housemaid.

"You're a woman," retorted Brittles, plucking up a little.

"Brittles is right," said Mr. Giles, nodding his head, approvingly; "from a woman, nothing else was to be expected. But we, being men, took a dark lantern, that was standing on Brittles's hob, and groped our way down stairs in the pitch dark, – as it might be so."

Mr. Giles had risen from his seat, and taken two steps with his eyes shut, to accompany his description with appropriate action, when he started violently, in common with the rest of the company, and hurried back to his chair. The cook and housemaid screamed.

"It was a knock," said Mr. Giles, assuming perfect serenity. "Open the door, somebody."

Nobody moved.

[…]

"If Brittles would rather open the door, in the presence of witnesses," said Mr. Giles, after a short silence, "I am ready to make one."

5 **unmitigated:** ungemindert, rein. | 8 **firm:** standhaft, fest. | 12 **to pluck up:** sich fassen. | 16 **in the pitch dark:** im Stockdunkeln. | 23 **serenity:** Gelassenheit. | 27 **presence:** Anwesenheit, Gegenwart.

"So am I," said the tinker, waking up, as suddenly as he had fallen asleep.

Brittles capitulated on these terms; and the party being somewhat reassured by the discovery (made on throwing open the shutters) that it was now broad day, took their way up stairs; with the dogs in front; and the two women, who were afraid to stay below, bringing up the rear. By the advice of Mr. Giles, they all talked very loud, to warn any evil-disposed person outside, that they were strong in numbers; and by a master-stroke of policy, originating in the brain of the same ingenious gentleman, the dogs' tails were well pinched, in the hall, to make them bark savagely.

These precautions having been taken, Mr. Giles held on fast by the tinker's arm (to prevent his running away, as he pleasantly said), and gave the word of command to open the door. Brittles obeyed; and the group, peeping timorously over each other's shoulders, beheld no more formidable object than poor little Oliver Twist, speechless and exhausted, who raised his heavy eyes, and mutely solicited their compassion.

"A boy!" exclaimed Mr. Giles, valiantly pushing the tinker into the background. "What's the matter with the – eh? – Why – Brittles – look here – don't you know?"

Brittles, who had got behind the door to open it, no sooner saw Oliver, than he uttered a loud cry. Mr. Giles, seizing the boy by one leg and one arm: fortunately not the broken limb:

3 **to capitulate:** aufgeben. | 7 **to bring up the rear:** die Nachhut bilden. | 8 **evil-disposed:** übel gesinnt. | 9 f. **master-stroke:** Meisterleistung. | 10 **policy:** Strategie. | **to originate:** entstehen, entspringen. | 10 f. **ingenious:** raffiniert, erfinderisch. | 11 **to pinch s.th.:** etwas kneifen. | 12 **savagely:** wild, wütend. | 13 **precaution:** Vorkehrung. | 14 f. **pleasantly:** scherzend. | 16 **to peep:** spähen. | **timorously:** furchtsam. | 17 **formidable:** schrecklich. | 18 **speechless:** stumm. | 19 **to solicit:** erflehen. | 20 **valiantly:** tapfer.

lugged him straight into the hall, and deposited him at full length on the floor thereof.

"Here he is!" bawled Giles, calling, in a state of great excitement, up the staircase; "here's one of the thieves, ma'am! Here's a thief, miss! Wounded, miss! I shot him, miss; and Brittles held the light."

[...]

The two women-servants ran up stairs to carry the intelligence that Mr. Giles had captured a robber; and the tinker busied himself in endeavouring to restore Oliver, lest he should die before he could be hanged. In the midst of all this noise and commotion, there was heard a sweet female voice, which quelled it, in an instant.

"Giles!" whispered the voice from the stair-head.

"I'm here, miss," replied Mr. Giles. "Don't be frightened, miss; I ain't much injured. He didn't make a very desperate resistance, miss; I was soon too many for him."

[...]

"Hush, pray; there's a good man!" rejoined the young lady. "Wait quietly one instant, while I speak to aunt."

With a footstep as soft and gentle as the voice, the speaker tripped away; and soon returned, with the direction that the wounded person was to be carried, carefully, up stairs to Mr. Giles's room; and that Brittles was to saddle the pony and betake himself instantly to Chertsey: from which place, he was to despatch, with all speed, a constable and doctor.

[...]

3 **to bawl:** brüllen, laut schreien. | 10 **to endeavour to do s.th.:** sich bemühen, etwas zu tun. | **to restore s.o.:** jdn. wiederherstellen. | 12 **commotion:** Tumult, Spektakel. | 13 **to quell:** bezwingen. | 14 **stair-head:** oberer Treppenabsatz. | 19 **there's a good man!:** seid so gut! | 22 **to trip:** trippeln. | 26 **constable:** Konstabler, Polizist.

Chapter XXIX

Has an introductory Account of the Inmates of the House, to which Oliver resorted

In a handsome room: though its furniture had rather the air of old-fashioned comfort, than of modern elegance: there sat two ladies at a well-spread breakfast-table. Mr. Giles, dressed with scrupulous care in a full suit of black, was in attendance upon them. […]

Of the two ladies, one was well advanced in years; but the high-backed oaken chair in which she sat, was not more upright than she. […] Her eyes, (and age had dimmed but little of their brightness), were attentively fixed upon her young companion.

The younger lady was in the lovely bloom and spring-time of womanhood; at that age, when, if ever angels be for God's good purposes enthroned in mortal forms, they may be, without impiety, supposed to abide in such as hers.

[…]

She was busily engaged in the little offices of the table. Chancing to raise her eyes as the elder lady was regarding her, she playfully put back her hair, which was simply braided on

2 **introductory:** einführend, einleitend. | 3 **to resort to s.th.:** Zuflucht in etwas suchen. | 4 **air:** Aussehen, Ausstrahlung. | 5 **comfort:** Behaglichkeit. | 6 **well-spread:** reichgedeckt. | 7 **scrupulous:** penibel, gewissenhaft. | **to be in attendance upon s.o.:** jdm. zu Diensten sein, jdm. aufwarten (*attendance:* Dienst). | 10 **high-backed:** mit hoher Rückenlehne. | **oaken:** aus Eichenholz. | 11 **to dim:** trüben. | 16 **to enthrone s.o.:** jdn. inthronisieren, einsetzen. | **mortal form:** sterbliche Hülle, menschliche Gestalt. | 17 **impiety:** Gottlosigkeit, Vermessenheit. | **to abide:** verweilen, wohnen. | 19 **little offices:** kleine Handreichungen. | 21 **braided:** geflochten.

her forehead; and threw into one beaming look, such a gush of affection and artless loveliness, that blessed spirits might have smiled to look upon her.

"And Brittles has been gone, upwards of an hour, has he?" asked the old lady, after a pause.

"An hour and twelve minutes, ma'am," replied Mr. Giles, referring to a silver watch, which he drew forth by a black ribbon.

[...]

Mr. Giles was apparently considering the propriety of indulging in a respectful smile himself, when a gig drove up to the garden-gate: out of which, there jumped a fat gentleman, who ran straight up to the door: and who, getting quickly into the house by some mysterious process, burst into the room, and nearly overturned Mr. Giles and the breakfast-table together.

"I never heard of such a thing!" exclaimed the fat gentleman. "My dear Mrs. Maylie – bless my soul – in the silence of night, too – I *never* heard of such a thing!"

[...]

The doctor seemed especially troubled by the fact of the robbery having been unexpected, and attempted in the night-time; as if it were the established custom of gentlemen in the housebreaking way to transact business at noon, and to make an appointment, by the twopenny post, a day or two previous.

1 **beaming:** strahlend. | **gush:** Aufwallung. | 2 **artless:** natürlich, ungekünstelt. | **spirit:** Seele, Geist. | 6 f. **to refer to s.th.:** sich auf etwas beziehen. | 7 **ribbon:** Band, Kordel. | 9 f. **to indulge in s.th.:** sich etwas erlauben. | 10 **gig:** leichter Einspänner. | 14 **to overturn:** umwerfen, umstoßen. | 22 **established custom:** alter Brauch. | 23 **housebreaking way:** Einbrecherzunft. | **to transact:** durchführen, abwickeln. | 24 **appointment:** Termin, Verabredung. | **twopenny post:** wörtl.: Zweipenny-Post; Form der Briefbeförderung in einem bestimmten Umkreis des Londoner Postamts.

"And you, Miss Rose," said the doctor, turning to the young lady, "I –"

"Oh! very much so, indeed," said Rose, interrupting him; "but there is a poor creature up stairs, whom aunt wishes you to see."

[...]

"'Gad that's true!" said the doctor. "Where is he? Shew me the way. I'll look in again, as I come down, Mrs. Maylie. That's the little window that he got in at, eh? Well, I couldn't have believed it!"

Talking all the way, he followed Mr. Giles up stairs; and while he is going up stairs, the reader may be informed, that Mr. Losberne, a surgeon in the neighbourhood, known through a circuit of ten miles round as "the doctor," had grown fat: more from good humour than from good living: and was as kind and hearty, and withal as eccentric an old bachelor, as will be found in five times that space, by any explorer alive.

[...] At length he returned; and in reply to an anxious inquiry after his patient, looked very mysterious, and closed the door, carefully.

"This is a very extraordinary thing, Mrs. Maylie," said the doctor, standing with his back to the door, as if to keep it shut.

"He is not in danger, I hope?" said the old lady.

"Why, that would *not* be an extraordinary thing, under the circumstances," replied the doctor; "though I don't think he is. Have you seen this thief?"

"No," rejoined the old lady.

"Nor heard anything about him?"

"No."

"I beg your pardon, ma'am," interposed Mr. Giles; "but I

7 **Gad:** *God.* | 14 **circuit:** Kreis, Umkreis. | 16 **eccentric:** verschroben. | **bachelor:** Junggeselle. | 17 **explorer:** Forschungsreisender.

was going to tell you about him when Doctor Losberne came in."

The fact was, that Mr. Giles had not, at first, been able to bring his mind to the avowal, that he had only shot a boy. Such commendations had been bestowed upon his bravery, that he could not, for the life of him, help postponing the explanation for a few delicious minutes; during which he had flourished, in the very zenith of a brief reputation for undaunted courage.

"Rose wished to see the man," said Mrs. Maylie, "but I wouldn't hear of it."

"Humph!" rejoined the doctor. "There is nothing very alarming in his appearance. Have you any objection to see him in my presence?"

"If it be necessary," replied the old lady, "certainly not."

"Then I think it is necessary," said the doctor; [...].

Chapter XXX

Relates what Oliver's new Visitors thought of him

[...]

"Now," said the doctor, in a whisper, as he softly turned the handle of a bedroom-door, "let us hear what you think of him. He has not been shaved very recently, but he don't look at all ferocious notwithstanding. Stop, though! Let me first see that he is in visiting order."

4 **avowal:** Eingeständnis. | 5 **commendation:** Lob. | **bravery:** Tapferkeit, Wagemut. | 6 **to postpone s.th.:** etwas verschieben, aufschieben. | 7 **to flourish:** (auf-, er)blühen. | 8 **zenith:** Gipfel, Höhepunkt. | **brief:** kurz, flüchtig. | **undaunted:** unerschrocken. | 22 **ferocious:** wild, grimmig. | 23 **to be in visiting order:** in der Lage sein, Besuch zu empfangen.

Stepping before them, he looked into the room. Motioning them to advance, he closed the door when they had entered; and gently drew back the curtains of the bed. Upon it, in lieu of the dogged, black-visaged ruffian they had expected to behold, there lay a mere child: worn with pain and exhaustion: and sunk into a deep sleep. His wounded arm, bound and splintered up, was crossed upon his breast; his head reclined upon the other arm, which was half hidden by his long hair, as it streamed over the pillow.

[…]

"What can this mean?" exclaimed the elder lady. "This poor child can never have been the pupil of robbers!"

"Vice," sighed the surgeon, replacing the curtain, "takes up her abode in many temples; and who can say that a fair outside shall not enshrine her?"

[…]

"But, can you – oh, sir! can you really believe that this delicate boy has been the voluntary associate of the worst outcasts of society?" said Rose.

The surgeon shook his head, in a manner which intimated that he feared it was very possible; and observing that they might disturb the patient, led the way into an adjoining apartment.

"But even if he has been wicked," pursued Rose, "think how young he is; think that he may never have known a mother's love, or the comfort of a home; and that ill-usage and blows, or

3 **in lieu of:** anstelle, anstatt. | 4 **dogged:** verstockt. | **black-visaged:** mit finsterem Gesicht. | 5 **worn:** erschöpft, todmüde. | 6 **bound:** verbunden (Verletzung). | 6f. **to splinter s.th. up:** etwas schienen. | 7 **to recline:** ruhen, liegen. | 13 **vice:** Laster. | 14 **temple:** Tempel. | **fair:** schön, hübsch. | 15 **to enshrine:** verwahren, beherbergen. | 17f. **delicate:** zart. | 18 **voluntary:** freiwillig. | **outcasts:** Ausgestoßene, Geächtete. | 22 **adjoining:** angrenzend, benachbart. | 26 **ill-usage:** Misshandlung.

the want of bread, may have driven him to herd with men who have forced him to guilt. Aunt, dear aunt, for mercy's sake, think of this, before you let them drag this sick child to a prison, which in any case must be the grave of all his chances of amendment. Oh! as you love me, and know that I have never felt the want of parents in your goodness and affection, but that I might have done so, and might have been equally helpless and unprotected with this poor child, have pity upon him before it is too late!"

"My dear love!" said the elder lady, as she folded the weeping girl to her bosom, "do you think I would harm a hair of his head?"

"Oh, no!" replied Rose, eagerly.

"No," said the old lady, with a trembling lip; "my days are drawing to their close; and may mercy be shewn to me as I shew it to others! What can I do to save him, sir?"

[…]

"I think if you give me a full and unlimited commission to bully Giles, and that little boy, Brittles, I can manage it. He is a faithful fellow and an old servant, I know; but you can make it up to him in a thousand ways, and reward him for being such a good shot besides. You don't object to that?"

"Unless there is some other way of preserving the child," replied Mrs. Maylie.

"There is no other," said the doctor. "No other, take my word for it."

1 **want of s.th.:** Mangel an etwas. | **to herd with s.o.:** sich jdm. anschließen. | 5 **amendment:** Besserung. | 8 **unprotected:** schutzlos. | 15 **to draw to one's close:** sich ihrem, seinem Ende nähern. | 18 **commission:** Vollmacht, Erlaubnis. | 19 **to bully s.o.:** jdn. drangsalieren. | 20 f. **to make it up to s.o.:** jdn. entschädigen. | 22 **shot:** Schütze. | 23 **to preserve s.o.:** jdn. schützen, schonen.

"Then my aunt invests you with full power," said Rose [...].

Finally, the treaty was entered into; and the parties thereunto, sat down to wait, with some impatience, until Oliver should awake.

The patience of the two ladies was destined to undergo a longer trial than Mr. Losberne had led them to expect; for hour after hour passed on, and still Oliver slumbered heavily. It was evening, indeed, before the kind-hearted doctor brought them the intelligence, that he was at length sufficiently restored to be spoken to. The boy was very ill, he said, and weak from the loss of blood; but his mind was so troubled with anxiety to disclose something, that he deemed it better to give him the opportunity, than to insist upon his remaining quiet until next morning: which he should otherwise have done.

The conference was a long one; for Oliver told them all his simple history: and was often compelled to stop, by pain and want of strength. It was a solemn thing, to hear, in the darkened room, the feeble voice of the sick child recounting a weary catalogue of evils and calamities which hard men had brought upon him. [...]

The momentous interview was no sooner concluded, and Oliver composed to rest again, than the doctor, after wiping his eyes, and condemning them for being weak all at once, betook himself down stairs to open upon Mr. Giles. And finding nobody about the parlours, it occurred to him, that he could perhaps originate the proceedings with better effect in the kitchen; so into the kitchen he went.

1 **to invest s.o. with s.th.:** jdn. mit etwas ausstatten. | 3 **treaty:** Übereinkunft. | 3 f. **thereunto:** dazu. | 7 **trial:** Prüfung. | 8 **to slumber:** schlummern. | 19 **to recount:** erzählen. | 20 **calamity:** Unglück, Schicksalsschlag. | 22 **momentous:** bedeutsam. | 26 **to occur to s.o.:** jdm. in den Sinn kommen. | 27 **to originate s.th.:** etwas beginnen.

There were assembled, in that lower house of the domestic parliament, the women-servants, Mr. Brittles, Mr. Giles, the tinker (who had received a special invitation to regale himself for the remainder of the day, in consideration of his services), and the constable. The latter gentleman had a large staff, a large head, large features, and large half-boots; and he looked as if he had been taking a proportionate allowance of ale, as indeed he had.

[...]

"How is the patient to-night, sir?" asked Giles.

"So-so;" returned the doctor. "I am afraid you have got yourself into a scrape there, Mr. Giles."

"I hope you don't mean to say, sir," said Mr. Giles, trembling, "that he's going to die. If I thought it, I should never be happy again. I wouldn't cut a boy off: no, not even Brittles here: not for all the plate in the country, sir."

[...]

"Then tell me this," said the doctor, "both of you – both of you! Are you going to take upon yourselves to swear that that boy up stairs is the boy that was put through the little window last night? Out with it! Come! We are prepared for you!"

The doctor, who was universally considered one of the best-tempered creatures on earth, made this demand in such a

1 **to assemble:** sich versammeln. | **lower house:** Anspielung auf das »Unterhaus« (*House of Commons*) des britischen Parlaments; die Küche befand sich zumeist im Souterrain. | **domestic:** häuslich. | 3 **to regale o.s.:** sich gütlich tun. | 4 **in consideration of:** als Belohnung für, in Anbetracht von. | 5 **staff:** (Amts-)Stab. | 7 **proportionate:** entsprechend. | **ale:** Ale (Biersorte). | 11 f. **to get o.s. into a scrape:** in die Bredouille geraten. | 15 **to cut s.o. off:** jdn. niederstrecken. | 16 **plate:** Tafelsilber. | 23 **universally:** allseits, allgemein. | 23 f. **best-tempered:** gutmütigste(r, s).

dreadful tone of anger, that Giles and Brittles, who were considerably muddled by ale and excitement, stared at each other in a state of stupefaction.

[...]

"It's a simple question of identity, you will observe," said the doctor.

"That's what it is, sir," replied the constable, coughing with great violence; for he had finished his ale in a hurry, and some of it had gone the wrong way.

"Here's a house broken into," said the doctor, "and a couple of men catch one moment's glimpse of a boy, in the midst of gunpowder-smoke, and in all the distraction of alarm and darkness. Here's a boy comes to that very same house, next morning, and because he happens to have his arm tied up, these men lay violent hands upon him; by doing which, they place his life in great danger, and swear he is the thief. Now, the question is, whether these men are justified by the fact; and if not, in what situation do they place themselves?"

The constable nodded profoundly. He said, if that wasn't law, he would be glad to know what was.

"I ask you again," thundered the doctor, "are you, on your solemn oaths, able to identify that boy?"

Brittles looked doubtfully at Mr. Giles; Mr. Giles looked doubtfully at Brittles; the constable put his hand behind his ear, to catch the reply; the two women and the tinker leant forward to listen; and the doctor glanced keenly round; when a ring was heard at the gate, and at the same moment, the sound of wheels.

2 **muddled:** konfus, benebelt. | 3 **stupefaction:** Bestürzung, Verblüffung, Betäubung. | 5 **identity:** Identität. | 12 **distraction:** Ablenkung. | 22 **oath:** Eid, Schwur. | 23 **doubtfully:** zweifelnd, unschlüssig. | 26 **keenly:** aufmerksam, eifrig.

"It's the runners!" cried Brittles, to all appearance much relieved.

"The what!" exclaimed the doctor, aghast in his turn.

"The Bow-street officers, sir," replied Brittles, taking up a candle; "me and Mr. Giles sent for 'em this morning."

"What!" cried the doctor.

"Yes," replied Brittles; "I sent a message up by the coachman, and I only wonder they weren't here before, sir."

"You did, did you? Then confound your – slow coaches down here; that's all," said the doctor, walking away.

Chapter XXXI

Involves a critical Position

"Who's that?" inquired Brittles, opening the door a little way, with the chain up, and peeping out: shading the candle with his hand.

"Open the door," replied a man outside; "it's the officers from Bow-street, as was sent to, to-day."

[…]

The man who had knocked at the door, was a stout personage of middle height: aged about fifty: with shiny black hair,

1 **Runners:** Gemeint sind die Bow Street Runners, 1749 von dem vor allem als Schriftsteller bekannten Henry Fielding begründet. Sie waren in Fieldings ehemaligem Amtssitz als Friedensrichter in der Bow Street stationiert und als Vorläufer der Metropolitan Police die ersten professionellen Polizeikräfte. Zuvor gab es lediglich die unbezahlten Konstabler der Gemeinden. Die Bow Street Runners wurden 1839 aufgelöst. | 3 **aghast:** entgeistert. | 9 **confound …:** zur Hölle mit … | 12 **to involve s.th.:** etwas mit sich bringen. | **critical:** bedenklich, schwierig.

cropped pretty close; half-whiskers; a round face; and sharp eyes. The other was a red-headed, bony man, in top-boots: with a rather ill-favoured countenance: and a turned-up, sinister-looking, nose.

"Tell your governor that Blathers and Duff is here, will you?" said the stouter man, smoothing down his hair, and laying a pair of handcuffs on the table. [...]

"Now, with regard to this here robbery, master," said Blathers. "What are the circumstances?"

Mr. Losberne, who appeared desirous of gaining time, recounted them at great length, and with much circumlocution. Messrs. Blathers and Duff looked very knowing meanwhile, and occasionally exchanged a nod.

[...]

"Now, what is this, about this here boy that the servants are a-talking on?" said Blathers.

"Nothing at all," replied the doctor. "One of the frightened servants chose to take it into his head, that he had something to do with this attempt to break into the house; but it's nonsense: sheer absurdity."

"Wery easy disproved if it is," remarked Duff.

"What he says is quite correct," observed Blathers, nodding his head in a confirmatory way, and playing carelessly with the handcuffs, as if they were a pair of castanets. "Who is the boy? What account does he give of himself? Where did he come from? He didn't drop out of the clouds, did he, master?"

1 **cropped pretty close:** ziemlich kurz geschnitten. | **half-whiskers:** Koteletten. | 3 **ill-favoured:** hässlich. | **turned-up nose:** Stupsnase. | 3 f. **sinister-looking:** unheilverkündend. | 5 **governor:** Herrschaft(en). | 7 **handcuffs:** Handschellen. | 10 **to gain time:** Zeit gewinnen. | 11 **circumlocution:** Weitschweifigkeit. | 12 **Messrs.:** Abk. für den Plural von *Mr.:* die Herren. | 20 **sheer:** rein, pur. | **absurdity:** Unsinn. | 23 **confirmatory:** bestätigend. | 24 **castanets:** Kastagnetten.

"Of course not," replied the doctor, with a nervous glance at the two ladies. "I know his whole history; but we can talk about that presently. You would like, first, to see the place where the thieves made their attempt, I suppose?"

"Certainly," rejoined Mr. Blathers. "We had better inspect the premises first, and examine the servants arterwards. That's the usual way of doing business."

[...]

Meanwhile, the doctor walked up and down the next room in a very uneasy state; and Mrs. Maylie and Rose looked on, with anxious faces.

[...]

"The more I think of it," said the doctor, "the more I see that it will occasion endless trouble and difficulty if we put these men in possession of the boy's real story. I am certain it will not be believed; and even if they can do nothing to him in the end, still the dragging it forward, and giving publicity to all the doubts that will be cast upon it, must interfere, materially, with your benevolent plan of rescuing him from misery."

"[...] We must make the best of it; and I bad be the best, it is no fault of ours. Come in!"

"Well, master," said Blathers, entering the room, followed by his colleague; and making the door fast, before he said any more. "This warn't a put-up thing."

[...]

"There was two of 'em in it," continued Blathers; "and they had a boy with 'em; that's plain from the size of the window. That's all to be said at present. We'll see this lad that you've got up stairs at once, if you please."

[...]

19 **materially:** wesentlich, erheblich. | 25 **warn't:** *wasn't.*

"Very curious, indeed," observed the doctor. "Now, if you please, you can walk up the stairs."

"If *you* please, sir," returned Mr. Blathers; and closely following Mr. Losberne, the two officers ascended to Oliver's bedroom: Mr. Giles preceding the party, with a lighted candle.

Oliver had been dozing; but looked worse, and was more feverish, than he had appeared yet. Being assisted by the doctor, he managed to sit up in bed for a minute or so; and looked at the strangers without at all understanding what was going forward: in fact, without seeming to recollect where he was, or what had been passing.

"This," said Mr. Losberne, speaking softly, but with great vehemence notwithstanding, "this is the lad, who, being accidentally wounded by a spring-gun in some boyish trespass on Mr. What-d'ye-call-him's grounds, at the back here, comes to the house for assistance this morning, and is immediately laid hold of, and maltreated, by that ingenious gentleman with the candle in his hand: who has placed his life in considerable danger, as I can professionally certify."

Messrs. Blathers and Duff looked at Mr. Giles, as he was thus recommended to their notice; the bewildered butler gazed from them towards Oliver, and from Oliver towards Mr. Losberne, with a most ludicrous mixture of fear and perplexity.

"You don't mean to deny that, I suppose?" said the doctor, laying Oliver gently down again.

"It was all done for the – for the best, sir!" answered Giles. "I

5 **to precede s.o.:** jdm. vorangehen. | 6 **to doze:** dösen. | 12 f. **vehemence:** Leidenschaft, Heftigkeit. | 14 **spring-gun:** Selbstschussanlage. | **trespass:** unbefugtes Betreten. | 15 **Mr. What-d'ye-call-him:** Herr Soundso, Herr Wie-heißt-er-noch-gleich. | 16 f. **to lay hold of s.o.:** jdn. packen. | 17 **to maltreat s.o.:** jdn. misshandeln. | 19 **professionally:** von Berufs wegen. | **to certify:** bestätigen, bescheinigen. | 23 **perplexity:** Verwirrtheit. | 24 **to mean s.th.:** etwas beabsichtigen.

am sure I thought it was the boy, or I wouldn't have meddled with him. I am not of an inhuman disposition, sir."

[...]

Mr. Losberne had been feeling the patient's pulse during this short dialogue; but he now rose from the chair by the bedside, and remarked, that if the officers had any doubts upon the subject, they would perhaps like to step into the next room, and have Brittles before them.

Acting upon this suggestion, they adjourned to a neighbouring apartment, where Mr. Brittles, being called in, involved himself and his respected superior in such a wonderful maze of fresh contradictions and impossibilities, as tended to throw no particular light on anything, but the fact of his own strong mystification; except, indeed, his declarations that he shouldn't know the real boy, if he were put before him that instant; that he had only taken Oliver to be he, because Mr. Giles had said he was; and that Mr. Giles had, five minutes previously, admitted, in the kitchen, that he began to be very much afraid he had been a little too hasty.

Among other ingenious surmises, the question was then raised, whether Mr. Giles had really hit anybody; and upon examination of the fellow pistol to that which he had fired, it turned out to have no more destructive loading than gunpowder and brown paper: a discovery which made a considerable impression on everybody but the doctor, who had drawn the ball about ten minutes before. Upon no one, however, did it make a greater impression than on Mr. Giles himself; who, af-

1 **to meddle with s.o.:** sich an jdm. vergreifen. | 2 **inhuman:** unmenschlich. | 9 **to adjourn to s.th.:** sich in, zu etwas zurückziehen. | 14 **mystification:** Verwirrung. | **declaration:** Erklärung, Aussage. | 17 **to admit:** zugeben, eingestehen. | 20 **surmise:** Vermutung. | 22 **fellow:** Gegenstück (eines Paares). | 23 **destructive:** zerstörerisch, vernichtend. | **loading:** Ladung. | 26 **ball:** Kugel.

ter labouring, for some hours, under the fear of having mortally wounded a fellow-creature, eagerly caught at this new idea, and favoured it to the utmost. Finally, the officers, without troubling themselves very much about Oliver, left the Chertsey constable in the house, and took up their rest for that night in the town [...].

Chapter XXXII

Of the happy life Oliver began to lead with his kind Friends

Oliver's ailings were neither slight nor few. In addition to the pain and delay attendant on a broken limb, his exposure to the wet and cold had brought on fever and ague: which hung about him for many weeks, and reduced him sadly. But, at length, he began, by slow degrees, to get better, and to be able to say sometimes, in a few tearful words, how deeply he felt the goodness of the two sweet ladies, and how ardently he hoped that, when he grew strong and well again, he could do something to shew his gratitude; [...].

"Poor fellow!" said Rose, when Oliver had been one day feebly endeavouring to utter the words of thankfulness that rose to his pale lips: "you shall have many opportunities of serving us, if you will. We are going into the country; and my aunt intends that you shall accompany us. The quiet place, the pure

1 f. **mortally:** lebensgefährlich. | 3 **to favour s.th.:** etwas für gut halten, befürworten. | 4 **to trouble o.s. about s.o.:** sich um jdn. kümmern. | 9 **ailings:** körperliche Leiden, Gebrechen. | 10 **(to be) attendant on s.th.:** etwas begleiten, mit etwas verbunden sein. | **exposure:** Ausgesetztsein. | 11 **ague:** Schüttelfrost. | 14 **tearful:** tränenreich. | 15 **ardently:** leidenschaftlich, inbrünstig. | 17 **gratitude:** Dankbarkeit. | 20 **to serve s.o.:** jdm. behilflich sein.

air, and all the pleasures and beauties of spring, will restore you in a few days; and we will employ you in a hundred ways, when you can bear the trouble."

[...]

"Oh yes, ma'am, yes!" replied Oliver, eagerly; "but I was thinking that I am ungrateful now."

"To whom?" inquired the young lady.

"To the kind gentleman, and the dear old nurse, who took so much care of me before," rejoined Oliver. "If they knew how happy I am, they would be pleased, I am sure."

"I am sure they would," rejoined Oliver's benefactress; "and Mr. Losberne has already been kind enough to promise that, when you are well enough to bear the journey, he will carry you to see them."

"Has he, ma'am?" cried Oliver, his face brightening with pleasure. "I don't know what I shall do for joy when I see their kind faces once again!"

In a short time Oliver was sufficiently recovered to undergo the fatigue of this expedition; and one morning he and Mr. Losberne set out, accordingly, in a little carriage which belonged to Mrs. Maylie. [...]

As Oliver knew the name of the street in which Mr. Brownlow resided, they were enabled to drive straight thither. When the coach turned into it, his heart beat so violently, that he could scarcely draw his breath.

"Now, my boy, which house is it?" inquired Mr. Losberne.

"That! That!" replied Oliver, pointing eagerly out of the window. "The white house. Oh! make haste! Pray make haste! I feel as if I should die; it makes me tremble so."

11 **benefactress:** Wohltäterin. | 19 **fatigue:** Anstrengung. | 23 **to reside:** wohnen, wohnhaft sein. | **to enable s.o. to do s.th.:** jdm. ermöglichen, etwas zu tun. | **thither:** dorthin.

"Come, come!" said the good doctor, patting him on the shoulder. "You will see them directly, and they will be overjoyed to find you safe and well."

"Oh! I hope so!" cried Oliver. "They were so good to me; so very very good to me."

The coach rolled on. It stopped. No; that was the wrong house; the next door. It went on a few paces, and stopped again. Oliver looked up at the windows, with tears of happy expectation coursing down his face.

Alas! the white house was empty, and there was a bill in the window. "To Let."

"Knock at the next door," cried Mr. Losberne, taking Oliver's arm in his. "What has become of Mr. Brownlow, who used to live in the adjoining house, do you know?"

The servant did not know; but would go and inquire. She presently returned; and said, that Mr. Brownlow had sold off his goods, and gone to the West Indies, six weeks before. Oliver clasped his hands, and sank feebly backwards.

"Has his housekeeper gone, too?" inquired Mr. Losberne, after a moment's pause.

"Yes, sir;" replied the servant. "The old gentleman, the housekeeper, and a gentleman who was a friend of Mr. Brownlow's, all went together."

"Then, turn towards home again," said Mr. Losberne to the driver; "and don't stop to bait the horses, till you get out of this confounded London!"

[…]

This bitter disappointment caused Oliver much sorrow and grief, even in the midst of his happiness; for he had pleased

9 **to course:** strömen, fließen. | 16 **presently:** bald, sogleich. | **to sell s.th. off:** etwas verkaufen. | 17 **goods:** Besitz, Güter. | **West Indies:** Westindische Inseln (Karibik). | 25 **to bait:** füttern.

himself, many times during his illness, with thinking of all that Mr. Brownlow and Mrs. Bedwin would say to him: and what delight it would be to tell them how many long days and nights he had passed in reflecting on what they had done for him, and in bewailing his cruel separation from them. The hope of eventually clearing himself with them, too, and explaining how he had been forced away, had buoyed him up, and sustained him, under many of his recent trials; and now, the idea that they should have gone so far, and carried with them the belief that he was an impostor and a robber: a belief which might remain uncontradicted to his dying day: was almost more than he could bear.

The circumstance occasioned no alteration, however, in the behaviour of his benefactors. After another fortnight: when the fine warm weather had fairly begun, and every tree and flower was putting forth its young leaves and rich blossoms: they made preparations for quitting the house at Chertsey, for some months. Sending the plate, which had so excited the Jew's cupidity, to the banker's; and leaving Giles and another servant in care of the house; they departed to a cottage at some distance in the country; and took Oliver with them.

Who can describe the pleasure and delight: the peace of mind and soft tranquillity: the sickly boy felt in the balmy air, and among the green hills and rich woods, of an inland village! [...]

4 **to reflect on s.th.:** über etwas nachdenken. | 5 **to bewail:** beklagen, betrauern. | **separation:** Trennung. | 5 f. **eventually:** schließlich, endlich. | 6 **to clear o.s.:** sich rechtfertigen. | 7 **to buoy s.o. up:** jdm. Mut machen. | **to sustain s.o.:** jdn. stärken, stützen. | 10 **impostor:** Betrüger, Schwindler. | 11 **uncontradicted:** unwidersprochen. | 16 **to put forth s.th.:** etwas hervorbringen. | 17 **to quit:** verlassen. | 19 **cupidity:** Begierde. | 22 f. **peace of mind:** Seelenfrieden. | 23 **tranquillity:** Ruhe, Beschaulichkeit. | **balmy:** mild, lau.

Chapter XXXIII

Wherein the Happiness of Oliver and his Friends, experiences a sudden Check

Spring flew swiftly by, and summer came; [...].

Still the same quiet life went on at the little cottage, and the same cheerful serenity prevailed among its inmates. Oliver had long since grown stout and healthy; but health or sickness made no difference in his warm feelings to those about him, though they do in the feelings of a great many people. He was still the same gentle, attached, affectionate creature that he had been when pain and suffering had wasted his strength; and when he was dependent for every slight attention and comfort on those who tended him.

One beautiful night, they had taken a longer walk than was customary with them; for the day had been unusually warm, and there was a brilliant moon; and a light wind had sprung up, which was unusually refreshing. Rose had been in high spirits, too, and they had walked on, in merry conversation, until they had far exceeded their ordinary bounds. Mrs. Maylie being fatigued, they returned more slowly home. The young lady, merely throwing off her simple bonnet, sat down at the piano, as usual; after running abstractedly over the keys for a few minutes, she fell into a low and very solemn air; and as she played it, they heard her sob, as if she were weeping.

"Rose, my dear!" said the elder lady.

[...]

3 **to experience:** erfahren, erleben. | **check:** Dämpfer. | 10 **attached:** anhänglich. | **affectionate:** liebevoll, herzlich. | 12 **to be dependent for s.th.:** von etwas abhängig, auf etwas angewiesen sein. | 17 f. **to be in high spirits:** in bester Stimmung sein. | 19 **to exceed s.th.:** (fig.) etwas überschreiten. | 22 **keys:** Tasten. | 23 **air:** Weise, Lied.

"I would not alarm you if I could avoid it," rejoined Rose; "but indeed I have tried very hard, and cannot help this. I fear I *am* ill, aunt."

[…]

Oliver, who watched the old lady anxiously, observed that she was alarmed by these appearances; and so, in truth, was he; but seeing that she affected to make light of them, he endeavoured to do the same, and they so far succeeded, that when Rose was persuaded by her aunt to retire for the night, she was in better spirits, and appeared even in better health: assuring them that she felt certain she should rise in the morning, quite well.

"I hope," said Oliver, when Mrs. Maylie returned, "that nothing is the matter? She don't look well to-night, but –"

The old lady motioned to him not to speak; and sitting herself down in a dark corner of the room, remained silent for some time. At length, she said, in a trembling voice:

"I hope not, Oliver. I have been very happy with her for some years: too happy, perhaps. It may be time that I should meet with some misfortune; but I hope it is not this."

"What?" inquired Oliver.

"The heavy blow," said the old lady, "of losing the dear girl who has so long been my comfort and happiness."

[…]

An anxious night ensued. When morning came, Mrs. Maylie's predictions were but too well verified. Rose was in the first stage of a high and dangerous fever.

"We must be active, Oliver, and not give way to useless grief," said Mrs. Maylie, laying her finger on her lip, as she looked steadily into his face; "this letter must be sent, with all

7 **to make light of s.th.:** etwas auf die leichte Schulter nehmen. | 20 **misfortune:** Unheil. | 26 **to verify s.th.:** etwas bestätigen. | 29 **grief:** Trauer.

possible expedition, to Mr. Losberne. It must be carried to the market-town, which is not more than four miles off, by the footpath across the fields; and thence despatched, by an express on horseback, straight to Chertsey. The people at the inn will undertake to do this; and I can trust to you to see it done, I know."

Oliver could make no reply, but looked his anxiety to be gone at once.

"Here is another letter," said Mrs. Maylie, pausing to reflect; "but whether to send it now, or wait until I see how Rose goes on, I scarcely know. I would not forward it, unless I feared the worst."

"Is it for Chertsey, too, ma'am?" inquired Oliver: impatient to execute his commission, and holding out his trembling hand for the letter.

"No," replied the old lady, giving it to him mechanically. Oliver glanced at it, and saw that it was directed to Harry Maylie, Esquire, at some great lord's house in the country; where, he could not make out.

"Shall it go, ma'am?" asked Oliver, looking up, impatiently.

"I think not," replied Mrs. Maylie, taking it back. "I will wait until to-morrow."

With these words, she gave Oliver her purse, and he started off, without more delay, at the greatest speed he could muster.

Swiftly he ran across the fields, and down the little lanes which sometimes divided them: now almost hidden by the high corn on either side, and now emerging in an open field, where the mowers and haymakers were busy at their work; nor did he stop once, save now and then, for a few seconds, to re-

3 f. **express:** Eilbote. | 11 **to forward:** absenden. | 18 **Esquire:** niedriger Adelstitel, dem Namen nachgestellt, oft auch nur als höfliche und respektvolle Wendung benutzt. | 23 **purse:** Geldbörse.

cover breath, until he came, in a great heat, and covered with dust, on the little market-place of the market-town.

Here he paused, and looked about for the inn. There was a white bank, and a red brewery, and a yellow town-hall; and in one corner there was a large house, with all the wood about it painted green: before which was the sign of "The George." To this he hastened, as soon as it caught his eye.

He spoke to a postboy who was dozing under the gateway; [...].

[...] the man set spurs to his horse, and rattling over the uneven paving of the market-place, was out of the town, and galloping along the turnpike-road, in a couple of minutes.

It was something to feel certain that assistance was sent for; and that no time had been lost. Oliver hurried up the inn-yard, with a somewhat lighter heart: and was turning out of the gateway when he accidentally stumbled against a tall man, wrapped in a cloak: who was at that moment coming out of the inn-door.

"Hah!" cried the man, fixing his eyes on Oliver, and suddenly recoiling. "What the devil's this?"

"I beg your pardon, sir," said Oliver; "I was in a great hurry to get home, and didn't see you were coming."

[...]

"Rot his bones!" murmured the man, in a horrible passion: between his clenched teeth; "if I had only had the courage to say the word, I might have been free of you in a night. Curses

4 **brewery:** Brauerei. | **town-hall:** Rathaus. | 6 **sign:** Wirtshausschild. | 8 **postboy:** Postreiter. | **gateway:** Toreinfahrt. | 10 **to set spurs to one's horse:** seinem Pferd die Sporen geben. | 12 **turnpike-road:** Chaussee (ursprünglich mautpflichtige, mit einem Schlagbaum [*turnpike*] versehene Landstraße). | 17 **wrapped:** eingehüllt. | 20 **to recoil:** zurückschrecken. | 24 **Rot his bones!:** Mögen seine Gebeine verfaulen! | **horrible:** entsetzlich, schrecklich.

on your head, and black death on your heart, you imp! What are you doing here?"

The man shook his fist, and gnashed his teeth, as he uttered these words incoherently. He advanced towards Oliver, as if with the intention of aiming a blow at him, but fell violently on the ground: writhing and foaming, in a fit.

Oliver gazed, for a moment, at the struggles of the madman (for such he supposed him to be); and then darted into the house for help. Having seen him safely carried into the hotel, he turned his face homewards: running as fast as he could, to make up for lost time: and recalling, with a great deal of astonishment and some fear, the extraordinary behaviour of the person from whom he had just parted.

[...]

When he reached home, Mrs. Maylie was sitting in the little parlour. Oliver's heart sank at sight of her; for she had never left the bedside of her niece; and he trembled to think what change could have driven her away. He learnt that she had fallen into a deep sleep, from which she would waken, either to recovery and life, or to bid them farewell, and die.

They sat, listening, and afraid to speak, for hours. The untasted meal was removed; and with looks which shewed that their thoughts were elsewhere, they watched the sun as he sank lower and lower, and, at length, cast over sky and earth those brilliant hues which herald his departure. Their quick

1 **black death:** der schwarze Tod, die Pest. | **imp:** böser Wicht, Kobold. | 3 **to gnash one's teeth:** mit den Zähnen knirschen. | 6 **to writhe:** sich krümmen, sich hin und her winden. | **to foam:** schäumen. | 11 **to recall s.th.:** sich an etwas erinnern. | 13 **to part from s.o.:** sich von jdm. trennen. | 18 **to learn:** in Erfahrung bringen. | 20 **to bid s.o. farewell:** jdm. Lebewohl sagen. | 25 **to herald s.th.:** etwas ankündigen. | **departure:** Abschied, Verschwinden. | 25 f. **quick ears:** gespitzte Ohren.

ears caught the sound of an approaching footstep; and they both involuntarily darted to the door, as Mr. Losberne entered.

"What of Rose?" cried the old lady. "Tell me at once! I can bear it; anything but suspense! Oh, tell me! in the name of Heaven!"

"You must compose yourself," said the doctor, supporting her. "Be calm, my dear ma'am, pray."

"Let me go, in God's name! My dear child! She is dead! She is dying!"

"No!" cried the doctor, passionately. "As He is good and merciful, she will live to bless us all, for years to come."

[...]

Chapter XXXIV

Contains some introductory Particulars relative to a young Gentleman who now arrives upon the Scene; and a new Adventure which happened to Oliver

It was almost too much happiness to bear. Oliver felt stunned and stupefied by the unexpected intelligence; he could not weep, or speak, or rest. He had scarcely the power of understanding anything that had passed, until, after a long ramble in the quiet evening air, a burst of tears came to his relief; and he seemed to awaken, all at once, to a full sense of the joyful change that had occurred, and the almost insupportable load of anguish which had been taken from his breast.

12 **to bless s.o.:** jdn. beglücken. | 15 **relative to:** betreffs, bezüglich. | 18 **stunned:** benommen. | 21 **ramble:** Wanderung, Streifzug. | 24 **insupportable:** unerträglich. | 25 **anguish:** Qual, Pein.

The night was fast closing in, when he returned homewards: laden with flowers which he had culled, with peculiar care, for the adornment of the sick chamber. As he walked briskly along the road, he heard behind him the noise of some vehicle, approaching at a furious pace. Looking round, he saw that it was a post-chaise, driven at great speed; and as the horses were galloping, and the road was narrow, he stood leaning against a gate until it should have passed him.

As it dashed on, Oliver caught a glimpse of a man in a white nightcap, whose face seemed familiar to him, although his view was so brief that he could not identify the person. In another second or two, the nightcap was thrust out of the chaise-window; and a stentorian voice bellowed to the driver to stop: which he did as soon as he could pull up his horses. Then, the nightcap once again appeared; and the same voice called Oliver by his name.

"Here!" cried the voice. "Master Oliver, what's the news? Miss Rose! Master O-li-ver!"

"Is it you, Giles?" cried Oliver, running up to the chaise-door.

Giles popped out his nightcap again, preparatory to making some reply, when he was suddenly pulled back by a young gentleman who occupied the other corner of the chaise, and who eagerly demanded what was the news.

"In a word!" cried the gentleman, "better or worse?"

"Better – much better!" replied Oliver, hastily.

1 **to close in:** herankommen, hereinbrechen. | 2 **to cull:** pflücken. | 3 **adornment:** Verschönerung. | **sick chamber:** Krankenzimmer (*chamber:* Kammer, Raum, Gemach). | 5 **furious:** rasend. | 6 **post-chaise:** Postkutsche. | 9 **to dash on:** dahinrasen, -jagen. | 13 **stentorian voice:** Stentorstimme (sehr laute Stimme). | 21 **to pop out s.th.:** etwas hinausstecken.

"Thank Heaven!" exclaimed the gentleman. "You are sure?"

"Quite, sir," replied Oliver. "The change took place only a few hours ago; and Mr. Losberne says, that all danger is at an end."

[...]

Mrs. Maylie was anxiously waiting to receive her son when he reached the cottage; and the meeting did not take place without great emotion on both sides.

"Mother!" whispered the young man; "why did you not write before?"

"I did," replied Mrs. Maylie; "but, on reflection, I determined to keep back the letter until I had heard Mr. Losberne's opinion."

[...]

"This is unkind, mother," said Harry. "Do you still suppose that I am a boy ignorant of my own mind, and mistaking the impulses of my own soul?"

"I think, my dear son," returned Mrs. Maylie, laying her hand upon his shoulder, "that youth has many generous impulses which do not last; and that among them are some, which, being gratified, become only the more fleeting. Above all, I think," said the lady, fixing her eyes on her son's face, "that if an enthusiastic, ardent, and ambitious man marry a wife on whose name there is a stain, which, though it originate in no fault of hers, may be visited by cold and sordid people upon her, and upon his children also: and, in exact proportion

6 **to receive s.o.:** jdn. empfangen. | 16 **to be ignorant of s.th.:** etwas nicht kennen. | **to mistake s.th.:** etwas verkennen. | 17 **impulse:** Regung. | 19 **generous:** großherzig. | 21 **to gratify s.th.:** etwas befriedigen, einer Sache nachgeben. | **fleeting:** flüchtig, vergänglich. | 23 **enthusiastic:** schwärmerisch. | **ambitious:** ehrgeizig. | 24 **stain:** Fleck, Makel. | 25 **to visit s.th. upon s.o.:** etwas gegen jdn. verwenden. | **sordid:** niedrig gesinnt, gemein.

to his success in the world, be cast in his teeth, and made the subject of sneers against him: he may – no matter how generous and good his nature – one day repent of the connection he formed in early life; and she may have the pain and torture of knowing that he does so."

"Mother," said the young man, impatiently, "he would be a selfish brute, unworthy alike of the name of man and of the woman you describe, who acted thus."

"You think so now, Harry," replied his mother.

"And ever will!" said the young man. "The mental agony I have suffered, during the last two days, wrings from me the avowal to you of a passion which, as you well know, is not one of yesterday, nor one I have lightly formed. On Rose, sweet, gentle girl! my heart is set, as firmly as ever heart of man was set on woman. I have no thought, no view, no hope, in life beyond her; and if you oppose me in this great stake, you take my peace and happiness in your hands, and cast them to the wind. Mother, think better of this, and of me, and do not disregard the warm feelings of which you seem to think so little."

"Harry," said Mrs. Maylie, "it is because I think so much of warm and sensitive hearts, that I would spare them from being wounded. But we have said enough, and more than enough, on this matter just now."

[...]

Oliver rose next morning, in better heart; and went about

1 **to cast s.th. in s.o.'s teeth:** jdm. etwas unter die Nase reiben. | 2 **sneers:** Spötteleien. | 3 **to repent of s.th.:** etwas bereuen. | 7 **selfish:** selbstsüchtig. | **brute:** Rohling. | **alike:** ebenso, gleicherweise. | 11 **to wring s.th. from s.o.:** jdm. etwas abnötigen. | 14 **to set one's heart on s.o.:** sein Herz an jdn. hängen. | 16 **great stake:** hehres Ansinnen. | 18 **to disregard:** geringschätzen. | 21 **sensitive:** empfindsam. | **to spare s.o. s.th.:** jdm. etwas ersparen. | 25 **(to be) in good heart:** guten Mutes sein.

his usual early occupations, with more hope and pleasure than he had known for many days. […]

He applied himself, with redoubled assiduity, to the instructions of the white-headed old gentleman: and laboured so hard that his quick progress surprised even himself. It was while he was engaged in this pursuit, that he was greatly startled and distressed by a most unexpected occurrence.

The little room in which he was accustomed to sit, when busy at his books, was on the ground-floor, at the back of the house. It was quite a cottage-room, with a lattice-window: […].

One beautiful evening, when the first shades of twilight were beginning to settle upon the earth, Oliver sat at this window, intent upon his books. He had been poring over them for some time; and as the day had been uncommonly sultry, and he had exerted himself a great deal; it is no disparagement to the authors: whoever they may have been: to say, that gradually and by slow degrees, he fell asleep.

There is a kind of sleep that steals upon us sometimes, which, while it holds the body prisoner, does not free the mind from a sense of things about it, and enable it to ramble at its pleasure. […]

Oliver knew, perfectly well, that he was in his own little room; that his books were lying on the table before him; and

3 f. **instruction:** Lektion, Unterweisung. | 4 **white-headed:** weißhaarig. | **to labour:** sich anstrengen, hart arbeiten. | 6 **pursuit:** Beschäftigung. | 7 **distressed:** erschüttert. | 8 **accustomed:** gewohnt. | 12 **twilight:** Dämmerung. | 14 **(to be) intent upon s.th.:** mit etwas eifrig beschäftigt sein. | **to pore over s.th.:** über etwas brüten. | 15 **sultry:** drückend, schwül. | 16 **to exert o.s.:** sich anstrengen. | **disparagement:** Verunglimpfung. | 20 **to hold s.o. prisoner:** jdn. gefangen halten. | 21 **sense:** Wahrnehmung, Empfindung. | **to ramble:** umherschweifen.

that the sweet air was stirring among the creeping plants outside. And yet he was asleep. Suddenly, the scene changed; the air became close and confined; and he thought, with a glow of terror, that he was in the Jew's house again. There sat the hideous old man, in his accustomed corner: pointing at him: and whispering to another man, with his face averted, who sat beside him.

"Hush, my dear!" he thought he heard the Jew say; "it is he, sure enough. Come away."

"He!" the other man seemed to answer; "could I mistake him, think you? If a crowd of devils were to put themselves into his exact shape, and he stood amongst them, there is something that would tell me how to point him out. If you buried him fifty feet deep, and took me across his grave, I should know, if there wasn't a mark above it, that he lay buried there. I should!"

The man seemed to say this, with such dreadful hatred, that Oliver awoke with the fear, and started up.

Good Heaven! what was that, which sent the blood tingling to his heart, and deprived him of his voice, and of power to move! There – there – at the window; close before him; so close, that he could have almost touched him before he started back: with his eyes peering into the room, and meeting his: there stood the Jew! And beside him, white with rage, or fear, or both, were the scowling features of the very man who had accosted him in the inn-yard.

It was but an instant, a glance, a flash, before his eyes; and they were gone. But they had recognised him, and he them;

1 **creeping plants:** Kletterpflanzen. | 3 **close:** stickig. | **confined:** drückend. | 3 f. **glow of terror:** kaltes Entsetzen. | 6 **to avert one's face:** das Gesicht abwenden. | 20 **to deprive s.o. of s.th.:** jdm. etwas rauben. | 25 **scowling:** finster dreinblickend.

and their look was as firmly impressed upon his memory, as if it had been deeply carved in stone, and set before him from his birth. He stood transfixed for a moment; and then, leaping from the window into the garden, called loudly for help.

Chapter XXXV

Containing the unsatisfactory result of Oliver's Adventure; and a Conversation of some importance between Harry Maylie and Rose

When the inmates of the house, attracted by Oliver's cries, hurried to the spot from which they proceeded, they found him, pale and agitated, pointing in the direction of the meadows behind the house, and scarcely able to articulate the words, "The Jew! the Jew!"

Mr. Giles was at a loss to comprehend what this outcry meant; but Harry Maylie, whose perceptions were something quicker, and who had heard Oliver's history from his mother, understood it at once.

"What direction did he take?" he asked, catching up a heavy stick which was standing in a corner.

"That," replied Oliver, pointing out the course the men had taken; "I missed them, in an instant."

"Then, they are in the ditch!" said Harry. "Follow! And keep as near me, as you can." So saying, he sprang over the hedge, and darted off with a speed which rendered it matter of exceeding difficulty for the others to keep near him.

[...]

2 **carved:** gemeißelt. | 3 **transfixed:** starr, versteinert. | 11 **agitated:** aufgeregt. | 14 **to be at a loss to do s.th.:** Schwierigkeiten haben, etwas zu tun. | 15 **perception:** Auffassungsgabe.

The search was all in vain. There were not even the traces of recent footsteps, to be seen. [...]

On the next day, further search was made, and the inquiries renewed; but with no better success. On the day following, Oliver and Mr. Maylie repaired to the market-town, in the hope of seeing or hearing something of the men there; but this effort was equally fruitless; and after a few days, the affair began to be forgotten, as most affairs are, when wonder, having no fresh food to support it, dies away of itself.

Meanwhile, Rose was rapidly recovering. She had left her room; was able to go out; and mixing once more with the family, carried joy into the hearts of all.

But although this happy change had a visible effect on the little circle; and although cheerful voices and merry laughter were once more heard in the cottage; there was, at times, an unwonted restraint upon some there: even upon Rose herself: which Oliver could not fail to remark. [...]

At length, one morning, when Rose was alone in the breakfast-parlour, Harry Maylie entered; and, with some hesitation, begged permission to speak with her for a few moments.

"A few: a very few: will suffice, Rose," said the young man, drawing his chair towards her. "What I shall have to say, has already presented itself to your mind; the most cherished hopes of my heart are not unknown to you, though from my lips you have not yet heard them stated."

[...] I give to you the heart so long your own, and stake my all upon the words with which you greet the offer."

2 **recent:** hier: frisch. | 3 **inquiries:** Nachforschungen. | 4 **renewed:** erneuert. | 7 **fruitless:** vergeblich, erfolglos. | 8 **wonder:** Verwunderung, Neugier. | 16 **restraint:** Zurückhaltung. | 21 **suffice:** genügen, ausreichen. | 23 **most cherished:** innigst gehegte(r, s). | 26 f. **to stake all upon s.th.:** alles auf etwas setzen. | 27 **to greet s.th.:** einer Sache begegnen, etwas aufnehmen.

"Your behaviour has ever been kind and noble," said Rose, mastering the emotions by which she was agitated. "As you believe that I am not insensible or ungrateful, so hear my answer."

"It is, that I may endeavour to deserve you; it is, dear Rose?"

"It is," replied Rose, "that you must endeavour to forget me; not as your old and dearly-attached companion, for that would wound me deeply: but, as the object of your love. Look into the world; think how many hearts you would be proud to gain, are there. Confide some other passion to me, if you will; I will be the truest, warmest, and most faithful friend you have."

[...]

"Another word, Rose," said Harry. "Your reason in your own words. From your own lips, let me hear it."

"The prospect before you," answered Rose, firmly, "is a brilliant one; all the honours to which great talents and powerful connections can help men in public life, are in store for you. But, those connections are proud; and I will neither mingle with such as hold in scorn the mother who gave me life; nor bring disgrace or failure on the son of her who has so well supplied that mother's place. In a word," said the young lady, turning away, as her temporary firmness forsook her, "there is a stain upon my name, which the world visits on innocent heads. I will carry it into no blood but my own; and the reproach shall rest alone on me."

"One word more, Rose. Dearest Rose! one more!" cried Harry, throwing himself before her. "If I had been less – less

3 **insensible:** gefühllos. | 10 **to confide s.th. to s.o.:** jdm. etwas gewähren, anvertrauen. | 13 **reason:** Beweggrund. | 17 **to be in store for s.o.:** jdn. erwarten, jdm. zur Verfügung stehen. | 20 **disgrace:** Schmach, Schande. | **failure:** Scheitern, Misserfolg. | 20 f. **to supply s.th.:** etwas ersetzen. | 22 **firmness:** Fassung, Festigkeit, Selbstbeherrschung. | **to forsake s.o.:** jdn. verlassen. | 24 f. **reproach:** Vorwurf; Schande.

fortunate, the world would call it; if some obscure and peaceful life had been my destiny; if I had been poor, sick, helpless; would you have turned from me then? Or has my probable advancement to riches and honour, given this scruple birth?"

[...]

"Then, if your lot had been differently cast," rejoined Rose; "if you had been even a little, but not so far, above me; if I could have been a help and comfort to you in any humble scene of peace and retirement, and not a blot and drawback in ambitious and distinguished crowds; I should have been spared this trial. I have every reason to be happy, very happy, now; but then, Harry, I own I should have been happier."

[...]

"I ask one promise," said Harry. "Once, and only once more, – say within a year, but it may be much sooner, – let me speak to you again on this subject, for the last time."

"Not to press me to alter my right determination," replied Rose, with a melancholy smile; "it will be useless."

"No," said Harry; "to hear you repeat it, if you will; finally repeat it. I will lay at your feet, whatever of station or fortune I may possess; and if you still adhere to your present resolution, will not seek, by word or act, to change it."

"Then let it be so," rejoined Rose; "it is but one pang the more, and by that time I may be enabled to bear it better."

1 **to be fortunate:** vom Glück begünstigt, erfolgreich sein. | **obscure:** unbedeutend, abgeschieden. | 3 f. **advancement:** (fig.) Aufstieg. | 4 **scruple:** Zweifel, Bedenken. | 6 **lot:** Los, Schicksal. | **to cast s.th.:** etwas formen, gestalten. | 9 **retirement:** Zurückgezogenheit. | **blot:** Schandfleck. | **drawback:** Hindernis. | 10 **distinguished:** vornehm. | 12 **to own:** zugeben. | 17 **determination:** Entscheidung. | 20 **fortune:** Reichtum. | 21 **to adhere to s.th.:** an etwas festhalten. | **present:** derzeitig, gegenwärtig. | **resolution:** Entschluss. | 22 **act:** Tat. | 23 **pang:** Schmerz.

She extended her hand again. But the young man caught her to his bosom; and imprinting one kiss on her beautiful forehead, hurried from the room.

Chapter XXXVI

Is a very short one, and may appear of no great importance in its place. But it should be read notwithstanding, as a Sequel to the last, and a Key to one that will follow when its time arrives

"And so you are resolved to be my travelling-companion this morning; eh?" said the doctor, as Harry Maylie joined him and Oliver at the breakfast-table. [...]

The post-chaise drove up to the door shortly afterwards; and Giles coming in for the luggage, the good doctor bustled out, to see it packed.

"Oliver," said Harry Maylie, in a low voice, "let me speak a word with you."

Oliver walked into the window-recess to which Mr. Maylie beckoned him; much surprised at the mixture of sadness and boisterous spirits, which his whole behaviour displayed.

"You can write well now?" said Harry, laying his hand upon his arm.

"I hope so, sir," replied Oliver.

"I shall not be at home again, perhaps for some time; I wish you would write to me – say once a fortnight: every alternate Monday: to the General Post Office in London. Will you?"

1 **to extend:** ausstrecken. | 7 **sequel:** Fortsetzung. | 13 f. **to bustle out:** geschäftig hinauseilen. | 18 **to beckon s.o. to s.th.:** jdn. zu etwas (herbei)winken. | 24 f. **every alternate Monday:** jeden zweiten Montag.

"Oh! certainly, sir; I shall be proud to do it," exclaimed Oliver, greatly delighted with the commission.

"I should like to know how – how my mother and Miss Maylie are," said the young man; "and you can fill up a sheet by telling me what walks you take, and what you talk about, and whether she – they, I mean, seem happy and quite well. You understand me?"

"Oh! quite, sir, quite," replied Oliver.

[...]

The doctor was in the chaise; Giles (who, it had been arranged, should be left behind) held the door open in his hand; and the women-servants were in the garden, looking on. Harry cast one slight glance at the latticed window, and jumped into the carriage.

[...]

And there was one looker-on, who remained with eyes fixed upon the spot where the carriage had disappeared, long after it was many miles away; for behind the white curtain which had shrouded her from view when Harry raised his eyes towards the window, sat Rose herself.

[...]

4 **sheet:** Bogen, Blatt (Papier).

Chapter XXXVII

In which the Reader may perceive a Contrast, not uncommon in Matrimonial Cases

Mr. Bumble sat in the workhouse parlour, with his eyes moodily fixed on the cheerless grate, whence, as it was summer time, no brighter gleam proceeded, than the reflection of certain sickly rays of the sun, which were sent back from its cold and shining surface. [...]

Nor was Mr. Bumble's gloom the only thing calculated to awaken a pleasing melancholy in the bosom of a spectator. There were not wanting other appearances, and those closely connected with his own person, which announced that a great change had taken place in the position of his affairs. The laced coat, and the cocked hat; where were they? He still wore knee-breeches, and dark cotton stockings on his nether limbs; but they were not *the* breeches. The coat was wide-skirted; and in that respect like *the* coat, but, oh, how different! The mighty cocked hat was replaced by a modest round one. Mr. Bumble was no longer a beadle.

There are some promotions in life, which, independent of the more substantial rewards they offer, acquire peculiar value and dignity from the coats and waistcoats connected with them. A field-marshal has his uniform; a bishop his silk apron; a counsellor his silk gown; a beadle his cocked hat. Strip the

3 **matrimonial:** ehelich. | 4 f. **moodily:** schlecht gelaunt, verdrossen. | 5 **grate:** Kaminrost. | **whence:** woher, von wo aus. | 7 **sickly:** trübe, matt. | 15 **nether limbs:** untere Gliedmaßen. | 16 **wide-skirted:** mit breiten Schößen. | 18 **modest:** bescheiden, schlicht. | 20 **promotion:** Beförderung. | 21 **more substantial reward:** höhere Entlohnung. | 23 **field-marshal:** Feldmarschall. | **apron:** Schurz. | 24 **counsellor:** Ratsherr. | **gown:** Robe. | **to strip:** entkleiden, entblößen.

bishop of his apron, or the beadle of his hat and lace; what are they? Men. Mere men. Dignity, and even holiness too, sometimes, are more questions of coat and waistcoat than some people imagine.

Mr. Bumble had married Mrs. Corney, and was master of the workhouse. Another beadle had come into power; and on him the cocked hat, gold-laced coat, and staff, had all three descended.

[...]

"I sold myself," said Mr. Bumble, pursuing the same train of reflection, "for six tea-spoons, a pair of sugar-tongs, and a milk-pot; with a small quantity of second-hand furniter, and twenty pound in money. I went very reasonable. Cheap, dirt cheap!"

"Cheap!" cried a shrill voice in Mr. Bumble's ear: "you would have been dear at any price; and dear enough I paid for you, Lord above knows that!"

Mr. Bumble turned, and encountered the face of his interesting consort, who, imperfectly comprehending the few words she had overheard of his complaint, had hazarded the foregoing remark at a venture.

"Mrs. Bumble, ma'am!" said Mr. Bumble, with sentimental sternness.

[...]

"Are you going to sit snoring there, all day?" inquired Mrs. Bumble.

2 **holiness:** Heiligkeit. | 6 **to come into power:** an die Macht kommen, in ein Amt eingesetzt werden. | 8 **to descend:** übergehen (Besitz). | 13 **reasonable:** (kosten)günstig. | **dirt cheap:** spottbillig. | 15 **dear:** teuer. | 17 f. **interesting consort:** reizende Gemahlin. | 18 **imperfectly:** unvollständig. | **to comprehend s.th.:** etwas verstehen. | 19 **complaint:** Klage, Beschwerde. | 19 f. **foregoing:** vorhergehend. | 20 **at a venture:** aufs Geratewohl. | 21 **sentimental:** gefühlsbetont. | 22 **sternness:** Strenge. | 24 **to snore:** schnarchen.

"I am going to sit here, as long as I think proper, ma'am," rejoined Mr. Bumble; "and although I was *not* snoring, I shall snore, gape, sneeze, laugh, or cry, as the humour strikes me; such being my prerogative."

"Your prerogative!" sneered Mrs. Bumble, with ineffable contempt.

"I said the word, ma'am," said Mr. Bumble. "The prerogative of a man is to command."

"And what's the prerogative of a woman, in the name of Goodness?" cried the relict of Mr. Corney, deceased.

"To obey, ma'am," thundered Mr. Bumble. "Your late unfort'nate husband should have taught it you; and then, perhaps, he might have been alive now. I wish he was, poor man!"

Mrs. Bumble, seeing at a glance, that the decisive moment had now arrived: and that a blow struck for the mastership on one side or other, must necessarily be final and conclusive: no sooner heard this allusion to the dead and gone, than she dropped into a chair; and with a loud scream that Mr. Bumble was a hard-hearted brute, fell into a paroxysm of tears.

But, tears were not the things to find their way to Mr. Bumble's soul; his heart was waterproof. Like washable beaver hats that improve with rain, his nerves were rendered stouter and more vigorous by showers of tears, which, being tokens of weakness, and so far tacit admissions of his own power,

1 **to think proper:** gut finden. | 3 **to gape:** gähnen. | **humour:** Laune, Stimmung. | **to strike s.o.:** jdm. in den Sinn kommen. | 4 **prerogative:** Vorrecht. | 5 **to sneer:** spötteln, höhnen. | **ineffable:** unsäglich. | 10 **relict:** Überbleibsel; hier: Witwe. | **deceased:** verstorben, selig. | 11 **late:** verstorben. | 11 f. **unfort'nate:** bedauernswert, unselig. | 14 **decisive:** entscheidend. | 16 **conclusive:** entscheidend. | 19 **paroxysm of tears:** Weinkrampf. | 21 **waterproof:** wasserdicht. | **washable:** waschecht. | **beaver hat:** Biberhut. | 24 **tacit:** unausgesprochen. | **admission:** Anerkennung.

pleased and exalted him. He eyed his good lady with looks of great satisfaction; and begged, in an encouraging manner, that she should cry her hardest: the exercise being looked upon, by the faculty, as strongly conducive to health.

"It opens the lungs, washes the countenance, exercises the eyes, and softens down the temper," said Mr. Bumble. "So, cry away."

[…]

Now, Mrs. Corney that was, had tried the tears, because they were less troublesome than a manual assault; but she was quite prepared to make trial of the latter mode of proceeding, as Mr. Bumble was not long in discovering.

The first proof he experienced of the fact, was conveyed in a hollow sound, immediately succeeded by the sudden flying off of his hat to the opposite end of the room. This preliminary proceeding laying bare his head, the expert lady, clasping him tightly round the throat with one hand, inflicted a shower of blows (dealt with singular vigour and dexterity) upon it with the other. This done, she created a little variety by scratching his face, and tearing his hair off; and having, by this time, inflicted as much punishment as she deemed necessary for the offence, she pushed him over a chair, which was luckily well situated for the purpose: and defied him to talk about his prerogative again, if he dared.

"Get up!" said Mrs. Bumble, in a voice of command. "And

1 **to exalt:** (fig.) erhöhen. | 4 **faculty:** Mediziner, Ärzte. | **conducive:** zuträglich, förderlich. | 10 **manual assault:** Handgreiflichkeiten. | 11 **mode of proceeding:** Vorgehensweise. | 13 **to convey s.th.:** etwas übermitteln, mitteilen. | 16 **expert:** sachkundig. | **to clasp s.o.:** jdn. umklammern. | 17 **to inflict:** zufügen, versetzen. | 18 **dexterity:** Geschicklichkeit. | 19 **variety:** Abwechslung. | 21 **to deem:** (für etwas) erachten, halten. | 23 **to defy:** herausfordern.

take yourself away from here, unless you want me to do something desperate."

Mr. Bumble rose with a very rueful countenance: wondering much what something desperate might be; and, picking up his hat, looked towards the door.

"Are you going?" demanded Mrs. Bumble.

"Certainly, my dear, certainly," rejoined Mr. Bumble, making a quicker motion towards the door. "I didn't intend to – I'm going, my dear! You are so very violent, that really I –"

At this instant, Mrs. Bumble stepped hastily forward to replace the carpet, which had been kicked up in the scuffle. Mr. Bumble immediately darted out of the room, without bestowing another thought on his unfinished sentence: leaving the late Mrs. Corney in full possession of the field.

[...]

It was too much. Mr. Bumble boxed the ears of the boy who opened the gate for him (for he had reached the portal in his reverie); and walked, distractedly, into the street.

He walked up one street, and down another, until exercise had abated the first passion of his grief; and then the revulsion of feeling made him thirsty. He passed a great many public-houses; and at length paused before one in a by-way, whose parlour, as he gathered from a hasty peep over the blinds, was deserted, save by one solitary customer. It began to rain, heavily, at the moment. This determined him. Mr. Bumble stepped in; and ordering something to drink, as he passed the bar, entered the apartment into which he had looked from the street.

The man who was seated there, was tall and dark: and wore a

10 f. **to replace:** zurechtrücken. | 11 **scuffle:** Rauferei, Handgemenge. |
14 **late:** ehemalig. | 16 **to box s.o.'s ears:** jdn. ohrfeigen. |
20 **to abate:** mäßigen, mindern. | **revulsion:** Umschwung. |
22 **by-way:** Nebenstraße. | 23 **blind:** Vorhang; hier: Halbgardine. |
24 **deserted:** verlassen, menschenleer. | **customer:** Gast, Kunde.

large cloak. He had the air of a stranger; and seemed, by a certain haggardness in his look, as well as by the dusty soils on his dress, to have travelled some distance. He eyed Bumble askance, as he entered [...].

"I have seen you before, I think?" said he. "You were differently dressed at that time, and I only passed you in the street, but I should know you again. You were beadle here, once; were you not?"

"I was," said Mr. Bumble, in some surprise; "porochial beadle."

"Just so," rejoined the other, nodding his head. "It was in that character I saw you. What are you now?"

"Master of the workhouse," rejoined Mr. Bumble, slowly and impressively, to check any undue familiarity the stranger might otherwise assume. "Master of the workhouse, young man!"

"You have the same eye to your own interest, that you always had, I doubt not?" resumed the stranger, looking keenly into Mr. Bumble's eyes, as he raised them in astonishment at the question. "Don't scruple to answer freely, man. I know you pretty well, you see."

"I suppose, a married man," replied Mr. Bumble, shading his eyes with his hand, and surveying the stranger, from head to foot, in evident perplexity, "is not more averse to turning an honest penny when he can, than a single one. Porochial officers are not so well paid that they can afford to refuse any little extra fee, when it comes to them in a civil and proper manner."

[...]

2 **haggardness:** Abgezehrtheit. | **soil:** Verschmutzung. | 4 **askance:** von der Seite. | 12 **character:** Eigenschaft, Funktion. | 14 **undue:** ungebührlich, unangemessen. | **familiarity:** Vertraulichkeit. | 19 **to scruple:** Bedenken haben. | 23 **to be averse to doing s.th.:** abgeneigt sein, etwas zu tun. | 23 f. **to turn an honest penny:** sein Geld redlich verdienen. | 26 **fee:** Entgelt, Verdienst.

"Now listen to me," said the stranger, after closing the door and window. "I came down to this place, to-day, to find you out; and, by one of those chances which the devil throws in the way of his friends sometimes, you walked into the very room I was sitting in, while you were uppermost in my mind. I want some information from you. I don't ask you to give it for nothing, slight as it is. Put up that, to begin with."

As he spoke, he pushed a couple of sovereigns across the table to his companion; carefully, as though unwilling that the chinking of money should be heard without. When Mr. Bumble had scrupulously examined the coins, to see that they were genuine: and had put them up, with much satisfaction, in his waistcoat-pocket: he went on:

"Carry your memory back – let me see – twelve years, last winter."

"It's a long time," said Mr. Bumble. "Very good. I've done it."

"The scene, the workhouse."

"Good!"

"And the time, night."

"Yes."

"And the place, the crazy hole, wherever it was, in which miserable drabs brought forth the life and health so often denied to themselves; gave birth to puling children for the parish to rear; and hid their shame, rot 'em, in the grave!"

"The lying-in room, I suppose?" said Mr. Bumble, not quite following the stranger's excited description.

5 **to be uppermost in s.o.'s mind:** jdn. sehr beschäftigen (in Gedanken). | 7 **to put up s.th.:** etwas einstecken. | 10 **chinking:** Geklimper. | 23 **to bring forth s.th.:** etwas gebären, hervorbringen. | 23 f. **to deny:** verweigern. | 24 **puling:** wimmernd. | 25 **to rear s.o.:** jdn. großziehen. | 26 **lying-in room:** Zimmer für Wöchnerinnen.

"Yes," said the stranger. "A boy was born there."

"A many boys," observed Mr. Bumble, shaking his head, despondingly.

"A murrain on the young devils!" cried the stranger, "I speak of one; a meek-looking, pale-faced hound, who was apprenticed down here, to a coffin-maker: I wish he had made his coffin, and screwed his body in it: and who afterwards ran away to London, as it was supposed."

"Why, you mean Oliver! Young Twist!" said Mr. Bumble; "I remember him, of course. There wasn't a obstinater young rascal –"

"It's not of him I want to hear; I've heard enough of him," said the stranger, stopping Mr. Bumble in the very outset of a tirade on the subject of poor Oliver's vices. "It's of a woman; the hag that nursed his mother. Where is she?"

"Where is she?" said Mr. Bumble, whom the gin-and-water had rendered facetious. "It would be hard to tell. There's no midwifery there, whichever place she's gone to; so I suppose she's out of employment any way."

"What do you mean?" demanded the stranger, sternly.

"That she died last winter," rejoined Mr. Bumble.

[...]

Mr. Bumble was cunning enough; and he at once saw that an opportunity was opened, for the lucrative disposal of some secret in the possession of his better half. He well remembered the night of old Sally's death, which the occurrences of that day had given him good reason to recollect, as the occasion on

2 f. **despondingly:** verzagt. | 4 **murrain:** Pest. | 5 **meek-looking:** etwa: schwächlich. | 10 **obstinate:** widerborstig. | 13 **outset:** Beginn. | 14 **tirade:** Wortschwall, Schimpftirade. | 15 **hag:** Vettel, altes Weib, Hexe. | 18 **midwifery:** Hebammenkunst, Geburtshilfe. | 24 **lucrative:** einträglich, lohnend. | **disposal:** Verkauf, Veräußerung.

which he had proposed to Mrs. Corney; and although that lady had never confided to him the disclosure of which she had been the solitary witness, he had heard enough to know that it related to something that had occurred in the old woman's attendance, as workhouse nurse, upon the young mother of Oliver Twist. Hastily calling this circumstance to mind, he informed the stranger, with an air of mystery, that one woman had been closeted with the old harridan shortly before she died; and that she could, as he had reason to believe, throw some light on the subject of his inquiry.

"How can I find her?" said the stranger [...].

"Only through me," rejoined Mr. Bumble.

"When?" cried the stranger, hastily.

"To-morrow," rejoined Bumble.

"At nine in the evening," said the stranger, producing a scrap of paper, and writing down upon it, an obscure address by the waterside, in characters that betrayed his agitation; "at nine in the evening, bring her to me there. I needn't tell you to be secret. It's your interest."

With these words, he led the way to the door: after stopping to pay for the liquor that had been drunk; and shortly remarking that their roads were different, departed, without more ceremony than an emphatic repetition of the hour of appointment for the following night.

On glancing at the address, the parochial functionary observed that it contained no name. The stranger had not gone far, so he made after him to ask it.

1 **to propose to s.o.:** jdm. einen Heiratsantrag machen. | 2 **disclosure:** (fig.) Enthüllung. | 16 **obscure:** anrüchig, zweifelhaft. | 17 **to betray s.th.:** etwas verraten, etwas erkennen lassen. | 18 f. **to be secret:** verschwiegen sein. | 25 **parochial functionary:** Gemeindediener.

"Who's that?" cried the man, turning quickly round, as Bumble touched him on the arm. "Following me!"

"Only to ask a question," said the other, pointing to the scrap of paper. "What name am I to ask for?"

"Monks!" rejoined the man; and strode, hastily, away.

Chapter XXXVIII

Containing an Account of what passed between Mr. and Mrs. Bumble, and Monks, at their nocturnal Interview

It was a dull, close, overcast summer evening: the clouds, which had been threatening all day, spread out in a dense and sluggish mass of vapour, already yielded large drops of rain, and seemed to presage a violent thunder-storm: when Mr. and Mrs. Bumble, turning out of the main street of the town, directed their course towards a scattered little colony of ruinous houses, distant from it some mile and a half, or thereabouts, and erected on a low unwholesome swamp, bordering upon the river.

They were both wrapped in old and shabby outer garments, which might, perhaps, serve the double purpose of protecting their persons from the rain, and sheltering them from observation. The husband carried a lantern, from which, however, no light yet shone; [...].

5 **to stride away:** davonschreiten. | 8 **nocturnal:** nächtlich. | 9 **overcast:** bewölkt, bedeckt. | 10 **dense:** dicht. | 11 **sluggish:** träge. | **vapour:** Dampf, Dunst. | **to yield s.th.:** etwas hervorbringen. | 12 **to presage:** ankündigen. | 14 **colony:** Siedlung. | 15 **thereabouts:** ungefähr. | 16 **to erect s.th.:** etwas errichten, erbauen. | **unwholesome:** ungesund. | **swamp:** Sumpf. | **to border upon s.th.:** an etwas grenzen. | 18 **shabby:** schäbig, abgetragen. | **outer garment:** Obergewand.

It was before this ruinous building that the worthy couple paused, as the first peal of distant thunder reverberated in the air, and the rain commenced pouring violently down.

"The place should be somewhere here," said Bumble, consulting a scrap of paper he held in his hand.

[...]

Mr. Bumble, who had eyed the building with very rueful looks, was apparently about to express some doubts relative to the advisability of proceeding any farther with the enterprise just then, when he was prevented by the appearance of Monks: who opened a small door, near which they stood, and beckoned them inwards:

"Come!" he cried impatiently, stamping his foot upon the ground. "Don't keep me here!"

The woman, who had hesitated at first, walked boldly in, without any further invitation. Mr. Bumble, who was ashamed or afraid to lag behind, followed: [...].

Bestowing something half-way between a smile and a scowl upon his two companions, and again beckoning them to follow him, the man hastened across the apartment, which was of considerable extent, but low in the roof. He was preparing to ascend a steep staircase, or rather ladder, leading to another floor of warehouses above: when a bright flash of lightning streamed down the aperture, and a peal of thunder followed, which shook the crazy building to its centre.

"Hear it!" he cried, shrinking back. "Hear it! Rolling and crashing on as if it echoed through a thousand caverns where the devils were hiding from it. I hate the sound!"

2 **peal of thunder:** Donnerschlag. | **to reverberate:** widerhallen. | 4 f. **to consult:** zurate ziehen. | 9 **advisability:** Ratsamkeit. | **enterprise:** Unternehmung. | 23 **warehouse:** Lagerraum, Speicher. | 25 **crazy:** baufällig. | 26 **to shrink back:** erschaudern. | **to roll:** grollen (Donner). | 27 **cavern:** Höhle.

He remained silent for a few moments; and then, removing his hands suddenly from his face, showed, to the unspeakable discomposure of Mr. Bumble, that it was much distorted, and discoloured.

"These fits come over me, now and then," said Monks, observing his alarm; "and thunder sometimes brings them on. Don't mind me now; it's all over for this once."

Thus speaking, he led the way up the ladder; and hastily closing the window-shutter of the room into which it led, lowered a lantern which hung at the end of a rope and pulley passed through one of the heavy beams in the ceiling: and which cast a dim light upon an old table and three chairs that were placed beneath it.

"Now," said Monks, when they had all three seated themselves, "the sooner we come to our business, the better for all. The woman knows what it is; does she?"

The question was addressed to Bumble; but his wife anticipated the reply, by intimating that she was perfectly acquainted with it.

"He is right in saying that you were with this hag the night she died; and that she told you something –"

"About the mother of the boy you named," replied the matron interrupting him. "Yes."

"The first question is, of what nature was her communication?" said Monks.

"That's the second," observed the woman with much deliberation. "The first is, what may the communication be worth?"

[…]

2 **unspeakable:** unsäglich. | 3 **discomposure:** Beunruhigung, Fassungslosigkeit. | **distorted:** verzerrt. | 4 **discoloured:** kreideweiß. | 10 **pulley:** Flaschenzug, Rolle. | 11 **beam:** Deckenbalken. | 17 f. **to anticipate:** vorwegnehmen. | 24 f. **communication:** Mitteilung.

"It may be nothing; it may be twenty pounds," replied Monks. "Speak out, and let me know which."

"Add five pounds to the sum you have named; give me five-and-twenty pounds in gold," said the woman; "and I'll tell you all I know. Not before."

[…]

He thrust his hand into a side-pocket; and producing a canvas bag, told out twenty-five sovereigns on the table, and pushed them over to the woman.

[…]

"When this woman, that we called old Sally, died," the matron began, "she and I were alone."

"Was there no one by!" asked Monks, in the same hollow whisper; "no sick wretch or idiot in some other bed? No one who could hear, and might, by possibility, understand?"

"Not a soul," replied the woman; "we were alone. *I* stood alone beside the body when death came over it."

"Good," said Monks, regarding her attentively. "Go on."

"She spoke of a young creature," resumed the matron, "who had brought a child into the world some years before; not merely in the same room; but in the same bed in which she then lay dying."

"Aye?" said Monks, with quivering lip, and glancing over his shoulder. "Blood! How things come about!"

"The child was the one you named to him last night," said the matron, nodding carelessly towards her husband; "the mother this nurse had robbed."

"In life?" asked Monks.

"In death," replied the woman, with something like a shud-

7f. **canvas:** Leinwand, Segeltuch. | 14 **wretch:** sieche, kranke Person. | **idiot:** Wahnsinnige(r). | 23 **quivering:** bebend, zitternd. | 24 **blood!:** hol's der Teufel!

der. "She stole from the corpse, when it had hardly turned to one, that which the dead mother had prayed her, with her last breath, to keep for the infant's sake."

"She sold it?" cried Monks, with desperate eagerness; "did she sell it? Where? When? To whom? How long before?"

"As she told me, with great difficulty, that she had done this," said the matron; "she fell back and died."

"Without saying more?" cried Monks, in a voice which, from its very suppression, seemed only the more furious. "It's a lie! I'll not be played with. She said more. I'll tear the life out of you both, but I'll know what it was."

"She didn't utter another word," said the woman, to all appearance unmoved (as Mr. Bumble was very far from being) by the strange man's violence; "but she clutched my gown, violently, with one hand, which was partly closed; and when I saw that she was dead, and so removed the hand by force, I found it clasped a scrap of dirty paper."

"Which contained –" interposed Monks, stretching forward.

"Nothing," replied the woman; "it was a pawnbroker's duplicate."

"For what?" demanded Monks.

"In good time I'll tell you," said the woman. "I judge that she had kept the trinket, for some time, in the hope of turning it to better account; and then, had pawned it; and had saved or scraped together, money to pay the pawnbroker's interest year by year, and prevent its running out; so that if anything came

9 **suppression:** Unterdrückung, Dämpfung. | 20 f. **pawnbroker's duplicate:** Pfandschein. | 23 **in good time:** beizeiten, rechtzeitig. | 24 **trinket:** Schmuck. | 24 f. **to turn s.th. to account:** etwas verwerten, losschlagen. | 25 **to pawn:** verpfänden. | 26 **to scrape s.th. together:** etwas zusammenkratzen. | **pawnbroker:** Pfandleiher.

of it, it could still be redeemed. Nothing had come of it; and, as I tell you, she died with the scrap of paper, all worn and tattered, in her hand. The time was out in two days; I thought something might one day come of it too; and so I redeemed the pledge."

"Where is it now?" asked Monks quickly.

"*There,*" replied the woman. And, as if glad to be relieved of it, she hastily threw upon the table, a small kid bag scarcely large enough for a French watch, which Monks pouncing upon, tore open with trembling hands. It contained a little gold locket: in which were two locks of hair, and a plain gold wedding-ring.

[...]

"Is that what you expected to get from me?" demanded the matron.

"It is," replied Monks. [...]

"What you propose to do with it? Can it be used against me?"

"Never," rejoined Monks; "nor against me either. See here! But don't move a step forward, or your life's not worth a bulrush!"

With these words, he suddenly wheeled the table aside, and pulling an iron ring in the boarding, threw back a large trap-door, which opened close at Mr. Bumble's feet, and caused that gentleman to retire several paces backward, with great precipitation.

"Look down," said Monks, lowering the lantern into the

1 **to redeem s.th.:** etwas auslösen. | 2 f. **tattered:** zerschlissen. | 5 **pledge:** Pfandstück. | 8 **kid:** Ziegenleder. | 9 f. **to pounce upon s.th.:** sich auf etwas stürzen. | 11 **locket:** Medaillon. | 20 f. **not to be worth a bulrush:** keinen Pfifferling wert sein. | 22 **to wheel:** schieben. | 23 **boarding:** Dielenbelag. | 23 f. **trap-door:** Falltür. | 25 f. **precipitation:** Eile, Hast.

gulf. “Don't fear me. I could have let you down, quietly enough, when you were seated over it, if that had been my game.”

[…] There had once been a water mill beneath; and the tide, and foaming and chafing round the few rotten stakes, and fragments of machinery that yet remained, seemed to dart onward, with a new impulse, when freed from the obstacles which had unavailingly attempted to stem its headlong course.

“If you flung a man's body down there, where would it be to-morrow morning?” said Monks, swinging the lantern to and fro in the dark well.

“Twelve miles down the river, and cut to pieces besides,” replied Bumble, recoiling at the very thought.

Monks drew the little packet from his breast, where he had hurriedly thrust it; and tying it to a leaden weight, which had formed a part of some pulley, and was lying on the floor, dropped it into the stream. It fell straight, and true as a die; clove the water with a scarcely audible splash; and was gone.

[…]

1 **gulf:** Abgrund, Schacht. | 4 **to chafe:** tosen. | **stake:** Pfahl. | 5 **machinery:** Maschinerie, Mechanismus. | 6 **impulse:** Antrieb. | **obstacle:** Hindernis. | 7 **unavailingly:** vergeblich. | **to stem s.th.:** etwas aufhalten. | **headlong:** ungestüm. | **course:** Lauf, Bahn. | 10 **well:** Schacht. | 14 **leaden:** bleiern. | 17 **clove:** Prät. von *to cleave:* spalten, teilen.

Chapter XXXIX

Introduces some respectable Characters with whom the Reader is already acquainted, and shews how Monks and the Jew laid their worthy Heads together

On the evening following that upon which the three worthies mentioned in the last chapter, disposed of their little matter of business as therein narrated, Mr. William Sikes, awakening from a nap, drowsily growled forth an inquiry what time of night it was.

The room in which Mr. Sikes propounded this question, was not one of those he had tenanted, previous to the Chertsey expedition, although it was in the same quarter of the town, and was situated at no great distance from his former lodgings. It was not, in appearance, so desirable a habitation as his old quarters: being a mean and badly-furnished apartment, of very limited size: lighted only by one small window in the shelving roof, and abutting on a close and dirty lane. [...]

The housebreaker was lying on the bed, wrapped in his white great-coat, by way of dressing-gown, and displaying a set of features in no degree improved by the cadaverous hue of illness, and the addition of a soiled nightcap, and a stiff, black beard of a week's growth. The dog sat at the bedside: now eyeing his master with a wistful look, and now pricking

5 **worthy:** treffliche Person. | 7 **to narrate:** erzählen, schildern. | 11 **to tenant:** bewohnen. | 14 **habitation:** Wohnstätte, Wohnung. | 15 **quarters** (pl.): Quartier, Unterkunft. | **mean:** armselig. | **furnished:** eingerichtet, möbliert. | 16 f. **shelving roof:** Dachschräge. | 17 **to abut on s.th.:** an etwas grenzen, stoßen. | 19 **by way of dressing-gown:** anstelle eines Schlafrocks. | 20 **cadaverous:** leichenblass. | 23 **wistful:** schwermütig, versonnen, wehmütig. | 23 f. **to prick one's ears:** die Ohren spitzen.

his ears, and uttering a low growl as some noise in the street, or in the lower part of the house, attracted his attention. Seated by the window, busily engaged in patching an old waistcoat which formed a portion of the robber's ordinary dress, was a female: so pale and reduced with watching and privation, that there would have been considerable difficulty in recognising her as the same Nancy who has already figured in this tale, but for the voice in which she replied to Mr. Sikes's question.

"Not long gone seven," said the girl. "How do you feel tonight, Bill?"

"As weak as water," replied Mr. Sikes, with an imprecation on his eyes and limbs. "Here; lend us a hand; and let me get off this thundering bed, anyhow."

Illness had not improved Mr. Sikes's temper; for, as the girl raised him up, and led him to a chair, he muttered various curses on her awkwardness: and struck her.

[...]

At any other time, this remonstrance, and the tone in which it was delivered, would have had the desired effect; but the girl being really weak and exhausted, dropped her head over the back of the chair, and fainted, before Mr. Sikes could get out a few of the appropriate oaths with which, on similar occasions, he was accustomed to garnish his threats. Not knowing, very well, what to do, in this uncommon emergency; for Miss Nancy's hysterics were usually of that violent kind which the patient fights and struggles out of, without much assistance;

3 **to patch:** flicken, ausbessern. | 4 **portion:** Bestandteil. | 5 **reduced:** abgezehrt. | **watching:** Wachen. | 5 f. **privation:** Entbehrung. | 8 **tale:** Geschichte, Erzählung. | 13 **to lend s.o. a hand:** jdm. helfen. | 15 **temper:** Naturell, Gemütsart. | 17 **awkwardness:** Ungeschicklichkeit. | 19 **remonstrance:** Zurechtweisung. | 24 **threat:** Drohung. | 26 **hysterics** (pl.): hysterischer Anfall.

Mr. Sikes tried a little blasphemy: and finding that mode of treatment wholly ineffectual, called for assistance.

"What's the matter here, my dear?" said the Jew, looking in.

"Lend a hand to the girl, can't you?" replied Sikes impatiently. "Don't stand chattering and grinning at me!"

With an exclamation of surprise, Fagin hastened to the girl's assistance, while Mr. John Dawkins (otherwise the Artful Dodger), who had followed his venerable friend into the room, hastily deposited on the floor a bundle with which he was laden; and snatching a bottle from the grasp of Master Charles Bates who came close at his heels, uncorked it in a twinkling with his teeth, and poured a portion of its contents down the patient's throat: previously taking a taste, himself, to prevent mistakes.

[...] The girl gradually recovered her senses; and, staggering to a chair by the bedside, hid her face upon the pillow: leaving Mr. Sikes to confront the new-comers, in some astonishment at their unlooked-for appearance.

"Why, what evil wind has blowed you here?" he asked of Fagin.

"No evil wind at all, my dear," replied the Jew; "for evil winds blow nobody any good; and I've brought something good with me, that you'll be glad to see. Dodger, my dear, open the bundle; and give Bill the little trifles that we spent all our money on, this morning."

In compliance with Mr. Fagin's request, the Artful untied his

1 **blasphemy:** gotteslästerliche Flüche. | 2 **ineffectual:** wirkungslos. | 6 **to chatter:** schwatzen. | 9 **venerable:** ehrbar. | 18 **to confront s.o.:** jdm. entgegentreten. | 19 **unlooked-for:** unerwartet. | 25 **trifles:** Kleinigkeiten. | 27 **in compliance with:** entsprechend, gemäß. | **request:** Bitte, Aufforderung. | **to untie:** aufschnüren.

bundle, which was of large size, and formed of an old table-cloth; and handed the articles it contained, one by one, to Charley Bates: who placed them on the table […].

"Ah!" said the Jew, rubbing his hands with great satisfaction. "You'll do, Bill; you'll do now."

"Do!" exclaimed Mr. Sikes; "I might have been done for, twenty times over, afore you'd have done anything to help me. What do you mean by leaving a man in this state, three weeks and more, you false-hearted wagabond?"

"Only hear him, boys!" said the Jew, shrugging his shoulders. "And us come to bring him all these beau-ti-ful things."

[…]

"It's all very well," said Mr. Sikes; "but I must have some blunt from you to-night."

"I haven't a piece of coin about me," replied the Jew.

"Then you've got lots at home," retorted Sikes; "and I must have some from there."

[…]

"Well, well!" said the Jew, with a sigh, "I'll send the Artful round presently."

"You won't do nothing of the kind," rejoined Mr. Sikes. "The Artful's a deal too artful, and would forget to come, or lose his way, or get dodged by traps and so be perwented, or anything for an excuse, if you put him up to it. Nancy shall go to the ken and fetch it, to make all sure; and I'll lie down and have a snooze while she's gone."

[…]

5 **you'll do:** du wirst schon wieder. | 6 **to be done for:** (fig.) erledigt sein. | 10 f. **to shrug one's shoulders:** mit den Achseln zucken. | 15 **blunt:** Moneten. | 24 **to get dodged:** erwischt werden. | **perwented:** *prevented.* | 25 **to put s.o. up to s.th.:** jdm. etwas einflüstern. | 26 **ken:** Bude. | 27 **snooze:** Nickerchen, Schläfchen.

In due course, they arrived at the Jew's abode, where they found Toby Crackit and Mr. Chitling intent upon their fifteenth game at cribbage, which it is scarcely necessary to say the latter gentleman lost; and with it, his fifteenth and last sixpence: much to the amusement of his young friends. [...]

"Now," said the Jew, when they had left the room, "I'll go and get you that cash, Nancy. This is only the key of a little cupboard where I keep a few odd things the boys get, my dear. I never lock up my money, for I've got none to lock up, my dear – ha! ha! ha! – none to lock up. It's a poor trade, Nancy, and no thanks; but I'm fond of seeing the young people about me; and I bear it all; I bear it all. Hush!" he said, hastily concealing the key in his breast; "who's that? Listen!"

[...]

Laying his skinny forefinger upon his lip, the Jew carried a candle to the door, as a man's step was heard upon the stairs without. He reached it, at the same moment as the visitor, who, coming hastily into the room, was close upon the girl before he observed her.

It was Monks.

"Only one of my young people," said the Jew, observing that Monks drew back, on beholding a stranger. [...]

The girl drew closer to the table, and made no offer to leave the room, although she could see that Monks was pointing to her. The Jew: perhaps fearing she might say something aloud about the money, if he endeavoured to get rid of her: pointed upwards, and took Monks out of the room.

"Not that infernal hole we were in before," she could hear the man say as they went up stairs. The Jew laughed; and mak-

1 **in due course:** zu gegebener Zeit. | 3 **cribbage:** Cribbage (Kartenspiel). | 22 **to draw back:** zurückweichen. | 26 **to get rid of s.o.:** jdn. loswerden. | 28 **infernal:** höllisch.

ing some reply which did not reach her, seemed, by the creaking of the boards, to lead his companion to the second story.

Before the sound of their footsteps had ceased to echo through the house, the girl had slipped off her shoes; and drawing her gown loosely over her head, and muffling her arms in it, stood at the door, listening with breathless interest. The moment the noise ceased, she glided from the room; ascended the stairs with incredible softness and silence; and was lost in the gloom above.

The room remained deserted for a quarter of an hour or more; the girl glided back with the same unearthly tread; and, immediately afterwards, the two men were heard descending. Monks went at once into the street; and the Jew crawled up stairs again for the money. When he returned, the girl was adjusting her shawl and bonnet, as if preparing to be gone.

"Why, Nance," exclaimed the Jew, starting back as he put down the candle, "how pale you are!"

"Pale!" echoed the girl, shading her eyes with her hand, as if to look steadily at him.

"Quite horrible," said the Jew. "What have you been doing to yourself?"

"Nothing that I know of, except sitting in this close place for I don't know how long and all," replied the girl carelessly. "Come! Let me get back; that's a dear."

With a sigh for every piece of money, Fagin told the amount into her hand. They parted without more conversation, merely interchanging a "good night."

[...]

2 **boards:** Dielen. | 3 **to cease:** aufhören. | 8 **incredible:** unglaublich. | 9 **gloom:** Finsternis, Dunkelheit. | 11 **unearthly:** unheimlich, gespenstisch. | **tread:** Tritt, Schritt. | 13 **to crawl:** kriechen. | 23 **carelessly:** unbekümmert, beiläufig. | 24 **that's a dear:** sei so gut. | 25 **to tell:** (ab)zählen. | 27 **to interchange:** austauschen.

Mr. Sikes, being weak from the fever, was lying in bed, taking hot water with his gin to render it less inflammatory; and had pushed his glass towards Nancy to be replenished for the third or fourth time, when these symptoms first struck him.

[...] Sikes drained the glass to the bottom, and then, with many grumbling oaths, called for his physic. The girl jumped up, with great alacrity; poured it quickly out, but with her back towards him; and held the vessel to his lips, while he drank off the contents.

[...] The grasp of his hand relaxed; the upraised arm fell languidly by his side; and he lay like one in a profound trance.

"The laudanum has taken effect at last," murmured the girl, as she rose from the bedside. "I may be too late, even now."

She hastily dressed herself in her bonnet and shawl: looking fearfully round, from time to time, as if, despite the sleeping draught, she expected every moment to feel the pressure of Sikes's heavy hand upon her shoulder; then, stooping softly over the bed, she kissed the robber's lips; and then, opening and closing the room-door with noiseless touch, hurried from the house.

[...]

When she reached the more wealthy quarter of the town, the streets were comparatively deserted; [...] and when she neared her place of destination, she was alone.

It was a family hotel in a quiet but handsome street near

2 **inflammatory:** erhitzend. | 3 **to replenish s.th.:** etwas wiederauffüllen. | 6 **grumbling:** mürrisch. | **to call for s.th.:** nach etwas verlangen. | **physic:** Medizin, Arznei. | 7 **alacrity:** Eilfertigkeit. | **to pour s.th. out:** etwas einschenken. | 8 **vessel:** Gefäß. | 11 **trance:** Bewusstlosigkeit. | 12 **laudanum:** Opiumtinktur. | 16 f. **sleeping draught:** Schlaftrunk. | 24 **comparatively:** vergleichsweise, verhältnismäßig. | 26 **family hotel:** Privatpension.

Hyde Park. [...] The porter's seat was vacant. She looked round with an air of incertitude, and advanced towards the stairs.

"Now, young woman!" said a smartly-dressed female, looking out from a door behind her, "who do you want here?"

"A lady who is stopping in this house," answered the girl.

"A lady!" was the reply, accompanied with a scornful look. "What lady?"

"Miss Maylie," said Nancy.

The young woman, who had, by this time, noted her appearance, replied only by a look of virtuous disdain; and summoned a man to answer her. To him, Nancy repeated her request.

[...]

The man ran up stairs. Nancy remained, pale and almost breathless, listening with quivering lip to the very audible expressions of scorn, of which the chaste housemaids were very prolific; and of which they became still more so, when the man returned, and said the young woman was to walk up stairs.

[...] Nancy followed the man with trembling limbs, to a small antechamber, lighted by a lamp from the ceiling. Here he left her, and retired.

1 **porter:** Portier, Pförtner. | **vacant:** leer, nicht besetzt. | 2 **incertitude:** Unsicherheit. | 5 **to stop:** logieren. | 10 **virtuous:** tugendhaft. | 10 f. **to summon s.o.:** jdn. herbeirufen. | 17 **to be prolific of s.th.:** reichlich über etwas verfügen. | 20 **antechamber:** Vorzimmer.

Chapter XL

A strange Interview, which is a Sequel to the last Chapter

The girl's life had been squandered in the streets, and among the most noisome of the stews and dens of London, but there was something of the woman's original nature left in her still; and when she heard a light step approaching the door opposite to that by which she had entered, and thought of the wide contrast which the small room would in another moment contain, she felt burdened with the sense of her own deep shame: and shrunk as though she could scarcely bear the presence of her with whom she had sought this interview.

[…]

She raised her eyes sufficiently to observe that the figure which presented itself was that of a slight and beautiful girl; […].

"Sit down," said Rose earnestly; "you distress me. If you are in poverty or affliction I shall be truly glad to relieve you if I can, – I shall indeed. Sit down."

"Let me stand, lady," said the girl, still weeping, "and do not speak to me so kindly till you know me better. It is growing late. Is – is – that door shut?"

"Yes," said Rose, recoiling a few steps, as if to be nearer assistance in case she should require it. "Why?"

"Because," said the girl, "I am about to put my life, and the lives of others, in your hands. I am the girl that dragged little Oliver back to old Fagin's, the Jew's, on the night he went out from the house in Pentonville."

3 **to squander:** vergeuden, verschwenden. | 4 **noisome:** übel, schädlich. | **stew:** Bordell. | 9 **burdened:** belastet. | 14 **slight:** schlank, zart. | 17 **affliction:** Bedrängnis, Not.

"You!" said Rose Maylie.

"I, lady!" replied the girl. "I am the infamous creature you have heard of, that lives among the thieves, and that never from the first moment I can recollect my eyes and senses opening on London streets have known any better life, or kinder words than they have given me, so help me God! Do not mind shrinking openly from me, lady. I am younger than you would think, to look at me, but I am well used to it. The poorest women fall back, as I make my way along the crowded pavement."

[...]

"I pity you!" said Rose, in a broken voice. "It wrings my heart to hear you!"

"Heaven bless you for your goodness!" rejoined the girl. "If you knew what I am sometimes, you would pity me, indeed. But I have stolen away from those who would surely murder me, if they knew I had been here, to tell you what I have overheard. Do you know a man named Monks?"

"No," said Rose.

"He knows you," replied the girl; "and knew you were here, for it was by hearing him tell the place that I found you out."

"I never heard the name," said Rose.

"Then he goes by some other amongst us," rejoined the girl, "which I more than thought before. Some time ago, and soon after Oliver was put into your house on the night of the robbery, I – suspecting this man – listened to a conversation held between him and Fagin in the dark. I found out, from what I heard, that Monks – the man I asked you about, you know –"

"Yes," said Rose, "I understand."

"– That Monks," pursued the girl, "had seen him accidental-

2 **infamous:** schändlich. | 9 **to fall back:** zurückweichen. | 11 f. **to wring s.o.'s heart:** jdm. sehr zu Herzen gehen. | 16 f. **to overhear:** belauschen. | 22 **to go by the name of ...:** unter dem Namen ... bekannt sein.

ly with two of our boys on the day we first lost him, and had known him directly to be the same child that he was watching for, though I couldn't make out why. A bargain was struck with Fagin, that if Oliver was got back he should have a certain sum; and he was to have more for making him a thief, which this Monks wanted for some purpose of his own."

"For what purpose?" asked Rose.

"He caught sight of my shadow on the wall as I listened, in the hope of finding out," said the girl; "and there are not many people besides me that could have got out of their way in time to escape discovery. But I did; and I saw him no more till last night."

"And what occurred then?"

"I'll tell you, lady. Last night he came again. Again they went up stairs, and I, wrapping myself up so that my shadow should not betray me, again listened at the door. The first words I heard Monks say were these: 'So the only proofs of the boy's identity lie at the bottom of the river, and the old hag that received them from the mother is rotting in her coffin.' They laughed, and talked of his success in doing this; and Monks, talking on about the boy, and getting very wild, said, that though he had got the young devil's money safely now, he'd rather have had it the other way; for, what a game it would have been to have brought down the boast of the father's will, by driving him through every jail in town, and then hauling him up for some capital felony, which Fagin could easily manage, after having made a good profit on him besides."

"What is all this!" said Rose.

15 **to wrap o.s. up:** sich einhüllen, sich vermummen. |
24 **boast:** Prahlerei. | 25 **to drive s.o.:** jdn. treiben. | 25 f. **to haul s.o. up:** jdn. zur Rechenschaft ziehen; jdn. aufknüpfen (hängen). |
26 **capital felony:** Kapitalverbrechen. | 27 **to make profit of s.th.:** aus etwas Gewinn herausschlagen.

"The truth, lady, though it comes from my lips," replied the girl. "Then, he said, with oaths common enough in my ears, but strange to yours, that if he could gratify his hatred by taking the boy's life without bringing his own neck in danger, he would; but, as he couldn't, he'd be upon the watch to meet him at every turn in life; and if he took advantage of his birth and history, he might harm him yet. 'In short Fagin,' he says, 'Jew as you are, you never laid such snares as I'll contrive for my young brother, Oliver.'"

"His brother!" exclaimed Rose.

"Those were his words," said Nancy, glancing uneasily round, as she had scarcely ceased to do, since she began to speak, for a vision of Sikes haunted her perpetually. "And more. When he spoke of you and the other lady, and said it seemed contrived by Heaven, or the devil, against him, that Oliver should come into your hands, he laughed, and said there was some comfort in that too, for how many thousands and hundreds of thousands of pounds would you not give, if you had them, to know who your two-legged spaniel was."

[…]

"But what can I do?" said Rose. "To what use can I turn this communication without you? Back! Why do you wish to return to companions you paint in such terrible colours? If you repeat this information to a gentleman whom I can summon in an instant from the next room, you can be consigned to some place of safety without half an hour's delay."

"I wish to go back," said the girl. "I must go back, because – how can I tell such things to an innocent lady like you? – because among the men I have told you of, there is one: the most

5 **to be upon the watch:** auf der Hut sein, achtsam sein. | 6 **turn:** Wendung. | 8 **snare:** Fallstrick. | **to contrive:** aushecken, ersinnen. | 13 **vision:** Vorstellung, Trugbild. | **perpetually:** ständig, fortwährend. | 19 **spaniel:** Spaniel (Hunderasse). | 28 **innocent:** arglos, anständig.

desperate among them all: that I can't leave; no, not even to be saved from the life I am leading now."

[...]

"What am I to do?" said Rose. "I should not let you depart from me thus."

"You should, lady, and I know you will," rejoined the girl, rising. "You will not stop my going because I have trusted in your goodness, and forced no promise from you, as I might have done."

"Of what use, then, is the communication you have made?" said Rose. "This mystery must be investigated, or how will its disclosure to me, benefit Oliver, whom you are anxious to serve?"

"You must have some kind gentleman about you that will hear it as a secret, and advise you what to do," rejoined the girl.

"But where can I find you again when it is necessary?" asked Rose. "I do not seek to know where these dreadful people live, but where will you be walking or passing at any settled period from this time?"

"Will you promise me that you will have my secret strictly kept, and come alone, or with the only other person that knows it; and that I shall not be watched or followed?" asked the girl.

"I promise you solemnly," answered Rose.

"Every Sunday night, from eleven until the clock strikes twelve," said the girl without hesitation, "I will walk on London Bridge if I am alive."

[...]

Thus speaking, and sobbing aloud, the unhappy creature

11 **to investigate s.th.:** etwas ergründen. | 12 **to benefit s.o.:** jdm. nützen, zugutekommen. | **to be anxious to do s.th.:** darauf bedacht sein, etwas zu tun. | 18 **settled period:** festgelegter Zeitraum.

turned away; while Rose Maylie, overpowered by this extraordinary interview, which had more the semblance of a rapid dream than an actual occurrence, sank into a chair, and endeavoured to collect her wandering thoughts.

Chapter XLI

Containing fresh Discoveries, and shewing that Surprises, like Misfortunes, seldom come alone

Her situation was, indeed, one of no common trial and difficulty. While she felt the most eager and burning desire to penetrate the mystery in which Oliver's history was enveloped, she could not but hold sacred the confidence which the miserable woman with whom she had just conversed, had reposed in her, as a young and guileless girl. Her words and manner had touched Rose Maylie's heart; and, mingled with her love for her young charge, and scarcely less intense in its truth and fervour, was her fond wish to win the outcast back to repentance and hope.

They only proposed remaining in London three days, prior to departing for some weeks to a distant part of the coast. It was now midnight of the first day. What course of action could she determine upon, which could be adopted in eight-and-forty hours? Or how could she postpone the journey without exciting suspicion?

2 **semblance:** Ähnlichkeit, Anschein. | **rapid:** flüchtig. | 3 **actual:** tatsächlich, wirklich. | 9 f. **to penetrate:** ergründen. | 10 **to envelop s.th.:** etwas einhüllen. | 11 **to hold s.th. sacred:** etwas als heilig erachten. | 12 f. **to repose confidence in s.o.:** Vertrauen in jdn. setzen. | 13 **guileless:** arglos. | 15 f. **fervour:** Eifer. | 16 **repentance:** Umkehr, Reue. | 18 f. **prior to s.th.:** einer Sache vorausgehend. | 22 f. **to excite:** erwecken, erregen.

Mr. Losberne was with them, and would be for the next two days; but Rose was too well acquainted with the excellent gentleman's impetuosity, and foresaw too clearly the wrath with which, in the first explosion of his indignation, he would regard the instrument of Oliver's re-capture, to trust him with the secret, when her representations in the girl's behalf could be seconded by no experienced person. […]

[…] After more communing with herself next day, she arrived at the desperate conclusion of consulting Harry.

"If it be painful to him," she thought, "to come back here, how painful it will be to me! But perhaps he will not come; he may write, or he may come himself, and studiously abstain from meeting me – he did when he went away. I hardly thought he would; but it was better for us both." And here, Rose dropped the pen, and turned away, as though the very paper which was to be her messenger should not see her weep.

She had taken up the same pen, and laid it down again fifty times, and had considered and reconsidered the first line of her letter without writing the first word, when Oliver, who had been walking in the streets, with Mr. Giles for a body-guard, entered the room in such breathless haste and violent agitation, as seemed to betoken some new cause of alarm.

"What makes you look so flurried?" asked Rose, advancing to meet him.

"I hardly know how; I feel as if I should be choked," replied

3 **impetuosity:** Ungestüm. | **to foresee:** vorhersehen. | 5 **instrument:** Werkzeug, Mittel. | **re-capture:** Wiederergreifung. | 6 **representation in s.o.'s behalf:** Vertretung, Eintreten für jdn. | 7 **to second s.th.:** etwas unterstützen, befürworten. | 8 **to commune with o.s.:** mit sich zurate gehen. | 12 **studiously:** geflissentlich. | 12 f. **to abstain from doing s.th.:** davon absehen, etwas zu tun. | 22 **to betoken:** verkünden, anzeigen. | 23 **flurried:** beunruhigt. | 25 **to choke s.o.:** jdn. ersticken, erwürgen.

the boy. "Oh dear! to think that I should see him at last, and you should be able to know that I have told you all the truth!"

"I never thought you had told us anything but the truth," said Rose, soothing him. "But what is this? – of whom do you speak?"

"I have seen the gentleman," replied Oliver, scarcely able to articulate, "the gentleman who was so good to me – Mr. Brownlow, that we have so often talked about."

"Where?" asked Rose.

"Getting out of a coach," replied Oliver, shedding tears of delight, "and going into a house. I didn't speak to him – I couldn't speak to him, for he didn't see me, and I trembled so, that I was not able to go up to him. But Giles asked, for me, whether he lived there, and they said he did. Look here," said Oliver, opening a scrap of paper, "here it is; here's where he lives – I'm going there directly! Oh, dear me, dear me! what shall I do when I come to see him and hear him speak again!"

With her attention not a little distracted by these, and a great many other incoherent exclamations of joy, Rose read the address, which was Craven-street, in the Strand, and very soon determined upon turning the discovery to account.

"Quick!" she said, "tell them to fetch a hackney-coach, and be ready to go with me. I will take you there directly, without a minute's loss of time. I will only tell my aunt that we are going out for an hour, and be ready as soon as you are."

Oliver needed no prompting to despatch, and in little more

5 **to soothe s.o.:** jdn. besänftigen, beruhigen, beschwichtigen. |
21 **Strand:** Straße in London. | 22 **to turn s.th. to account:** sich etwas zunutze machen. | 23 **hackney-coach:** Mietdroschke. |
27 **prompting:** Drängen, Antreiben. | **to despatch:** aus-, durchführen.

than five minutes they were on their way to Craven-street. When they arrived there, Rose left Oliver in the coach, under pretence of preparing the old gentleman to receive him; and sending up her card by the servant, requested to see Mr. Brownlow on very pressing business. The servant soon returned, to beg that she would walk up stairs; and, following him into an upper room, Miss Maylie was presented to an elderly gentleman of benevolent appearance, in a bottle-green coat. At no great distance from whom, was seated another old gentleman, in nankeen breeches and gaiters: who did not look particularly benevolent, and who was sitting with his hands clasped on the top of a thick stick, and his chin propped thereupon.

"Dear me," said the gentleman, in the bottle-green coat, hastily rising with great politeness, "I beg your pardon, young lady – I imagined it was some importunate person who – I beg you will excuse me. Be seated, pray."

"Mr. Brownlow, I believe, sir?" said Rose, glancing from the other gentleman to the one who had spoken.

"That is my name," said the old gentleman. "This is my friend, Mr. Grimwig. Grimwig, will you leave us for a few minutes?"

"I believe," interposed Miss Maylie, "that at this period of our interview, I need not give that gentleman the trouble of going away. If I am correctly informed, he is cognizant of the business on which I wish to speak to you."

Mr. Brownlow inclined his head. Mr. Grimwig, who had made one very stiff bow, and risen from his chair, made another very stiff bow, and dropped into it again.

3 **pretence:** Vorwand. | 5 **pressing:** dringend. | 16 **importunate:** aufdringlich, lästig. | 25 **to be cognizant of s.th.:** über etwas unterrichtet sein.

"I shall surprise you very much, I have no doubt," said Rose, naturally embarrassed; "but you once shewed great benevolence and goodness to a very dear young friend of mine, and I am sure you will take an interest in hearing of him again."

"Indeed!" said Mr. Brownlow.

"Oliver Twist you knew him as," replied Rose.

[...]

Mr. Brownlow was no less surprised, although his astonishment was not expressed in the same eccentric manner. He drew his chair nearer to Miss Maylie's, and said,

"Do me the favour, my dear young lady, to leave entirely out of the question that goodness and benevolence of which you speak, and of which nobody else knows anything; and if you have it in your power to produce any evidence which will alter the unfavourable opinion I was once induced to entertain of that poor child, in Heaven's name put me in possession of it."

[...]

Rose, who had had time to collect her thoughts, at once related, in a few natural words, all that had befallen Oliver since he left Mr. Brownlow's house; reserving Nancy's information for that gentleman's private ear, and concluding with the assurance that his only sorrow, for some months past, had been the not being able to meet with his former benefactor and friend.

"Thank God!" said the old gentleman. "This is great happiness to me; great happiness. But you have not told me where he is now, Miss Maylie. You must pardon my finding fault with you, – but why not have brought him?"

2 **naturally:** verständlicherweise. | **embarrassed:** verlegen. | 2 f. **benevolence:** Wohlwollen. | 11 f. **to leave s.th. out of question:** etwas beiseite lassen. | 14 **evidence:** Beweis, Beleg. | 19 **natural:** einfach, schlicht. | 20 **to reserve s.th.:** etwas zurückhalten. | 21 **private:** vertraulich. | 27 **to find fault with s.o.:** jdn. tadeln.

"He is waiting in a coach at the door," replied Rose.

"At this door!" cried the old gentleman. With which he hurried out of the room, down the stairs, up the coach-steps, and into the coach, without another word.

[...] Mr. Brownlow returned accompanied by Oliver, whom Mr. Grimwig received very graciously; and if the gratification of that moment had been the only reward for all her anxiety and care in Oliver's behalf, Rose Maylie would have been well repaid.

"There is somebody else who should not be forgotten, by the bye," said Mr. Brownlow, ringing the bell. "Send Mrs. Bedwin here, if you please."

[...]

"God be good to me!" cried the old lady [...]; "it is my innocent boy!"

"My dear old nurse!" cried Oliver.

[...]

Leaving her and Oliver to compare notes at leisure, Mr. Brownlow led the way into another room; and there, heard from Rose a full narration of her interview with Nancy, which occasioned him no little surprise and perplexity. Rose also explained her reasons for not making a confident of her friend Mr. Losberne in the first instance; the old gentleman considered that she had acted prudently, and readily undertook to hold solemn conference with the worthy doctor himself. To afford him an early opportunity for the execution of this design, it was arranged that he should call at the hotel at eight o'clock that evening, and that in the mean time Mrs. Maylie should be

6 **graciously:** liebenswürdig. | **gratification:** Genugtuung, Freude, Belohnung. | 9 **to repay s.o.:** jdn. entlohnen, entschädigen. | 18 **to compare notes:** Erfahrungen austauschen. | **at leisure:** nach Belieben, nach Herzenslust. | 21 **to occasion s.o. s.th.:** jdm. etwas verursachen. | 22 **confident:** Vertraute(r). | 26 **design:** Plan, Vorhaben.

cautiously informed of all that had occurred. These preliminaries adjusted, Rose and Oliver returned home.

Rose had by no means overrated the measure of the good doctor's wrath. Nancy's history was no sooner unfolded to him, than he poured forth a shower of mingled threats and execrations; threatened to make her the first victim of the combined ingenuity of Messrs. Blathers and Duff; [...].

"Not exactly that," rejoined Mr. Brownlow laughing; "but we must proceed gently and with great care."

"Gentleness and care!" exclaimed the doctor. "I'd send them one and all to –"

"Never mind where," interposed Mr. Brownlow. "But reflect whether sending them anywhere is likely to attain the object we have in view."

"What object?" asked the doctor.

"Simply, the discovery of Oliver's parentage, and regaining for him the inheritance of which, if this story be true, he has been fraudulently deprived."

"Ah!" said Mr. Losberne, cooling himself with his pocket-handkerchief; "I almost forgot that."

"You see," pursued Mr. Brownlow; [...].

"[...] It is quite clear that we shall have extreme difficulty in getting to the bottom of this mystery, unless we can bring this man, Monks, upon his knees. That can only be done by stratagem, and by catching him when he is not surrounded by these people. [...]

1 f. **preliminaries:** vorbereitende Maßnahmen. | 3 **to overrate:** überschätzen. | 4 **to unfold s.th. to s.o.:** jdm. etwas offenlegen. | 5 **to pour forth s.th.:** etwas ausstoßen, von sich geben. | **shower:** Fülle. | 5 f. **execration:** Verwünschung. | 6 f. **combined:** vereint. | 7 **ingenuity:** Scharfsinn. | 16 **parentage:** Abstammung, Herkunft. | **to regain:** wiedererlangen, zurückgewinnen. | 17 **inheritance:** Erbe. | 18 **fraudulently:** auf betrügerische Weise. | 24 f. **stratagem:** List.

[…] But, before we can resolve upon any precise course of action, it will be necessary to see the girl; to ascertain from her whether she will point out this Monks, on the understanding that he is to be dealt with by us, and not by the law; or, if she will not, or cannot do that, to procure from her such an account of his haunts and description of his person, as will enable us to identify him. She cannot be seen until next Sunday night; this is Tuesday. I would suggest that, in the mean-time, we remain perfectly quiet, and keep these matters secret, even from Oliver himself."

Although Mr. Losberne received with many wry faces a proposal involving a delay of five whole days, he was fain to admit that no better course occurred to him just then; and as both Rose and Mrs. Maylie sided very strongly with Mr. Brownlow, that gentleman's proposition was carried unanimously.

[…]

1 **to resolve upon s.th.:** etwas beschließen. | 1 f. **course of action:** Handlungsweise. | 3 **to point out s.o.:** jdn. zeigen, auf jdn. hinweisen. | **understanding:** Voraussetzung, Abmachung. | 4 **to deal with s.o.:** mit jdm. zu tun haben. | 5 **to procure:** besorgen, beschaffen. | 6 **haunt:** Schlupfwinkel. | 11 **wry face:** säuerliche Miene. | 12 **to be fain to do s.th.:** genötigt sein, etwas zu tun. | 14 **to side with s.o.:** für jdn. Partei ergreifen, sich auf jds. Seite stellen. | 15 **to carry s.th. unanimously:** etwas einstimmig annehmen.

Chapter XLII

An old Acquaintance of Oliver's, exhibiting decided marks of Genius, becomes a public Character in the Metropolis

Upon the very same night when Nancy, having lulled Mr. Sikes to sleep, hurried on her self-imposed mission to Rose Maylie, there advanced towards London, by the Great North Road, two persons, upon whom it is expedient that this history should bestow some attention.

They were a man and woman; or perhaps they would be better described as a male and female; for the former was one of those long-limbed, knock-kneed, shambling, bony people, to whom it is difficult to assign any precise age, – looking as they do, when they are yet boys, like under-grown men, and when they are almost men, like overgrown boys. The woman was young, but of a robust and hardy make, as she need have been to bear the weight of the heavy bundle which was strapped to her back. Her companion was not encumbered with much luggage, as there merely dangled from a stick, which he carried over his shoulder, a small parcel wrapped in a common handkerchief, and apparently light enough. [...]

Thus, they toiled along the dusty road, taking little heed of any object within sight, [...] when the foremost traveller stopped, and called impatiently to his companion,

"Come on, can't yer? What a lazybones yer are, Charlotte."

[...]

3 **public:** allgemein bekannt, öffentlich. | 4 **to lull s.o. to sleep:** jdn. zum Einschlafen bringen. | 5 **self-imposed:** selbst auferlegt. | 7 **expedient:** angebracht, ratsam, nützlich. | 11 **knock-kneed:** x-beinig. | **shambling:** watschelnd. | 13 **under-grown:** kleinwüchsig. | 14 **overgrown:** übergroß. | 15 **hardy:** zäh. | **make:** Körperbau. | 16 **to strap:** festbinden, schnallen. | 24 **lazybones:** (hum.) Faultier.

"Is it much farther?" asked the woman, resting herself against a bank, and looking up with the perspiration streaming from her face.

"Much farther! Yer as good as there," said the long-legged tramper pointing out before him. "Look there! Those are the lights of London."

"They're a good two mile off, at least," said the woman despondingly.

"Never mind whether they're two mile off, or twenty," said Noah Claypole; for he it was; "but get up and come on, or I'll kick yer, and so I give yer notice."

[...]

"Well, you needn't be so cross," said his companion.

"A pretty thing it would be, wouldn't it, to go and stop at the very first public-house outside the town, so that Sowerberry, if he come up after us, might poke in his old nose, and have us taken back in a cart with handcuffs on," said Mr. Claypole in a jeering tone. "No! I shall go and lose myself among the narrowest streets I can find, and not stop till we come to the very out-of-the-wayest house I can set eyes on. 'Cod, yer may thank yer stars I've got a head; for if we hadn't gone, at first, the wrong road a purpose, and come back across country, yer'd have been locked up hard and fast a week ago, my lady. And serve yer right for being a fool."

"I know I ain't as cunning as you are," replied Charlotte; "but don't put all the blame on me, and say *I* should have been locked up. You would have been if I had been, any way."

2 **bank:** Böschung. | 5 **tramper:** Wandersmann. | 11 **to give s.o. notice:** jdm. Bescheid geben. | 13 **to be cross:** böse sein. | 16 **to poke in:** hineinstecken. | 20 **out-of-the-way:** abgelegen. | **'Cod:** *God.* | 23 **hard and fast:** garantiert. | 24 **to serve s.o. right:** jdm. recht geschehen.

"Yer took the money from the till, yer know yer did," said Mr. Claypole.

"I took it for you, Noah, dear," rejoined Charlotte.

[...]

In pursuance of this cautious plan, Mr. Claypole went on, without halting, until he arrived at the Angel at Islington, where he wisely judged, from the crowd of passengers and number of vehicles, that London began in earnest. [...]

Through these streets, Noah Claypole walked, dragging Charlotte after him; now stepping into the kennel to embrace at a glance the whole external character of some small public-house; and now jogging on again, as some fancied appearance induced him to believe it too public for his purpose. At length, he stopped in front of one, more humble in appearance and more dirty than any he had yet seen; and, having crossed over and surveyed it from the opposite pavement, graciously announced his intention of putting up there, for the night.

"So give us the bundle," said Noah, unstrapping it from the woman's shoulders, and slinging it over his own; "and don't yer speak, except when yer spoke to. What's the name of the house – t-h-r – three what?"

"Cripples," said Charlotte.

"Three Cripples," repeated Noah, "and a very good sign too. Now, then! Keep close at my heels, and come along." With these injunctions, he pushed the rattling door with his shoulder, and entered the house, followed by his companion.

There was nobody in the bar but a young Jew, who, with his

1 **till:** Ladenkasse. | 5 **in pursuance of:** gemäß. | 10 f. **to embrace s.th.:** etwas erfassen. | 11 **external:** äußerlich. | 14 **humble:** ärmlich. | 17 **to put up:** (in einem Gasthof oder Hotel) absteigen. | 19 **to unstrap s.th.:** etwas losbinden, abschnallen. | 20 **to sling:** werfen. | 23 **cripple:** Krüppel.

two elbows on the counter, was reading a dirty newspaper. He stared very hard at Noah, and Noah stared very hard at him.

[…]

"Is this the Three Cripples?" asked Noah.

"[…] We want to sleep here to-night."

"I'b dot certaid you cad," said Barney, who was the attendant sprite; "but I'll idquire."

"Show us the tap, and give us a bit of cold meat and a drop of beer while yer inquiring, will yer?" said Noah.

Barney complied by ushering them into a small back-room, and setting the required viands before them; having done which, he informed the travellers that they could be lodged that night, and left the amiable couple to their refreshment.

Now, this back-room was immediately behind the bar, and some steps lower, so that any person connected with the house, undrawing a small curtain which concealed a single pane of glass fixed in the wall of the last-named apartment, about five feet from its flooring, could not only look down upon any guests in the back-room without any great hazard of being observed (the glass being in a dark angle of the wall, between which and a large upright beam the observer had to thrust himself), but could, by applying his ear to the partition, ascertain with tolerable distinctness, their subject of conversation. The landlord of the house had not withdrawn his eye from this place of espial for five minutes, and Barney had only

6 **I'b dot certaid you cad:** *I'm not certain you can.* | 6 f. **attendant sprite:** dienstbarer Geist. | 8 **tap:** *tap-room.* | 10 **to comply:** (einem Wunsch) nachkommen. | 11 **viands** (pl.): Lebensmittel. | 12 **to lodge:** logieren. | 13 **refreshment:** Imbiss, Stärkung. | 17 **pane of glass:** Glasscheibe, Fensterscheibe. | 18 **flooring:** Fußboden. | 19 **hazard:** Gefahr, Risiko. | 22 **partition:** Trennwand. | 23 **tolerable:** erträglich, passabel. | **distinctness:** Deutlichkeit. | 25 **espial:** Spähen, Auskundschaften.

just returned from making the communication above related, when Fagin, in the course of his evening's business, came into the bar to inquire after some of his young pupils.

"Hush!" said Barney: "stradegers id the next roob."

"Strangers!" repeated the old man in a whisper.

"Ah! Ad rub uds too," added Barney. "Frob the cuttry, but subthig in your way, or I'b bistaked."

Fagin appeared to receive this communication with great interest. Mounting a stool, he cautiously applied his eye to the pane of glass, from which secret post he could see Mr. Claypole taking cold beef from the dish, and porter from the pot, and administering homoeopathic doses of both to Charlotte, who sat patiently by, eating and drinking at his pleasure.

[...]

"So I mean to be a gentleman," said Mr. Claypole, kicking out his legs, and continuing a conversation, the commencement of which Fagin had arrived too late to hear. "No more jolly old coffins, Charlotte, but a gentleman's life for me; and, if yer like yer shall be a lady."

"I should like that well enough, dear," replied Charlotte; "but tills ain't to be emptied every day, and people to get clear off after it."

"Tills be blowed!" said Mr. Claypole; "there's more things besides tills to be emptied."

"What do you mean?" asked his companion.

"Pockets, women's ridicules, houses, mail-coaches, banks!" said Mr. Claypole, rising with the porter.

"But you can't do all that, dear," said Charlotte.

"I shall look out to get into company with them as can," re-

6 **ad rub uds:** *and rough ones.* | **cuttry:** *country.* | 11 **pot:** Krug. | 23 **... be blowed:** zum Teufel mit .... | 26 **ridicule:** *reticule:* Damenhandtasche. | 27 **to rise:** in Fahrt geraten.

plied Noah. "They'll be able to make us useful some way or another. Why, you yourself are worth fifty women; I never see such a precious sly and deceitful creetur as yer can be when I let yer."

[...]

After expressing this opinion, Mr. Claypole looked into the porter-pot with an aspect of deep wisdom; and having well shaken its contents, nodded condescendingly to Charlotte, and took a draught, wherewith he appeared greatly refreshed. He was meditating another, when the sudden opening of the door, and the appearance of a stranger, interrupted him.

The stranger was Mr. Fagin. And very amiable he looked, and a very low bow he made, as he advanced, and, setting himself down at the nearest table, ordered something to drink of the grinning Barney.

"A pleasant night, sir, but cool for the time of year," said Fagin, rubbing his hands. "From the country, I see, sir?"

"How do yer see that?" asked Noah Claypole.

"We have not so much dust as that in London," replied the Jew, pointing from Noah's shoes to those of his companion, and from them to the two bundles.

"Yer a sharp feller," said Noah. "Ha! ha! only hear that, Charlotte!"

"Why, one need be sharp in this town, my dear," replied the Jew, sinking his voice to a confidential whisper; "and that's the truth."

The Jew followed up this remark by striking the side of his nose with his right forefinger, – a gesture which Noah attempted to imitate, though not with complete success, in consequence of his own nose not being large enough for the pur-

3 **deceitful:** hinterlistig. | 9 **draught:** Schluck. | 10 **to meditate s.th.:** etwas erwägen. | 27 **to strike s.th.:** auf etwas klopfen, tippen.

pose. However, Mr. Fagin seemed to interpret the endeavour as expressing a perfect coincidence with his opinion, and put about the liquor which Barney re-appeared with, in a very friendly manner.

"Good stuff that," observed Mr. Claypole, smacking his lips.

"Dear!" said Fagin. "A man need be always emptying a till, or a pocket, or a woman's reticule, or a house, or a mail-coach, or a bank, if he drinks it regularly."

Mr. Claypole no sooner heard this extract from his own remarks than he fell back in his chair, and looked from the Jew to Charlotte with a countenance of ashy paleness and excessive terror.

"Don't mind me, my dear," said Fagin, drawing his chair closer. "Ha! ha! it was lucky it was only me that heard you by chance. It was very lucky it was only me."

"I didn't take it," stammered Noah, no longer stretching out his legs like an independent gentleman, but coiling them up as well as he could under his chair; "it was all her doing: yer've got it now, Charlotte, yer know yer have."

"No matter who's got it, or who did it, my dear!" replied Fagin, glancing, nevertheless, with a hawk's eye at the girl and the two bundles. "I'm in that way myself, and I like you for it."

[...]

"I'll tell you more," said the Jew, after he had reassured the girl, by dint of friendly nods and muttered encouragements. "I have got a friend that I think can gratify your darling wish, and

2 **coincidence:** Übereinstimmung. | 2 f. **to put about s.th.:** etwas herumgehen lassen. | 5 f. **to smack one's lips:** schmatzen. | 10 **extract:** Auszug, Stück. | 12 **excessive:** außerordentlich. | 17 **to stretch out:** ausstrecken. | 18 **to coil s.th. up:** etwas aufwickeln. | 22 **hawk:** Habicht; Falke. | 26 **encouragement:** Ermutigung. | 27 **to gratify:** erfüllen. | **darling wish:** Herzenswunsch.

put you in the right way, where you can take whatever department of the business you think will suit you best at first, and be taught all the others."

[...]

"When could I see him?" asked Noah doubtfully.

"To-morrow morning," replied the Jew.

[...]

"Will ten do?" asked the Jew, adding, as Mr. Claypole nodded assent, "What name shall I tell my good friend?"

"Mr. Bolter," replied Noah, who had prepared himself, for such an emergency. "Mr. Morris Bolter. This is Mrs. Bolter."

"Mrs. Bolter's humble servant," said Fagin, bowing with grotesque politeness. "I hope I shall know her better very shortly."

[...]

Chapter XLIII

Wherein is shown how the Artful Dodger got into Trouble

"And so it was you that was your own friend, was it?" asked Mr. Claypole, otherwise Bolter, when, by virtue of the compact entered into between them, he had removed next day to Fagin's house. "'Cod, I thought as much last night!"

"Every man's his own friend, my dear," replied Fagin, with his most insinuating grin. "He hasn't as good a one as himself anywhere."

1 f. **department:** Abteilung, Zweig, Branche. | 8 **to add:** hinzufügen. | 12 **humble servant:** ergebener Diener. | 13 **grotesque:** übersteigert, übertrieben. | 19 **by virtue of:** aufgrund, kraft. | **compact:** Pakt, Abkommen, Übereinkunft. | 20 **to remove:** umziehen (Quartier wechseln). | 23 **insinuating:** vielsagend.

[…] "My best hand was taken from me, yesterday morning."

"Yer don't mean to say he died?" cried Mr. Bolter.

"No, no," replied Fagin, "not so bad as that. Not quite so bad."

"What, I suppose he was –"

"Wanted," interposed the Jew. "Yes, he was wanted."

"Very particular?" inquired Mr. Bolter.

"No," replied the Jew, "not very. He was charged with attempting to pick a pocket, and they found a silver snuff-box on him, – his own, my dear, his own, for he took snuff himself, and was very fond of it. They remanded him till to-day, for they thought they knew the owner. Ah! he was worth fifty boxes, and I'd give the price of as many to have him back. You should have known the Dodger, my dear; you should have known the Dodger."

"Well, but I shall know him, I hope; don't yer think so?" said Mr. Bolter.

"I'm doubtful about it," replied the Jew, […] when the dialogue was cut short by the entry of Master Bates, with his hands in his breeches-pockets, and his face twisted into a look of semi-comical woe.

"It's all up, Fagin," said Charley, when he and his new companion had been made known to each other.

"What do you mean?" asked the Jew with trembling lips.

"They've found the gentleman as owns the box; two or three more's a-coming to 'dentify him; and the Artful's booked

1 **hand:** Helfer, Gehilfe. | 6 **wanted:** (polizeilich) gesucht. | 9 **to pick a pocket:** Taschendiebstahl begehen. | 11 **to remand s.o.:** jdn. in Gewahrsam behalten. | 19 **to cut s.th. short:** etwas unterbrechen. | 20 **twisted:** verzerrt. | 21 **semi-comical:** tragikomisch. | **woe:** Kummer, Schmerz.. | 25 **as owns:** *who owns.* | 26 **'dentify:** *identify.* | 26 f. **booked for a passage out:** für eine Überfahrt gebucht (gemeint ist die Strafe der Deportation per Schiff nach Australien).

for a passage out," replied Master Bates. "I must have a full suit of mourning, Fagin, and a hatband, to wisit him in, afore he sets out upon his travels. To think of Jack Dawkins – lummy Jack – the Dodger – the Artful Dodger – going abroad for a common twopenny-halfpenny sneeze-box! I never thought he'd a done it under a gold watch, chain, and seals, at the lowest. Oh, why didn't he rob some rich old gentleman of all his walables, and go out *as* a gentleman, and not like a common prig, without no honour nor glory!"

[…]

Chapter XLIV

The Time arrives, for Nancy to redeem her Pledge to Rose Maylie. She fails

Adept as she was, in all the arts of cunning and dissimulation, the girl Nancy could not wholly conceal the effect which the knowledge of the step she had taken, wrought upon her mind. She remembered that both the crafty Jew and the brutal Sikes had confided to her, schemes, which had been hidden from all others: in the full confidence that she was trustworthy and beyond the reach of their suspicion. […]

It was Sunday night, and the bell of the nearest church struck the hour. Sikes and the Jew were talking, but they paused to

1 f. **suit of mourning:** Traueranzug. | 3 **lummy:** gewieft, vorzüglich. | 4 **abroad:** nach Übersee. | 5 **sneeze-box:** Schneuzdose. | 6 **seal:** Petschaft. | **at the lowest:** mindestens. | 7 **walables:** *valuables:* Wertsachen. | 8 **prig:** Langfinger. | 14 **adept:** geschickt, geübt. | **cunning:** List. | **dissimulation:** Verstellung, Verheimlichung. | 18 **scheme:** Plan, Komplott. | 19 **trustworthy:** vertrauenswürdig, zuverlässig.

listen. The girl looked up from the low seat on which she crouched, and listened too. Eleven.

[…]

"Hallo!" cried Sikes. "Nance. Where's the gal going to at this time of night?"

"Not far."

"What answer's that?" returned Sikes. "Where are you going?"

"I say, not far."

"And I say where?" retorted Sikes. "Do you hear me?"

"I don't know where," replied the girl.

"Then I do," said Sikes, more in the spirit of obstinacy than because he had any real objection to the girl going where she listed. "Nowhere. Sit down."

"I'm not well. I told you that before," rejoined the girl. "I want a breath of air."

"Put your head out of the winder," replied Sikes.

"There's not enough there," said the girl. "I want it in the street."

"Then you won't have it," replied Sikes. With which assurance he rose, locked the door, took the key out, and pulling her bonnet from her head, flung it up to the top of an old press. "There," said the robber. "Now stop quietly where you are, will you."

"It's not such a matter as a bonnet would keep me," said the girl turning very pale. "What do you mean, Bill? Do you know what you're doing?"

"Know what I'm – Oh!" cried Sikes turning to Fagin, "she's out of her senses, you know, or she daren't talk to me in that way."

4 **gal:** *girl.* | 14 **to list:** wünschen. | 17 **winder:** *window.* | 22 **press:** Kleiderschrank. | 29 **to be out of one's senses:** von Sinnen sein, den Verstand verloren haben.

"You'll drive me on to something desperate," muttered the girl placing both hands upon her breast, as though to keep down by force some violent outbreak. "Let me go, will you, – this minute – this instant –"

"No!" said Sikes.

"Tell him to let me go, Fagin. He had better. It'll be better for him. Do you hear me?" cried Nancy stamping her foot upon the ground.

"Hear you!" repeated Sikes turning round in his chair to confront her. "Aye! And if I hear you for half a minute longer, the dog shall have such a grip on your throat as'll tear some of that screaming voice out. Wot has come over you, you jade! Wot is it?"

"Let me go," said the girl with great earnestness; then sitting herself down on the floor, before the door, she said, "Bill, let me go; you don't know what you are doing. You don't, indeed. For only one hour – do – do."

"Cut my limbs off one by one!" cried Sikes, seizing her roughly by the arm, "if I don't think the gal's stark raving mad. Get up."

"Not till you let me go – not till you let me go – Never – never!" screamed the girl. Sikes looked on, for a minute, watching his opportunity, and suddenly pinioning her hands dragged her, struggling and wrestling with him by the way, into a small room adjoining, where he sat himself on a bench, and thrusting her into a chair, held her down by force. She struggled and implored by turns until twelve o'clock had struck, and then, wearied and exhausted, ceased to contest the point any further. With a caution, backed by many oaths, to make no more efforts

12 **jade:** Weibsstück. | 19 **stark** (adv.): gänzlich, völlig. | **raving:** rasend, tobend. | 24 **to wrestle:** ringen. | 27 **to implore:** flehen. | **by turns:** abwechselnd. | 28 **to contest s.th.:** etwas ausfechten.

to go out that night, Sikes left her to recover at leisure and rejoined the Jew.

"Whew!" said the housebreaker wiping the perspiration from his face. "Wot a precious strange gal that is!"

"You may say that, Bill," replied the Jew thoughtfully. "You may say that."

[...]

Fagin walked towards his own home, intent upon the thoughts that were working within his brain. He had conceived the idea – not from what had just passed, though that had tended to confirm him, but slowly and by degrees – that Nancy, wearied of the housebreaker's brutality, had conceived an attachment for some new friend. Her altered manner, her repeated absences from home alone, her comparative indifference to the interests of the gang for which she had once been so zealous, and, added to these, her desperate impatience to leave home that night at a particular hour, all favoured the supposition, and rendered it, to him at least, almost matter of certainty. The object of this new liking was not among his myrmidons. He would be a valuable acquisition with such an assistant as Nancy, and must (thus Fagin argued) be secured without delay.

[...]

3 **whew!:** uff!, puh! | 5 **you may say that:** das kann man wohl sagen. | 12 f. **to conceive an attachment for s.o.:** zu jdm. Zuneigung fassen. | 14 f. **indifference:** Gleichgültigkeit, Teilnahmslosigkeit. | 16 **zealous:** begeistert. | 17 f. **supposition:** Annahme, Vermutung. | 19 f. **myrmidons:** Gefolgsleute, Getreue. | 20 **acquisition:** Verstärkung. | 21 **to secure s.o.:** jdn. gewinnen.

Chapter XLV

Noah Claypole is employed by Fagin on a secret Mission

The old man was up, betimes, next morning, and waited impatiently for the appearance of his new associate, who, after a delay that seemed interminable, at length presented himself, and commenced a voracious assault on the breakfast.

[…]

"I want you, Bolter," said Fagin, leaning over the table, "to do a piece of work for me, my dear, that needs great care and caution."

"I say," rejoined Bolter, "don't yer go shoving me into danger […]. That don't suit me, that don't; and so I tell yer."

"There's not the smallest danger in it – not the very smallest," said the Jew; "it's only to dodge a woman."

[…]

"Who is she?" inquired Noah.

"One of us."

"Oh Lor!" cried Noah, curling up his nose. "Yer doubtful of her, are yer?"

"She has found out some new friends, my dear, and I must know who they are," replied the Jew.

"I see," said Noah. "Just to have the pleasure of knowing them, if they're respectable people, eh? Ha! ha! ha! I'm your man."

[…] Six nights passed – six long weary nights – and on each, Fagin came home with a disappointed face, and briefly intimated that it was not yet time. On the seventh, he returned

3 **betimes:** zeitig, beizeiten. | 5 **interminable:** endlos. |
6 **assault:** Angriff. | 11 **to shove:** stoßen, drängeln. | 14 **to dodge s.o.:** jdn. heimlich beschatten. | 18 **to curl up one's nose:** die Nase rümpfen. |
18 f. **to be doubtful of s.o.:** an jdm. zweifeln.

earlier, and with an exultation he could not conceal. It was Sunday.

"She goes abroad to-night," said Fagin, "and on the right errand, I'm sure; for she has been alone all day, and the man she is afraid of, will not be back much before daybreak. Come with me. Quick!"

Noah started up without saying a word; for the Jew was in a state of such intense excitement that it infected him. They left the house stealthily, and, hurrying through a labyrinth of streets, arrived at length before a public-house, which Noah recognised as the same in which he had slept, on the night of his arrival in London.

It was past eleven o'clock, and the door was closed. It opened softly on its hinges as the Jew gave a low whistle. They entered, without noise; and the door was closed behind them.

Scarcely venturing to whisper, but substituting dumb show for words, Fagin, and the young Jew who had admitted them, pointed out the pane of glass to Noah, and signed to him to climb up and observe the person in the adjoining room.

"Is that the woman?" he asked, scarcely above his breath.

The Jew nodded yes.

[…]

"I see her now," cried the spy.

"Plainly?" asked the Jew.

"I should know her among a thousand."

He hastily descended, as the room-door opened, and the girl came out. […]

1 **exultation:** Hochstimmung. | 3 **abroad:** aus dem Haus. | 8 **to infect s.o.:** jdn. anstecken. | 16 **to substitute:** ersetzen. | 17 **to admit s.o.:** jdn. einlassen. | 18 **to sign to s.o. to do s.th.:** jdm. bedeuten, etwas zu tun. | 23 **spy:** Späher, Kundschafter.

Chapter XLVI

The Appointment kept

The church clocks chimed three quarters past eleven, as two figures emerged on London Bridge. One, which advanced with a swift and rapid step, was that of a woman, who looked eagerly about her as though in quest of some expected object; the other figure was that of a man, who slunk along in the deepest shadow he could find, and, at some distance, accommodated his pace to hers: stopping when she stopped: and, as she moved again, creeping stealthily on […].

The girl had taken a few restless turns to and fro – closely watched meanwhile by her hidden observer – when the heavy bell of St. Paul's tolled for the death of another day. Midnight had come upon the crowded city. The palace, the night-cellar, the jail, the madhouse: the chambers of birth and death, of health and sickness, the rigid face of the corpse and the calm sleep of the child: midnight was upon them all.

The hour had not struck two minutes, when a young lady, accompanied by a grey-haired gentleman, alighted from a hackney-carriage within a short distance of the bridge, and, having dismissed the vehicle, walked straight towards it. They had scarcely set foot upon its pavement, when the girl started, and immediately made towards them.

They walked onward, looking about them with the air of persons who entertained some very slight expectation which had little chance of being realised, when they were suddenly joined by this new associate. They halted with an exclamation

3 **to chime:** läuten, schlagen. | 6 **in quest of s.th.:** auf der Suche nach etwas. | 8 **to accommodate:** in Einklang bringen. | 13 **to toll:** läuten, schlagen. | 14 **night-cellar:** etwa: Räuberhöhle. | 16 **rigid:** starr, steif. | 27 **to halt:** anhalten.

of surprise, but suppressed it immediately; for a man in the garments of a countryman came close up – brushed against them, indeed – at that precise moment.

"Not here," said Nancy hurriedly. "I am afraid to speak to you here. Come away – out of the public road – down the steps yonder!"

As she uttered these words, and indicated, with her hand, the direction in which she wished them to proceed, the countryman looked round, and roughly asking what they took up the whole pavement for, passed on.

The steps to which the girl had pointed, were those which, on the Surrey bank, and on the same side of the bridge as Saint Saviour's church, form a landing-stairs from the river. To this spot, the man bearing the appearance of a countryman, hastened unobserved; and after a moment's survey of the place, he began to descend.

These stairs are a part of the bridge; they consist of three flights. Just below the end of the second, going down, the stone wall on the left terminates in an ornamental pier or pedestal facing towards the Thames. At this point, the lower steps widen: so that a person turning that angle of the wall, is necessarily unseen by any others on the stairs who chance to be above him, if only a step. The countryman looked hastily round, when he reached this point; and as there seemed no better place of concealment, and, the tide being out, there was plenty of room, he slipped aside, with his back to the pier, [...].

1 **to suppress s.th.:** etwas unterdrücken, dämpfen. | 2 **garments** (pl.): Kleidung. | **countryman:** Landbewohner. | **to brush against s.o.:** jdn. streifen, leicht berühren. | 3 **precise:** genau, exakt. | 13 **Saviour:** Erlöser. | **landing-stairs** (pl.): Anlegestelle. | 19 **ornamental pier or pedestal:** Zierpfeiler oder Vorsprung. | 20 f. **to widen:** breiter werden. | 25 **concealment:** Versteck. | **the tide being out:** da Ebbe herrschte. | 26 **to slip:** schlüpfen.

[…] He was on the point of emerging from his hiding-place, and regaining the road above, when he heard the sound of footsteps, and directly afterwards of voices almost close at his ear.

He drew himself straight upright against the wall, and, scarcely breathing, listened attentively.

[…]

"This young lady," the gentleman began, "has communicated to me, and to some other friends who can be safely trusted, what you told her nearly a fortnight since. I confess to you that I had doubts, at first, whether you were to be implicitly relied upon, but now I firmly believe you are."

"I am," said the girl earnestly.

"I repeat that I firmly believe it. To prove to you that I am disposed to trust you, I tell you without reserve, that we propose to extort the secret, whatever it may be, from the fears of this man Monks. But if – if –" said the gentleman, "he cannot be secured, or, if secured, cannot be acted upon as we wish, you must deliver up the Jew."

"Fagin," cried the girl, recoiling.

"That man must be delivered up by you," said the gentleman.

"I will not do it! I will never do it!" replied the girl. "Devil that he is, and worse than devil as he has been to me, I will never do that."

"You will not?" said the gentleman, who seemed fully prepared for this answer.

"Never!" returned the girl.

"Tell me why?"

10 **to confess:** gestehen. | 11 **implicitly:** bedingungslos, ohne Vorbehalt. | 11 f. **to rely upon s.o.:** jdm. vertrauen. | 16 **to extort s.th. from s.o.:** jdm. etwas abnötigen. | 18 **to secure s.o.:** jdn. stellen, aufspüren. | 19 **to deliver up s.o.:** jdn. ausliefern, preisgeben.

"For one reason," rejoined the girl firmly, "for one reason, that the lady knows and will stand by me in, I know she will, for I have her promise; and for this other reason, besides, that, bad life as he has led, I have led a bad life too; there are many of us who have kept the same courses together, and I'll not turn upon them, who might – any of them – have turned upon me, but didn't, bad as they are."

"Then," said the gentleman, quickly, as if this had been the point he had been aiming to attain; "put Monks into my hands, and leave him to me to deal with."

[...]

"Monks would never learn how you knew what you do?" said the girl, after a short pause.

"Never," replied the gentleman. "The intelligence should be so brought to bear upon him, that he could never even guess."

"I have been a liar, and among liars from a little child," said the girl after another interval of silence, "but I will take your words."

After receiving an assurance from both, that she might safely do so, she proceeded in a voice so low that it was often difficult for the listener to discover even the purport of what she said, to describe, by name and situation, the public-house whence she had been followed that night. From the manner in which she occasionally paused, it appeared as if the gentleman were making some hasty notes of the information she communicated. When she had thoroughly explained the localities of the place, the best position from which to watch it without exciting observation, and the night and hour on which Monks was most in the habit of frequenting it, she seemed to consider

5 f. **to turn upon s.o.:** sich gegen jdn. wenden. | 9 **to attain:** erreichen. | 21 **purport:** Inhalt, Bedeutung, Sinn. | 26 **thoroughly:** gründlich, ausführlich. | **localities:** Örtlichkeiten. | 29 **to frequent:** aufsuchen.

for a few moments, for the purpose of recalling his features and appearance more forcibly to her recollection.

"He is tall," said the girl, "and a strongly made man, but not stout; he has a lurking walk; and as he walks, constantly looks over his shoulder, first on one side, and then on the other. Don't forget that, for his eyes are sunk in his head so much deeper than any other man's, that you might almost tell him by that alone. His face is dark, like his hair and eyes; and, although he can't be more than six or eight and twenty, withered and haggard. His lips are often discoloured and disfigured with the marks of teeth; for he has desperate fits, and sometimes even bites his hands and covers them with wounds – why did you start?" said the girl, stopping suddenly.

The gentleman replied, in a hurried manner, that he was not conscious of having done so, and begged her to proceed.

"Part of this," said the girl, "I've drawn out from other people at the house I tell you of, for I have only seen him twice, and both times he was covered up in a large cloak. I think that's all I can give you to know him by. Stay though," she added. "Upon his throat: so high that you can see a part of it below his neckerchief when he turns his face: there is –"

"A broad red mark, like a burn or scald?" cried the gentleman.

"How's this!" said the girl. "You know him!"

The young lady uttered a cry of surprise, and for a few moments they were so still that the listener could distinctly hear them breathe.

"I think I do," said the gentleman, breaking silence. "I should

2 **forcibly:** eindringlich. | 4 **to lurk:** lauern, schleichen. | 7 **to tell s.o. by s.th.:** jdn. an etwas erkennen. | 10 **disfigured:** entstellt, verunstaltet. | 11 **mark:** Abdruck. | 15 **to be conscious of doing s.th.:** bewusst etwas tun. | 19 **stay!:** bleibt!, wartet!, Moment! | 22 **burn:** Brandmal. | **scald:** Verbrühung.

by your description. We shall see. Many people are singularly like each other. It may not be the same."

As he expressed himself to this effect, with assumed carelessness, he took a step or two nearer the concealed spy, as the latter could tell from the distinctness with which he heard him mutter, "It must be he!"

"Now," he said, returning: so it seemed by the sound: to the spot where he had stood before, "you have given us most valuable assistance, young woman, and I wish you to be the better for it. What can I do to serve you?"

"Nothing," replied Nancy.

[...]

[...] "I am chained to my old life. I loathe and hate it now, but I cannot leave it. I must have gone too far to turn back, – and yet I don't know, for if you had spoken to me so, some time ago, I should have laughed it off. But," she said, looking hastily round, "this fear comes over me again. I must go home."

[...]

"This purse," cried the young lady. "Take it for my sake, that you may have some resource in an hour of need and trouble."

"No!" replied the girl. "I have not done this for money. Let me have that to think of. And yet – give me something that you have worn: I should like to have something – no, no, not a ring – your gloves or handkerchief – anything that I can keep, as having belonged to you, sweet lady. There. Bless you! God bless you. Good night, good night!"

[...] The astonished listener remained motionless on his post for some minutes afterwards, and having ascertained, with many cautious glances round him, that he was again

1 **singularly:** eigentümlich, seltsam. | 3f. **carelessness:** Gleichgültigkeit, Unbekümmertheit. | 13 **to loathe s.th.:** etwas hassen, verabscheuen. | 16 **to laugh s.th. off:** etwas mit Freuden aufgeben. | 20 **resource:** (Geld-) Mittel. | 27 **motionless:** regungslos, bewegungslos. | 28 **post:** Posten.

alone, crept slowly from his hiding-place, and returned, stealthily and in the shade of the wall, in the same manner as he had descended.

Peeping out, more than once, when he reached the top, to make sure that he was unobserved, Noah Claypole darted away at his utmost speed, and made for the Jew's house as fast as his legs would carry him.

Chapter XLVII

Fatal Consequences

It was nearly two hours before daybreak; that time which, in the autumn of the year, may be truly called the dead of night; when the streets are silent and deserted; when even sounds appear to slumber, and profligacy and riot have staggered home to dream; it was at this still and silent hour, that the Jew sat watching in his old lair, with face so distorted and pale, and eyes so red and bloodshot, that he looked less like a man, than like some hideous phantom: moist from the grave, and worried by an evil spirit.

[...]

Stretched upon a mattress on the floor, lay Noah Claypole, fast asleep. Towards him the old man sometimes directed his eyes for an instant, and then brought them back again to the candle; which with a long-burnt wick drooping almost double,

9 **fatal:** verhängnisvoll; tödlich. | 11 **dead of night:** tiefste Nacht, totenstille Nacht. | 13 **profligacy:** Lasterhaftigkeit. | **riot:** Ausschweifung. | 15 **lair:** Schlupfwinkel. | 16 **bloodshot:** blutunterlaufen. | 17 **phantom:** Gespenst. | **moist:** feucht. | 23 **wick:** Docht. | **to droop:** herabhängen.

and hot grease falling down in clots upon the table, plainly shewed that his thoughts were busy elsewhere.

[...]

He sat without changing his attitude in the least, or appearing to take the smallest heed of time, until his quick ear seemed to be attracted by a footstep in the street.

"At last," muttered the Jew, wiping his dry and fevered mouth. "At last!"

The bell rang gently, as he spoke. He crept up stairs to the door, and presently returned accompanied by a man muffled to the chin, who carried a bundle under one arm. Sitting down, and throwing back his outer coat, the man displayed the burly frame of Sikes.

"There!" he said, laying a bundle on the table. "Take care of that, and do the most you can with it. It's been trouble enough to get; I thought I should have been here, three hours ago."

Fagin laid his hand upon the bundle, and locking it in the cupboard, sat down again without speaking. But he did not take his eyes off the robber, for an instant, during this action; and now that they sat over against each other, face to face, he looked fixedly at him, with his lips quivering so violently, and his face so altered by the emotions which had mastered him, that the housebreaker involuntarily drew back his chair, and surveyed him with a look of real affright.

"Wot now?" cried Sikes. "Wot do you look at a man so for?"

The Jew raised his right hand, and shook his trembling forefinger in the air; but his passion was so great, that the power of speech was for the moment gone.

1 **grease:** Talg, Kerzenfett. | **clot:** Klümpchen. | 5 **quick ear:** geübtes Ohr, scharfes Gehör. | 12 **burly:** kräftig, vierschrötig. | 22 **to master s.o.:** jdn. beherrschen. | 24 **affright:** Schrecken.

[...]

Sikes looked with an aspect of great perplexity into the Jew's face, and reading no satisfactory explanation of the riddle there, clenched his coat-collar in his huge hand and shook him soundly.

"Speak, will you!" he said; "or if you don't, it shall be for want of breath. Open your mouth and say wot you've got to say in plain words. Out with it, you thundering old cur, out with it!"

"Suppose that lad that's lying there –" Fagin began.

Sikes turned round to where Noah was sleeping, as if he had not previously observed him. "Well!" he said, resuming his former position.

"Suppose that lad," pursued the Jew, "was to peach – to blow upon us all – first seeking out the right folks for the purpose, and then having a meeting with 'em in the street to paint our likenesses, describe every mark that they might know us by, and the crib where we might be most easily taken. Suppose he was to do all this, and besides to blow upon a plant we've all been in, more or less – of his own fancy; not grabbed, trapped, tried, earwigged by the parson and brought to it on bread and water, – but of his own fancy; to please his own taste; stealing out at nights to find those most interested against us, and peaching to them. Do you hear me?" cried the Jew, his eyes flashing with rage. "Suppose he did all this, what then?"

"What then!" replied Sikes with a tremendous oath. "If he

8 **cur:** Hundesohn. | 14 **to peach:** denunzieren, verraten. | 15 **to blow upon s.o.:** jdn. verpfeifen, auffliegen lassen. | 16 f. **to paint s.o.'s likeness:** eine genaue Beschreibung von jdm. geben (*likeness:* Porträt). | 19 **plant:** krummes Ding. | 20 **fancy:** Einfall, Lust, Laune. | 21 **trapped:** eingesperrt, gefangen. | **tried:** vor Gericht gestellt. | **earwigged:** ausgehorcht. | **parson:** Pfaffe. | 23 **taste:** Gefällen, Neigung.

was left alive till I came, I'd grind his skull under the iron heel of my boot into as many grains as there are hairs upon his head."

"What if *I* did it!" cried the Jew almost in a yell. "*I*, that know so much, and could hang so many besides myself!"

[...]

"I don't care who," replied Sikes impatiently. "Whoever it was, I'd serve them the same."

Fagin again looked hard at the robber; and, motioning him to be silent, stooped over the bed upon the floor, and shook the sleeper to rouse him. [...]

[...] Noah rubbed his eyes, and, giving a heavy yawn, looked sleepily about him.

"Tell me that again – once again, just for him to hear," said the Jew, pointing to Sikes as he spoke.

"Tell yer what?" asked the sleepy Noah, shaking himself pettishly.

"That about – NANCY," said the Jew, clutching Sikes by the wrist, as if to prevent his leaving the house before he had heard enough. "You followed her?"

"Yes."

"To London Bridge?"

"Yes."

"Where she met two people?"

"So she did."

"A gentleman, and a lady that she had gone to of her own accord before, who asked her to give up all her pals, and Monks first, which she did – and to describe him, which she did – and to tell her what house it was that we meet at, and go to, which she did – and where it could be best watched from, which she did – and what time the people went there, which she did. She

1 **to grind:** zermalmen. | 2 **grain:** Körnchen. | 17 **pettishly:** mürrisch.

did all this. She told it all every word without a threat, without a murmur – she did – did she not?" cried the Jew, half mad with fury.

"All right," replied Noah, scratching his head. "That's just what it was!"

[…]

"Hell's fire!" cried Sikes, breaking fiercely from the Jew. "Let me go!"

Flinging the old man from him, he rushed from the room, and darted, wildly and furiously, up the stairs.

[…]

Without one pause, or moment's consideration; without once turning his head to the right, or left, raising his eyes to the sky, or lowering them to the ground, but looking straight before him with savage resolution: his teeth so tightly compressed that the strained jaw seemed starting through his skin; the robber held on his headlong course, nor muttered a word, nor relaxed a muscle, until he reached his own door. He opened it, softly, with a key; strode lightly up the stairs; and entering his own room, double-locked the door, and lifting a heavy table against it, drew back the curtain of the bed.

The girl was lying, half-dressed, upon it. He had roused her from her sleep, for she raised herself with a hurried and startled look.

"Get up!" said the man.

"It *is* you, Bill!" said the girl, with an expression of pleasure at his return.

[…]

The robber sat regarding her, for a few seconds, with dilated

4 **to scratch one's head:** sich am Kopf kratzen. | 7 **to break from s.o.:** sich von jdm. losreißen. | 15 **with savage resolution:** wild entschlossen. | 15 f. **compressed:** zusammengepresst. | 16 **strained:** angespannt. | 29 **dilated:** geweitet.

nostrils and heaving breast; and then, grasping her by the head and throat, dragged her into the middle of the room, and looking once towards the door, placed his heavy hand upon her mouth.

"Bill, Bill!" gasped the girl, wrestling with the strength of mortal fear, – "I – I – won't scream or cry – not once – hear me – speak to me – tell me what I have done!"

"You know, you she devil!" returned the robber, suppressing his breath. "You were watched to-night; every word you said was heard."

[...]

The housebreaker freed one arm, and grasped his pistol. The certainty of immediate detection if he fired, flashed across his mind even in the midst of his fury; and he beat it twice with all the force he could summon, upon the upturned face that almost touched his own.

She staggered and fell: nearly blinded with the blood that rained down from a deep gash in her forehead; but raising herself, with difficulty, on her knees, drew from her bosom a white handkerchief – Rose Maylie's own – and holding it up, in her folded hands, as high towards Heaven as her feeble strength would allow, breathed one prayer for mercy to her Maker.

It was a ghastly figure to look upon. The murderer staggering backward to the wall, and shutting out the sight with his hand, seized a heavy club and struck her down.

1 **to heave:** sich heben und senken; keuchen. | 6 **mortal fear:** Todesangst. | 8 **she devil:** Teufelin. | 13 **detection:** Entdeckung. | 18 **gash:** klaffende Wunde. | 23 **Maker:** Schöpfer(gott). | 24 **figure:** Gestalt; Bild. | 25 **to shut out s.th.:** etwas aussperren, ausschließen. | 26 **club:** Knüppel.

Chapter XLVIII

The Flight of Sikes

[...]

He had not moved; he had been afraid to stir. There had been a moan and motion of the hand; and, with terror added to hate, he had struck and struck again. Once he threw a rug over it; but it was worse to fancy the eyes, and imagine them moving towards him, than to see them glaring upward, as if watching the reflection of the pool of gore that quivered and danced in the sunlight on the ceiling. He had plucked it off again. And there was the body – mere flesh and blood, no more – but such flesh, and so much blood!

He struck a light, kindled a fire, and thrust the club into it. There was hair upon the end, which blazed and shrunk into a light cinder, and, caught by the air, whirled up the chimney. Even that frightened him, sturdy as he was; but he held the weapon till it broke, and then piled it on the coals to burn away, and smoulder into ashes. He washed himself, and rubbed his clothes; there were spots that would not be removed, but he cut the pieces out, and burnt them. How those stains were dispersed about the room! The very feet of the dog were bloody.

All this time he had, never once, turned his back upon the corpse; no, not for a moment. Such preparations completed, he moved, backward, towards the door: dragging the dog with

2 **flight:** Flucht. | 5 **moan:** Stöhnen. | 6 **rug:** grobe Wolldecke. | 7 **to fancy s.th.:** sich etwas vorstellen, ausmalen. | 9 **reflection:** Spiegelung, Widerschein. | **gore:** (geronnenes) Blut. | 10 **to pluck s.th. off:** etwas wegreißen. | 13 **to strike a light:** einen Funken schlagen. | **to kindle s.th.:** etwas entzünden, anfachen. | 14 **to blaze:** auflodern. | 15 **cinder:** Asche. | 17 **to pile:** stapeln, schichten. | 18 **to smoulder:** (ver)glühen. | 20 f. **dispersed:** verstreut, verspritzt. | 21 **very:** sogar.

him, lest he should soil his feet anew and carry out new evidences of the crime into the streets. He shut the door softly, locked it, took the key, and left the house.

He crossed over, and glanced up at the window, to be sure that nothing was visible from the outside. There was the curtain still drawn, which she would have opened to admit the light she never saw again. It lay nearly under there. *He* knew that. God, how the sun poured down upon the very spot!

The glance was instantaneous. It was a relief to have got free of the room. He whistled on the dog, and walked rapidly away.

[...]

With the same perversity of feeling and irresolution that had fastened upon him, despite himself, all day, the murderer [...] turned back up the town, and getting out of the glare of the lamps of a stage-coach that was standing in the street, was walking past, when he recognised the mail from London, and saw that it was standing at the little post-office. He almost knew what was to come; but he crossed over, and listened.

The guard was standing at the door, waiting for the letter-bag. A man, dressed like a gamekeeper, came up at the moment, and he handed him a basket which lay ready on the pavement.

"That's for your people," said the guard. "Now, look alive in there, will you. Damn that 'ere bag, it warn't ready night afore last; this won't do, you know!"

"Anything new up in town, Ben?" asked the gamekeeper,

9 **instantaneous:** augenblicklich, kurz. | 12 **perversity:** Verdrehtheit, Verkehrung. | **irresolution:** Unentschlossenheit. | 13 **to fasten upon s.o.:** jdn. im Griff haben. | **despite o.s.:** gegen den eigenen Willen, ungewollt. | 14 **to turn back:** umkehren. | 19 **guard:** Schirrmeister. | 19 f. **letter-bag:** Postsack. | 20 **gamekeeper:** Wildhüter. | 23 **look alive!:** Beeilung!

drawing back the window-shutters, the better to admire the horses.

"No, nothing that I knows on," replied the man, pulling on his gloves. "Corn's up a little. I heerd talk of a murder, too, down Spitalfields way, but I don't reckon much upon it."

"Oh, that's quite true," said a gentleman inside, who was looking out of the window. "And a dreadful murder it was."

"Was it, sir?" rejoined the guard, touching his hat. "Man or woman, pray, sir?"

"A woman," replied the gentleman. "It is supposed –"

"Now, Ben," replied the coachman impatiently.

"Damn that 'ere bag," said the guard; "are you gone to sleep in there?"

"Coming!" cried the office keeper, running out.

"Coming," growled the guard. "Ah, and so's the young 'ooman of property that's going to take a fancy to me, but I don't know when. Here, give hold. All ri – ight!"

The horn sounded a few cheerful notes, and the coach was gone.

Sikes remained standing in the street, apparently unmoved by what he had just heard, and agitated by no stronger feeling than a doubt where to go. At length he went back again, and took the road which leads from Hatfield to St. Albans.

He went on doggedly; but as he left the town behind him, and plunged into the solitude and darkness of the road, he felt a dread and awe creeping upon him which shook him to the core. […]

4 **corn's up a little:** das Getreide ist ein wenig (im Preis) gestiegen. | 5 **to reckon much upon s.th.:** viel auf etwas geben. | 11 **coachman:** Kutscher. | 16 **'ooman:** *woman.* | **to take a fancy to s.o.:** an jdm. Gefallen finden. | 17 **give hold!:** her damit! | 18 **horn:** Posthorn. | 25 **to plunge into s.th.:** in etwas eintauchen. | 26 f. **to the core:** bis ins Mark.

For now, a vision came before him, as constant and more terrible than that from which he had escaped. Those widely staring eyes, so lustreless and so glassy, that he had better borne to see them than think upon them, appeared in the midst of the darkness; light in themselves, but giving light to nothing. There were but two, but they were everywhere. [...]

He hurried off, and walked till he almost dropped upon the ground; then lay down in a lane, and had a long, but broken and uneasy sleep. He wandered on again, irresolute and undecided, and oppressed with the fear of another solitary night.

Suddenly, he took the desperate resolution of going back to London.

"There's somebody to speak to there, at all events," he thought. "A good hiding-place, too. They'll never expect to nab me there, after this country scent. Why can't I lie by for a week or so, and, forcing blunt from Fagin, get abroad to France? Damme, I'll risk it."

[...]

The dog, though, – if any descriptions of him were out, it would not be forgotten that the dog was missing, and had probably gone with him. This might lead to his apprehension as he passed along the streets. He resolved to drown him, and walked on, looking about for a pond: picking up a heavy stone and tying it to his handkerchief as he went.

The animal looked up into his master's face while these preparations were making; and, whether his instinct apprehended something of their purpose, or the robber's sidelong

1 **constant:** beständig. | 3 **lustreless:** glanzlos, stumpf. | 9 **uneasy:** unruhig. | 9 f. **undecided:** unschlüssig. | 10 **oppressed:** bedrückt. | 15 **to nab s.o.:** jdn. schnappen. | **scent:** Fährte, Spur. | **to lie by:** (fig.) untertauchen. | 16 **abroad:** außer Landes. | 21 **apprehension:** Festnahme, Verhaftung. | 23 **pond:** Teich, Tümpel. | **to pick up s.th.:** etwas aufheben, zur Hand nehmen. | 27 f. **sidelong look:** Seitenblick.

look at him was sterner than ordinary, he skulked a little farther in the rear than usual, and cowered as he came more slowly along. When his master halted at the brink of a pool, and looked round to call him, he stopped outright.

"Do you hear me call? Come here!" cried Sikes.

The animal came up from the very force of habit; but as Sikes stooped to attach the handkerchief to his throat, he uttered a low growl and started back.

"Come back!" said the robber, stamping on the ground.

The dog wagged his tail, but moved not. Sikes made a running noose and called him again.

The dog advanced, retreated, paused an instant, turned, and scoured away at his hardest speed.

The man whistled again and again, and sat down and waited in the expectation that he would return. But no dog appeared, and at length he resumed his journey.

Chapter XLIX

Monks and Mr. Brownlow at length meet.
Their Conversation, and the Intelligence that interrupts it

The twilight was beginning to close in, when Mr. Brownlow alighted from a hackney-coach at his own door, and knocked softly. The door being opened, a sturdy man got out of the coach and stationed himself on one side of the steps, while another man, who had been seated on the box, dismounted too,

2 **to cower:** sich ducken. | 3 **brink:** Rand, Ufer. | **pool:** Tümpel. | 10 **to wag one's tail:** mit dem Schwanz wedeln. | 10 f. **running noose:** laufende Schlinge. | 13 **to scour away:** davonjagen. | 24 **box:** (Kutsch-) Bock. | **to dismount:** absteigen.

and stood upon the other side. At a sign from Mr. Brownlow, they helped out a third man, and taking him between them, hurried him into the house. This man was Monks.

[...]

"By what authority am I kidnapped in the street and brought here by these dogs?" asked Monks, looking from one to the other of the men who stood beside him.

"By mine," replied Mr. Brownlow. "Those persons are indemnified by me. [...]

[...] "If you wish me to prefer my charges publicly, and consign you to a punishment the extent of which, although I can, with a shudder, foresee, I cannot control, once more, I say, you know the way. If not, and you appeal to my forbearance, and the mercy of those you have deeply injured, seat yourself, without a word, in that chair. It has waited for you two whole days."

[...]

Monks looked at the old gentleman, with an anxious eye; but, reading in his countenance nothing but severity and determination, walked into the room, and, shrugging his shoulders, sat down.

[...]

"This is pretty treatment, sir," said Monks, throwing down his hat and cloak, "from my father's oldest friend."

"It is because I was your father's oldest friend, young man," returned Mr. Brownlow; "it is because [...] he knelt with me beside his only sister's death-bed when he was yet a boy, on the morning that would – but Heaven willed otherwise – have made her my young wife; [...] it is of all these things that I am

5 **authority:** Befehl, Befugnis. | 8 f. **to indemnify s.o.:** jdn. ermächtigen. | 10 **to prefer:** (Klage) erheben. | **charges:** Anschuldigungen. | 13 **to appeal to s.th.:** an etwas appellieren. | **forbearance:** Nachsicht. | 18 **severity:** Strenge, Härte.

moved to treat you gently now – yes, Edward Leeford, even now – and blush for your unworthiness who bear the name."

[…]

"This is all mighty fine," said Monks (to retain his assumed designation) after a long silence, during which he had jerked himself in sullen defiance to and fro, and Mr. Brownlow had sat, shading his face with his hand. "But what do you want with me?"

"You have a brother," said Mr. Brownlow, rousing himself: "a brother, the whisper of whose name in your ear when I came behind you in the street, was, in itself, almost enough to make you accompany me hither, in wonder and alarm."

"I have no brother," replied Monks. "You know I was an only child. Why do you talk to me of brothers? You know that, as well as I."

"Attend to what I do know, and you may not," said Mr. Brownlow. "I shall interest you by and by. I know that of the wretched marriage, into which family pride, and the most sordid and narrowest of all ambition, forced your unhappy father when a mere boy, you were the sole and most unnatural issue."

[…]

"Well, they were separated," said Monks, "and what of that?"

"When they had been separated for some time," returned Mr. Brownlow, "and your mother, wholly given up to continental frivolities, had utterly forgotten the young husband ten

2 **to blush:** rot werden, erröten. | **unworthiness:** Unwürdigkeit. | 5 **designation:** Benennung, Bezeichnung. | 5 f. **to jerk o.s.:** sich ruckweise bewegen. | 6 **defiance:** Trotz. | 12 **hither:** hierher. | 16 **to attend to s.th.:** etwas beachten. | 20 **sole:** einzig. | **unnatural:** widernatürlich, abscheulich. | 21 **issue:** Spross, Abkömmling. | 26 f. **continental:** kontinental, europäisch. | 27 **frivolities:** Lustbarkeiten.

good years her junior, who, with prospects blighted, lingered on at home, he fell among new friends. *This* circumstance, at least, you know already."

[...]

"I have nothing to disclose," rejoined Monks. "You must talk on if you will."

"These new friends, then," said Mr. Brownlow, "were a naval officer retired from active service, whose wife had died some half a year before, and left him with two children – there had been more, but, of all their family, happily but two survived. They were both daughters; one a beautiful creature of nineteen, and the other a mere child of two or three years old."

[...]

"They resided, [...] in a part of the country to which your father in his wanderings had repaired, and where he had taken up his abode. [...] As the old officer knew him more and more, he grew to love him. I would that it had ended there. His daughter did the same."

[...]

"The end of a year found him contracted, solemnly contracted, to that daughter; the object of the first, true, ardent, only passion of a guileless, untried girl."

"Your tale is of the longest," observed Monks, moving restlessly in his chair.

"It is a true tale of grief and trial, and sorrow, young man," returned Mr. Brownlow, "and such tales usually are; if it were one of unmixed joy and happiness, it would be very brief. At length one of those rich relations to strengthen whose interest

1 **to blight s.th.:** etwas vereiteln, zerstören. | 7f. **naval officer:** Marineoffizier. | 20 **(to be) contracted to s.o.:** mit jdm. verlobt sein. | 27 **unmixed:** unvermischt, ungetrübt. | 28 **relations** (pl.): Verwandte, Verwandtschaft. | **to strengthen:** stärken.

and importance your father had been sacrificed, as others are often – it is no uncommon case – died, and to repair the misery he had been instrumental in occasioning, left him *his* panacea for all griefs – Money. It was necessary that he should immediately repair to Rome, whither this man had sped for health, and where he had died, leaving his affairs in great confusion. He went; was seized with mortal illness there; was followed, the moment the intelligence reached Paris, by your mother who carried you with her; he died the day after her arrival, leaving no will – *no will* – so that the whole property fell to her and you."

At this part of the recital Monks held his breath, and listened with a face of intense eagerness, though his eyes were not directed towards the speaker. As Mr. Brownlow paused, he changed his position with the air of one who has experienced a sudden relief, and wiped his hot face and hands.

"Before he went abroad, and as he passed through London on his way," said Mr. Brownlow slowly, and fixing his eyes upon the other's face, "he came to me."

"I never heard of that," interrupted Monks in a tone intended to appear incredulous, but savouring more of disagreeable surprise.

"He came to me, and left with me, among some other things, a picture – a portrait painted by himself – a likeness of this poor girl – which he did not wish to leave behind, and could not carry forward on his hasty journey. He was worn by anxiety and remorse almost to a shadow; [...] and I never saw him more."

[...]

1 **to sacrifice s.o.:** jdn. opfern. | 2 **to repair s.th.:** etwas wiedergutmachen. | 3 **to be instrumental in doing s.th.:** dabei mitwirken, etwas zu tun. | **panacea:** Allheilmittel. | 5 **to speed:** eilen. | 21 **incredulous:** ungläubig. | **to savour of s.th.:** etwas ahnen lassen. | 27 **remorse:** Reue.

Monks drew his breath yet more freely, and looked round with a smile of triumph.

"When your brother," said Mr. Brownlow, drawing nearer to the other's chair, "When your brother: a feeble, ragged, neglected child: was cast in my way by a stronger hand than chance, and rescued by me from a life of vice and infamy –"

"What?" cried Monks.

"By me," said Mr. Brownlow. "I told you I should interest you before long. I say by me – I see that your cunning associate suppressed my name, although, for aught he knew, it would be quite strange to your ears. When he was rescued by me, then, and lay recovering from sickness in my house, his strong resemblance to this picture I have spoken of, struck me with astonishment. […] You have a brother; you know it, and him. There was a will, which your mother destroyed, leaving the secret and the gain to you at her own death. It contained a reference to some child likely to be the result of this sad connection, which child was born, and accidentally encountered by you, when your suspicions were first awakened by his resemblance to his father. You repaired to the place of his birth. There existed proofs – proofs long suppressed – of his birth and parentage. Those proofs were destroyed by you, and now […], Edward Leeford, do you still brave me!"

"No, no, no!" returned the coward, overwhelmed by these accumulated charges.

"Every word!" cried the old gentleman, "every word that has passed between you and this detested villain, is known to me. Shadows on the wall have caught your whispers, and

4 f. **neglected:** vernachlässigt. | 6 **infamy:** Schande. | 10 **aught:** alles mögliche. | 12 f. **resemblance:** Ähnlichkeit. | 16 **gain:** Gewinn, Vermögen. | 16 f. **reference:** Hinweis. | 23 **to brave s.o.:** jdm. trotzen, mutig entgegentreten. | 24 **overwhelmed:** überwältigt. | 25 **accumulated:** angehäuft. | 27 **detested:** abscheulich.

brought them to my ear; the sight of the persecuted child has turned vice itself, and given it the courage and almost the attributes of virtue. Murder has been done, to which you were morally if not really a party."

"No, no," interposed Monks. "I – I – know nothing of that; I was going to inquire the truth of the story when you overtook me. I didn't know the cause. I thought it was a common quarrel."

"It was the partial disclosure of your secrets," replied Mr. Brownlow. "Will you disclose the whole?"

"Yes, I will."

"Set your hand to a statement of truth and facts, and repeat it before witnesses?"

"That I promise too."

"Remain quietly here, until such a document is drawn up, and proceed with me to such a place as I may deem most advisable, for the purpose of attesting it?"

"If you insist upon that, I'll do that also," replied Monks.

[...]

While Monks was pacing up and down, meditating with dark and evil looks on this proposal and the possibilities of evading it: torn by his fears on the one hand and his hatred on the other: the door was hurriedly unlocked, and a gentleman (Mr. Losberne) entered the room in violent agitation.

"The man will be taken," he cried. "He will be taken tonight!"

"The murderer?" asked Mr. Brownlow.

"Yes, yes," replied the other. "His dog has been seen lurking

1 **persecuted:** verfolgt. | 2f. **attribute:** Eigenschaft. | 3 **virtue:** Tugend. | 4 **party:** Beteiligter. | 6 **to overtake s.o.:** jdn. ereilen, stellen. | 12 **statement:** Erklärung. | 17 **to attest s.th.:** etwas beglaubigen, bestätigen. | 20 **to pace up and down:** auf und ab gehen. | 22 **to evade s.th.:** etwas vermeiden. | 28 **to lurk:** herumstreichen.

about some old haunt, and there seems little doubt that his master either is, or will be, there, under cover of the darkness. Spies are hovering about in every direction. I have spoken to the men who are charged with his capture, and they tell me he cannot escape. A reward of a hundred pounds is proclaimed by Government to-night."

[…]

Chapter L

The Pursuit and Escape

Near to that part of the Thames on which the church at Rotherhithe abuts, where the buildings on the banks are dirtiest and the vessels on the river blackest with the dust of colliers and the smoke of close-built low-roofed houses, there exists, at the present day, the filthiest, the strangest, the most extraordinary of the many localities that are hidden in London, wholly unknown, even by name, to the great mass of its inhabitants.

[…]

In such a neighbourhood, beyond Dockhead in the Borough of Southwark, stands Jacob's Island, surrounded by a muddy ditch, six or eight feet deep and fifteen or twenty wide when the tide is in, once called Mill Pond, but known in these days as Folly Ditch. […]

In Jacob's Island, the warehouses are roofless and empty; the walls are crumbling down; the windows are windows no

3 **to hover about:** ausschwärmen. | 5 **to proclaim s.th.:** etwas ausrufen, verkünden. | 12 **vessel:** (Wasser-)Fahrzeug. | **collier:** Kohlenschiff. | 19 **borough:** (Stadt-)Bezirk. | 21 f. **when the tide is in:** bei Flut. | 25 **to crumble down:** einstürzen.

more; the doors are falling into the streets; the chimneys are blackened, but they yield no smoke. [...]

In an upper room of one of these houses [...] there were assembled three men, who, regarding each other every now and then with looks expressive of perplexity and expectation, sat for some time in profound and gloomy silence. One of these was Toby Crackit, another Mr. Chitling, and the third a robber of fifty years, whose nose had been almost beaten in, in some old scuffle, and whose face bore a frightful scar which might probably be traced to the same occasion. This man was a returned transport, and his name was Kags.

"I wish," said Toby turning to Mr. Chitling, "that you had picked out some other crib when the two old ones got too warm, and had not come here my fine feller."

"Why didn't you blunder-head?" said Kags.

"Well, I thought you'd have been a little more glad to see me than this," replied Mr. Chitling, with a melancholy air.

[...]

"When was Fagin took then?"

"Just at dinner-time – two o'clock this afternoon. Charley and I made our lucky up the wash'us chimney, and Bolter got into the empty water-butt, head downwards; but his legs were so precious long that they stuck out at the top, and so they took him too."

[...]

"Wot's come of young Bates?" demanded Kags.

5 **(to be) expressive of s.th.:** etwas ausdrücken. | 9 **scar:** Narbe. | 11 **transport:** (nach Australien) Deportierter. | 14 **warm:** heiß (gefährlich). | 15 **blunder-head:** Blödmann, Dummkopf. | 17 **melancholy:** traurig, düster. | 19 **to take s.o.:** jdn. ergreifen, schnappen. | 21 **to make one's lucky:** entwischen. | **wash'us:** *wash-house:* Waschküche. | 22 **water-butt:** Regentonne. | 26 **to come of s.o.:** aus jdm. werden.

"He hung about, not to come over here afore dark, but he'll be here soon," replied Chitling. "There's nowhere else to go to now, for the people at the Cripples are all in custody, and the bar of the ken – I went up there and see it with my own eyes – is filled with traps."

[...]

The horror-stricken witness of this scene pressed his hands upon his ears, and with his eyes closed got up and paced violently to and fro, like one distracted.

While he was thus engaged, and the two men sat by in silence with their eyes fixed upon the floor, a pattering noise was heard upon the stairs, and Sikes's dog bounded into the room. They ran to the window, down stairs, and into the street. The dog had jumped in at an open window; he made no attempt to follow them, nor was his master to be seen.

"What's the meaning of this!" said Toby, when they had returned. "He can't be coming here. I – I – hope not."

[...]

It being now dark, the shutter was closed, and a candle lighted and placed upon the table. The terrible events of the last two days had made a deep impression on all three, increased by the danger and uncertainty of their own position. They drew their chairs closer together, starting at every sound. They spoke little, and that in whispers, and were as silent and awe-stricken as if the remains of the murdered woman lay in the next room.

They had sat thus, some time, when suddenly was heard a hurried knocking at the door below.

1 **to hang about:** sich herumdrücken. | 4 **bar:** Schankstube. | **ken:** Spelunke. | 7 **horror-stricken:** von Entsetzen gepackt. | 9 **distracted:** Wahnsinnige(r), Verwirrte(r). | 11 **to patter:** trappeln. | 12 **to bound:** springen. | 24 **awe-stricken:** ehrfürchtig. | 25 **remains:** sterbliche Überreste.

[…]

Crackit went to the window, and, shaking all over, drew in his head. There was no need to tell them who it was; his pale face was enough. The dog too was on the alert in an instant, and ran whining to the door.

"We must let him in," he said, taking up the candle.

[…]

Crackit went down to the door, and returned followed by a man with the lower part of his face buried in a handkerchief, and another tied over his head under his hat. He drew them slowly off. Blanched face, sunken eyes, hollow cheeks, beard of three days' growth, wasted flesh, short thick breath; it was the very ghost of Sikes.

[…]

Sikes carried his eyes slowly up the wall behind him: rather trying to turn his head than actually doing it: and said, "Is – it – the body – is it buried?"

They shook their heads.

"Why isn't it!" he retorted with the same glance behind him. "Wot do they keep such ugly things above the ground for? – Who's that knocking?"

Crackit intimated, by a motion of his hand as he left the room, that there was nothing to fear; and directly came back with Charley Bates behind him. Sikes sat opposite the door, so that the moment the boy entered the room he encountered his figure.

"Toby," said the boy falling back, as Sikes turned his eyes towards him, "why didn't you tell me this, down stairs?"

[…]

4 **to be on the alert:** auf der Hut, hellwach sein. | 5 **to whine:** winseln, wimmern. | 11 **blanched:** bleich geworden. | 12 **wasted flesh:** abgemagert. | **thick breath:** schwerer Atem.

"Why, Charley!" said Sikes, stepping forward, "don't you – don't you know me?"

"Don't come nearer me," answered the boy, still retreating, and looking, with horror in his eyes, upon the murderer's face. "You monster!"

The man stopped half-way, and they looked at each other; but Sikes's eyes sunk gradually to the ground.

"Witness you three," cried the boy shaking his clenched fist, and becoming more and more excited as he spoke. "Witness you three – I'm not afraid of him – if they come here after him, I'll give him up; I will. I tell you out at once. He may kill me for it if he likes, or if he dares, but if I am here I'll give him up. I'd give him up if he was to be boiled alive. Murder! Help! If there's the pluck of a man among you three, you'll help me. Murder! Help! Down with him!"

Pouring out these cries, and accompanying them with violent gesticulation, the boy actually threw himself, single-handed, upon the strong man, and in the intensity of his energy, and the suddenness of his surprise, brought him heavily to the ground.

[...]

The contest, however, was too unequal to last long. Sikes had him down, and his knee was on his throat, when Crackit pulled him back with a look of alarm, and pointed to the window. There were lights gleaming below, voices in loud and earnest conversation, the tramp of hurried footsteps – endless they seemed in number – crossing the nearest wooden bridge. One man on horseback seemed to be among the crowd; for there was the noise of hoofs rattling on the uneven pavement.

11 **to give s.o. up:** jdn. ausliefern. | 14 **pluck:** Mut, Schneid, Mumm. | 17 f. **single-handed:** eigenhändig, im Alleingang. | 18 **intensity:** Ausmaß, Stärke. | 22 **contest:** Kampf. | 26 **tramp:** Stapfen, Getrampel.

The gleam of lights increased; the footsteps came more thickly and noisily on. Then, came a loud knocking at the door, and then a hoarse murmur from such a multitude of angry voices as would have made the boldest quail.

"Help!" shrieked the boy in a voice that rent the air. "He's here! Break down the door!"

"In the King's name," cried voices without; and the hoarse cry arose again, but louder.

"Break down the door!" screamed the boy. "I tell you they'll never open it. Run straight to the room where the light is. Break down the door!"

Strokes, thick and heavy, rattled upon the door and lower window-shutters as he ceased to speak, and a loud huzzah burst from the crowd; giving the listener, for the first time, some adequate idea of its immense extent.

"Open the door of some place where I can lock this screeching Hell-babe," cried Sikes fiercely; running to and fro, and dragging the boy, now, as easily as if he were an empty sack. "That door. Quick!" He flung him in, bolted it, and turned the key. [...]

"The tide," cried the murderer, as he staggered back into the room [...], "the tide was in as I came up. Give me a rope, a long rope. They're all in front. I may drop into the Folly Ditch, and clear off that way. Give me a rope, or I shall do three more murders and kill myself at last."

The panic-stricken men pointed to where such articles were kept; the murderer, hastily selecting the longest and strongest cord, hurried up to the house-top.

3 **multitude:** Vielzahl, Menge. | 4 **to quail:** verzagen. | 5 **to rend the air:** die Luft zerschneiden. | 13 **huzzah:** Hurra. | 15 **adequate:** hinreichend, genau. | 16 f. **screeching:** kreischend. | 17 **hell-babe:** Satansbraten. | 26 **panic-stricken:** kopflos, von Panik erfasst. | 28 **cord:** Schnur, Seil. | **house-top:** Dach.

[…]

Roused into new strength and energy, and stimulated by the noise within the house which announced that an entrance had really been effected, he set his foot against the stack of chimneys, fastened one end of the rope tightly and firmly round it, and with the other made a strong running noose by the aid of his hands and teeth almost in a second. He could let himself down by the cord to within a less distance of the ground than his own height, and had his knife ready in his hand to cut it then and drop.

At the very instant when he brought the loop over his head previous to slipping it beneath his arm-pits, […] at that very instant the murderer, looking behind him on the roof, threw his arms above his head, and uttered a yell of terror.

"The eyes again!" he cried in an unearthly screech.

Staggering as if struck by lightning, he lost his balance and tumbled over the parapet. The noose was on his neck. It ran up with his weight, tight as a bow-string, and swift as the arrow it speeds. He fell for five-and-thirty feet. There was a sudden jerk, a terrific convulsion of the limbs; and there he hung, with the open knife clenched in his stiffening hand.

[…]

2 **to stimulate s.o.:** jdn. anspornen. | 3 f. **to effect an entrance:** sich Zutritt verschaffen. | 4 f. **stack of chimneys:** Schornsteine. | 6 **by the aid of:** mit Hilfe. | 11 **loop:** Schlinge. | 12 **arm-pit:** Achselhöhle. | 15 **screech:** Schrei. | 17 **to tumble:** taumeln, stürzen. | **parapet:** Brüstung. | 18 **bow-string:** Bogensehne.

Chapter LI

Affording an Explanation of more Mysteries than One, and comprehending a proposal of Marriage with no Word of Settlement or Pin-money

The events narrated in the last chapter were yet but two days old, when Oliver found himself, at three o'clock in the afternoon, in a travelling-carriage rolling fast towards his native town. Mrs. Maylie, and Rose, and Mrs. Bedwin, and the good doctor, were with him; and Mr. Brownlow followed in a post-chaise, accompanied by one other person whose name had not been mentioned.

They had not talked much upon the way; for Oliver was in a flutter of agitation and uncertainty which deprived him of the power of collecting his thoughts, and almost of speech, and appeared to have scarcely less effect on his companions, who shared it, in at least an equal degree. He and the two ladies had been very carefully made acquainted by Mr. Brownlow with the nature of the admissions which had been forced from Monks; and although they knew that the object of their present journey was to complete the work which had been so well begun, still the whole matter was enveloped in enough of doubt and mystery to leave them in endurance of the most intense suspense.

[...]

3 **to comprehend s.th.:** etwas enthalten. | 4 **settlement:** Mitgift. | **pin-money:** Nadelgeld (Summe, die Ehemänner ihren Frauen für den persönlichen Gebrauch und Bedarf zur Verfügung stellen). | 7 f. **native town:** Geburtsort. | 13 **flutter:** hier: (aufgeregter) Zustand. | 18 **admission:** Eingeständnis. | 22 **endurance:** Aushalten, Ertragen. | **intense:** stark, heftig.

They drove straight to the door of the chief hotel (which Oliver used to stare up at, with awe, and think a mighty palace, but which had somehow fallen off in grandeur and size); and here was Mr. Grimwig all ready to receive them, kissing the young lady, and the old one too, when they got out of the coach, as if he were the grandfather of the whole party, all smiles and kindness, [...].

At length, when nine o'clock had come, and they began to think they were to hear no more that night, Mr. Losberne and Mr. Grimwig entered the room, followed by Mr. Brownlow and a man whom Oliver almost shrieked with surprise to see; for they told him it was his brother, and it was the same man he had met at the market-town, and seen looking in with Fagin at the window of his little room. Monks cast a look of hate, which, even then, he could not dissemble, at the astonished boy, and sat down near the door. Mr. Brownlow, who had papers in his hand, walked to a table near which Rose and Oliver were seated.

"This is a painful task," said he, "but these declarations, which have been signed in London before many gentlemen, must be in substance repeated here. I would have spared you the degradation, but we must hear them from your own lips before we part, and you know why."

"Go on," said the person addressed, turning away his face. "Quick. I have almost done enough, I think. Don't keep me here."

"This child," said Mr. Brownlow, drawing Oliver to him, and laying his hand upon his head, "is your half-brother; the illegitimate son of your father, my dear friend Edwin Lee-

1 **chief:** beste(r, s). | 3 **to fall off:** abnehmen, nachlassen. | **grandeur:** Pracht. | 15 **to dissemble s.th.:** etwas verhehlen. | 22 **degradation:** Erniedrigung. | 29 **illegitimate:** unehelich.

ford, by poor young Agnes Fleming, who died in giving him birth."

[...]

"Listen then! You!" returned Monks. "His father being taken ill at Rome, was joined by his wife, my mother, from whom he had been long separated, who went from Paris and took me with her – to look after his property, for what I know, for she had no great affection for him, nor he for her. He knew nothing of us, for his senses were gone, and he slumbered on till next day, when he died. Among the papers in his desk, were two, dated on the night his illness first came on, directed to yourself;" he addressed himself to Mr. Brownlow; "and enclosed in a few short lines to you, with an intimation on the cover of the package that it was not to be forwarded till after he was dead. One of these papers was a letter to this girl Agnes; the other, a will."

[...]

Monks was silent.

"The will," said Mr. Brownlow, speaking for him, "was in the same spirit as the letter. He talked of miseries which his wife had brought upon him; of the rebellious disposition, vice, malice, and premature bad passions of you, his only son, who had been trained to hate him; and left you, and your mother, each an annuity of eight hundred pounds. The bulk of his property he divided into two equal portions – one for Agnes Fleming, and the other for their child, if it should be born alive and ever come of age. If it were a girl, it was to inherit the money unconditionally; but if a boy, only on the

8 **to know of s.o.:** jdn. (er)kennen. | 11 **directed:** gerichtet, adressiert. | 12 **enclosed:** beigefügt. | 14 **package:** Päckchen, Bündel. | 23 **to leave s.o. s.th.:** jdm. etwas hinterlassen. | 24 **annuity:** jährliche Rente. | **bulk:** Großteil, Hauptteil. | 27 **to come of age:** erwachsen werden. | 28 **to inherit:** erben. | **unconditionally:** bedingungslos, ohne Vorbehalt.

stipulation that in his minority he should never have stained his name with any public act of dishonour, meanness, cowardice, or wrong. He did this, he said, to mark his confidence in the mother, and his conviction – only strengthened by approaching death – that the child would share her gentle heart, and noble nature. If he were disappointed in this expectation, then the money was to come to you; for then, and not till then, when both children were equal, would he recognise your prior claim upon his purse, who had none upon his heart, but had, from an infant, repulsed him with coldness and aversion."

"My mother," said Monks, in a louder tone, "did what a woman should have done – she burnt this will. [...]"

"The father of the unhappy Agnes had *two* daughters," said Mr. Brownlow. "What was the fate of the other – the child?"

"The child," replied Monks, "when her father died in a strange place, in a strange name, without a letter, book, or scrap of paper that yielded the faintest clue by which his friends or relatives could be traced – the child was taken by some wretched cottagers, who reared it as their own."

"Go on," said Mr. Brownlow, signing to Mrs. Maylie to approach. "Go on!"

"You couldn't find the spot to which these people had repaired," said Monks, "but where friendship fails, hatred will often force a way. My mother found it, after a year of cunning search – aye, and found the child."

"She took it, did she?"

1 **stipulation:** Vorbehalt, Bedingung. | **minority:** Unmündigkeit, Minderjährigkeit. | **to stain:** beschmutzen, beflecken. | 2 **dishonour:** Ehrlosigkeit. | **meanness:** Niedertracht. | 2 f. **cowardice:** Feigheit. | 3 **wrong:** Unrecht. | 8 **to recognise:** anerkennen. | **prior:** älter, früher. | 9 **claim:** Anspruch. | 10 **to repulse:** zurückweisen, abstoßen. | **aversion:** Abneigung, Widerwillen. | 17 **faintest:** geringste(r, s). | 19 **cottager:** Häusler (ärmlicher Kleinbauer).

"No. The people were poor, and began to sicken – at least the man did – of their fine humanity; so she left it with them, giving them a small present of money which would not last long, and promising more, which she never meant to send. She didn't quite rely, however, on their discontent and poverty for the child's unhappiness, but told the history of the sister's shame, with such alterations as suited her; bade them take good heed of the child, for she came of bad blood; and told them she was illegitimate, and sure to go wrong at one time or other. The circumstances countenanced all this; the people believed it; and there the child dragged on an existence, miserable enough even to satisfy us, until a widow lady, residing, then, at Chester, saw the girl by chance, pitied her, and took her home. There was some cursed spell, I think, against us; for in spite of all our efforts she remained there and was happy. I lost sight of her, two or three years ago, and saw her no more until a few months back."

"Do you see her now?"

"Yes. Leaning on your arm."

"But not the less my niece," cried Mrs. Maylie, folding the fainting girl in her arms; "not the less my dearest child. I would not lose her now, for all the treasures of the world. My sweet companion, my own dear girl!"

[...]

"Not aunt," cried Oliver, throwing his arms about her neck: "I'll never call her aunt – sister, my own dear sister, that something taught my heart to love so dearly from the first! Rose, dear, darling Rose!"

1 **to sicken of s.th.:** einer Sache überdrüssig werden. |
2 **humanity:** Menschlichkeit. | 3 **to last:** reichen. | 7 f. **to take heed of s.o.:** auf jdn. achtgeben. | 8 **blood:** Abstammung, Familie. |
10 **to countenance:** unterstützen. | 14 **cursed:** verflucht, verwünscht. |
spell: Zauber, Bann. | 20 **not the less:** nichtsdestoweniger.

[...]

They were a long, long time alone. A soft tap at the door, at length announced that some one was without. Oliver opened it, glided away, and gave place to Harry Maylie.

"I know it all," he said, taking a seat beside the lovely girl. "Dear Rose, I know it all."

"I am not here by accident," he added after a lengthened silence; "nor have I heard all this to-night, for I knew it yesterday – only yesterday. Do you guess that I have come to remind you of a promise?"

"Stay," said Rose. "You *do* know all?"

"All. You gave me leave, at any time within a year, to renew the subject of our last discourse."

"I did."

"Not to press you to alter your determination," pursued the young man, "but to hear you repeat it, if you would. I was to lay whatever of station or fortune I might possess at your feet, and if you still adhered to your former determination, I pledged myself, by no word or act, to seek to change it."

[...] "My hopes, my wishes, prospects, feeling: every thought in life except my love for you: have undergone a change. I offer you, now, no distinction among a bustling crowd; no mingling with a world of malice and detraction, where the blood is called into honest cheeks by aught but real disgrace and shame; but a home – a heart and home – yes, dearest Rose, and those, and those alone, are all I have to offer."

"What do you mean!" she faltered.

"I mean but this – that when I left you last, I left you with a

11 **to stay:** innehalten. | 13 **discourse:** Gespräch, Unterredung. | 18 f. **to pledge o.s.:** sich verpflichten. | 22 **distinction:** (hohes) Ansehen. | **bustling:** emsig, geschäftig. | 23 **detraction:** Schmähung, Verleumdung.

firm determination to level all fancied barriers between yourself and me; resolved that if my world could not be yours, I would make yours mine; that no pride of birth should curl the lip at you, for I would turn from it. This I have done. Those who have shrunk from me because of this, have shrunk from you, and proved you so far right. Such power and patronage: such relatives of influence and rank: as smiled upon me then, look coldly now; but there are smiling fields and waving trees in England's richest county; and by one village church – mine, Rose, my own – there stands a rustic dwelling which you can make me prouder of, than all the hopes I have renounced, measured a thousandfold. This is *my* rank and station now, and here I lay it down!"

[...]

Chapter LII

The Jew's last Night alive

[...]

They led him through a paved room under the court [...] into the interior of the prison.

Here, he was searched, that he might not have about him the means of anticipating the law; this ceremony performed, they

1 **to level:** einebnen, niederreißen. | **barrier:** Schranke, Hindernis. |
3 **pride of birth:** Standesdünkel. | 3f. **to curl the lip at s.o.:** etwa: verächtlich über jdn. die Nase rümpfen. | 5 **to shrink from s.o.:** von jdm. abrücken. | 6 **patronage:** Gönnerschaft. | 7 **rank:** Rang. |
10 **rustic:** schlicht, einfach. | **dwelling:** Wohnhaus, Behausung. |
11 **to renounce s.th.:** etwas aufgeben. | 18 **court:** Gerichtshof. |
20 **to search s.o.:** jdn. durchsuchen.

led him to one of the condemned cells, and left him there – alone.

He sat down on a stone bench opposite the door, which served for seat and bedstead; and casting his blood-shot eyes upon the ground, tried to collect his thoughts. After a while, he began to remember a few disjointed fragments of what the judge had said: though it had seemed to him, at the time, that he could not hear a word. These gradually fell into their proper places, and by degrees suggested more: so that in a little time he had the whole, almost as it was delivered. To be hanged by the neck, till he was dead – that was the end. To be hanged by the neck till he was dead.

As it came on very dark, he began to think of all the men he had known who had died upon the scaffold; some of them through his means. They rose up, in such quick succession, that he could hardly count them. He had seen some of them die, – and had joked too, because they died with prayers upon their lips. With what a rattling noise the drop went down; and how suddenly they changed, from strong and vigorous men to dangling heaps of clothes!

[...]

Saturday night. He had only one night more to live. And as he thought of this, the day broke – Sunday.

It was not until the night of this last awful day, that a withering sense of his helpless, desperate state came in its full intensity upon his blighted soul; not that he had ever held any defined or positive hope of mercy, but that he had never been able to consider more than the dim probability of dying so soon. He had spoken little to either of the two men, who relieved each

1 **condemned cell:** Todeszelle. | 14 **scaffold:** Schafott. | 15 **succession:** Folge. | 18 **drop:** Falltür (unterm Galgen). | 24 f. **withering:** vernichtend. | 27 **positive:** eindeutig. | 28 **probability:** Wahrscheinlichkeit.

other in their attendance upon him; and they, for their parts, made no effort to rouse his attention. He had sat there, awake, but dreaming. Now, he started up, every minute, and with gasping mouth and burning skin, hurried to and fro, in such a paroxysm of fear and wrath that even they – used to such sights – recoiled from him with horror. He grew so terrible, at last, in all the tortures of his evil conscience, that one man could not bear to sit there, eyeing him alone; and so the two kept watch together.

He cowered down upon his stone bed, and thought of the past. He had been wounded with some missiles from the crowd on the day of his capture, and his head was bandaged with a linen cloth. His red hair hung down upon his bloodless face; his beard was torn, and twisted into knots; his eyes shone with a terrible light; his unwashed flesh crackled with the fever that burnt him up. Eight – nine – ten. If it was not a trick to frighten him, and those were the real hours treading on each other's heels, where would he be, when they came round again! Eleven! Another struck, before the voice of the previous hour had ceased to vibrate. At eight, he would be the only mourner in his own funeral train; at eleven –

Those dreadful walls of Newgate, which have hidden so much misery and such unspeakable anguish, not only from the eyes, but, too often and too long, from the thoughts, of men, never held so dread a spectacle as that. The few who lingered as they passed, and wondered what the man was doing who was to be hung to-morrow, would have slept but ill that night, if they could have seen him.

7 **evil conscience:** schlechtes Gewissen. | 8 **to keep watch:** Wache halten. | 11 **missile:** Wurfgeschoss. | 13 **linen cloth:** Leinentuch. | 14 **twisted into knots:** verfilzt. | 15 **to crackle:** knistern. | 20 **to vibrate:** schwingen, hallen. | 21 **funeral train:** Leichenzug. | 22 **Newgate:** berüchtigtes Gefängnis in London.

From early in the evening until nearly midnight, little groups of two and three presented themselves at the lodge-gate, and inquired, with anxious faces, whether any reprieve had been received. These being answered in the negative, communicated the welcome intelligence to the clusters in the street, who pointed out to one another the door from which he must come out, and shewed where the scaffold would be built, and, walking with unwilling steps away, turned back to conjure up the scene. By degrees they fell off, one by one; and, for an hour, in the dead of night, the street was left to solitude and darkness.

[…]

Day was dawning when they again emerged. A great multitude had already assembled; the windows were filled with people, smoking and playing cards to beguile the time; the crowd were pushing, quarrelling, and joking. Everything told of life and animation, but one dark cluster of objects in the centre of all – the black stage, the cross-beam, the rope, and all the hideous apparatus of death.

2 **lodge-gate:** Pforte. | 3 **reprieve:** Strafaufschub, Begnadigung. | 5 **cluster:** (Menschen-)Ansammlung. | 8 **to conjure up s.th.:** etwas heraufbeschwören. | 9 **by degrees:** allmählich, nach und nach. | 13 **to dawn:** dämmern. | 15 **to beguile the time:** sich die Zeit vertreiben. | 17 **animation:** Lebhaftigkeit, Munterkeit. | 18 **stage:** Gerüst, Plattform. | **cross-beam:** Querbalken. | 19 **apparatus:** Gerät(e), Instrumentarium.

Chapter LIII

And Last

The fortunes of those who have figured in this tale, are nearly closed. The little that remains to their historian to relate, is told in few and simple words.

Before three months passed, Rose Fleming and Harry Maylie were married, in the village church which was henceforth to be the scene of the young clergyman's labours; on the same day they entered into possession of their new and happy home.

Mrs. Maylie took up her abode with her son and daughter-in-law, to enjoy, during the tranquil remainder of her days, the greatest felicity that age and worth can know – the contemplation of the happiness of those on whom the warmest affections and tenderest cares of a well-spent life, have been unceasingly bestowed.

[...]

Mr. Brownlow adopted Oliver as his son. Removing with him and the old housekeeper to within a mile of the parsonage-house, where his dear friends resided, he gratified the only remaining wish of Oliver's warm and earnest heart, and thus linked together a little society, whose condition approached as nearly to one of perfect happiness as can ever be known in this changing world.

[...]

4 **to close s.th.:** etwas abschließen. | 7 **henceforth:** fortan. | 8 **labour:** Arbeit, Tätigkeit. | 11 **tranquil:** ruhig, beschaulich. | 12 **felicity:** Glück. | **worth:** Würde. | 14 **care:** Fürsorge. | **well-spent:** rechtschaffen. | **unceasingly:** ohne Unterlass. | 18 f. **parsonage-house:** Pfarrhaus. | 20 **earnest:** aufrichtig. | 21 **to link together:** miteinander verbinden, zusammenführen. | 23 **changing:** unbeständig.

Editorische Notiz

Der englische Text folgt der Ausgabe: Charles Dickens, *Oliver Twist*, edited, and with an introduction by Kathleen Tillotson, Oxford: Clarendon Press, 1966. Diese maßgebliche Ausgabe bietet den Text der von Dickens revidierten Ausgabe von 1846.

Das Glossar enthält alle Wörter, die nicht im *Thematischen Grund- und Aufbauwortschatz Englisch* von Gernot Häublein und Recs Jenkins (Stuttgart: Ernst Klett Sprachen, 2001) verzeichnet sind. Im Zweifelsfall wurde großzügig verfahren, d. h. eher eine Vokabel mehr aufgenommen.

Im Glossar verwendete englische Abkürzungen

fig.	figuratively (übertragen)
hum.	humorously (scherzhaft)
Lat.	Latin
o.s.	oneself
pl.	plural
s.o.	someone
s.th.	something

Literaturhinweise

Davies, B. R., *A Street Map of London 1843*, Nachdr. Devon: Old House Books, 1992.

Dexter, Walter (Hrsg.), *The Letters of Charles Dickens*, Bloomsbury: The Nonesuch Press, 1938.

Dickens, Charles, *Oliver Twist*, New York: W. W. Norton, 1993 (Norton Critical Edition).

Eisner, Will, *Fagin the Jew: A Graphic Novel*, New York: Doubleday, 2003. [Erzählt die Geschichte aus der Sicht Fagins.]

House, Madeline / Storey, Graham (Hrsg.), *The Letters of Charles Dickens*, Oxford: Oxford University Press, 1965.

Lean, David, *Oliver Twist*, [DVD mit dem Film von 1948 und dokumentarischem Material] 2000.

Marcus, Steven, »Who is Fagin?«, in: Charles Dickens, *Oliver Twist*, New York: W. W. Norton, 1993, S. 478–495.

Schmidt, Johann N., *Dickens*, Reinbek bei Hamburg: Rowohlt, 1978 (rororo Bildmonographie).

Tomalin, Claire, *The Invisible Woman. The Story of Nelly Ternan and Charles Dickens*, Harmondsworth: Penguin, 1991. [Die spannende Geschichte von Dickens' heimlicher Liebschaft mit einer Schauspielerin, die er während der letzten zwölf Jahre seines Lebens unterhielt.]

Tomlin, E. W. F. (Hrsg.), *Die Welt des Charles Dickens*, übers. von Eva Gärtner, Hamburg: Hoffmann und Campe, 1969.

Williams, Emlyn, »Dickens und das Theater«, in: E. W. F. Tomlin (Hrsg.), *Die Welt des Charles Dickens*, S. 178–195.

Nachwort

Charles Dickens (1812–1870) kann mit Fug und Recht als literarischer Chronist des viktorianischen Zeitalters (Königin Victoria, 1819–1901, regierte von 1837 bis 1901) gelten. Zu Beginn dieser Ära erzielte Dickens mit den *Pickwick Papers* (1836/37) seinen Durchbruch als Schriftsteller. Alle folgenden Werke spiegeln die sich wandelnden gesellschaftlichen Zustände und Probleme des britischen Empire, das auf dem Höhepunkt seiner Macht ein Viertel der Erdoberfläche und ein Drittel der Weltbevölkerung umfasste.

Es fällt heute schwer, sich auch nur eine ungefähre Vorstellung von Dickens' Popularität und Ruhm zu machen. Überall warteten die Menschen auf die Fortsetzungen seiner Geschichten, deren Veröffentlichung zumeist in wöchentlichen oder monatlichen Lieferungen erfolgte. In England galoppierten nachts Reiter durch die Dörfer und verkündeten: »Carker ist tot!« (eine Figur aus *Dombey and Son*).[1] In New York drängte sich eine Menschenmenge am Kai eines aus England einlaufenden Schiffes und rief den Passagieren die bange Frage zu: »Ist Little Nell gestorben?« (Figur aus *The Old Curiosity Shop*).[2] Beim Abschied zu seiner zweiten Amerikareise richtete man Dickens in London ein Staatsbankett aus, im Hafen von Boston wurde er mit einem Feuerwerk empfangen. In New York standen Menschen in eiskalter Winternacht stundenlang an, um für seine Lesung Karten zu bekommen, mit denen Schwarzhändler bis zu zweitausend Prozent Profit machten. Und schon damals gab es ein modern anmutendes »Merchandising« (an

1 E. W. F. Tomlin, *Die Welt des Charles Dickens*, übers. von Eva Gärtner, Hamburg: Hoffmann und Campe, 1969, S. 18.
2 Johann N. Schmidt, *Dickens*, Reinbek bei Hamburg: Rowohlt, 1978, S. 58.

dem Dickens jedoch nichts verdient haben dürfte): Mit den Konterfeis des Autors und seiner Figuren wurde nicht nur für Tinte und Schreibfedern geworben, sondern auch für Tee, Zigarren, Hüte, Liederbücher und Kordhosen. Die unübersehbare Zahl der Übersetzungen und das weltweite Presseecho auf seinen Tod bezeugen, dass Dickens' Popularität nicht auf die englischsprachigen Länder beschränkt war.

Oliver Twist (1837/38) erschien zur Zeit der Thronbesteigung Königin Victorias, die das Buch, das bei den höheren Gesellschaftsschichten Englands für Unmut gesorgt hatte, mochte und verteidigte. Die *Pickwick Papers* spielen noch im Postkutschen-Universum des Merry Old England, das aus Gasthäusern, Poststationen, Landpartien, Salons und Cottages besteht. Wahrscheinlich war Dickens während des Schreibens nicht bewusst, dass er damit bereits einen Abgesang verfasste auf dieses Zeitalter, das der stählernen Macht der Eisenbahnen (deren Möglichkeiten zum schnellen Reisen der rastlose Dickens exzessiv nutzte – Claire Tomalin nennt ihn einen »Flying Dutchman of the railways«[3]) weichen musste.

Parallel zu den monatlichen Folgen der *Pickwick Papers* beginnt Dickens bereits an *Oliver Twist* zu schreiben. Schon in diesem Roman, anfangs angeregt durch die neuen Armengesetze von 1834, die Dickens scharf attackierte, erzählt er von den dunklen Schatten, die auf den Glanz der viktorianischen Zeit fallen und mit dem industriellen Aufschwung einhergehen: Armut, Kriminalität, Prostitution und die Verelendung breiter Gesellschaftsschichten, worauf die Bessergestellten zum großen Teil mit Ignoranz, Zynismus und Gefühlskälte reagieren.

Zu diesen äußeren Anstößen für die Geschichte gesellen

3 Claire Tomalin, *The Invisible Woman. The Story of Nelly Ternan and Charles Dickens*, Harmondsworth: Penguin, 1991, S. 102.

sich Konflikte, die in Dickens' Seele gären. Es sind die traumatischen Erlebnisse seiner Kindheit, als 1824 zum einen sein Vater ins Londoner Schuldgefängnis Marshalsea kommt – wohin ihn die gesamte Familie bis auf den kleinen Charles begleitet – und er selbst in Warren's Schuhwichsfabrik Flaschen abfüllen und mit Etiketten bekleben muss, was der bildungshungrige Zwölfjährige, der sich bereits seiner schöpferischen Talente bewusst ist, als soziale Degradierung und Erniedrigung empfindet. Wie tief dieser Stachel sitzt, lässt sich daran ablesen, dass Dickens diese Kindheitsepisode später selbst gegenüber engen Familienangehörigen verschwieg und sie erst postum von seinem Freund und Biographen John Forster öffentlich gemacht wurde. Das Sujet des unglücklichen, allein gelassenen und bedrohten Kindes, das in Dickens' Werk immer von neuem wiederkehren wird, nimmt in der Geschichte von Oliver Twist erstmals feste Gestalt an. Dabei wirkt der Titelheld selbst über weite Strecken seltsam blutleer, unwirklich und leblos. Er agiert nicht wie ein im Armenhaus aufgewachsener Waisenjunge, sondern wie ein kleiner Gentleman (»the young Gentleman« wurde Dickens bei Warren's gerufen). Und so spricht er auch. Übrigens ebenso wie der alte Hehler Fagin, bei dem es glaubwürdiger wirkt, denn er könnte durchaus bessere Zeiten in vornehmeren Verhältnissen erlebt haben.

Damit wären wir bei dem bekannten Phänomen, dass die Schurken einer Geschichte zumeist interessanter sind als ihre Helden. Gegen Fagin, den Dodger und Nancy sind Brownlow, Oliver und Rose im wahrsten Sinne des Wortes blasse Gestalten. Fagin ist jedoch nicht allein die interessanteste (kein Wunder, dass Alec Guinness darauf bestand, in David Leans cineastischem Meisterwerk von 1948 den Fagin zu spielen!), sondern zugleich auch die problematischste Gestalt des *Oliver Twist*. Geradezu erschreckend auf den heutigen Leser wirken die antisemitischen Stereotype, die Dickens verwendet hat, um möglichst eindrücklich die Gestalt eines *stage jew*, eines Bühnenjuden, zu zeichnen, etwa nach Art des Shakespeareschen Shylock. Eine Ursache dieser drastischen Darstellungsweise ist sicher in der engen und leidenschaftlichen Verbundenheit, die Dickens mit dem Theater pflegte, zu suchen.

Ein anderer Grund ist schlicht der, dass sich bei Dickens, wie eingangs schon erwähnt, natürlich auch die Einstellung der viktorianischen Gesellschaft widerspiegelt. Um 1830 wurden Juden in England gesellschaftlich noch massiv diskriminiert. Sie konnten in der City of London keine Geschäfte eröffnen, wurden nicht als Anwälte bei Gericht zugelassen, bekamen keine Universitätsabschlüsse verliehen und durften auch nicht ins Parlament einziehen. Zwischen 1830 und 1860 verbesserte sich ihre Stellung dann kontinuierlich, eine Entwicklung, die 1858 symbolisch einen Höhepunkt erreicht, als Baron Lionel Rothschild, der bereits 1847 ins House of Commons gewählt worden war, endlich seinen Parlamentssitz einnehmen und einen abgeänderten Amtseid, bei dem der ausdrücklich aufs Christentum bezogene Passus (»upon the true faith of a Christian«) weggelassen wurde, ablegen durfte, was ihm bis dahin verweigert worden war.

In dem Roman *Our Mutual Friend*, den Dickens in den Jahren 1864/65 schrieb und der sein letztes vollendetes Werk ist, folgt die betont positive Darstellung des alten Juden Mr. Riah zum einen diesem Wandel der Zeit, zum anderen mutet es an, als habe Dickens diesen Charakter bewusst als Gegenbild und Korrektur zu Fagin geschaffen.

Als in den Jahren 1867/68 eine neue Ausgabe seiner Werke erscheint, streicht Dickens in *Oliver Twist* an zahlreichen Stellen das Wort »Jude« und ersetzt es durch »Fagin«. Auch in den Texten, die er für seine berühmten szenischen Lesungen bearbeitet hat, fungiert Fagin lediglich als »Hehler«.

Die Gestalt Fagins steht aber ebenfalls in enger Verbindung

zu Dickens' Kindheitstrauma, seiner Knechtschaft in Warren's Schuhwichsfabrik. Wie er in einem autobiographischen Fragment gesteht, hat Dickens sich von einem anderen der Jungen, die dort arbeiten, den Namen für den alten Hehler entliehen: »Two or three boys were kept at similar duty downstairs on similar wages. One of them came up, in a ragged apron and a paper cap, on the first Monday morning, to show me the trick of using the string and tying the knot. His name was Bob Fagin; and I took the liberty of using his name, long afterwards, in *Oliver Twist*.«[4]

Obwohl Bob Fagin eine Art Beschützerrolle für den jungen Charles übernimmt, bleibt er für Dickens bei all seiner Hilfsbereitschaft dennoch mit zwiespältigen Gefühlen verbunden, da dieser Angehörige der untersten Schichten ihn stets an seine gesellschaftliche Degradierung gemahnt.

Diese Zwiespältigkeit zeigt sich auf vielerlei Weise auch in dem alten Hehler, der keineswegs durchweg negativ gezeichnet ist. Er nimmt Oliver auf, bewahrt ihn im Grunde vor dem Hungertod auf den Straßen Londons und kümmert sich, wenn auch nicht ohne Hintergedanken, auf eine Weise um das Kind, wie es die ehrbaren Respektspersonen der Gesellschaft in Kinderheim, Armenhaus oder seinen Lehrbetrieben nie getan haben. Allem unterwürfigen Gehabe zum Trotz muss Fagin auch sehr viel Mut besitzen, um mit jähzornigen und zu Gewaltausbrüchen neigenden Verbrechern wie Bill Sikes sein Spiel zu treiben.

Es ist bezeichnend, dass Dickens sich im Alter wieder verstärkt diesem Frühwerk und damit den traumatischen Erlebnissen seiner Kindheit zuwandte. Gegen Ende seiner Karriere unternahm er ausgedehnte Lesetourneen, die sich durchweg

4 Zit. nach: Steven Marcus, »Who is Fagin?«, in: Charles Dickens, *Oliver Twist*, New York: W. W. Norton, 1993, S. 478–495, hier S. 483.

als triumphale Erfolge erwiesen. Der ansonsten eher skeptische Emlyn Williams schreibt darüber: »Dickens' Auftritte müssen, selbst unter Abzug journalistischer Übertreibungen in diesbezüglichen Schilderungen, eine ganz außergewöhnliche Wirkung gehabt haben. [...] Dickens war eine legendäre Figur, ein Zauberer des Wortes, der mit eigener Stimme eigene Worte aus Büchern sprach, die sein Publikum auswendig kannte, und der dieses Publikum von dem Augenblick an, in dem er auftrat, in Hypnose versetzte.«[5]

Höhepunkt dieser Lesungen waren stets Auszüge aus *Oliver Twist*, die in dem eindringlich vorgetragenen Mord an Nancy gipfelten. Dickens versetzte seine Zuhörer dermaßen in Schrecken, dass etliche von ihnen regelmäßig aufschrien, in Ohnmacht fielen und »steif und starr« aus dem Saal getragen werden mussten. Noch verheerender waren jedoch die Auswirkungen auf den Schriftsteller selbst. Auf der Lesebühne begann sein Puls zu rasen, der Blutdruck stieg in lebensbedrohliche Höhen und seine Gesichtsfarbe wechselte von aschfahl zu violett. Nach dem Auftritt dauerte es immer geraume Zeit, bis er wieder ansprechbar war. Diese Lesungen gerieten für Dickens zur Obsession, die er gegen die Weisungen seiner Ärzte fortsetzte. Der Biograph Edgar Johnson behauptet nicht ganz zu Unrecht, Dickens habe mit der Entscheidung, den Mord an Nancy ins Repertoire aufzunehmen, sein Todesurteil unterzeichnet.

Am 8. März 1870 fand die letzte Lesung aus *Oliver Twist* statt, am 15. März folgte Dickens' endgültige Abschiedsvorstellung. Am 9. Juni verstarb der Schriftsteller im Alter von 68 Jahren.

5 Emlyn Williams, »Dickens und das Theater«, in: E. W. F. Tomlin (Hrsg.), *Die Welt des Charles Dickens*, übers. von Eva Gärtner, Hamburg: Hoffmann und Campe, 1969, S. 178–195, hier S. 191.

Das Faszinosum, das Geheimnis, das von *Oliver Twist* ausgeht, wird sich, wie jedes echte Geheimnis, nie vollständig ergründen lassen. Am ehesten kommen wir ihm auf die Spur, wenn wir Charles Dickens selbst sprechen lassen, der seinem Verleger Richard Bentley schrieb: »I have thrown my whole heart and soul into Oliver Twist.«[6]

Axel Monte

6 Zit. nach: Charles Dickens, *Oliver Twist*, New York: W. W. Norton, 1993, S. 374.

Inhalt